PRAISE

"*Image Breaker* is a breathtaking rarity—a novel that begins in faithlessness and strives toward hope, a takedown of intellectual excess that is unabashedly learned, a quest for love that never loses sight of the human comedy. Mark E. Leib's much-praised dramatic skills are on full display in this moving, provocative, and entertaining novel, one you'll think about—and talk with friends about—well beyond its generous conclusion."
JOHN FLEMING, AUTHOR OF *SONGS FOR THE DEAF*

"Mark Leib writes beautifully, and he knows how to tell a story. His protagonist Tristan Wishnasky is a writer on a mission, not just to be the best there is, but to undo the bleakness of his past writings. He faces a crisis of belief, in the deepest sense; and because of that crisis, he must confront everything he previously believed, including the non-existence of a Higher Power in his own life. Only a writer as good as Mark Leib is could pull off this literary juggling act, of writing an entertainment that moves the reader, but also he gives us a book that may just change our lives. Reader, be forewarned. Here is a writer asking you directly if you are ready for the challenge."
M. G. STEPHENS, AUTHOR OF *KING EZRA*

"*Image Breaker* tells the story of Tristan Wishnasky, a successful novelist, who experiences an unexpected vision that threatens to upend his seemingly comfortable life. Part academic satire, part existential quest, *Image Breaker* is a perfectly structured book filled with delicious literary allusions, hilarious moments, and crackling dialogue. In this deeply moving story of a middle-aged man attempting to come to terms with faith, love, and of course, himself, Mark Leib establishes his genius."
HEATHER SELLERS, AUTHOR OF *YOU DON'T LOOK LIKE ANYONE I KNOW*

ABOUT THE AUTHOR

Mark E. Leib's short stories and essays have appeared in *Boston Review, Two Bridges Review, JewishFiciton.net, Commentary, American Theatre, Harvard Magazine,* and *Stage Directions.* His theatre plays have been produced in New York, Chicago, Cambridge, Tampa/St. Petersburg, Edinburgh, and Singapore. His drama criticism for the alternative newspaper *Creative Loafing* has won seven awards from the Society of Professional Journalists. He received his MFA in Playwriting from the Yale School of Drama and was the first American playwright produced at Harvard's American Repertory Theatre. He lives in Tampa with his wife, Elizabeth, and teaches at the University of South Florida.

markeleib.me

IMAGE BREAKER

MARK E. LEIB

www.vineleavespress.com

To my wife, Elizabeth, and our son, Jeremy
Love comes first.

PART ONE

1.

TRISTAN WISHNASKY, the famous novelist of despair, was making his way through Camus's *Myth of Sisyphus* in French, and finding the experience exceedingly rewarding.

He'd first read the celebrated essay in English translation when he was sixteen or seventeen, and had immediately found the writer convincing. Of course, Camus was right: We are exiles in a world we don't understand and that gives us nothing to hope for, there is a divorce between our needs and our reality, and we are lost between our endless desire for sense and our inescapable knowledge that there is no such thing. Twenty years later, reading these words in his warm, book-lined study, it wasn't just the truth of the writer's sentiments that comforted Wishnasky, but the memory of being an adolescent confused about his future, alienated from his parents, conscious that death would play no favorites in the end ... and then discovering this little paperback book, with its gray and blue cover showing a half-naked man shoving a boulder up the side of a mountain. What a relief it had been to discover Camus and *Sisyphus*! What a clear, courageous view this French author had of life! After reaching the last page, teenaged Wishnasky had been so enthused, he'd gone straight to the Lexington library to check out *The Stranger*—which he didn't begin to understand, but which mysteriously moved him—and then *The Plague,* which taught so powerfully the sort of heroism demanded of decent humans in a murderously arbitrary world. It was *Sisyphus* that had started Wishnasky's quest through modern and not-so-modern classics for the answer to his conundrums, and by the time he had graduated in History and Literature at Harvard, he'd built a pantheon of such names as Sartre and Beauvoir, Kafka and Brecht, Beckett and Pinter and a dozen other writers who all agreed, whatever their differences, that we live on an exurban rock in an accidental solar system in an unimportant galaxy in a meaningless universe. And of course, when Wishnasky at twenty-six published his first novel—*No One From Nowhere*, which sold comfortably, to even his publisher's surprise—it was this philosophy of heroic desolation, first encountered in *Sisyphus,* that motivated his characters as they stumbled through a post-nuclear California in search of durable identities unencumbered by that cheat called "the future." Three years later, his second novel, *The Anguish of the Condemned,* was nearly a bestseller with its tale of the doomed lovers, Rico and Marissa, and their valiant but abortive quest with the help of mescaline, LSD, and psilocybin mushrooms, to justify the life they'd come to despise near Nova Scotia's dramatic Bay of Fundy. And then finally, four years later, had come his masterpiece—so it was called by the *Times*—the 919-page *Craters of the Spirit,* in which no fewer than a dozen interlocking narratives followed a polyglot assembly of characters on four continents as they strove to prevent the one man they all cherished—the brilliant, anguished physicist Nigel Zimmerberg—from immolating himself in an active volcano. *Craters* had handily won a National Book Critics Circle Award, and Wishnasky had been acclaimed as a literary trailblazer, all the more valuable in that he was still only in his mid-thirties.

And now, in the living room of his home in Newton Corner (bought with proceeds from the film deal for *Craters*), Wishnasky was again reading Camus. Truth be told, it wasn't just the philosophy that gladdened him. Affirming, too, was the legend around this sainted author: his courage in the Resistance, his moral refusal to ignore Stalin's infamies, his philosophy-confirming death in an automobile accident when he still had his best days ahead of him. Sometimes, Wishnasky's mind wandered from the page and he imagined Camus smoking yet another Gauloise, his searching eyes observing the pitiless futility around him, his open face affirming that even in the Void, one can be compassionate. Truly, this was an admirable stance: to see so clearly into the emptiness and to hold oneself upright nonetheless. Truly, this was the only kind of dignity possible in our troubled age.

Just now Wishnasky came upon a patch that was particularly convincing. The fundamental fact, Camus was saying, is life's utter unintelligibility, and even a slightly rigorous mind will admit that there is nothing rational about the cosmos, no chance to find in its chaos anything but obstacles to the human yearning for sense, a yearning that finally one has to jettison and replace with surrender to the certitude of nothingness—

And then something strange happened.

The book itself didn't move—Wishnasky was holding it in one hand while sitting in his favorite black leather desk chair, and there wasn't the slightest agitation of the light paperback in his grip. But two French paragraphs shifted, two blocks of print suddenly parted, one going north and one south, and in the middle a sentence in English appeared:

You know better than this.

Wishnasky started—huh? He looked back at the page and there was nothing, just the simple but eloquent French he'd been enjoying. Was he daydreaming? He actually thought for a moment that two fixed blocks of text separated in front of him and a line of English appeared between them. Too strange. He must be tired. He must not be dining well. The brain runs on glucose, and he'd been eating nothing but protein. He'd have to pick up some fresh fruit before Vanessa arrived for the evening.

He resumed his reading. Now Camus was saying that not only is the universe unknowable, but so is the self, that we are strangers twice over, to the world and to our own minds, we can never hope to discern the truth because reality is written in a foreign language, and all the pretenders to understanding are so many fools and deceivers—It happened again.

The French on the page parted into two walls of print, and between them he read:

You don't have time to waste.

Wishnasky slapped the book shut, as if it had delivered an electric shock. He closed his eyes and tried to quiet his mind. But when he opened to his place and looked again, there was yet another message, three words in English:

Search for Me.

Wishnasky tossed the book on the table beside him, rose and stalked into the kitchen, to the cabinet where he kept the gin. He shakily poured himself a glass, took a sip, returned to his living room and picked up *Sisyphus*. With trepidation he found his place and looked for the English words. They weren't there. There was only French Camus, and the pathos of Absurd Man. Wishnasky turned the pages quickly, searching for other messages, but there were none. He felt silly, then frightened, then worried for his sanity. He put the book down, leaned back in his chair and drank his gin cautiously. What had he seen? *You know better than this?* Better than what? He closed his eyes, brought the glass to his lips and tried to believe that he wasn't going psychotic.

2.

WHEN VANESSA WALKED IN, Wishnasky was still in his study, working on his new novel, tentatively entitled *Traveler in the Abyss*. Only work, he had decided, could quiet his mind after the unusual occurrences of the afternoon. And just as he'd hoped, the challenge of advancing in *Abyss* mostly banished his nervousness. He had now reached the part where Ozono, his protagonist, discovered that his life's savings had been plundered by his trusted but corrupt investment advisors. Prior to this, he had lost his job at the computer company he'd nurtured to dominance, lost his wife to his greatest rival, and lost his two grown daughters to a contempt so definitive, they refused to again speak to him even to remind him of their hatred. Wishnasky intended to strip away one by one all the artificial supports and distractions that made up Ozono's life, 'til at the end—which was still a hundred pages and many losses away—he would have nothing but the unaccommodated human animal: isolated, Godless, aware for the first time of the truth of truths, that we're all half-insane refugees on an Earth that refuses to make itself anything like our home. Then he intended to finish with a long stream-of-consciousness rant against the lies humankind tells itself in order not to face the music.

Still, smoothly as the work was going, he couldn't quite forget that other thing: the words he had seen on the page of *Sisyphus*, especially: *You know better than this.* Did he? And what about: *You don't have time to waste?* Working hard not to think about it, he wrote:

When he walked out of the elevator onto the thirty-first floor, Ozono was surprised to find a crowd of people milling around the lobby, among whom were two uniformed policemen. The door to the Parmalee and Retz interior was open, but there was a third officer, a woman, standing there with her arms folded, and no one at all was in the glassed-in receptionist's area. Confused and vaguely frightened, Ozono turned to an oval-faced young man who was writing on a stenographer's pad.

"What's going on?" he said. "Why are the police here?"

"Who are you?" asked the young man, his fashionably shaved cranium shining under the fluorescent lights.

"Edward Ozono. Has there been some crime? Are you a reporter?"

"Yeah, L.A. Times. Do you have any investments here? If you don't mind, I'd like to take a statement."

"About what? Where's Micky Parmalee?"

"He's somewhere back there," said the journalist, pointing to the area behind the policewoman. "And in just a few more minutes, he's going to be in the back of a patrol car headed for his arraignment."

Ozono's heart dropped. He thought: no—it can't be possible. Things don't happen that way. "What has he done?" he said, trying to sound untroubled.

"Him and Retz both," said the reporter. "Fraud, embezzlement, grand theft, you name it. I really hope you didn't have any investments with these assholes. If you did, you're in deep trouble. So, Mr. Ozono—" He put the tip of his pen on his pad. "How much were you taken for?"

■

"Hey," said Vanessa, stepping just inside the study. "It's been a day. Let's go to dinner."

Wishnasky turned from his computer. "Sure," he said, noting the tiredness in her blue eyes but admiring, as always, her strikingly long dark hair and proud aristocratic face. "Where do you want to go?"

"You know," she said. She meant Hermione's, their favorite restaurant when there was no special occasion. "Just give me a few minutes to wash up." She turned in the doorway, heading for the bathroom. Wishnasky saved his document, stood up and walked into the kitchen.

He and Vanessa had been together for a year and a half now. It was a good, strong relationship, all the better since Vanessa, dean of students at a small college on the highway between Boston and Worcester, was so intelligent and articulate. Wishnasky had been married once before, to his college girlfriend, but the marriage had foundered on repetition and boredom. With Vanessa there was no such danger: she was alive to every impulse in the cool New England air, read everything, and explored everything. It was she who had introduced him to the novels of Jean Rhys, the pre-Socratic philosophers, *The*

Second Sex, the essays of Nicola Chiaromonte. Long before he had won his Book Critics Circle Award, it was Vanessa who told him *Craters of the Spirit* was a masterpiece. He trusted her judgment more than that of any professional critic.

They drove in his gray Camry through the heavy traffic on Brookline Avenue. Now that it was autumn, darkness was falling earlier, so the storefronts on either side of the street were already illuminated, and pedestrians hurried to their destinations in light coats and sweaters. Wishnasky kept his driver's-side window slightly cracked so he could enjoy the not-yet-frigid breeze.

"Quite a challenge today," Vanessa said. "A transgender student came to see me. He's transitioning from female to male and wants the registrar to change all the college record information. But the registrar is a Neanderthal who won't do it till the new semester starts. I think the student's going to sue us."

"I had a strange day myself," said Wishnasky.

"He already looks like a man," said Vanessa, "though the breasts are barely noticeable. He's been taking hormone treatments, seeing a counselor, uses the men's bathroom, but it's a hard time for him. He started to cry in my office: apparently his parents are mortified, his father told him not to come home next summer. Imagine the revolution he's going through, and then Deb Neely insists on calling him Staci. He's about as much Staci as I'm Vincent."

"I think I had some kind of hallucination today."

"I'm bushed. Tell me at the restaurant. He spent an hour with me, crying and spilling his guts. I wanted to hug him." She passed her hand over her forehead. Wishnasky drove up the crowded road, burning to reveal what he'd seen.

Hermione's was unusually empty. They were taken directly to a crimson-and-black booth, just a few yards from the open kitchen where the smell of broiling steak was sweet and pungent. When their wine was served, Vanessa drank gratefully, in long drafts. The potion seemed to revive her; her eyes no longer looked haunted. Wishnasky thought he saw his moment.

"I was reading Camus just for fun," he began. Then he told her the whole story, including the three lines in English. He tried to laugh as he told it, just in case she might scoff.

When he finished, she looked somber. "So, what are you saying?" she said. "You saw Jesus? You're born again?"

"Not Jesus," he said. "But something. And I'm supposed to search for It. Him. Her. And I'm supposed to admit to myself that I don't believe my own novels."

"It's burnout," Vanessa said. "How's work on *Traveler* going?"

"All right. A little trouble making the business crisis exciting."

"That's it," Vanessa said. "'You know better than this' is about poor Ozono. 'You don't have time to waste'—well, your deadline's pending, isn't it? And '*Search for Me*'—it's 'Search for a fresher plotline.'"

"I wasn't thinking about my novel. I was reading Camus."

"Look, you're not going to get religious on me. You're not going to turn into a tie-dyed freak handing out leaflets for salvation. You have an inspiration about your new novel and you're interpreting it to mean you've been contacted by the Stratosphere. You're not going to turn into my grandmother."

Vanessa's grandmother was a pious Catholic whom Vanessa avoided as much as possible.

"No," said Wishnasky. "I just thought it was kind of strange."

"It was. Your inner critic manifested herself. So don't become a Hare Krishna. Have a little wine and get your head straight."

She's right, Wishnasky thought. It was all about the new novel. As usual, Vanessa saw directly to the marrow of things, and all in an instant. He loved this woman.

"I'm hungry," he said gratefully, as if a burden had been lifted. "I'm ordering the Surf 'n' Turf." So much for his huge Religious Experience. Of course, the subject had been his novel: What else? Now, with Vanessa's help, he could forget the shock and all his worries, now he could put it out of his head.

3.

HE COULDN'T PUT IT OUT OF HIS HEAD.

He was at a reading at Boston University, arranged by his editor Darryl Kamfort "to keep your brand from disappearing while you're finishing the next monument." As he read a twenty-minute excerpt from *Craters of the Spirit*, he found himself questioning every prize-winning word, sentence, and paragraph. He was on the section about Sandra Eisenheim, the historian of the Holocaust, who had left her job and family to play blackjack in Las Vegas, and who had moved on from there to gambling dens in Grand Bahama Island, Helsinki, and Macau. "It's what there is," she told Wayne Wister, the ex-police detective hired by her husband to bring her home. "That's all: a bet on a beer-stained craps table where the house always wins, a wager in the dark on a doctored roulette wheel no one can see spinning. I just can't go on pretending." Wishnasky read these desolate sentiments to the wall-to-wall spectators in the amphitheater-like classroom and tried his best to make Eisenheim sound insightful, astute. But what kept coming to mind all the time he was reading was: *You know better than this.* And sometimes, more worrisome still: *You don't have time to waste.*

Didn't he? He came to the passage where Eisenheim challenged Wister to ditch his agency and travel with her to other smoky rooms in Bangkok and Manila where they could live honestly, authentically. "'We'll be free,' said passionate Eisenheim. 'Freer than all the sad fools slaving for a salary and watching themselves evaporate. We'll be living the only truth that this papier-mâché palace can deliver.'" When he said the word "deliver," he paused for a moment to look out at his audience. They were mostly young college students, and they were rapt, nodding in agreement. On Wishnasky's authority, they were learning—or had they already known?—that human existence was a lost cause.

He finished the excerpt, feeling a discomfort he couldn't quite identify. The applause strangely worried him. Then it was time for questions.

A lanky young man, pimply, with blond hair brushed over one eye, was first. "Your book reminds me of Pascal," he said. "Were you influenced in your writing by Pascal's picture of the human condition?"

"For all his worry about the 'terrifying silence of the empty spaces,'" Wishnasky began, "Pascal allowed himself the comfort of believing in God. I can't in good conscience avail myself of that illusion. Aside from that, yes, I feel Pascal's relevance."

Search for Me.

Another student, this one a curly-haired girl with enormous glasses, said. "If I understand your book correctly, a bourgeois life denies reality. How do you recommend that young people like us, who are just starting out in life, carry out that task truly? What are our options?"

"I can't tell you how to live," said Wishnasky, used to this question. "When you realize just how nonsensical everything on earth is, you have two choices and two only. Either you construct a lie you can live with—what Wallace Stevens meant by a 'necessary fiction'—or you go nuts. I can't recommend the latter." There was a smattering of laughter. "As to what fiction you choose, that's entirely personal. Each to her own fantasy."

The young woman wasn't finished. "What fiction do *you* choose?" she asked with what sounded a little like hostility. "How do *you* endure the meaninglessness you write about all the time?"

"That's easy enough," he said in a cheerful tone. "I choose art. To write a novel, that gives me pleasure. At the very least, the craftsman's pleasure in the craft. But do my books really matter? I know better. What takes three years of my valuable time will only occupy a fraction of the consciousness of the occasional reader, and is, I'm sure, entirely forgotten in a few weeks. So what's the lie that I tell myself? That I make a difference. That my audience needs me. And does this fantasy do its job, keep me going, and make me want to get out of bed in the morning? Yes, it does, so I embrace it. But at my best moments, I remember that I'm a lowly speck of felt living on a moldering pool table in a deteriorating juke joint that's been slated for demolition day after tomorrow."

You don't have time to waste.

The young woman sat down, looking dissatisfied, and Wishnasky became conscious of tightness in his chest, behind his sternum, right between the

nipples. It was the symptom of some emotion he didn't recognize immediately, something between sadness and panic, and it made him want to rush out
of the auditorium immediately. But another young woman was waving her
hand so insistently he felt an obligation to call on her. She was pretty, plump,
wearing a knee-length blue dress and white blouse, and her light brown hair
was cut short.

"Mr. Wishnasky," she began, "I really want to thank you for saving my life.
I was brought up by parents who didn't ever admit that there was anything
wrong with the world, that there was anything out there besides sunshine
and bluebirds. And I knew this was wrong, I knew it from the first time I
was bullied or sick or when a car ran over my favorite border collie. Then,
when I started high school and was looking for someone who had a more
credible vision, I came across your book, *The Anguish of the Condemned,* and
I was so very impressed. I read it over and over. I got a copy at the bookstore and another for my e-reader; I can quote passages from it like it was the
Gettysburg Address. And I just want to say thank you, a hundred times thank
you for teaching me and thousands of others what utter garbage the world is,
what a load of vomit and shit we all have to pass through, what an ordeal it is
to survive and endure on this junk heap with everyone else who—"

The pain in his chest was getting more and more severe, his head was swimming, and he felt he had to get out of the auditorium at once or make a spec-
tacle of himself. "Yes, that's fine, thanks," he mumbled, grabbed the volume of
Craters and rushed off the podium, up the aisle past the startled students, and
out the door. Once on the outside, he turned left and right, trying to regain
his senses, then remembered where he'd parked his car and ran for it. He was
panting when he fell heavily into the front seat, and the panting didn't stop
for minutes. Finally, he dried his eyes—tears had begun to fall—and turned the
key in the ignition.

You don't have time to waste.

"SO LET ME UNDERSTAND," said bug-eyed, wild-haired Ion Petrescu, sitting back in his chair and crossing his legs. "You live for two reasons only, writing novels and getting laid, and you're shocked when your brain says, 'I can't take it anymore; I need a change'?"

"So that's all it was?" asked Wishnasky, hopefully. "My need for a breather? A vacation, a mental holiday?"

Scrawny Ion leaned forward in his blue, four-wheeled business chair and smiled at Wishnasky, who was seated in the velvet-covered armchair he always chose during these sessions. There was another seat he might have selected—a black, wooden one that looked like it had been lifted from a grade school—but only a masochist (or so Wishnasky reasoned) would prefer its pitiless rigidity. There was also a lime green sofa against one wall of Ion's small office, which, Wishnasky assumed, was for couples or families.

"The Mind wants balance," said Rumanian-born Ion. "Spend all your time chasing *haute cuisine*, the Mind will give you food poisoning. I had a client who cared about nothing but horses: raising them, riding them, studying them like an encyclopedia. What happened? The man she fell in love with was allergic to hay. Stables made him violently ill. And she *needed* this joker. Happenstance? Or the Mind conjuring its opposite for its sly purposes?"

"But that's not natural," said Wishnasky. "You're acting as if life has some sort of credible shape. My whole career has been based on the opposite of that sentiment."

"And so of course you get these messages," said Ion with a shrug. "I had a client whose passion was singing, only singing. Love, money, children, these things didn't matter next to Cole Porter, Johnny Mercer, Harold Arlen. So what happened? You guessed it: polyps on her vocal cords. The more melody, the more damage. When she came to me, she had to whisper the whole story.

And I told her what I'm telling you: the Mind can't bear one-sidedness. Either you elect to have balance or the Mind will force the issue."

"So it's not that I've been contacted by God?" asked Wishnasky. "My own brain projected these messages onto the page of *Sisyphus*? I'm free to go on my way?"

"You make that mistake, you'll get even more messages. And louder ones. More demanding. Your whole problem is that you've been pointed in one direction so long, you're ready to explode."

"But I'm a success," said Wishnasky. "I like my one direction."

"Who said it's about what you like?" said Ion, smiling cunningly. "The Mind couldn't care less; it's primordial, aboriginal, and older than any of us. It carries all the memory of the human species from crawling out of the swamp to writing the Ninth Symphony. Speaking of which, ever wonder why Beethoven went deaf?"

This was too much. "What kind of reasoning is that? Most composers *didn't* go deaf! Mozart didn't go deaf!"

"Poor Mozart had worse problems. Poverty. Health issues. A spectacular childhood he couldn't recapture. Don't talk to me about Mozart."

"So let me understand," said exasperated Wishnasky. "What I thought I saw, I really saw. You're saying there's a God and God arranges these upheavals."

"I don't know what you're talking about," said Ion, miffed. "Whoever said I believed in God? Are you trying to insult me?"

"Then you believe that in a Godless universe, the human mind has secret purposes and enough willpower of its own to turn the tables on unsuspecting citizens. Where do you get this idea? Is this Jung? Is this the Collective Unconscious?"

"Ion Petrescu," said Ion Petrescu. "Who's been practicing psychotherapy for twenty-six years and who hasn't missed the clever patterns that hundreds of his clients have fallen into. Yes, I said 'patterns': set by the Mind, the deep human Mind. Which notices everything you do, everything you think, and then arranges things."

"So you *do* believe in God," said Wishnasky. "You just call it 'Mind' and then you give it all the powers that other people attribute to the Deity."

"You are refusing to hear me," said Ion, grimacing. "I don't believe in a Creator, a Law-Giver, a Judge at the hour of death. Nothing that I've seen in twenty-six years convinces me that there's a God. But Mind—oh, it's there.

Watching, dispensing, upsetting, even punishing. And right now, it's telling you to change your stripes—or else!"

"Well, I don't believe in your shrewd incorporeal Mind any more than I believe in Jehovah or Jesus or Gautama Buddha. I had a hallucination and I expect you to comfort me and warn me against overwork. Instead, you're talking like a priest."

"I'm unaffected by your outrage," said Ion. "You've been contacted. Now listen, or face even worse shocks. You can't escape your own brain."

"That's your diagnosis?"

"That's my diagnosis. And you'll see that I'm right."

"My mind says otherwise."

"See you when you get more impossible messages."

5.

THEY WERE AT A PARTY in Chestnut Hill, given by Maura Stokes, the *Boston Review* publisher, for whom Wishnasky wrote the occasional essay on Life in the Urban Wilderness. The house was elegant, brightly modern, a testament to good taste and wealth. The minimalist living room in which Wishnasky was standing featured calming indoor foliage, large urns inscribed with Native American runes, tan leather couches, floor-to-ceiling windows. There were thirty artists, editors, and critics drinking, arguing, laughing heartily and peering around anxiously. There was enough intellectual firepower to bring down a civilization.

Vanessa was talking with Boris Bulovich, the filmmaker. His movie *Spite* had become an instant classic with its tale of a father who chooses to squat in a slum just so he can be near his heroin-addicted daughter and her crystal meth-addled husband. At the end of the film, the father shoots up for the first time and the three lost souls lie in a filthy alley together, near-dead but a loving family. The *Boston Globe* had said it was "a parable for our time," and even *Variety* had called it "a tear-jerker from the front pages." Boris's more recent movie, *Landfill,* hadn't been nearly as successful, but its message of hopelessness on the Great Plains still found avid spectators among the nineteen to twenty-five demographic.

"For me, there's no one but Dostoevsky," Vanessa was saying. "Especially *Notes from the Underground.* Plato says that evil is caused by ignorance, that to know the good is to do the good. Dostoevsky comes along and says, Why not admit that one can choose the wrong path deliberately, because it's the wrong path? Why not admit that at bottom we love our bloody-minded freedom a hundred times more than we want to do right."

"I would like to make a movie of Dostoevsky's youth," said bald, bespectacled Boris, gesturing with the half-filled martini glass in his right hand.

"At the climax he's taken out to be executed by firing squad. Then, at the last moment, the tsar gives him a reprieve and sends him to Siberia. I see it as a metaphor for the contemporary predicament: death or Siberia. I would get Eric Schiaparelli to play Dostoevsky." Schiaparelli was a young singing star who had recently made his first movie. He had a fresh-faced, hopeful look that in no way appeared Russian or irrational.

"Schiaparelli would be a great choice," said Vanessa. "With a week's worth of stubble on his cheeks he'd be shattering." Vanessa loved actors who played against type. Conferring with desperately troubled students all day left her in search of harmless, playful paradoxes.

"Of course, the key is to find the funding," Boris said. "Even *Spite* cost sixty million. Outside Hollywood and Zurich, no one understands money." Boris always managed to mention *Spite* in conversation, no matter how far off the topic. No chance he was going to let anyone forget his few months on top of the heap.

Wishnasky wandered in, touched Vanessa's shoulder. "And what are you two gabbing about?" he said. He'd just been asked for the tenth time about the novel he was working on. Tonight, the question made him uneasy; in past days, he'd gloried in dispensing a tantalizing preview.

"Your beautiful partner and I are going to put Dostoevsky on film," said Boris. "And you're going to write the script."

"I am?"

"You will be paid for the six weeks' work on the screenplay fifty times more than you've made in a lifetime writing novels."

"I love your novels," said Stella Lombardo, the painter, gliding into the discussion with seamless charm. "I'll kill you if you go to Hollywood."

Wishnasky looked to Stella with gratitude. She was tall, brown-skinned, and muscular, and gazed out from two steel-gray eyes that seemed to pierce through your skull to something on the wall behind you. She was also wildly successful. Her paintings of the severed heads of celebrities had been hailed by *Artforum* as "a testament to contemporary death-consciousness and guilt." Although few would admit it, to be depicted by Stella with blood caked around your half-missing neck was the new emblem of High Achievement in New York and Los Angeles.

"Where's your guillotine?" asked Boris. "How will you conduct your Reign of Terror? Don't forget, Robespierre also ended up losing his skull."

"I love you too, Boris," said Stella. "And I only bring my guillotine when I'm working. This is pleasure." She looked through Wishnasky. "Or at least it's supposed to be."

"How are you?" said Wishnasky.

"I was fine until I saw this charlatan's *Landfill*," said Stella, gesturing at Boris. "You have your hero soldiering on at the end, dear Boris. You know that's disingenuous. You know that in any real world, he'd be as dead as his lover."

"You don't understand Hollywood," said Boris. "They won't finance honesty. They give you a choice: a little uptick at the finale or they toss you into the Pacific. If Galileo could fudge the facts, so can Boris Bulovich."

"Have you seen it?" asked Stella to Wishnasky and Vanessa.

"We haven't had the chance yet," said Vanessa. "I'm sure it's terrific."

"The distributor did focus groups," said Boris with a guilty look.

"Look, we're grownups here, right?" said Stella, now impaling Boris with her eyes. "And we know how things go. When you finish with your main character walking unbowed into the setting sun, you suggest there's a future. But ask Tristan: there's no future. None of us has any place to go at the finale. To intimate otherwise is just hypocrisy."

"We filmed three endings," said Boris. "The distributor chose the one you saw."

"Dishonest," said Stella.

"Pragmatic," said Boris.

"Wouldn't it be interesting," said Wishnasky suddenly, "if there was something to hope for after all?"

There was a pause. Then Stella said gently, "What do you mean, Tristan?"

Wishnasky felt his forehead begin to pulse. "Wouldn't it be interesting ... if while we were all rendering everything in gray and black ... if in fact there was something ... more colorful, let's say ... worthy of our ... searching?"

Another pause. Stella and Boris looked blankly at anxious Wishnasky. "What would that be, Tristan?" said Vanessa delicately, as if warning him not to make a fool of himself.

"Maybe there's not a name for it," offered Wishnasky, blushing. "But maybe it's something like ... what people mean ... when they speak of ... I mean, what if ... there's actually a ... you know ... something beyond us?"

There was a total silence—and then Boris and Stella burst out laughing.

"Get me the *Enquirer*," said Boris, shaking with mirth. "Get me *People* and *TMZ*. Tristan Wishnasky, the author of *Craters of the Spirit* just said he believes in God!"

"Oh, Tristan," said Stella, "you're hilarious! What a jester!" But Vanessa was ashen, silent.

"Trying to get a rise out of us, Tristan?" Boris said as he heaved with laughter. "May I quote you? What a comic!"

"I didn't say I believed it," said Wishnasky, feeling miserable. "But wouldn't it be ... fascinating ... if ... if we knew better than ... to claim otherwise. And maybe there is something to ... point ourselves toward. And we don't have endless time."

Vanessa grabbed his arm tightly and whispered, "I need to talk to you," as she pulled him away from the other two. "Are you ill?" she said, distraught. "Do you need to go home?"

"What did I say?" said Wishnasky, as they weaved through the crowd. "Where are you taking me?"

"Away from those two before you make an even bigger idiot of yourself. Do you remember who you are?"

"Of course I do. What's gotten into you?"

"You are Tristan Wishnasky. You are contemporary America's most trusted guide to the Bleak Nothingness. You are a fearless witness to the absence of all Purpose."

"You sound like my book jacket."

"You need to reread your book jacket. You have one little incident falling asleep over Camus and you're going to turn into Billy Graham? Do you realize how you sound? And in front of this crowd? This crowd gossips! This crowd gets interviewed! Have you lost your mind?"

"Stop pulling on me. I just said 'if.'"

"We're going outside."

She pulled him through the front door, smiling and waving at a couple flirting with each other on the front step. Out in the semicircular driveway, a sleek black BMW was just pulling up. There was no one else within earshot. "Now, I'm going to say this once and once only," Vanessa said. "You have a life people dream of. You're a critical and a popular success, you've moved tens of thousands to see the wasteland they're all crawling through, you bought a house on your fucking movie deal. Don't throw it away because of some brain fart one hot afternoon. Don't waste your enormous luck—yes, I said 'luck'—on some Seventh Day Adventist adventure in your reading room. I saved your ass just a moment ago." She looked toward the doorway through which they had just passed. "But I can't do that 24/7. Pull yourself together, catch your breath, then get back in there and tell them you were joking."

Wishnasky looked at her and saw that she was trying to help him.

"I don't know if I was," he said. "I've got to think about it a little."

"Then drive me home."

"Why?

"Because I'm concerned for you. Because I don't want you to blow it."

"I didn't mean to offend you," said Wishnasky. "I was just thinking aloud."

"Drive me home, please. Go get the car. We'll talk again in the morning."

He was too confused to argue and too surprised at himself to protest. He headed for his car feeling guilty and vulnerable.

6.

OF COURSE, VANESSA WAS RIGHT. She had to be.

He lay supine in the darkened bedroom, staring at the ceiling, trying to gather his troubled thoughts. Vanessa, sleeping on her stomach beside him, was breathing regularly, peacefully. He looked over at the digital clock radio on his night table: it said 1:46. Almost two in the morning and he was still working the thing through. Well, then, fine, that's what he'd do. Reason it out and put it to rest.

There were two possibilities: he'd been contacted by ... Something and was supposed to act somehow in response, or else he'd gone momentarily crazy, was seeing imaginary messages in a passing fit of schizophrenia. All indications pointed toward possibility two. Possibility one was ... unacceptable. God didn't exist. Freud had it right: God was an infantile wish fulfillment, a projection of one's father. Humans were alone in the universe and shouldn't tell themselves otherwise. God was a neurotic symptom.

You know better than this. Did he? Nothing he'd written in his three published novels had been anything less than heartfelt. He'd tried to look honestly at the world, without prejudice, without presumption, and he'd reported faithfully what he'd found—and, more to the point, what not. A personal God who could actually address you in nouns and verbs: never. Only in mythologies. Like the Bible, that book of counterfeits.

You know better than this. Was it true? He thought back to his childhood: saw himself in synagogue at age twelve with other unruly kids, preparing for a bar mitzvah neither he nor his parents thought anything more than a pricy formality. Sure, he'd kind of believed then—that's what childhood was, nonstop credulity. But then he'd wised up—first in high school, then at Harvard, oh, definitely at Harvard. Where he looked around and no one, *no one* took religion seriously. Not a single male friend, girlfriend, teaching fellow, professor.

He'd roomed for four years with two Protestants and a Catholic, but none of them thought Christmas anything more than a retailers' bonanza, or so much as bothered to go to church on Easter. God was a joke at Harvard, a wisecrack, a punchline, He only came up in late-night bull sessions over marijuana and beer, then was forgotten even before the pot smell had dissipated. It would have been embarrassing, no, *humiliating,* to admit believing in God at Harvard. And it was embarrassing now—he could only cringe at the thought of what Vanessa might say about it, or his agent Roland, or his critics ... *And then he took a new job teaching Sunday School at Oral Roberts University, and no one ever heard from him again.* Oh, how they would laugh. *And then he threw away his meteoric career to publish hortatory pamphlets on how to keep kosher.*

He thought for a moment about Vanessa lying beside him: how much good she did, and without an iota of religious faith. Yes, this was what all the rabbis and priests and ministers didn't want known: that one could be a decent person, an exceedingly generous human being, without imagining a God demanding decency and generosity. True, Vanessa could be sharp-tongued at times, but it wasn't long after meeting her that he'd discovered the enormous reservoir of goodness in her heart. Atheist though she was, she'd saved lives, ended abuses, treated the kids at her college like the most delicate of organisms to be rescued from brutal parents, hateful fellow-students, an unfeeling, often vicious unnatural habitat. If Vanessa was possible without God, what other heights could people reach without that ancient hypothesis? And wasn't he himself, Tristan Wishnasky, proof that you didn't need a deity in order to carry on a good life? Wasn't he caring, polite, modest in spite of his attainments? Who needed God if an entirely attractive life was possible without Him?

Yes, Vanessa was right, and so were Boris and Stella and Joyce and Beckett and, perhaps not least, Wishnasky. And no mental glitch could move him from an atheism that not only felt justified but provided the material for his books and fame. Religion? The only reason he'd ever given it a second thought was because of those writers—Eliot, Claudel, Auden—who'd chosen faith sooner or later, in spite of their times. But he'd always assessed Eliot's Anglicanism the same way he'd understood Brecht's communism: as a lie the poet cravenly backed into after too potent an encounter with the ghastly, terrifying truth. And that truth was the Wilderness, the Wasteland, the Jungle of the Cities. Could one honestly say otherwise?

Search for Me. What kind of God wouldn't just say, Here I am and *do this*? Why "search"? It made no sense. So maybe he *hadn't* seen the three messages. Maybe he'd seen a momentary after-image of some words in the Camus, something about the futile *search* for certainty and the sense, as one quested, that one didn't have *time to waste.* Yes, that was it: he'd invented the messages, and now he was back to normal, now he could hold his course as a convinced atheist. With a great feeling of relief, he strained his neck to look at the clock. But instead of blue numbers on its LED face, he saw, burning brightly:

You're Losing Time.

No—it couldn't be happening again. His heart leapt, he felt himself blanch, he fought an impulse to weep, to get out of bed and run. But before he did, he looked back at the clock and now it said:

Why Do You Ask My Name?

This was too much. "Vanessa," he cried out. She didn't wake. "Vanessa!" Now the clock face read: *Search for Me.*

"What?" said Vanessa groggily. "What's wrong? What are you doing?"

"What does it say?" asked Wishnasky. "The clock. Tell me what you see there."

She rose up on one elbow. "1:48. What's the matter? What's going on here?"

He looked and she was right: the clock was simply telling the time. He felt shaken and ashamed. "A dream. No, I'm sorry. Go back to sleep. It was just—a nightmare."

"You're getting weirder and weirder," she mumbled and buried her head back in her pillow.

He looked at the clockface: 1:48.

But he knew what he'd seen.

7.

"ALL RIGHT," SAID RABBI DIAMANT. "You had a mysterious experience and you think the Holy One might have been behind it. Now, what can I do for you?"

It was a Wednesday afternoon. They sat at a round table near the center of the rabbi's book-lined modern office in a synagogue Wishnasky hadn't entered in twenty-three years. The rabbi was a friendly, clean-faced woman who couldn't have been more than thirty, had medium-length black hair and wore a lime green suit that might have been appropriate on an executive. Wishnasky had made the appointment the first thing that morning and had suggested to the rabbi's secretary that the occasion was personal and very possibly an emergency. His emotions upon seeing the synagogue again—it stood out proudly on the top of a hill between Lexington and Bedford—had been worry, fear, and embarrassment. He felt that at any minute the editors of the *New York Review of Books* were going to burst through the door with microphones and photographers. He felt that the specters of Arthur Schopenhauer and Bertrand Russell were floating near his head, shaking their fingers at him. He was betraying his readers, his critics, himself. How could he have ever decided to take this silly step? But he couldn't imagine where else to pursue the mystery.

"Well, first," said Wishnasky, "is it possible that it was what it appeared to be? Does God contact people who read Camus? Does He send them English messages on an LED clock-radio screen?"

"The Holy One does what the Holy One wants," said the rabbi with a smile. "Were you contacted? It's not impossible. Were you hallucinating? Also possible. I'd like to believe that the first case is the true one. But of course, I'm prejudiced. You might say my whole career is based on the possibility that what you think happened did happen."

"Is there a precedent for this? Have other people been contacted this way?"

"In your particular way, not that I know of. But it's said in our tradition that when the Children of Israel stood at Mount Sinai, each one had a unique experience of the Divine, tailored to his or her capacity. Perhaps you were contacted in a way appropriate to you only."

"But I'm not a believer."

"Maybe someone wants you to reconsider."

Wishnasky peered at the rabbi and tried to decide how far to trust her. She didn't look particularly wise: her clear, smiling face lacked the valleys of a deep thinker. Still, he would give her a chance to authenticate herself.

"Tell me about your background," he said, trying to sound pleasant. "I'd like to know who's giving me life lessons."

"I graduated from Seminary three years ago," she said. "Before that I studied sociology at Johns Hopkins. This is my first congregation. Married, one child so far. My husband is an attorney in the Public Defender's office. Now you."

"My story?"

"That's right."

Wishnasky recounted his biography, emphasizing wherever possible his atheism. He especially pointed to his youthful fascination with Modernist literature, his studies in French and German at Harvard, his senior thesis on the transgressive novels of Jean Genet. He spoke modestly of his writing successes, leaving out the awards, and only touched the surface of his first marriage and its breakup. When he was finished, he found himself watching the rabbi's reaction. But he couldn't tell: that clear-skinned, straightforward face betrayed nothing.

"So now that we know each other, what do you recommend?" he said. "One of the messages said '*Search for Me.*' What does that mean?"

"It doesn't mean, 'Get out your telescope,'" said the rabbi. "There's a famous Jewish maxim: the world stands on three things: *Torah, Avodah,* and *Gemilut Hasidim. Torah* means the study of Jewish texts. *Avodah* means Jewish ritual. *Gemilut Hasidim* means doing acts of loving-kindness, especially for the poor and oppressed. Which sounds most attractive to you? That's where your search starts."

"Well, I'm most comfortable with texts. But there are a lot of them, aren't there?" He gestured to the tall bookcases lining the walls of the rabbi's office.

"That's right: there's *Torah* and *Talmud* and Commentaries. There are Codes like *Shulhan Aruch* and there's the classical *Midrash*. There's the *Responsa* litera-ture and all sorts of contemporary interpretations. Any of it sound familiar?"

"I had to study *Torah* for my bar mitzvah a couple of decades ago. Haven't looked at it since."

"Did it make an impression at the time?"

"I thought it was frightening. A lot of 'Thou Shalt Nots.'"

"All right, that's good to know." She stood up and walked over to the nearest bookshelf, which stretched a couple of feet above her. She ran her hands over the backs of the volumes in one section, then, after a hesitation, pulled one out. She looked briefly at the cover and walked over to Wishnasky and handed it to him. It was a paperback, no more than 120 pages, called *The Purpose of the Law* by Daniel Pawel Kagan, Jr. Wishnasky examined the cover art, an abstract drawing in blue and white, then looked up at the rabbi, who hadn't retaken her seat.

"This is short," he said. "Should only take a few hours. Then what do I do?"

"See me and let's talk about it."

"What if I hate it?"

"Then be good enough to say so."

"I have to warn you," said Wishnasky. "I can be ridiculously judgmental. I'm the sort of reader who looks for all sorts of flaws in his reading."

"You share that tendency with all the rabbis in the *Talmud*. Criticize away." She didn't sit down again.

"I'll hold you to that," said Wishnasky, rising. "Is there anything else?"

"No," said the rabbi. "But make an appointment once you've finished."

"You'll be available in a few days?"

"Well, Rosh Hashanah is coming and scheduling's tight. But talk to my secretary. She'll know when we can meet again."

"Thank you," said Wishnasky, and left the office clutching his prize.

He walked back to his car. So he was doing it after all: acting as if the eerie messages really mattered. Well, Mr. Kagan, Jr. wasn't going to have an easy sell. Tristan Wishnasky had been impatient with everything religious for over two decades, and he wasn't about to change his mind because of some visions that were most likely symptoms of an ophthalmic migraine. What's more, Mr. Wishnasky had Conrad and Chekhov and Umberto Eco in his corner. And Sartre and Foucault.

He opened his car door, tossed the book onto the passenger seat, and climbed in. He was beginning to entertain a more palatable theory, troubling enough but still credible: he was simply going mad. It had happened to a lot of writers before him, and now it was his turn. As he drove down the hill from the synagogue, he thought of McLean Hospital in nearby Belmont, where Robert Lowell, Anne Sexton, Sylvia Plath and other luminaries had spent days and months. That was probably where he was heading. Well, if so, he was in good company. Better than Kagan Jr., anyway. And there was a certain glamour in madness.

The Purpose of the Law: he was in no hurry to learn it.

8.

He and Vanessa were at his parents' house. It was their monthly dinner, and it was going as badly as ever.

Wishnasky's mother didn't like Vanessa, and Vanessa felt the same toward Wishnasky's mother. When the two were together, it was only a matter of time before they sprang for each other's throats. Wishnasky's father, oblivious as always to the bad blood between the two women, was no help at all, and in fact occasionally provided the spark that set them at each other. As for Wishnasky himself, his peacekeeping mission had failed so often, he could barely muster enough energy to make the usual mitigating gestures.

They were sitting in the spacious, well-lit powder-blue dining room, eating baked chicken in barbecue sauce with roast broccoli and boiled potatoes. Wishnasky and Vanessa sat on one side of the glass table, his parents, both looking small and intense, on the other. Unfortunately, Vanessa had somehow ended up directly opposite his mother. The subject was the local congressman, Alvin "Pudgy" Oppenheim. Wishnasky's mother, Mia, was singing his praises.

"He's a mensch," said Mia Wishnasky, her dyed blonde hair looking radiant though unconvincing. "He cares for the poor. He's got good, strong Jewish values."

Mia Wishnasky, atheist, saw Judaism as a set of socio-political attitudes. As Oppenheim had those attitudes, he was, in her mind, perfectly Jewish.

"He's a narcissist," said Vanessa. "I have no time for Alvin Oppenheim. There's probably no one in Washington more enamored of himself."

"This chicken is wonderful," said Wishnasky, hopelessly.

"Why don't you like Alvin Oppenheim?" asked Morris, unhelpfully. His wavy white hair and wide eyes made him look more knowing than he was.

"He came to the university to give a lecture a few years ago," said Vanessa. "I was tapped to introduce him. The whole time I was with him he talked of

35

nothing but himself, his opinions, his complaints, the wonderful time he and his wife had just had vacationing in Alaska. I could hardly get a word in about the students or their needs."

"A man like that does so much, "said Mia Wishnasky. "You have to excuse him his foibles."

"I don't have to excuse any man who's so obtuse and narcissistic that he doesn't even want to know who he's talking to."

"You know, the problem with you—"

Wishnasky's heart dropped.

"What," said Vanessa in her frostiest voice, "is the problem with me?"

"The problem with you," said Mia, unfazed, "is that you've never had children. With children, you learn to excuse a certain self-regard. You come to see it as healthy. It's even a sign of character."

Vanessa, in an earlier dinner, had revealed to Mia and Morris that she had no desire to raise children. Since that moment, the issue had generated contention.

"I see more kids in one day's work than most parents see in a year," said Vanessa. "All I do all day is deal with children. I can't believe what you just said to me."

"When they're *your* kids, it's different," said Wishnasky's mother, undeterred. "Other people's children don't tear at the heart the same way."

"You know, Vanessa is right, Mom," said Wishnasky with his best disarming smile. "She has a parent's problems times three hundred at that school. She could write a book on parenting."

Morris Wishnasky, missing everything that was going on, had a thought. "You know, in ancient Jewish times, you couldn't be a judge if you didn't have children. It was forbidden. Isn't that interesting?"

Morris Wishnasky, atheist, saw being Jewish as having a certain history. If you knew and respected that history—especially its worst moments: the Crusades, the Inquisition, and the Holocaust—you were, in his mind, an excellent Jew.

"Because I don't have children of my own," said Vanessa, barely suppressing her indignation, "I'm able to give more attention, during and after hours, to a bunch of desperately needy late adolescents whose biological parents are usually the reason they're screwed up in the first place. I'm shocked that you don't appreciate that. How would you feel if I said you hated the homeless because you hadn't taken any into your keeping this week?"

Wishnasky's mother, confident that she had drawn blood, relented a little.

"Maybe you're right," she said humbly. "Still, I'd vote for Pudgy Oppenheim whatever he was running for. Dogcatcher or President, he has my vote."

"An egomaniac," said Vanessa. "Dogcatcher's too good for him."

There was a moment of pained silence. Then Morris spoke up.

"So how's your new novel going?" he said to Wishnasky. "Are we going to be able to understand this one a little?"

"You'll understand it fine," said Wishnasky, glad for the new subject.

"I still don't get the last one. That child who wouldn't open his eyes. What was the point of it? Was he sick? Was he making some sort of statement?"

"He *was* making a statement. About what passes for appearances in the world he was thrown into. About refusing to buy into false hopes."

"There are blind people who would give everything they own in order to see," said Morris. "But your little boy chose the opposite. I find that strange."

"It was a symbol, wasn't it?" asked Mia like a bright undergraduate. "He was based on *Oedipus Rex*—he didn't feel he deserved his eyesight."

"Yeah, there was some Oedipus in him," said Wishnasky. "Thanks for the comparison. But Oedipus blinds himself because he realizes he's committed crimes too terrible to go unpunished. My character blinds himself because of *other* people's crimes. Because all he can see of life is selfishness and greed. And on the subject of intertextuality, there's also an allusion to Gide's *Pastoral Symphony*, which features a blind girl who kills herself when her sight is restored."

"All so bleak," said Mia. "But I suppose that's the fashion."

"It's not a question of fashion," said Wishnasky. "I wrote that little boy's character because I understood his objections. They're my objections too. They're anyone's objections who sees how much evil is triumphant in the world and how much innocence is crushed. I looked around and I was honest."

"But you were such a happy child," said Mia, pouting. "How could you enjoy such a pleasant upbringing and then write books where life is desperate?"

"You know, Mia," ventured Vanessa, "Tristan's novels only say what a great many people believe. That's why they've sold so well in spite of their literary quality. A lot of people feel despondent about this world we're all living in."

"You're thirty-six years old," said Mia to Wishnasky, deliberately ignoring Vanessa's interjection. "At sixteen, we fully expected you to be a rebel and cut your hair funny. But you're older now, you're an adult. And if you don't notice now just how beautiful the world is, then the one with the eyes closed is you, not your little boy character."

"You know, she's right," said Morris.

"And that's not all you're missing. There's an appropriate age for everything in this world and you're letting it slip away. At thirty-six, isn't it time you were remarried and raised children?" She glanced at Vanessa, who glared in response.

"We were talking about literature," said Wishnasky. "And why the modern novel is so often pessimistic."

"Is that why you don't want to have children?" said Mia to Vanessa. "Because you hate the world like Tristan?"

"Mia," said Vanessa, "I deal with children every day, five days a week, from eight to four, five, and sometimes six. I spend untold hours counseling children, calming children, and analyzing children. If I haven't chosen to produce any of my own, I deserve better than to be told that I'm a criminal on the earth."

"What's wrong with wanting children?" Mia said, her voice rising. "It's not normal, and meanwhile, you're keeping my son from his real life."

"I'm keeping ..." sputtered Vanessa. "Tristan, am I keeping you from anything?"

"Everybody, stay calm," said Wishnasky, watching the train wreck right on schedule. "Please. Nobody be unreasonable."

"Unreasonable?" said Vanessa. "I come here and absorb a hundred insults building to an attack on my life choices and I'm unreasonable?" Her voice was raised and her eyes were widening. "You're taking her side in this *mugging*?"

"I'm not taking anybody's side," said Wishnasky. "I'm thinking we should eat in peace and avoid all controversial—"

Vanessa stood up. "We're going," she said. "Say your goodbyes."

"Sweetheart," said Wishnasky. "Sit down. Please. My mother doesn't mean it."

"I mean every word I say," said Mia. "She and her peculiar ways are the reason I don't have grandchildren."

"Tristan," said Vanessa. "Stand up. Now."

"Tristan, if you walk out on me in the middle of dinner, I will be very deeply insulted," said Mia, tears coming to her innocent eyes.

"But it's okay to insult me?" said Vanessa.

Wishnasky knew there was no hope. "Vanessa, please sit," he said stupidly. "Everything's all right. There's no problem."

"Oh, there's no problem?" said Vanessa. "I give most of my life to the welfare of my students, only to be told that I'm a misanthrope and a family-wrecker? Come with me now or don't even think to spend another minute enjoying my company."

"I gotta go," said Wishnasky, rising. "I really wish you'd be more tactful, Ma."

"Sometimes it takes a little truth to wake a person up," said Mia.

"What's the matter?" said Morris. "Why aren't we enjoying dinner?"

"I'm coming," Tristan told Vanessa. They headed for the door.

"Such an excitable person," said Mia, innocent as a puppy. "What did I say?"

9.

IT TURNED OUT THAT Daniel Pawel Kagan, Jr. had a very precise understanding of Jewish law. Its purpose, he said early in his book, was to take morally clumsy, semi-bestial oafs, and turn them into ethical giants, blessings on the earth, and conscious representatives of a God who was entirely good. The *Torah*, he said, was the greatest self-help manual ever written, and had succeeded, over three millennia, in making personal improvement the fundamental theme of Western life from Mesopotamia to Oahu. Prior to *Torah*, Kagan Jr. explained, the occasional call to moral uprightness had been fatally mixed with savagery, torture, and bloodlust, and every abomination up to and including child sacrifice. The God of Israel would have none of it. He protected babies from their parents, the elderly from contempt, the whole world from homicide and larceny, and arrogant humanity from daily hubris. The *Torah* vision of the world was one of righteousness, compassion, peace—meaning not only tranquility but complete equity and the ability to freely enjoy the miracle of life. Any Jew who departed notably from any of these ideals was not being fully a Jew. Any gentile who lived up to them was as Jewish as Abraham.

Wishnasky closed the book and sat back in his armchair. His first instinct was defiant: Didn't the God of the Bible order all sorts of violence and punishment? So why all this talk about His profound respect for life? And even more important, where was the proof that the God who supposedly commanded these things really existed? Kagan Jr. took it for granted that God had indeed spoken at Sinai, but weren't the other religions just as certain that Jesus or Mohammed or Vishnu was equally loquacious? Wishnasky looked at the spine of the book on his desk and thought of the religion section at the Boston University Bookstore where he often browsed. Every faith had its shelf and every book purported to speak the unique Truth. How was Kagan Jr. any different?

True, there'd been one section of Kagan Jr.'s book that had given him pause. In a passage about the Jewish call to social justice, the author observed that most modern Americans lived hugely selfish lives—that outside their work and families, they spent next to no time helping others in a cosmos full of suffering. Wishnasky winced when he read this and thought defensively: Was it really selfishness if one spent his time edifying the fiction-buying public as to the meaninglessness of life? But the twinge in his conscience was impossible to deny, and he concluded, all right, maybe there was the smallest bit of truth in the assertion: people could be more generous. Not that it mattered in the end.

Besides this, the book mostly worked on his nostalgia. He saw himself as a child, learning Hebrew or singing Psalms in the narrow schoolhouse next to the main synagogue building on Grovener Hill. Maybe he really had believed at that time. But then came adolescence, and with it the realization that God was only a legend, a tall tale not corroborated by anything the universe really offered. And finally he'd come across Camus in the school library, and later the Hemingway of "A Clean Well-Lighted Place" (a sort of anthem of atheism) and the Fitzgerald of *Gatsby* (the enormous, empty eyes of Dr. T. J. Eckleburg), and Kleist and Virginia Woolf and Malraux and Genet ... Real life was there, with his literary heroes, not with a God he'd never truly noticed in thirty-six years of sentient life. Anyway, if God existed, why the horrors of World War II? Why the Armenian genocide, the atrocities in Cambodia, Rwanda, the Balkans and so many other places? Let the rabbi answer those questions and then maybe he'd consider the presumptuous Kagan Jr. and his arbitrary claims about an unverifiable deity.

And the words he'd seen while reading *Sisyphus? You know better than this.* Maybe, maybe not. *You don't have time to waste.* Well, neither did Kagan Jr., who, if the copyright was any indication, had already passed into the great darkness. *Search for Me.* All right, that was precisely what he was doing. And not finding, to be honest.

He closed his eyes and realized that the whole time he'd been reading, he'd been stifling a feeling of profound embarrassment. If his public only knew how he'd spent the last couple of hours. How let-down they'd feel, how cheated, betrayed. And they'd be right. He resolved to see the rabbi one last time, to thank her and tell her he wasn't convinced.

Search for me.

As if one could.

10.

It was a bright Monday afternoon, and Wishnasky was walking along fashionable Newbury Street with Roland Furbis, his crackerjack literary agent. As always with Roland, Wishnasky was uncomfortable: the man regularly made him feel naïve, a yokel. Still, Roland was a terrific agent. It was he who got *No One From Nowhere* a top imprint when Wishnasky was unknown, it was he who made sure that Wishnasky's contract for *The Anguish of the Condemned* compelled its publisher to go all-out promoting it, it was Roland who had negotiated such a high advance on the film deal for *Craters of the Spirit* that Wishnasky had been able to swing a mortgage on his house in Newton Corner.

And now tough-looking Roland—he served as a Marine, well-muscled with crewcut brown hair and thick glasses—was up from New York. They'd just finished a tense lunch at a crêpe place near Arlington Street; as usual Wishnasky had been made to feel ignorant of the world of publishing, a lamb among wolves. Then Roland had suggested they stroll together so he could have a parting look at bad old Boston. Wishnasky, as usual, was too intimidated to demur.

"These galleries," said Roland, gesturing at a show window with paintings in it. "All of them run by crooks, white-collar criminals who control the fine-arts market, create a career and destroy it in a single week if it'll line their pockets."

"I don't know much about it," said Wishnasky.

"I know too much," said Roland. "I represent half-a-dozen writers who put out fancy coffee-table tombstones, on Rothko or Schnabel or Judy Chicago. Working with the galleries is like working with hyenas. After they kiss you, count your teeth."

They walked by a shop that sold ski equipment and winter coats. "Then I'm glad I don't know them," said Wishnasky, trying to sound innocuous.

"You've got problems of your own," said Roland. "Darryl Kamfort. That reptile. That boa constrictor. It's no accident the man has been married four times. What woman could stomach living near that septic tank for more than a few weeks? That ugly, malevolent python."

Kamfort was Wishnasky's editor on his last two books. Wishnasky liked him and found his personal style rather pleasant.

"Darryl's always been good to me," he said with a smile.

"That's his M.O., don't you know," said Roland, squinting aggressively. "He draws his victims in with compliments, generosity, a gentle manner. Then when he's got you, he's into your private life, your weaknesses, which he manipulates so shrewdly, you don't even feel the poison enter your entrails. I've got to admire your ability to work with him all this time. Most of my clients get a close whiff and they run."

"He's been a good editor," said Wishnasky.

"You're lucky. Most of his authors are overwhelmed by the stink. And the lies. And the demands. Speaking of which, we hurried through lunch without mentioning *Traveler*. Are you on deadline? Will you finish on time?"

"I've had a few setbacks. It's not coming as quickly as I'd like."

The fact was he'd spent less and less time on *Traveler in the Abyss* ever since he'd seen the messages in the Camus book and on the clock radio. At first there'd been no problem. But to produce his protagonist's downward spiral from Digital Baron to common beggar, he had to believe that he was describing something true not just about Edward Ozono but about humanity in general: its real prospects in the Cosmic Sahara. And though he didn't like to admit it, that first phrase—*You know better than this*—kept getting in the way. One steadfast principle that Wishnasky held to as a writer—the very basis of his success, he suspected—was his refusal to express anything he didn't fully believe. But thinking on that message, he'd begun to wonder if it was possible—just barely possible—that he'd been a little presumptuous. Maybe the Ozonos of the world regularly failed to commit suicide not because of a blind will to live but because there were some good things—not God, not the hope of heaven, certainly, but physical pleasure and earthly love and satisfying work, for example—that they didn't want to miss. He hadn't thought it out fully yet—he knew how to let an idea simmer inside him, for months if need be—but till he'd decided one way or another, he couldn't put Edward Ozono through the degradation he'd originally plotted. Which meant the novel was stalled.

"My clients don't miss deadlines," said Roland gruffly, stopping in the middle of the sidewalk. "I use every weapon in my arsenal to get you a good contract, and what that crapulous publisher Rebecca Mallory gets in return is a manuscript in PDF format one minute before midnight on the agreed-upon date. Are you honestly telling me you're going to miss your deadline?"

"I don't know. I can't control these things."

"You can't control—Are you a *paramecium*? I gave you three years to write *Traveler*, you *swore* to me that that was enough time. What have you been doing, contemplating your *vacuole*?"

"I've been showing up at the writing desk, if that's what you're asking. But it's not moving along. Maybe it will again tomorrow. Let's walk."

"How can I walk? You're going to humiliate me in front of every publisher in New York!"

"Given the way my third book sold for her, I think Rebecca will be forgiving."

"That's giving her the power! The one who forgives is the one with the power! You're going to ruin me in this business!"

Wishnasky started walking again and after half a moment, Roland caught up with him.

"All right," said Roland. "I'll talk to Rebecca Mallory. That bitch. That medusa. I'll tell her you've had a terrible family tragedy and it's affecting your work."

"Rebecca knows I'm not the sort to treat deadlines cavalierly."

"That cesspool. That walking horror. It's no wonder her daughter's addicted to cocaine. If I had a mother like that, I'd do nothing but take cocaine."

They strolled in silence for a few moments more, crossed Gloucester Street along with a crowd of students and a few middle-aged adults, and then continued up Newbury. It was a cold mid-afternoon: the store windows reflected the unobscured three o'clock sun. Looking at all the traffic, Wishnasky wondered if he'd been right to call these streets an abyss. To be absolutely honest, they didn't, at this moment, appear very abysmal. In fact, most everyone around him seemed animated, sprightly, even joyful. He looked for the usual exceptions—the insane, the vagrants—and sure enough, he saw a strung-out-looking beggar with scraggly gray hair and a cardboard sign: "Anything helps. God bless you." All right, who was the world-historical character: this unhappy mendicant or the young blonde laughing with her girlfriend in front of the shoe store? True, the young blonde and her kind were in the majority here.

But on other continents, weren't the beggars the rule, weren't the impoverished and the hopeless the ones dominating the village streets? Which was false then: this upscale Disneyland or a dirty alley in Bangladesh? And if both were true, could one believe in an all-caring God?

"You've made me sad," Roland was saying. "I come to Boston to meet with my favorite nihilist workhorse and I find he's been spending all night twiddling his *cilia*. You've made me despondent."

But Wishnasky wasn't listening. He was now entirely aware of the beggar with the cardboard sign, and the words, "God bless." He felt a guilty impulse to take a dollar bill from his pocket and give it to the unhappy man, but he also felt that if he did, Roland would eviscerate him. On the other hand, he thought about the book he'd just finished—Kagan Jr. had written about the words "charity" and "justice" being identical in Hebrew—and he felt a slight itch, the merest temptation … The beggar looked up at him: time to decide. No, he'd just spend it on whiskey. Or crack cocaine. And he didn't feel like being mocked. They walked past, Roland chattering on the whole time.

"She's a banshee," the agent said, about someone Wishnasky couldn't identify. "She's a garbage can on two legs. Stay away from her like you would if you came upon a mound of dog turds. I'm just telling you this for your own good."

"Wait a minute," said Wishnasky, suddenly stopping his forward progress. "Wait, there's something I've got to do." Not fully understanding why, he reached into his back pocket, removed his wallet and looked for a dollar bill. Only a couple of twenties. He searched his pants pockets for change.

"What are you up to?" asked Roland. "What are you looking for?"

"Nothing." He glanced at Roland. The agent was watching him incredulously, ready to pounce when he saw Wishnasky pull off the good deed. The heart went out of him. He looked up again at the beggar, but the poor guy was already walking away, bent and pathetic. Meanwhile, Roland glared like a cheetah about to strike.

"What's gotten into you?" asked Roland.

"Nothing," said Wishnasky as, with a sigh, he began to walk again. Well, he'd spared himself some grief. Still, he felt uncomfortable. "How far do you want to go?" he asked.

"Up to the Mass Ave.," said Roland. "Then I'll catch the first cab to Logan."

Wishnasky felt unsettled. He didn't know why he'd almost given money, but was glad—he thought—that it hadn't worked out. Still, just to give a little change … He walked along the street, barely hearing Roland destroy the reputations of all his colleagues. He felt dizzy. He wondered why he'd hesitated so fatally. He wondered if he'd failed some sort of test.

"She's got the morals of a character out of Edgar Allan Poe," Roland was saying about someone. "She's got a private life out of H.P. Lovecraft."

They walked through the cold afternoon as Roland expertly obliterated yet another unsuspecting personality.

11.

VANESSA HAD BEEN DIFFERENT to him since the troubled evening with his parents. He'd tried to restore good relations, but something was bothering her and in her usual stubborn way, she was waiting for him to broach the subject. Finally, he called her and said, "Okay, I surrender. When do you want to talk about it?"

"Come over at seven," she said. "I'll pour you a glass of your favorite wine." Then he knew it was important, and no doubt, about their relationship. He hoped he'd survive.

Vanessa's apartment was in Cambridge, a few blocks from Harvard Law School in one direction and Hilles Library in the other. It was upstairs in a wooden two-family house that was one-quarter rented to Vanessa, one-quarter to her downstairs neighbor, and one-half still in the possession of their landlady and her family. When Wishnasky finally found parking—a cramped space between two SUVs—he took a quick look around him—well-kept pastel homes all along one side of the street, a monolithic brick condominium building opposite—and used his key to get in the front door. At the top of the stairs, he found the door to Vanessa's apartment already open. She was waiting in the living room, wearing a pink knit sweater and slim black jeans. Her blue eyes were sparkling and her dark hair was freshly washed: she looked as alluring as she ever had. Something was up.

After the kiss, the small talk, the pouring of the Pouilly Fuissé, she inhaled sharply. Then she began:

"I'm not going through that again," she said. "I'm not going to let you put me in a position where I have to absorb insult after insult from your dreadful mother. That was the last of it."

"Look," said Wishnasky. "I endure your brother and his reactionary politics, not to mention your friend Yolanda and her contempt for anything with testosterone. If I can survive those two, you can handle harmless Mia."

"I don't think you understand. She hates me because I'm Catholic, she hates me because I don't want children, and most of all she hates me because her little boy is so satisfied fucking me, he doesn't have time for her twenty-nine days out of thirty."

"It's a comedy," said Wishnasky. "People. Family. See it as a comedy and then you won't get hurt."

"To see it as a comedy would require that I have calluses the thickness of tree bark. But I don't; that's your malady. Meanwhile, I sense it when someone cuts me. I feel the rusty knife."

"All right, I'll talk to my mother. I'll tell her if she insults you even one more time, we'll stop visiting altogether."

"I'm not going back. From here on, she'll have to take target practice on someone else."

Wishnasky sipped his wine and tried to understand how best to defuse Vanessa's anger. He'd tried many times to assure her that his mother's barbs weren't aimed at her in particular: they were directed at any woman who dared claim her son's affection. Wishnasky had been enduring this jealousy since he'd been in high school, and he expected the women he went with to endure it also. Most of them did; as always, Vanessa was exceptional.

"Okay," he said. "No more dinner visits with my parents, at least for a while. Now, end the emotional lockout. Tell me the combination."

"What do you want from me, Tristan?" asked Vanessa, importunate.

"What I—your company," he said. "Your mind. Your body. Everything about you. Haven't I made that clear?"

"But to what end?" said Vanessa. "Are you going to ask me to marry you? And if so, when? In five years? After your parents pass? What's the strategy?"

"Strategy?"

"What's the scheme? I don't imagine you ever play anything by ear."

Wishnasky looked down at his wineglass and tried to formulate his response. Since the end of his marriage and before meeting Vanessa, he'd steadily dated three other women, none of whom he'd come to love. As for Vanessa, she was different. He felt affection for her that might be love (it was certainly in the vicinity) and he could think of no other woman whose intellect he more admired. Of course, she wanted to know if they'd marry: they were both too old not to wonder. But he didn't know the answer.

"I figure," he said finally, "that we'll continue to see each other as we've been doing. And either one thing will lead to another or it won't. I can't predict."

"That's not good enough anymore," said Vanessa. "I want a time frame. A deadline. You say you care for me, well, tell me to marry you or not and let's get this thing over with, one way or another."

"All right, six months," he said.

"Six weeks."

"Six weeks is nothing. With my writing and your work at the college, six weeks adds up to very few hours together."

"Six weeks, and the next time we see your parents is to announce our engagement or disbandment. Agreed?"

"No, not agreed. Are you offering me a choice?"

"I suppose not. I suppose I'm giving you an ultimatum. I'm sorry. I don't like doing that."

He didn't know how to answer; still, maybe an impasse would be productive. "All right, six weeks," he said finally. "If you insist. But I'd rather we let this thing develop more naturally."

"Six weeks is lots of time for nature to show its face," said Vanessa. "More than enough. Good, now we've decided."

She smiled at him, picked up her wineglass and brought it to her lips. Watching her, Wishnasky tried to understand his feelings. Maybe this love thing was overrated. He'd loved his ex-wife and that hadn't mattered in the end, so maybe something else—respect, affection, friendship—was what he should be valuing. Or maybe the key was admiration. Perhaps the admiration he felt for Vanessa could evolve into love—though it was disturbing to think that didn't seem to be happening. On the other hand, what if the attachment he felt now was as strong as he'd ever feel for any woman in the future, and to abandon it would be the greatest error of his life? What if years from now he was remembering that he could have been happy with a woman he profoundly esteemed, but here he was, sixty years old, lonely, and no Vanessa?

She put down her glass and stood up. "Let's make love," she said, and the smile on her face was dazzling. Wishnasky rose and they embraced and walked together through the narrow passageway leading to her bedroom.

At least on one level there was no question about their compatibility. As they fell onto her bed, Wishnasky put all worries out of his mind. It was good to know Vanessa. It was possibly the best thing in his life.

12.

"VERY GOOD," SAID THE RABBI. "What did you think of Kagan's book?"

Wishnasky was sitting in the rabbi's office, legs crossed, the book on the round table in front of them. The rabbi, seated opposite him, was wearing a brown dress with a Star of David pin on the broad collar. She looked at Wishnasky with an encouraging smile.

"I think that if you'd given me six books by six writers from six different religions, each would have claimed with the same confidence that his or her view was the truthful one."

"I didn't give you six books," she said. "I gave you this one. And I'm wondering what you thought of it."

Wishnasky considered telling her his reaction to the section on modern selfishness, but decided against too personal a revelation. "It's got a nice perspective," he said instead. "It's cute that Mr. Kagan Jr. wants to turn me into an ethical paragon. But when he says that it's God's will, I get the feeling that, no, it's Kagan Jr.'s will. And I don't know why I should be changing my life to please Kagan Jr."

"There's nothing he says that's not directly from *Torah*," said the rabbi. "It's all right if you disagree with it. But then it's *Torah* you disagree with, not the writer who paraphrased it. Do you find you disagree with *Torah*?"

"Not really," said Wishnasky. "But since the *Torah*'s writers were probably as human as you or I, that's who I found: Mr. Schwartz and Ms. Cohen. I didn't find God."

"I didn't expect you to," said the rabbi. "Your search is just beginning. Now, how did you feel about the part where the author says the on-the-ground purpose of Judaism is to create admirable human beings? Generous, unselfish activists? How did you respond to that?"

"It sounds like no sex."

Rabbi Diamant laughed. "Just the contrary. Sex between husband and wife is a *mitzvah*, a commandment. And most Conservative Jews like myself are rather liberal when it comes to consensual premarital sex as well. If that's what you're worried about, ease up: you can still spend a weekend in Las Vegas with your sweetie." She laughed again.

"That's a great relief."

"Any other thoughts that the book provoked?"

"Yeah, as a matter of fact. If God's so anxious to have people listen to Him, why is He relying on people like Kagan Jr. for publicity? Why doesn't He just blast a word or two from heaven?"

"You may have had, for a very few seconds, a contact with the Divine. And look how it's affected you. How do you think it would change people if God were actually to appear and begin commanding this or that behavior? What would it do to people's free will? To their personal consciences?"

"You're saying that God chooses not to appear to people in order to preserve their freedom?"

"That's precisely what I'm saying."

"Well, that's a pretty convenient thought. What about all those moments when I really need God to appear, not to inform me of His existence but to save me from danger? What happens when a Fenway thug holds a gun to my temple and I need God to intervene to save me?"

"Maybe God will."

"And maybe not."

"Is that really the sort of world you want? Harmless as a stuffed bear?"

"Yes, as a matter of fact."

"Just think what you're saying: you want a world where any time a gun is fired, the bullets turn to marshmallows before they reach their target. If a tree were to fall, it would become a tower of Jell-O before it hit a nearby lumberjack. Before a car hit another car, both would turn into ocean foam. Is that what you crave, a global daycare center? A world where the laws of nature cease to apply anytime someone's endangered? Is that your concept of God's grace?"

"Is the only alternative one where the bullet hits its target?"

"Isn't it? Or do you prefer a playpen, where everything's made of soap bubbles?" Wishnasky paused for a moment. Of course, he wanted a real world with genuine pleasures and meaningful transactions. But was the only alternative a child's playground? There must be something missing from the rabbi's reasoning. "You're saying that God wants the world to be real. Even real enough to hurt."

"That's right. And something else: God wants you to have enormous freedom in this reality. To do good. Or ill. Entirely up to you."

"So when millions of people were murdered in the Holocaust—"

"Freedom," said the rabbi. "Same as before. Even for great evil."

"Then you're a deist," said Wishnasky, "like Benjamin Franklin or Thomas Jefferson. God created everything, and now He just sits back and watches."

"Not at all," said the rabbi. "The Holy One appeared at Sinai to tell us how we're to live. And when God chooses, the Jews are saved from Seleucid persecution. And D-Day is effective. And Israel wins its War of Independence. Some things the Holy One leaves to freedom, in other cases the Almighty gets involved. Not just the kindly clockmaker."

"Does He answer prayers?"

"Yes, some of them."

"How do you know?"

"Because the Holy One's answered so many of mine."

"I wish I could believe that."

"Do better than believe. Try it. Not just once, but as you develop a relationship with the Holy One, ask for the right things. Not a winning lottery ticket, but something consistent with your genuine needs. You might be surprised."

Wishnasky didn't know which he liked least: the idea that he had to develop a relationship with a God whose existence he doubted, or the thought of formulating prayer. The one seemed like an abdication of his rationality, the other a ridiculous diversion from real life.

"Look," he said. "The fact is, as a novelist, as a human being, my eyes are wide open. And what they see isn't infused with God. What they see is a lot of poverty, despair, confusion, war. There's no way God is involved with this mess."

"I don't understand."

"It's too screwed up," said Wishnasky, with a depth of emotion that surprised him.

"Whatever gave you the idea that it's not supposed to be?"

The question baffled him. "Well, the Bible, since you ask. Which wants me to believe that there's a benevolent Almighty keeping things peachy."

"Are you serious? The Bible never paints the world like that. Our patriarch Abraham faced famine, war, the kidnapping of his wife, the banishment of one of his sons. Isaac was bound on an altar and just barely escaped, was deceived by his wife and his child in old age, and eventually went blind. Jacob had to flee a murderous brother, was duped by his employer into a marriage he didn't want, lost his favorite son Joseph for years, and his beloved Rachel in childbirth. And these were people in contact with God, sometimes day to day. Wherever did you get the idea that life is supposed to be easy? Certainly not from the Bible."

Wishnasky felt uncomfortable. If what the rabbi said was true, there was even less reason to believe in God than before. Didn't she realize it?

"If you can worship God and still have a messed-up life, why worship Him?" he said.

"A few reasons. One of them's in Psalms: 'Many are the afflictions of the righteous, but the Lord delivers him out of them all.' Which is another way of saying, when things do go wrong, it's nice to have God in your corner."

"Other reasons?"

"We Jews believe in a heaven, a life after life. There's that prospect to keep in mind."

"Other reasons?"

"God created you. God allows you to have an exciting career as a writer and a lover and an intellectual seeker. A little gratitude wouldn't be out of order."

Wishnasky was silent again. Then, cautiously—he didn't want to seem credulous—he said, "Why would God create a world that's so messed up? What's the intention behind it?"

"The classical *Midrash* answers that too. Do you know what *Midrash* is?"

"No."

"Call it Biblical interpretation-*cum*-literary criticism. And it reminds us that *Torah* says God created the world 'for making.' '*Bara la-asot.*' The Holy One did the creating. And then left the making to human beings."

"The world is supposed to be screwed up?"

"Incomplete, *Torah* would say. And we're to complete it—'repair it under the sovereignty of the Almighty,' according to the *Aleinu* prayer. And in the process of repairing it, and of facing the difficulties every life includes, we become better: more caring, more courageous, more morally adult. Yes, that's basic *Torah* doctrine."

Wishnasky pinched the bridge of his nose with his thumb and forefinger. He looked around the office, saw the smiling photographs of past synagogue presidents, not one of whom looked likely to have escaped life's vicissitudes. Still, he was searching for that defect in the rabbi's argument, the defect he knew had to be there. "How do you know all this?" he finally said. "Excuse me for mentioning it, but you're not that old. Where do you get this information?"

The rabbi laughed. "I get it precisely as you can: from study and prayer. I read the main Jewish texts, especially *Talmud*, which you'll get to. When I'm stumped, I find prayer often precedes my sudden light bulb. But there's nothing that I've learned that you can't discover just as well. In the old days, every Jew—well, every male Jew—was supposed to be a scholar. Not just rabbis. Are you ready for your next assignment?"

"I don't know," said Wishnasky, feeling that he'd failed himself somehow. "I don't know that I need another book."

"I'm not thinking of another book. I want you to try something else. I want you to try one heartfelt prayer to God between now and our next meeting."

"Out of the prayer book?"

"The prayer book is wonderful, but no, not yet. A Jew is supposed to have a personal relationship with the Holy One. That's only possible if you pray personally."

"What would I pray about?"

"Prayer has four elements: praise, confession, thanksgiving, supplication. Try one for size."

"How can I praise God if I'm not sure He's there?"

"Make that part of your prayer. Start with, 'God, I don't think you're listening.' Then talk."

The rabbi stood up and Wishnasky rose too. He had a sudden desire to drive home, banish all this religious nonsense from his mind and bring old Ozono to desolation as originally intended. He felt resentful: at the rabbi, at Kagan Jr., at the words in the Camus book and on his clock radio. He'd been sailing along smoothly, making good progress in his life when all this foolish interference had come out of nowhere. But then the thought returned to him: The world is supposed to be messed up? Incomplete? All right, that was a new way to look at things. That was possibly useful. But the idea of asking God for anything was still unattractive. Praying to empty air.

"Why do I feel so uncomfortable about all this?" he asked Rabbi Diamant. "If you're this prodigy of *Torah*, tell me. Why does all your talk of God, *Torah* and the screwed-up world make me so anxious?"

"Do you want the honest answer?" she said.

"Of course."

"Because you were a child when your faith was taught to you, and not very illogically, it was taught as if to children. But you're an adult now, and I'm not going to rehash all that infantile information. Stop worrying: you're about to learn the adult version of your religion."

Wishnasky nodded—not knowing what the gesture meant—thanked the rabbi and left her office. All the way to his car he tried to understand how he had missed the point that, yes, the main characters in the Bible all had challenging lives: Noah and King David and Esther and all the rest. All right, so God being in charge wasn't contradicted by a troubled world. But still, if God really existed, wouldn't He make it more obvious to more people more often? And then what about those people who didn't respond to life's difficulties by becoming wiser, more moral? What about those who became bitter or criminal or insane? Was that part of God's intention?

Something had to be wrong with the rabbi's deep certainty.

13.

WISHNASKY WAS IN THE locker room of his athletics club, changing into his tennis clothes along with his good friend and former college roommate, Chet Remington. Chet, thirty-seven, still had a mop of blond hair, black-rimmed glasses, and the slender body of a swimmer, which he'd been on the Harvard team. He and Wishnasky, along with their buddies Rick and Quentin, had roomed together fifteen years earlier. Now Chet was a lecturer at the Fletcher School of International Diplomacy at Tufts and a part-time attorney who specialized in obtaining asylum for political refugees. He was also a tennis player approximately on Wishnasky's level; when they found time to play, either one of them might triumph. Lately, Wishnasky had had the victories, but Chet was faster on the courts and regularly scooped up shots that a slower runner never would have reached. Whoever won would, as usual, buy the other's lunch at the club café.

Their changing finished, the two men walked out to the playing area. It comprised four clay courts, all under an expandable roof that the club erected every September and took down in late spring. On three of the courts, players were slamming yellow felt balls back and forth, occasionally grunting as they sent their topspin drives into each other's forehands. The temperature inside the dome, controlled by the sports club, was as pleasant as a day in April or May. Reservations were for ninety minutes: just enough for a warm-up, a long set and a few games more. The two men joked with each other as they removed their racquets from their cases, set them down on the green metal bench between courts and took up position on opposite sides of the net. Then they began their practice.

Wishnasky found it difficult to keep his emotions out of the action. He repeatedly hit the ball too hard, batting it way beyond the baseline and forcing Chet to retreat to the back wall in order to retrieve it. Wishnasky apologized a few times and then made precisely the same error. Meanwhile, Chet's strokes were sizzling and accurate, low and right down the middle, arching a little on forehands and straight as a bullet on backhands. Wishnasky sensed he was going to lose but didn't care—he just wanted to think about something, anything, besides the message in the Camus book, Vanessa's ultimatum, and his paralysis on the new novel. With so much to worry him, creaming the ball felt cathartic.

After the warm-up, they started playing. Wishnasky won the coin toss and served the first game. But his first, hard serves kept overshooting the mark, his second had little power, and within a few seconds Chet was off to the win. He took the first set 6-3, and was ahead 3-1 in the second when they ran out of time. As they collected their tennis bags and walked toward the club café, Wishnasky was still thinking of all the problems he was facing, and barely hearing Chet's opinion that Wishnasky was having an off day.

At the café where the two men sat with their fruit juices, Wishnasky asked Chet about his work for refugees. "I've got a couple of important cases," Chet said. "One is a group of indigenous workers from Colombia. A huge farming company is trying to scare them off their land and has murdered several of them with impunity. Many have stayed in Colombia to fight, but my clients feel sure that they're high on the list of targets. My other interesting case is a gay man from Ghana, where homosexuality is against the law. His house was burned down by a self-styled vigilante group, he's been beaten up by police, his life and freedom are in danger if he sets foot back in Ghana, and still the US is seeking to forcibly deport him. He's in a prison in Pennsylvania now while Immigration officials try to dispatch him to his death." Chet sipped his mango juice. "It's amazing what's happened to this country the last few years," he said. "Lady Liberty's not nearly as welcoming as she advertises."

Wishnasky tasted his own grapefruit concoction, his mind still juggling several subjects. "Listen, Chet," he said. "All the good deeds you do for these refugees—it's all *pro bono*, right? They don't pay you a thing."

"They would if they could," said Chet. "They're mostly broke. If they have any money, they need it for food."

"So why do you do it? You're not religious, right?"

"That's right. Not since high school."

"What's the philosophy behind your altruism? If you're going to spend part of your non-academic time lawyering, you could earn a lot more with a different sort of client."

"I don't really know," said Chet. "I guess it's how I was raised. Both my parents were pretty committed Methodists, and they always taught us the John Wesley thing: 'Do all the good you can, by all the means you can, in all the ways you can.' I think that was drilled into my sisters and myself so much that it stayed. Even when the religion didn't."

Wishnasky thought about his own parents and their mixed messages about charity: admire the charitable but don't yourself get bamboozled. Then he thought of the beggar on Newbury Street. Why hadn't he helped the poor guy? Because the mendicant would have wasted it on drink or drugs? Wasn't there just as much likelihood that he would have spent it on fruit and meat?

A waiter brought over a wide brown bowl filled with tortilla chips and asked if the two men were ready with their orders. Chet's winnings were to be a turkey club and cole slaw, and Wishnasky chose a vegetable wrap with a side of potato chips. As the waiter walked away, Wishnasky thought of something that his reading of Kagan Jr., had begun to suggest to him.

"Listen, Chet," he said. "If I ask you a somewhat personal question, will you promise to answer truthfully? Even if it might feel that I'm asking you to criticize me?"

"No, I don't think your tennis is a hopelessly lost cause. One of these days you're going to beat me again."

"Not the question."

"All right. Shoot."

Wishnasky looked around the café, hoping that no one else could hear him. Then he charged ahead: "Do you think it would be accurate to say I'm a selfish person?"

"You? Not at all."

"Why not? What's your reasoning? I don't take pro bono cases for asylum seekers from Ghana. I don't even teach the occasional creative writing class like I used to. Why am I not selfish?"

"Your writing is why. It's full of jewels—great ideas, beautiful expressions, new ways of seeing what life is and how to live it. I think you provide a real service."

"But what sort of jewels have I brought to my readers?" said Wishnasky. "In three novels I've told them that life is a bad joke and people have to bushwhack their way through the jungle in any crazy way they can. How is that 'providing a service?'"

"I think you're misreading your own message," said Chet. "Which is 'Live this mess with dignity. Slog through it with real honor.' At least, that's what I've always gotten from it. I feel you've helped me."

"Look," said Wishnasky, articulating, with some effort, a thought that was new to him. "I sit in my office six hours a day, writing novels that, if they connect, bring me money and fame and other personal pleasures. I'm not raising a family, I'm not looking after a wife and kids. If I give a free talk at a bookstore it's only to stimulate more book sales. I hardly donate anything to charity—maybe if there's some sort of major disaster, but on a regular basis, no, it never occurs to me. And at the end of the day, nothing I've created has made anyone better off or safer or stronger. Someone I read recently suggested that people have some sort of obligation to look after others, and I wonder, if I truly knew myself, whether I'd see what this all adds up to: that for most of my adult life, I've been pretty much a narcissist."

"You do a lot," said comradely Chet with his most helpful smile. "You've got no reason to criticize yourself. Just keep digging up jewels."

"Nobody can eat jewels," said Wishnasky. "You can't build a shelter with them, and they don't cure any diseases."

"Man, what's going on with you? What's happening with Vanessa? I'll bet this is about her somehow."

Reluctantly—because he sensed it was off the subject—Wishnasky told Chet about the latest flap at his parents' house and Vanessa's demands afterward. But before Chet could opine, Wishnasky changed the subject. "Also, I've been looking at Judaism," he said. "Having some conferences with a rabbi so that I can work out what I believe."

"Great," said Chet. "I've been meaning to investigate Methodism one day and see if it still touches me. Hey, it's wonderful that you're on this path. Just more information to consider and maybe add to your novels."

"I don't know that it's helping. I suspect its real effect is to make me unhappy with myself."

"That's probably good, too. You don't want to be the same old Tristan day in and day out."

"I embarrassed myself a little while ago," said Wishnasky. "I was at a party with Vanessa and I suggested that maybe there was a possibility something existed beyond the material world. I was laughed out of the room by the people I said it to, then excoriated by my date as if I'd uttered a vulgarity."

"What's Vanessa's beef with religion?"

"She had a terrible ordeal with it," said Wishnasky. "Fanatical parents and grandparents, tough nuns, prurient confessors. She was taught as a basic principle that women were responsible for bringing sin into the world. When she rebelled, she went all the way."

"Well, you've got to respect her pain on the subject."

"It's weird," said Wishnasky. "It may be that the only real obscenity in the circles I travel in is the mention of God. That's the real expletive. You can admit any number of sexual fetishes, financial machinations, and neurotic manias. But make reference to religion and shame on you, you've crossed a line, you ought to have your ugly mouth washed out." He took another sip of his drink. "Is this ridiculous? Do I strike you as ludicrous?"

"Not at all. Just Tristan Wishnasky. Doing his usual spelunking."

"Against my will."

"Against your will?"

"I know; it's crazy. But that's how I feel these days."

The two friends drank in silence for a few moments, and Wishnasky looked around to make sure that none of the other patrons had heard his God-talk. He was safe: the café's diners were too consumed in their own conversations to notice one frazzled novelist.

"Tristan," Chet said finally. "The way you were playing a few minutes ago, that was too intense. Whatever you're going through, let up a little, take it easy. Set a pace yourself and hold to it."

"Hard to do, Chet. Not simple at all."

"Why is it so hard?"

"I'm thirty-six years old," said Wishnasky. "I thought I knew what I believed. I'm not ready to spend a year investigating its opposite."

"Then don't. Take a breather."

Wishnasky remembered the messages in the Camus book. "I feel obliged," he said. "To look into it. Come what may."

"Just go slowly then. Not everything at once."

"I may not know how to go slowly."

"Well, you'd better try. Cause the way you were slamming that ball at me twenty minutes ago, that wasn't good form. All it got you was a loss."

"I know. Hey, here come our sandwiches."

14.

IT WAS JUST AFTER MIDNIGHT in Vanessa's apartment. In her spacious bedroom, with a *La Traviata* poster and photographs of Cape Cod on the wall, Vanessa was asleep and Wishnasky was awake beside her, sitting up in the moonlight that poured in from her bedroom window, watching his lover breathe in and out so beautifully, he didn't ever want to look away. But there was something he had to do.

With an effort, he climbed out of bed, slipped into the thick blue terrycloth robe he always kept at her apartment, and crept into the kitchen. He closed the door and turned on the light. He'd decided he was going to get it over with, to do as Rabbi Diamant had instructed and pray to a God he suspected wasn't there. He figured he'd better act on it sooner, not later; if he allowed himself to wait, he'd most likely do absolutely nothing.

First problem: he assumed he should cover his head as in synagogue. But he didn't own a yarmulke, and the nearest hat in Vanessa's apartment was the detachable hood on her pink ski parka in the closet near the foyer. That would have to do. He padded quietly to the closet, found the parka, unbuckled the hood and put it on. He felt silly wearing the thing indoors in a warm apartment and worried that Vanessa would wake up and see him. But he remembered what he'd learned in childhood about praying: one had to wear a head covering.

Where to pray? Standing or sitting? Standing was too tense: he'd sit at the kitchen table, fold his hands, close his eyes—why should he close his eyes? No, that was silly. He'd fold his hands, leave his eyes open, and do it. Address God. Praise or Thanks or ... what were the other two? Confession. But he had nothing to confess. And the fourth one ... Supplication. To ask for something. What should he ask for?

He sat down, clasped his hands, and closed his eyes even though he'd decided not to. And began:

"Dear God ... If you're there ... If I haven't entirely gone insane ... I want to ... tell you how things are going." He paused to recollect. "Of course, if You're God, You already know how things are going, so there's no point in telling You. In which case, I'll use this rare occasion ... to thank You for the success you've given me in my writing life ... Which I don't understand, since the premise of just about everything I've ever published is that You don't exist, and we humans are on our own ... But in any case, if You're there, I want to ... thank You for your ... patience with a guy who's not only denied You, but done so for lots of readers, including some who may even get their opinions about You from me ... In which case, if You're really there, I apologize and ask Your ... forgiveness ... and also thank you for contacting me in the Camus book and on the radio, though I'm not sure I wasn't hallucinating thanks to the low-sugar diet I've done off and on over the last couple of months ... and as for what I want, well, please help me make progress in the new novel, which is on ice since the *Sisyphus* thing ... And help me figure out whether I should marry Vanessa ... and maybe ... I hope this isn't too presumptuous ... maybe just give me one sign more ... something more or less irrefutable ... to let me know you're really out there ... and that it wasn't just a couple of neuronal misfires. And that's it. If You're listening. Which I doubt. But I promised I'd do this."

He opened his eyes, looked quickly around—just in case Vanessa was standing there, disapproving—rose, removed the parka hood, walked back to the closet and reattached it to the parka. Then he waited in the semi-dark foyer for a sign.

Nothing. No fire from heaven, not even thunder and lightning. After what he reasoned was a decent interval, he crept back to Vanessa's bedroom. As he removed his robe, he saw lovely Vanessa looking more like a child than a mature woman, a child whom he very much wanted to protect.

He slipped in beside her and tried to sleep.

15.

THE RABBI SEEMED DISTRACTED when Tristan saw her next, and Tristan had to ask her if she was all right.

"Not completely, no," she said. "I spent Wednesday at the funeral of a fourteen-year-old boy who died in an auto accident. I knew him well—I presided over his bar mitzvah just a few months ago. He was a wonderful child and would have lived a beautiful life. I'm devastated by his loss."

They were seated in the rabbi's office, but this time she hadn't come from behind her desk to join him at the round table. So Wishnasky had taken a seat in one of the ladderback chairs facing her and was noticing a puffy area under her eyes, a sign that she'd been weeping. He realized, as he spoke to her, that it had never occurred to him that clergy cried too; he'd always imagined them being too wise and understanding to do so.

"But as a believer aren't you satisfied that he's in heaven now, enjoying eternity?" asked Wishnasky. "I thought that your doctrine would buffer you against unhappiness."

"We're on the earth to live," said Rabbi Diamant. "At least till seventy, perhaps till one hundred twenty. To die long before that is a catastrophe that the boy's parents will never get over, that has kept him from having offspring, that has reduced God's image by who knows how many more exemplars. We make no fetish of death in Judaism: even at the end of a long life we don't welcome it. The *Torah* says 'Choose life.' That boy was meant to live. I am so sad, I can hardly express it."

"So this freedom thing has some tough implications," said Wishnasky.

"Yes, the freedom thing is hard to bear at times. I think I understand why the Holy One insists on it, but sometimes it's burdensome."

"Do you think the boy is in heaven?"

"Yes."

"Then isn't that cause for some rejoicing, that he's so happy now?"

"He was put on earth to live," said the rabbi. "Not die. To live his appointed years." She picked up a pen and tapped its end against her desk as if to underscore her words. Then she sighed and put the pen back down. "But we've got to move forward," she said, and Wishnasky wondered if she was speaking to herself or him. "Tell me, how did your prayer go?"

He told her all that he remembered, adding that he didn't honestly feel that God had heard him. If there was a God, if he hadn't merely been speaking to the four walls of Vanessa's kitchen. He also mentioned the difficulty he was having with his novel—how the possibility of God was making it so difficult now to remove all of his protagonist's main props as planned.

The rabbi seemed interested. "What's the point?" she said. "What is it you're trying to prove with this character Ozono?"

"That we're all alone. That we're born alone, die alone, and live most of our lives, no matter how social, alone."

"But that's clearly false."

"How is it false?"

"The human being is always in relationship," said the rabbi. "Conception of the fetus is only possible because of the conjunction of male and female, then one is totally in relation to one's mother for nine months, after birth the helpless infant depends on any number of other humans, growing into and through adulthood one encounters parents, teachers, friends, lovers, spouse, children of one's own, grandchildren—it never ends. At the very least we're interdependent, and much of the time fully dependent. Isolation's not only impossible, it would be deadly. We'd never get out of infancy."

"We at least die alone."

"Jewish law requires that someone sit with the body the entire night before the burial. Not alone even then."

"Then why do I feel it so sharply?" asked Wishnasky. "Why can I sit in my office and feel entirely isolated from the rest of humanity? That's not artificial."

"But is it true?" said the rabbi. "I don't know your office, but let me guess that you sit in a room built by an architect and contractors, on a chair imagined by designers, using a computer built by factory workers, at a desk littered with proof of other human beings: electric bills, photos of your girlfriend, a calendar, an antique barometer ... Alone you'd starve, have no home, no lover, not even anything to write with. You're always in community. At this moment, as you and I speak, there are hundreds of other people with us, perhaps thousands. We couldn't survive without them. Anyway, you've started," said the rabbi. "You've prayed. That's good. Now, I want you to know that observant Jews do that three times a day: morning, noon, and night. How familiar are you with the prayer book?"

"A little. From my days in Hebrew School, anyway. Why three times a day?"

"Why do you eat three times a day?"

"It's what the body requires."

"It's what the soul requires. Lest it lose essential nutrients. Now, you should also know that observant Jews have their own *siddurim* so that they can pray at home or at work. Not everyone has the free time to come to synagogue. I'm going to give you a prayer book."

"Rabbi—"

"Yes?"

"I have to tell you: I'm not advancing at the rate you want. I may not be advancing at all. I said a prayer like you suggested, but God didn't answer in any way I can fathom. I still have loads of objections to religion in general, Judaism in particular. Maybe we should conclude this is a bad idea and call it a day. This isn't working."

"Let's hear some objections."

"Do you really want to? I'm just going to offend you."

"Please, some objections. Stop at nothing."

Wishnasky sat back in the chair and sighed. There were so many things he could say, but he felt all of them would register as insults to a true believer. Still, if she insisted … "To begin with," he said, "it's so violent. As I remember, the *Torah* is full of savagery and murder and for every other sin there's the death penalty. It's really off-putting."

"But Judaism isn't the religion of the *Torah*," said the rabbi. "It's the religion of the *Talmud*. Do you know the difference?"

"I'm not sure. I thought that *Talmud* was a big commentary—"

"An evolution," said the rabbi, "that's more normative than *Torah*. In the *Torah*, as you said, there are lots of transgressions solved with capital punishment, but in the *Talmud*, capital punishment is virtually abolished. In fact, in one famous passage, a great *Talmud*ic rabbi insists that even one death penalty in seventy years is enough to brand a court as unacceptably destructive. Even for a murder charge. And for the lesser sins, tell me, are you aware in the last thousand years of a single Jewish court killing anyone for adultery?"

"No."

"Of course not. The rabbis of *Talmud* made it clear a hundred different times that the prime commandments were compassion, love of neighbor, social justice, and charity. Do you know any traditional Jews?"

"I guess I've met some—"

"Do they strike you as savage? Quite the opposite: the humble, kind, good-hearted Jew is what the *Talmud* demands, and your picture of Jewish doctrine hasn't been definitive in two thousand years."

"So why do they still read *Torah* in synagogue every Saturday?"

"It's the sacred seed from which the *Talmud* flowered. It has sanctity unlike any other book. But it's *Talmud* that rules the life of the observant Jew, and it's *Talmud* that insists on gentleness and mercy."

"That's news to me."

"No doubt it is, but as I said before, with me you'll get the adult version of your religion. And to quote from *Talmud*, the whole essence of the *Torah* is 'Love Your Neighbor as Yourself.' Or to cite *Talmud* elsewhere, the call of every Jew is to be righteous, modest, and perform deeds of loving kindness. Or elsewhere, the highest of all human attributes is a "*lev tov*": a good heart. Does that sound like a call to savagery?"

Wishnasky lowered his head and tried to think. As a twelve-year-old studying for his own bar mitzvah, he'd been told that the *Torah* portion for the week was to be studied, along with a section from Prophets that he was trained to recite. There'd been nothing about *Talmud*—a volume of which he'd never even seen. "Do you have a book of *Talmud* I could look at?" he said to the rabbi.

"Of course. Eventually, we'll even study it together. But first: any further objections?"

He sat back in his chair and tried to find the right words. "Who wrote the *Talmud*?" he said.

"A great number of brilliant rabbis between approximately 200 BCE and 500 CE. Perhaps you could call them 'inspired.'"

The next question was hard to formulate. "So, if God wrote the *Torah*—but some rabbis wrote the *Talmud* ... what right did they have to interfere with God's word?"

"They had the highest authorization: God's word itself."

"Meaning?"

"Deuteronomy 17: 'If there arise a matter too hard for you in judgment ... come to the judge there shall be in those days.' And then again in the Jerusalem *Talmud*: 'The Lord declared: there are no pre-existent final truths in doctrine or law; the truth is the considered judgment of the majority of authoritative interpreters in every generation.'"

Wishnasky felt confused. "That wasn't my understanding. I need to think about this awhile."

"Then think about one more thing: you're worried that the God who created the world might be too violent or severe. Well, look around you. Look around at the millions of people with their thousands of beliefs. What kind of God do you imagine would countenance so many people of so many faiths pursuing their happiness in so many ways and having what in many cases is a rather good time? Is it an intolerant God? Is it an unmerciful one?"

Wishnasky was about to answer when the rabbi's phone buzzed and her secretary's voice said, "Rabbi, it's Mrs. Gerstein. She says it's important."

"The mother of the deceased boy," the rabbi said to Wishnasky. "I've got to take her call."

Wishnasky rose. "Of course," he said.

"No, wait." She pushed a button on her phone. "Tell her I'll be on in just a minute, please." She rose also and walked over to one of her bookshelves. "I want you to have a prayer book. I want you to take things a step further."

"I should tell you," said Wishnasky. "Vanessa and I are going on vacation next Wednesday. I won't be able to see you again for two weeks."

"Still, you can pray. Where are you going?"

"St. Lucia. It's an island in the southern Caribbean. The poet Derek Walcott was born there. And a poet friend, Richard Dey, has written about it a bunch of times. I'm finally going to see it for myself."

"Then on St. Lucia, I want you to pray again, but this time start with the set words in the prayer book. As for your personal prayer, add that at the end. I want you to see what the rabbis of the *Talmud* thought everyone should say if brought into the presence of the Holy One. Before speaking for oneself." She handed a book with a blue cloth cover to Wishnasky. "You'll be put off by the length of the morning service," she said, "so I want you to just say *Ma'ariv*, in the evening. That also contains the *Shema*. Do you know what that is?"

"Yes—'God is One.' I remember it from Hebrew School."

"Good. So, that's your assignment: To develop your relationship with God a little further. Call me for an appointment when you get back."

"I have to warn you, rabbi. I still harbor lots of doubts."

"So do I. But now I have to take this call." Wishnasky put the prayer book under his arm, thanked the rabbi and left. As he was going, he heard the rabbi say into the phone, "Naomi, I'm still so stricken. Tell me, please, how you're faring."

He walked to his car feeling that at least he was searching, even if he hadn't quite managed to find. He thought of Vanessa and her opposition to all religion. She wouldn't be too happy if she knew how he'd just spent the last half hour. Then he had another thought: Vanessa with her good works at the college—if kindness was what mattered, she was miles ahead of him. Still, this was a lesson he didn't dare convey to her.

He drove home deciding where he would hide the prayer book.

16.

"INTERESTING," SAID ION PETRESCU as he leaned back in his office chair, looking like a deranged CEO. "I have to respect your girlfriend's courage and initiative. To demand that you answer one way or the other on the marriage question takes strength—and spunk. I would like to know such a woman. Can you predict what you'll decide?"

Wishnasky was sitting in his usual chair, facing crazy-haired Ion across the desk on which sat a single book: Fritz Perls's *Gestalt Therapy Verbatim*. There was also a yellow legal pad beside it, on which Ion made a few notes—very few—from time to time. Wishnasky wondered why some of his statements seemed more noteworthy than others, but he could find no pattern, and even wondered if Ion himself had any sort of system.

"I really don't know. And I'm fearful of making an enormous mistake."

"What do you feel for her?"

"I admire her. I don't think I've ever spent time with a more impressive woman. And she's caring: she's saved hundreds of kids at that school from drugs and pregnancies and suicides and parental abuse. And she takes it all in stride: all the tragedy and intractable facts of the job, she's like an engineer just looking for the next problem to solve. I kind of wonder at her."

"So marry her."

"I don't know. I don't know if I feel it."

"You care for her and admire her. What is it you're missing?"

"Before I married my first wife, whom I also cared for and kind of admired, I had the suspicion that something was missing in our relationship. It's hard to explain: some subterranean agreement between her and me, something primal and binding, I can't say it any better. And sure enough, after we married, there was nothing to … hold us together once the surfaces got familiar and the sex became predictable and days began to resemble each other … There's this ungraspable agreement real lovers have on some profound level beneath all the usual congruencies. And I don't know that on that level Vanessa and I are a match. On that deep, even primitive level of attachment."

"Congratulations. You've discovered the unconscious."

"Is that what it is?"

"Tell Freud, I hear he's interested."

"Am I boring you, Ion?"

"I've tried to alert you many times to the excess of consciousness in your three dismal novels. Finally, you admit that there's another source of human behavior—and 'subterranean' is a fine word for it. Tell me, have you ever felt this 'subterranean' agreement with any woman?"

"I don't know if I have. And I also don't know why I'm absolutely sure it's really out there. Maybe I'm kidding myself."

Ion was silent for a few moments and closed his protruding eyes: not his usual style. Then he blinked his eyes open, wrinkled his shiny forehead. "You're not kidding yourself," he said. "This deeper realm exists. It's a good sign that you're becoming aware of it." He rubbed his forehead for a moment, and Wishnasky wondered what it must be like to counsel troubled clients all day and week and month. "But I sense there's something more. Has any other recent event struck you as relevant to this therapy?"

Wishnasky hesitated. "Well, just one. It happened a few days ago, when my agent came to visit." He told Ion all about his walk with Roland on Newbury Street, the appearance of the beggar, and his awkward indecision. He admitted that his fear of Roland's ridicule had finally stopped him, but he didn't understand the weight of guilt he felt afterwards. Maybe Ion could advise him as to how he should have reacted to a filthy, smelly drug addict with a cardboard sign. So he didn't contribute a dollar toward any one of the man's vices. Should he therefore feel culpable?

Ion raised his two index fingers, put the tips of them together, and rested his nose on them, all the while watching Wishnasky. Then he quietly said, "You may perhaps know La Rochefoucauld's aphorism: 'In the country of our self-love, there is always undiscovered territory.' Are you familiar with this *bon mot*?"

"No, I'm not. Why are you saying it?"

"It reminds me of something else: in the country of our generosity, there too we have realms to discover. I think you almost discovered one. In yourself. And I think that's hopeful."

"So, I should have slipped the guy a dollar."

"Are you so afraid of your agent?"

"Who wants to be sneered at? It's a normal human impulse to protect oneself from scorn."

"Tristan, it was not your agent whom you feared at that moment."

"Then who?"

"I don't wish to say. This is for you to discover, preferably out there, in the world."

"You're not going to tell me?"

"The answer will mean more when you come upon it yourself."

"You're really going to leave me in suspense?"

"Nothing I've said since we began this therapy years ago has had a tenth of the impact of what you've gleaned for yourself. I can point you in the right direction, but it's you who has to see what lies waiting there."

"In that case," said Wishnasky, "I know precisely why I felt fearful of Roland. He represents authority to me. I can't bear the thought of being mocked by a figure of authority."

"That is not the correct answer," said Ion.

"That's precisely it," said Wishnasky, feeling like fighting. "That's it *in toto*."

"Tristan," said Ion, gently. "Would you say that you're a person who knows himself very well? Do you think that's a fair description?"

Wishnasky hesitated: it seemed like a trick question and he didn't want to be tricked. "Pretty well, I think. Being a writer means having to engage in a lot of self-examination. I'm used to it by now, and I think I've learned some things."

"Tristan," said Ion, "you are one of my favorite clients. You have looked into yourself regularly, consistently, for years. But in all that time, you've not found something essential, of the greatest importance. This thing which you're missing, which you've been missing as long as I've known you."

"And that is?"

"Humility, of course. Humility before the great mystery of existence. Humility before the enormous enigma of human life. Humility when I ask you to investigate your art, your relationship with your lover, the words that came to you from *Sisyphus*. You do not know yourself, my friend. The merest hints, the barest glimpses, and you assume you've seen to the core. If you take nothing more from this therapy than the beginnings of humility, I will count our meetings a great success."

"And how does this relate to the beggar on Newbury Street?"

"I will leave you to consider that. As well as all your other issues. This is the time to dig deep, Tristan. In each person's life there comes such a moment and this is yours. You must profit from it. So dig: you may never be so capable again." He picked up his pen and jotted a few words on his legal pad. "Now, you're going on vacation."

"That's right. Any suggestions?"

"Some new scenery should clear your mind. Disrupt the old habits of thought. Use the time to become acquainted with those parts of yourself that in your usual world have become routine."

"That's it?"

"That's a lot. And continue down this road of religious experimentation. Don't allow yourself to be deterred from it. Mind never lies."

"I'll call you when I get back, Ion. I'll fill you in on what happened."

"You're almost ready to make real progress," said Ion. "Keep at it. Don't stop."

17.

VANESSA LOVED TRAVELING, and she made the preparations for the trip so pleasant, Wishnasky couldn't help but feel that all tension between them had dissolved. They'd packed lightly—mostly sun things, like shorts, swimming trunks, and light hats. Vanessa had bought half a dozen bottles of sunblock, and she tossed them into her suitcase along with the books she wanted to read while on St. Lucia—the poems of Sharon Olds, Sidney Hook's *From Hegel to Marx,* Simone de Beauvoir's *She Came to Stay,* George Steiner's slim volume on Heidegger. Wishnasky packed his only bathing suit, one pair of white shorts and one pair of khakis, a few knit shirts and his copy of Sinclair Lewis's *Elmer Gantry.* He also brought his laptop so he could work on the new novel, and—furtively, so Vanessa wouldn't see it—the prayer book that the rabbi had given him. He also brought a baseball cap with the Boston Celtics logo on it to wear as a yarmulke. Vanessa, seeing it, congratulated him on remembering to protect his head in the bright island sun.

At Logan Airport, things moved more smoothly than he could have hoped. The lines advanced quickly, the security checks were not more exasperating than usual, and there were several available chairs in the waiting area by the gate. Once on the plane, Vanessa produced the Simone de Beauvoir, and Wishnasky fished out his *Elmer Gantry.* As the airplane began its taxi along the runway, Wishnasky considered praying for a safe journey, but then decided that was cowardice and instead read the first pages of Lewis's attack on religious charlatanry. The plane lifted off without mishap, and they were on their way to a southern idyll.

Several hours passed. Vanessa was napping quietly beside him, Wishnasky at the window was reading the Lewis book, and the hum of the plane's jets was comforting: all was well. He was particularly glad to be reacquainting himself with the Lewis novel, in which an alcoholic, womanizing hypocrite becomes a preacher and destroys lives all around him in pursuit of his own pleasure. What a revolution this must have been in its time, this exposé of faith as a swindler's game. After so many centuries when the clergy had the power to regulate human life, how refreshing to admit that they were mostly mountebanks and con artists, feeding on credulity, abusing their power, and no more faithful themselves than the most unregenerate atheist. And it wasn't just Lewis who said so, it was all Wishnasky's heroes from Diderot to Dawkins.

He looked over the top of the seats in front of him to the long row of passengers making this same journey to the island. Everyone different, everyone with a story that could fill three or four good novels. He couldn't remember when it first occurred to him that *every* adult had a fascinating trajectory; it was simply impossible to spend twenty-one or more years with a human psyche in contemporary society and *not* become interesting. So, the problem of writing wasn't how to create something new; the problem was how to distill from the overwhelming repertoire of human variety just a few of the details needed for a coherent tale. Of course, you couldn't choose wisely if you were unclear on your own convictions. Sinclair Lewis, by all appearances, knew exactly what he believed, and *Elmer Gantry* had a persuasive shape and texture. As for Tristan Wishnasky, who'd started a brilliant career tracing the implications of a Godless universe and was now supposed to think that he might have been mistaken … Well, clarity would come. A nice vacation on some sandy beaches, a few nights of lovemaking with beautiful Vanessa, and he would know what he believed. And then his writing would take off again. Then he wouldn't be leaving any Ozonos stranded in the offices of their financial advisors.

Wishnasky closed his eyes. He remembered something an old girlfriend had said in an email on her most recent birthday. She said, "I've been through so many lifetimes already. Can't wait to see what the next one is like." All right, maybe Tristan Wishnasky was facing a new lifetime. He hoped it would be full of pleasure. He fell asleep, not knowing.

18.

SOMEONE WAS RUBBING his shoulder, saying "Wake up, it's so lovely." He opened his eyes, forced himself to remember where he was, and then heard Vanessa say, "Look out the window. You're not going to believe it." He looked and was immediately struck by a display of dozens of green mountains, orange-roofed towns and brown beaches. A flight attendant was walking down the aisle handing customs forms to all the passengers, and Vanessa was smiling so broadly he instantly realized that he was crazy about her and only wanted to make her happy. He pecked her on the cheek and said, "Things are lovely everywhere I look." She laughed and pointed out the window again. "Are we really going *there?*"

Once off the plane they were herded into a building where a snaking line led up to six booths, each occupied by a customs inspector. All the inspectors mostly seemed bored by the endless job of examining passports, collecting customs cards, and sending people on to the baggage area. The fleshy woman who looked at Tristan and Vanessa's papers didn't once smile, and only glanced briefly to compare their passport photos and their faces. Then she hurried them along and called out to the next passenger.

It took another twenty minutes to get their rental car—reserved back in the States—and to set off on the forty-five-minute journey to their resort. Wishnasky felt uncomfortable driving on the left side of the street in a car with its steering wheel on the right, but the greater challenge was the tortuously twisting road through the mountains to Soufrière. The road was barely wide enough to let two cars pass safely, and the difficult uphill sections put a worrying strain on the rental car's engine. Still, they reached their destination with only one shock—a sizeable pothole on the way down a mountain—and Tristan was fascinated by the ramshackle town with its narrow streets and dozens of men and women watching from the sidewalks as if *he* were the attraction. A street out of the city led up another mountain and then there was the sign for Serenity Cove. He took a hard left into the entrance and stopped the car outside a two-story wooden structure that he assumed was the hotel office.

A few minutes later a slender woman named Glenda led them to cottage number seven and gave them a brief tour. On the first level was a kitchenette with working stove, microwave, and refrigerator; just beyond it was a living/dining room decorated with red, yellow, and green plaid curtains that exactly matched the tablecloth. Upstairs was a bathroom, then the master bedroom—with king-size bed, over which hung a Gauguin poster of a naked, impassive Polynesian woman—and beyond the bedroom was a spacious balcony, with rocking chair, a small table, upright chairs, and a hammock. The view from the balcony was spectacular: the two pitons, high triangles made of lava from an ancient volcano and now covered in lush green foliage, as well as other mountains also covered in rainforests. Glenda handed them their room key and the key to a small safe, wished them a happy stay, and departed. They were alone.

"What do you think?" said Tristan, putting his arm around Vanessa.

"It's too near perfect," she said. "Things aren't supposed to look this stunning."

"That bed doesn't look too uninviting either."

"Don't be in such a hurry. We'll get to that eventually."

"I'm just saying."

"I know what you're saying."

"In that case, I'm hungry. The guidebook says there are two markets in Soufrière. Or would you rather go to a restaurant and do the shopping tomorrow?"

"Restaurant."

"I saw one on the drive up the mountain."

"Let's do it."

They got back into the rental car and drove halfway down the mountain till they saw a sign announcing "*Le Papillon.*" Tristan was about to pull into the small parking area when an older-looking Black man near the entrance waved at them to stop and roll their windows down. Vanessa said, "Ignore him. He's probably a beggar."

"I don't know," said Tristan. "Maybe we're not supposed to park here."

"He's going to ask you for money."

"I'm not so sure." He rolled down his window. "Yes?" he said. "What is it?"

"You go to *Le Papillon*?" said the man, whose old brown skin was lined and tired-looking.

"Yes," said Tristan. "I'm about to park."

"I show you where to park," said the man, and pointed at a space outside the sign to the restaurant. "That's where you wish to park."

"All right, thanks," said Tristan, and maneuvered the car into the space. The old man watched without moving. But when Tristan and Vanessa got out of the car, he hurried over to Tristan.

"American?" he said.

"Yes," said Tristan. "Thanks for the information."

"I'm the head of the children's football team. We play all over the island."

"Good," said Tristan. "Now we're very hungry—"

"We need uniforms," said the man. "We need petrol for transport. You have five dollars?"

"What did I tell you?" said Vanessa.

"Not interested," said Tristan. "Goodbye. Thanks again for the parking—"

"We need five dollars," said the man. "For the children. So they can play football."

Wishnasky felt a tightening in his stomach. He remembered too well the beggar on Newbury Street and his regret at not having offered him some change. An impulse came to him: he wasn't going to make the same mistake this time, even if Vanessa disagreed.

"I'm going to give him a dollar," he said, trying to sound offhand. He opened his wallet and found an American bill. He offered it to the man, who took it without looking at it.

"The children need five dollars," he said. "Not just one. For the petrol."

"I've got to go," said Wishnasky, and took Vanessa by the arm.

"God will bless you for five dollars," said the man sadly as they walked off. "It's for the children."

They walked to the restaurant, Vanessa fuming all the way.

"It was only a dollar," said Wishnasky, feeling strangely joyful.

The meal was mediocre: overcooked tuna and some sort of diced potatoes and breadfruit. But the joy of being on the island was more potent than the quality of the food or the tension caused by the beggar. Vanessa relaxed into sweetness as the meal progressed, and when they left the restaurant she put her hand around Wishnasky's back and rested her head on his shoulder. "This is so overdue," she said.

"I feel the same," he said and turned his head to kiss her dark hair.

It was dusk. Back at the cottage, they went out to the balcony and sat beside each other. There was an almost-full moon, and pinpoints of light distributed unevenly among the mountains and hills. The two pitons were strikingly beautiful in the distance, and Wishnasky wondered about the volcano that had formed them millions of years ago, back before there were humans to stare at them and call them stunning. Was this what Ion meant by "humility"? The earth was so old! And how strange that it should have existed for eons before these strange creatures humans appeared and were able to say, *look, the sight of those peaks is sublime.*

Later, in the bedroom, he and Vanessa made love quietly, with tenderness and deliberation. Afterward, they lay awake listening to the high chatter, almost like birdsong, of thousands of frogs. They fell asleep with limbs entwined, and it didn't even occur to Wishnasky to feel grateful for the pleasure of sex, or to rise and dress and say the evening prayer.

19.

IN THE MORNING, after a breakfast of sliced mangos, cereal, and an omelet, they took a tour of the island. Their driver's name was Desmond, and his dark brown face was often illuminated by a smile that showed several missing teeth. Vanessa sat in the front seat of his blue Nissan beside him, and Wishnasky was in the back. When Wishnasky remarked that he was unfamiliar with this particular style of sedan, Desmond said, "It doesn't meet American standards, you know, so they don't sell it there." How it failed to reach those standards was unclear—and worrisome—but Wishnasky didn't feel it would be polite to pursue it.

They headed north to Castries, the capital city and the site of a market that Vanessa had read about in a guidebook. The way there was again through twisting mountain roads, hairpin turns, and bridges just wide enough for one car, steep ascents and plunging descents. But what struck Wishnasky most was the poverty he saw everywhere: dilapidated houses; low, half-painted, abandoned-looking shops; old, gutted cars parked in tiny front yards; "yards" that were four-fifths dirt. These were sights for which the guidebook hadn't prepared him, and they made him feel embarrassed to have money, to be able to fly in and out while so many men, women and children were trapped—was that the word?—with no prospects of anything better.

"Desmond," he said. "Have you ever been to the US?"

"No, never. But I drive many Americans."

"Are you curious to see it?"

"Oh yeah. But it's not easy to get a visa."

"Do you like living on St. Lucia?"

"Not really, no."

"Why not?"

"No jobs."

"Does driving tourists keep you busy?"

"Not enough. But I'm thinking: maybe I can get work on a cruise ship. Lots more money there, you know."

Now Vanessa joined in. "Desmond, are you married?"

"Yes," he said. "For nine years."

"Do you have any children?"

"Two children: one six years old, one seven months."

"Does your wife work?"

"Oh yes, she's a tailor. She stitches clothes from our home. But she also has to look after the children."

"Is it hard to raise two children on St. Lucia?" said Vanessa. "On your two salaries?"

"I don't wish to say yes," said Desmond. "But yes, it's difficult to do it well."

They pressed on through an area where the ramshackle houses seemed barely able to withstand a strong wind, where glum-looking adults stared curiously after them and children sat in the dirt, baffled at the sight of a car. Now the rabbi's words about Genesis came back to him: God had created the world for "making." This part of the world looked unfinished, not sufficiently "made." He remembered the beggar from the day before, asking for five dollars. What if he'd given him the amount he'd asked for, or double or triple that? Would it have alleviated even a little the blight that was all over this island?

"Desmond," he said. "What's the government like here?"

"Pretty corrupt, you know. They look after themselves."

"Do the British help at all? You were a British colony until not too long ago."

"Oh yeah, they help a lot," said Desmond. "They still are looking after us."

Viewing the shabby houses they were passing, Wishnasky didn't think that anyone was looking after St. Lucia. And then a strange thought came to consciousness. He had been to a poor island in the Caribbean once before—to Jamaica, with his then-wife—and at the time he had only felt that the poverty, briefly glimpsed in Kingston, was an unfortunate fact of nature, nothing that was relevant to *him*. Now he felt something different: the possibility, the bizarre possibility, that the poverty on this island was a problem he was personally called upon to solve. But wasn't that absurd? He remembered something he'd read on the internet recently: that in the most recent Super Bowl, a thirty-second commercial had cost five million dollars. Five million dollars! Imagine what that amount could do for this squalid island! How many schools, clinics, shelters could be built with money that instead exhorted consumers to eat more Fritos? Wasn't it obscene? Perverse? Was this how a Jew was supposed to think?

They were on a road so badly pitted that the car was lurching from side to side as they slowly progressed up a steep slope. Vanessa asked if the local government didn't feel obligated to fix the streets.

"Oh no," said Desmond. "And anyway this road is private."

"This is private? Who owns it?"

"The resort I'm taking you to. Where you'll have lunch."

"Why doesn't the resort do something about all these potholes?"

"They don't want to, you know. The beach is public, and they don't want the locals coming up here to use it. So they keep the road in bad shape. They're very clever. Works well."

At the top of the road, there was a guardhouse and a manually operated wooden arm. Desmond opened his window, shouted something in Creole to the guard, and said, "You walk through there and you'll see the restaurant. I'll be back here when you're finished." Wishnasky and Vanessa climbed out of the car, walked past the guard on a wide white path and to a spacious, outdoor restaurant with a bar in the center. Tourists, most of them white, were sitting comfortably, drinking and talking. A colorfully-dressed Black woman took them to a table and handed them menus.

"Did you see all that poverty?" Wishnasky said after she left. "Did you see those houses?"

"I know," Vanessa said. "It was terrible."

"Should we be embarrassed to be here? To throw around our money and then scoot?"

"Are you kidding? Tourism is all they've got. The dollars we're spending today are the best thing that's ever happened to them."

"I feel bad. The Ugly American."

"I can't think of it," said Vanessa. "If I do, I won't be able to enjoy the vacation. Anyway, I warned you it was going to be like this."

"You warned me? When?"

"You probably weren't even listening. I told you that we could choose between one of the chichi resorts on the northern coast or a more authentic hotel near Soufrière. You said 'authentic,' I figured you knew what that meant."

"I don't even remember the conversation."

"Well, that's not new, is it? Had nothing to do with sex or writing."

"You sound just like my therapist."

"No, I don't. You listen to your therapist."

They ordered drinks—Vanessa took a Scotch, Wishnasky a gin and tonic—and enjoyed the piped-in Creole music. Wishnasky wished the rabbi had been there to answer his questions: What was the Jewish interpretation of this stratified world? What did a religious person do when faced with so much want? He remembered that he'd promised to pray from the prayer book while he was on St. Lucia, and that he hadn't chosen to do so the previous night. Well, he could aim for it in the coming evening. Maybe out on the balcony, facing the pitons and the lower mountains—yes, that would feel spiritual. Couldn't let Vanessa know, of course, not if he didn't want to set her off on the subject of religious fanaticism. All right, he'd wait till she was asleep, then walk out on the balcony, face the mountains and pray. And she'd never know. He felt embarrassed to be hiding anything in his behavior from his lover, but that's how things were: that's what religion was in the milieu he knew best, something to conceal.

They drank, ordered lunch, then had another drink and finally walked back to the guardhouse. Someone had put two folding chairs by Desmond's car and he and another Black man were gabbing happily when they approached. Wishnasky wondered what Desmond must think—here he'd just spent close to a hundred dollars on food and drink, and would probably spend triple that before the day was over. Wasn't it criminal in some way, to have so much more than other people on the earth, to use it on delicacies while all around people were scraping for essentials?

They drove on to Castries. It was the opposite of all the small towns they'd passed through: modern, dirty, noisy with traffic and honking horns. The market consisted of dozens of booths side by side featuring clothing, crockery, fabrics and raw food. Desmond parked right in front—there were no parking meters or other indications of what was permissible—and bounded out of the car to open Vanessa's front door.

"I take you first to see my sister," he said to Vanessa and Wishnasky, and guided them through the maze of booths to a table patrolled by an overweight, middle-aged woman with her hair wrapped in green and yellow cloth. "She gives you what you need," said Desmond, and then, to the woman, "These are Americans."

Wishnasky looked at the goods on the table before him: purses and shopping bags adorned with pictures of the island, carved wood that said "St. Lucia," cut to resemble the two pitons, men's belts, decorated coffee cups, and ash trays painted the same red, yellow and green as the curtains back at the resort. There was nothing he wanted. He said to Vanessa, "Let's move on."

"It's his sister," she said quietly. "We've got to buy something."

"But I don't want anything here."

"It's his sister and we're going to help," said Vanessa. Then she turned to the portly woman and said, "I'd like that carved sign with the two pitons."

"Very good choice," said Desmond's sister, and plucked it off the table. "That is twenty dollars American."

"It's charming," said Vanessa as the woman wrapped it in yellow paper.

They spent a half hour at the market looking at clothing and knickknacks and more coffee cups saying "St. Lucia" than there could be coffee drinkers in the hemisphere. Desmond followed them wherever they went and didn't seem to consider that they might value some privacy as they cruised the various booths. After determining that there was nothing else she particularly wanted, Vanessa bought some sweet potatoes to cook back at the cottage. Wishnasky, feeling guilty about being a moneyed American, purchased a set of coasters with island scenes printed on them. Then, they were ensconced in Desmond's car and taking the long, twisting ride back to Soufrière. Wishnasky felt satisfied that in buying the coasters, he'd helped these impoverished people. At the same time, he was conscious of how appalling their penury was.

After they pulled into the resort, Desmond took a business card out of his shirt pocket and handed it to Wishnasky. "Anytime you want to tour the island, you call me," he said. "Much more to see: the botanical gardens, the sulphur spring, many beautiful beaches." Wishnasky took the card and paid him for the day's travels—a hundred and fifty, American—and he and Vanessa walked back to their cottage with their purchases. "Let's get in the pool," said Vanessa. "I'm broiled."

"Me too," said Wishnasky. He put down his packages and sighed: the day's sights were troubling him still. Wasn't the luxury he and Vanessa were enjoying something shameful? Shouldn't he be spending his time in Castries, talking redevelopment and job creation with its corrupt politicians? Were these thoughts insane?

The pool was deserted except for three young Black women immersed to their waists, talking energetically with one another. Wishnasky hoped they were guests: it was consoling to believe that someone besides whites could enjoy this getaway. He took off his shirt and laid it on one of the lawn chairs by the pool, then slipped into the water moments before Vanessa did. He swam around aimlessly for a few seconds, glided to the opposite side and climbed out. There was a narrow walkway dividing the pool from a wide balustrade. He sat on the balustrade and looked down a hill to the roofs of Soufrière, mostly orange and beautiful, and beyond them the beach. "Come look at this," he said to Vanessa. When she joined him, he said, "From this vantage point, you'd never know there were so many poor people."

"You're bringing that up again," said Vanessa. "Am I witnessing the birth of a social conscience?"

"I don't know. Have I been so self-centered till now?"

"You said the word, not me."

"Then I'm glad I'm changing."

"Terrific," said Vanessa. "Next, you'll be noticing that I spend almost every day working at a college with poverty, mental illness, sexual abuse, and would-be suicides."

They looked down at Soufrière again, then slipped back into the pool. The three Black women were standing by their chairs now, toweling off and laughing. Wishnasky took encouragement from their laughter. He hoped they had much to laugh about.

20.

IT WAS AFTER MIDNIGHT. Wishnasky heard the sleeping Vanessa breathing easily beside him as he carefully got to his feet and put on his clothes. He found the green and white Celtics cap he'd brought just for this reason, put it on, then felt around in his suitcase for the prayer book the rabbi had given him. He felt a shape he guessed was it, pulled it free, put it in his left hand and with his right quietly unlatched the door to the balcony. Outside, the full moon was bathing the mountain view with an uncanny glimmer. This would be a good place for prayer. You couldn't ask for a more spiritual vista.

He turned on a lamp—the moonlight wasn't strong enough for reading—and leafed through the prayer book looking for the evening service. He found it— Hebrew on one page, English on the opposite. He'd agreed to read the entire prayer service from first to last, so in English he whispered, "And He being merciful grants atonement for iniquity and does not destroy." Why start a prayer with talk of iniquity and destruction? Was the point to be frightened? He read on: "And many times He turns away His anger, and does not stir up all His wrath." More talk about a fearsome God. But hadn't the rabbi insisted on God's kindness? On God's compassion? "Oh Lord, save, the King, may he answer us on the day that we call." All right, that much made emotional sense: one sensibly was asking God to hear one's human voice. All right, maybe this prayer would work after all.

He read on, all in English except the *Shema*, the Hebrew of which he remembered from childhood. Then, there were the supplications of the *Amidah*, for knowledge, health, forgiveness, peace, and then it was time for his personal prayer. "Dear God," he said "If you're out there at all: thank you for this beautiful island, and for our safe journey here. But there looks to be such misery just a few minutes from where I'm standing: inspire me to know what I'm supposed to be doing about it, if anything. Besides feeling distressed. So thank you. Good night."

He said the concluding *Aleinu* prayer, closed the prayer book, took off his cap and crept back into the bedroom. He slipped in beside Vanessa and in a few minutes was asleep.

20.

21.

THE DAYS WERE FILLED with sightseeing, restaurants, and snorkeling. Wishnasky got used to the short drive down the mountain and into Soufrière, and even began to feel comfortable walking through the narrow Soufrière streets with all their poor, some of whom occasionally asked him for money. He gave on those occasions when Vanessa wasn't there to rebuke him, and the rest of the time just shook his head and said, "Sorry." He tried to see Vanessa's viewpoint: that if they gave every time they were asked, they'd soon have nothing left for their holiday. But if it was only a question of a few dollars ... Maybe there was a middle ground on which to tread.

They bought groceries in a small shop near the center of downtown, and one afternoon took a motorboat tour of the coast. The sights were spectacular: high cliffs, rocky beaches, a cleft between two mountains from which you could hear the thousands of bats crying out in the darkness. Back at the resort, they read, drank Mount Gay rum, and made love. Every night, after Vanessa slept, Wishnasky made his way out onto the balcony and prayed from the book the rabbi had given him. He was beginning to feel comfortable with the scripted prayers and even had the sense, in his personal supplications, that he wasn't speaking to the void. *Search for Me,* he thought. He guessed he was doing so. But he wished he didn't have to do so in secret.

One early evening he and Vanessa came in from a dinner near the botanical gardens, put their purchases on the chest of drawers facing the bed, and collapsed onto the mattress. "I'm beat," said Vanessa. "I've got to sleep. Just a nap. Then I'll get up and wash and all that." She turned over on her stomach and, fully clothed, fell instantly asleep. Wishnasky listened to her even breathing and tried to determine his own course of action.

He wasn't sleepy and didn't feel like reading the last chapters of *Elmer Gantry.* He knew what he'd do: it was earlier than usual, but why not say the evening prayer now instead of at midnight? He reached into his suitcase and found his prayer book, grabbed his Celtics cap off the night table, and quietly went out to the balcony. It was almost nine o'clock, and there were clouds blocking the moon, so all one could see was a formless, shimmering haze above the mountains. He turned on the standing lamp, leafed through the book to the evening service, and began quietly, "And He being merciful grants atonement for iniquity and does not destroy. Many a time He turns away His anger and does not stir up all His wrath. Oh Lord, save, the King, may He answer us on the day—"

"What are you doing?"

Wishnasky turned around. There was Vanessa, eyes still sleepy, standing in the doorway between the bedroom and the balcony. "What are you doing, Tristan?"

"I'm ... experimenting with a prayer. Saying a prayer. Out of ... the prayer book."

"You're saying a prayer?"

"That's right. You know, after those words I saw—"

"Don't tell me again about that hallucination. I know all about it and how it's interfered with your thinking. But since when do you pray from a prayer book? How many times have you done this?"

"Look, I just want to try something that—"

"Didn't I tell you what I went through because of religion? Disciplined, castigated, branded a sinner and treated like garbage, the whole apparatus of oppression I had to escape just to stay sane?"

"I know and I deeply sympathize. But this isn't about you, Vanessa, this is about me and my—"

"Is this about us getting married?"

"Huh?"

"Is that the reasoning behind this? Because you *know* I won't ever share bed and board with a religious man, is this your clever way to cast me off so that it looks like the decision was mine and not yours?"

"No, that's not at all what this is about—"

"Put away the prayer book."

"What?"

"Put it away. Don't ever open it again in my sight. Or give it to me and I'll tear it into shreds. Give it to me now."

"Are you kidding?"

"I'm not kidding. I barely escaped a stultifying religious childhood with my life, with my mental health, and I'm not about to stand by quietly while my lover turns into a maniac."

"I'm not a maniac! I'm just a man who's trying out a little personal prayer on the slim chance there really is a God out there to say thanks to and to ask forgiveness for—"

"To say thanks! For what? For a world of war and poverty and disease and despair? For all those poor people down in Soufrière, for the mountains here that were caused not by God, not by His Holiness, but by volcanoes and earthquakes and natural forces that never needed a God—"

"All right, look, go back to bed; we can talk about this later—"

"Give me the prayer book, Tristan. Give it to me now and I'll burn it with all the other ugly things nobody wants out in the open. Give it to me now if you ever want to kiss my lips or touch my body. This is not a negotiation. I won't have this back in my life."

Wishnasky hesitated. He could give her the book and have her companionship, not just now but forever. He could avoid a terrible blow-up and keep the woman he cared for most in the world.

Then he saw the words: *You know better than this. You don't have time to waste. Search for Me.*

"Look, Vanessa," he said. "This is a terribly important subject. Instead of having a scene here, let's go back to bed and in the morning we'll see how we—"

"Give me the prayer book now, Tristan. Or you'll never touch me again."

He paused. She was serious. But it occurred to him that it wasn't only religion she was challenging. It was his freedom to seek any sort of truth unhampered. And seeking truth was his vocation, had been since he started writing. It was, now that he thought about it, perhaps the only honestly good thing about him.

"I can't," he said. "I'm kind of considering this stuff recently. I have to see where it leads."

"Don't come near me," said Vanessa. "The next time you can come near me is when I see that book in a thousand pieces. Where it can't hurt me."

She burst into tears. She turned and walked back into the bedroom, lay down on the bed and wept. Wishnasky wanted to comfort her but knew she'd explode. He looked out at the green mountains that were beginning to disappear in the gathering darkness.

Perhaps tomorrow Vanessa would relent. Perhaps not. He prayed, "Help me through this, Lord. If You're out there." And he stared out at the vanishing mountains.

22.

IN THEIR LAST TWO DAYS of vacation, Vanessa hardly spoke to him. They ate breakfast together with a minimum of interaction, then went about their business—a dip in the pool, a walk around the hotel grounds—as if they hardly knew each other. On both afternoons, Vanessa conducted her life as if Wishnasky wasn't there: taking a taxi into Soufrière alone to do more shopping, disappearing with the Sidney Hook volume for several hours without announcing her whereabouts, packing for the flight back to the States without a word. On the drive to Hewanorra Airport she kept silent, smiling only at the car rental agent when he wished them a happy return to the mainland. On the plane, she read her Sidney Hook and barely glanced at Tristan once. He made a few failed attempts to strike up a civil conversation, then gave up entirely. He tried to finish *Elmer Gantry* but couldn't manage to concentrate.

Back in the US, on the cab ride to his house, she spoke to him coldly, in a business-like tone.

"I want a few hours alone at your house so I can collect my things. Do you think you can stoop to granting me that?"

"Vanessa, this does not have to be the end of our time together—"

"That's precisely what it is. And my only question is how shrewdly meditated it was, how much of it was your deliberate strategy for breaking us up—"

"I'm not breaking us up. *You're* breaking us up."

"As you knew I would. After what I've gone through. Can you give me a couple of hours? To clear my stuff out of your holy house, where the holy candlesticks are just a few holy days from appearing, where your holy skullcaps will show up in the holy bedroom before long, where we'll have to kiss the holy doorposts each time we enter and exit —"

"Vanessa, if you knew how you sound—"

"If *I* knew? Explain *this* to your agent. Explain it to your editor. Explain it to your readers!"

"I just want the freedom to see where things lead—"

"Do I have the couple of hours?"

"Of course. More if you want."

"Two hours is enough. Then you can light your incense and fall on your knees."

"Vanessa, I'm still committed to this relationship—"

"Don't delude yourself."

The cab deposited them at his house in Newton Corner. After he and Vanessa brought their suitcases inside, he left her and drove into Boston, into a neighborhood near the Longfellow Bridge. He had two hours to fill. Leaving his car at a meter, he walked down to the Charles River, stood quietly beside it, and wondered if he'd just thrown away his last chance for happiness.

PART TWO

23.

WISHNASKY SAT IN HIS KITCHEN, depressed and in pain. Vanessa had taken everything that belonged to her, not only her clothes from the drawers and closets, but favorite photos of the two of them together in a Manhattan restaurant (what lovely spare ribs they'd enjoyed that evening), on Duval Street in Key West (he'd actually convinced her to spend an hour with him in a strip joint), and with his parents on his mother's birthday (well, that tug-of-war wouldn't be missed). In the linen closet, most of the towels were missing. In the kitchen, her tea kettle, coffee mugs, energy bars, Swedish toaster. It had really happened: Vanessa was gone and he was alone, bereft.

It'll be good for the writing, he tried to persuade himself: fewer distractions, fewer obligations. On the other hand, he'd always been a better writer when he shared his life with a woman ... Well, damn it if he wouldn't find another one! And this time his lover wouldn't fault him for his religious seeking, would let him pursue his own quarry as he allowed her to pursue hers. Maybe she'd even be religious herself; wouldn't *that* be poetic justice! Yes, that was his future!

As for the present: devastation. He stood up, walked over to the counter and made a cup of instant coffee. Something he might as well get around to: alert his closest friends of the breakup. He took the cup into his study and sent a group email to Chet, Quentin, and Rick: *Back from St. Lucia. Good time, but Vanessa and I kaput. Any beautiful single women out there?* He hit "send" with mixed feelings. He next emailed Roland. *Back on track with novel,* he lied. *But can't promise deadline.* Next, his parents: *Returned from vacation this afternoon. Anticipating family dinner.* Then he remembered the mail that would have piled up during his vacation. He trudged outside to retrieve it, took it into his study and spent a half hour paying bills and throwing away junk. That done, he made another cup of coffee, brought it into his study and sat down in front of the computer. He found the most recent page of *Traveler in the Abyss* and punched "enter," as if to start a new paragraph.

Dejection overwhelmed him. Vanessa was gone. Elegant, brilliant Vanessa, whom he'd cared for so deeply. He'd sent her away. He'd never find a more felicitous lover.

He stared stupidly at the monitor, then closed the document. He wandered into his bedroom, lay down and allowed his poor heart to ache.

24.

"SO YOU STOOD UP FOR yourself and lost a few nights of sexual satisfaction as a result," said Ion Petrescu, his gray hair pointing in six directions. "This will not win you a medal. It's painful to have principles. Welcome to the adult world."

"But I almost loved her. I was this close to loving her."

"You'll feel pain for a while, then after a time, you won't. At the end, you'll hardly notice the scar in the great herbarium of scars life plants on the average human being by the age of forty."

"Then you don't think I was wrong to keep investigating my religion?"

"You know my opinion. Your Mind wants this. Intensely. Deny it at your risk. Then you'll really need my help."

"But I don't know that I believe! I don't know if I was defending my faith or just refusing to be ordered around!"

"You made a stand, period. If you can't see this as honorable, there's no point in my telling you."

"Ion, I still don't get your support on this subject. How can you encourage me when you yourself aren't a believer?"

"Do you know how old the Mind is? At the youngest, one-point-eight million years."

"Meaning what?"

"Meaning Ion Petrescu adopts a position of humility in all things concerning this primordial mystery. And recognizes in the message you had in the Camus book the Mind's warning that you were in need of a correction. Do I understand how the Mind acquired its wisdom over the millennia? Not at all. But I respect it. Its reality. Its effects. Its concern that there be nothing lacking in the life of the human."

"And how do you personally shape your life around this great knowledge?"

"I am one of the Mind's interpreters. More a village shaman than I'm comfortable admitting. And the Mind allows me this vocation so long as I conduct my business prudently. But when I err, it lets me know."

"How? What does it do when you're in error?"

"No tyrant is as irritable as the misconstrued Mind," said gnomic Ion. "I won't explain beyond that."

"Great," said Wishnasky. "My therapist thinks he's a witch doctor in the Amazon, and I miss my lover. I have a terrible pain under my sternum. What do you suggest I do?"

"You have two choices. You try to ignore your distress, and day by day you feel the agony not only of your lost love affair but of your refusal to grieve. Or you mourn. Lie down on your sofa and listen to Maria Callas sing "Addio del Passato" from the last act of *La Traviata,* on an endless loop. Cry hot tears. If Ms. Callas is not available, I dare to recommend Renata Scotto with, alas, reservations. This way your suffering will last three weeks before it expires. Any other method will last three months and will appear interminable. Follow my directions and you will soon return to something like working order."

"Will I ever find another woman as right for me as Vanessa?"

"I don't think you know who Vanessa was. I don't think you understand anyone's life, least of all your own."

"If you're so smart, what about *your* life? Are you utterly happy, knowing everything you know?"

"I am as happy as the world permits," said wise Ion. "I don't aspire to more."

"Your marriage? It's going smoothly?"

"There's hostility in these questions. And it's not directed at me; it's directed at a cosmos that is shaping you to its ends. No more questions. Sit back and tell me more about St. Lucia. And don't interpret anything; you don't have the training. If you had the capacity to interpret this miasma, you wouldn't have gotten into it. Now talk: time is vanishing."

25.

RABBI DIAMANT WAS WRITING on her computer when Wishnasky walked in for their appointment. She was dressed in a dark gray suit and had a small yarmulke pinned to her hair. When she saw him, she said, "Just a minute," and continued typing. After a time, she got up, walked over to the round table where they usually met, and sat.

"How was your vacation?" she asked.

"Not perfect," Wishnasky said. He told her about the breakup with Vanessa, the argument over his prayer, the last nights of cold rejection. She absorbed it all placidly, not showing her emotion even when Wishnasky emphasized his regret that his religious search had separated him from his lover.

"I'm sorry about your girlfriend," the rabbi said finally. "But it's perhaps better that the break happen now rather than after you've made more of a commitment."

"I thought religion was this great binding force," said Wishnasky. "How come I'm finding it divisive?"

"We're at a strange point in history," said the rabbi. "The progressive strains of religion are losing adherents and the fundamentalists are booming. The misnamed Conservative Jewish movement was followed by forty percent of Americans in 1970; now it's down to seventeen percent. I wish I could say that many of these lost congregants are choosing some other Jewish denomination, but they're not. They're leaving the synagogue altogether. A lot of people are disaffected. That's what you're facing."

"Any theories as to why so many people are angry at religion?"

"When the great grandparents of today's Jews arrived from East and Central Europe, their solidarity with newly-minted Americans like themselves naturally centered around the neighborhood *shul*. Who could understand them better than other Jews who'd made the same voyage? The next generation didn't have this identity problem. The generation after, even less. And so on and so on: more dilution every thirty years. Add astronomical rates of marriage with non-Jews, and the result is our present perplexity."

"So, I'm going against the current."

"You and a few others. But getting back to St. Lucia: you said that your girl-friend interrupted you saying the *Ma'ariv* prayer. On the evenings before that, how did the prayer make you feel?"

"Awkward with all the praises of God. I still can't get used to them."

"The sections of praise are meant to place you in an appropriate relation to your Creator."

"Does God need my praise?"

"Not at all. But you need it. To discover your deference, your smallness. Did the praise section remind you that at the moment of prayer, you stand before Someone tremendous, transcendent?"

"I don't know. Maybe a little."

"Did you remember to add your personal supplications to the *Amidah*?"

"Yeah. And I felt childish, asking for God's help."

"It's not childish. The great theologian Heschel says there are two reasons people spurn God: they feel too small or too big. 'Small' means inconsequential—why would the Holy One even bother to notice me? 'Big' means self-sufficient—I'm too adult to need God. The latter sounds like your malady. Examine yourself and see if your embarrassment isn't really a form of pride. As if to say, 'I'm too grown up for this. I don't need anyone but myself.'"

"Rabbi, just relying on myself, I was doing pretty well. In work and love both. I wasn't flailing around for help."

"You know how the Holy One expresses divine anger? God says, 'I was so exasperated with these humans, I let them follow their own hearts.' Do you get that? Having only oneself to rely on isn't a privilege in *Torah*; it's a punishment. You're *supposed* to depend on God and know it. And it's all right to declare your needs. The Holy One wants this."

"And you meant it when you said that He answers your prayers?"

"Some of them, yes," said the rabbi. "And sometimes, to be honest, the answer has been 'no.' But ask anyone who prays regularly and you'll hear the same: of course God answers prayers. Now, there are ways that you can show yourself more worthy of this attention." She paused a moment, and Wishnasky had the sense from the way she was peering at him that she was making a decision.

"I want to try something with you," she said finally. "I want to jump ahead in your education, show you a world I usually keep back from my students until they've had much more preparation. But your story about St. Lucia convinces me you're ready. Can you give me two hours Thursday evening around 6:30?"

"This Thursday? Well, you know, I tend to write during the early evenings." He didn't mention that he hadn't written anything in weeks.

"Can you skip it this Thursday? To go seek God, like your message said? I know a potent method, if you'll only give it a try."

"I'm not sure," said Wishnasky, "Can you furnish more details?"

"I don't think I want to," said the rabbi. "But I promise to take you to a place where people find God regularly. Including myself. I'm not exaggerating."

Search for Me.

"All right, I'll try it."

"6:30 Thursday," said the rabbi. "Come here to synagogue and I'll drive you." She smiled as if the expectation alone were pleasing. "Now tell me more about your argument with your girlfriend. When you defended your faith."

26.

HE WAS AT HIS FRIEND Chet's house, meeting with his ex-Harvard roommates and their wives for the express purpose of commiserating over the loss of Vanessa. Several times over the years they'd organized similar conclaves—to encourage Quentin's wife, Katie, when she was in treatment for cancer, to celebrate Chet's second marriage and introduce Lena to the group, to congratulate Rick on the publication of his book on Mies van der Rohe. Now it was Wishnasky's turn, and he was basking in the warmth of his friends and their spouses as they rallied around him. He was even vaguely aware that the world, in the guise of these six loving souls, was offering him consolation of a sort that his novels disputed.

They were all seated in Chet and Lena's spacious living room, drinking brown German beer or white California wine, snacking on Stoned Wheat Thins and Gouda cheese, and enjoying the great pleasure they took in one another's company. Wishnasky had the easy chair next to the foosball table; the others were on the sofa or in the captain's chairs on either side of the bookcase. Finally, the question of the hour came up—reacquainting Wishnasky with love.

"Are you sure you want this?" Chet said. "Shouldn't you wait till the hurt over Vanessa has receded?"

"It's too rough being alone," said Wishnasky. "I would be so much happier if I were dating other women."

"I've got a friend from work," said Katie carefully. Copper-haired Katie, sitting on the sofa with Chet and Lena, was a tough labor arbitrator, though one would never guess it observing her five-foot frame. "She's newly divorced, really sweet, and loves Jane Austen. I could set you up with one phone call."

"Wait a minute," said Quentin. With his thick black hair and often-smiling face, he was the group's pragmatist, quick to perform a cost/benefit analysis on any suggested course of action. "Are you talking about Tara?"

"Yeah. She'd be great for Tristan."

"Listen, Tristan," said Quentin. "Tara's terrific. Only not very much in the looks department."

"Quentin!" said Katie.

"I know Tristan." said Quentin, blushing almost as red as his flannel shirt. "He's into physical beauty. Don't forget what Vanessa looked like."

"And don't forget what she looked like walking out on him!"

"Tristan," said Quentin. "Do looks matter? Do you care?"

"Well," Wishnasky said guiltily. "Physical attraction doesn't hurt."

"Tara is attractive!" said Katie. "And she's got a beautiful body! And I can't believe that you're making me talk like this!"

"You have lots of other friends," said Quentin to his wife. "Suggest Ashley. Or Cass."

"Okay, Ashley. She's attractive and, I don't know, formidable. She's a doctor. A neurologist. And she's divorced and casting around for a relationship."

"Terrific, Ashley," said Wishnasky. "The lovely neurologist.'" He looked around the room. "Other suggestions?"

"Barbara," said Julie. She was a tall brunette, an actress and playwright, and her marriage to Rick was the longest-standing in the room. "She's originally from Missouri. She's a performer who also works as office manager in an attorney's office. She's not a knockout, but she's striking. Has a wonderful voice, once you hear it you'll never forget it. And she's outstanding on stage. I'm pretty sure she wants to meet someone."

"Good, Barbara," said Wishnasky. "I like actresses. Is she playing in anything these days? Maybe I could get a sense of her."

"You mean a *look*," said Katie.

"She's in a Beckett play at the Raft Theatre in Allston. Have you been there?" Tristan hadn't. "And I think I have a picture of her on my phone. Hold on." Julie took her phone out of her back pocket and scrolled through her photo library.

"While you're looking," said Wishnasky. "I'll consider others." He glanced around the room. Chet's wife, Lena, long-haired and willowy, shrugged as if to say that she didn't condone this sort of consultation. To the others, he said "Who've you got? This could be the most important question you're asked all year."

"Tristan," said Rick. He was tall, light-haired, mustached, a 1940s idea of a gentleman mountain climber. "You haven't asked if any of these women are Jewish. If you're really looking into your religion these days, is that a qualification that matters to you?"

"I don't think so," said Wishnasky. "I've hardly ever gone out with any Jewish women. I mean, when I was sixteen, and then a couple of times in college. But no, that's not a requirement."

"What if I told you about an Orthodox Jewish woman who happens to be single?"

"Oh," said Julie, looking up from her phone. "You're talking about Andrea."

"That's right." Rick looked to Wishnasky. "Are you interested?"

"How Orthodox is she?" said Wishnasky. "Would she even consider dating a guy who doesn't keep kosher, doesn't observe the *Sabbath*, and hardly knows a word of Hebrew?"

"I think she would," said Rick. "I've met a couple of the guys she's gone out with in the past, and I don't think they were observant. So, she's not too rigid. And I'm almost sure she'd find a novelist fascinating."

"She works at Dan Hibbert's office," said Julie. "She's just a few years out of architecture school."

"Okay, I'll try her," said Wishnasky. "Why not?"

"What does 'try her' mean?" said Katie, frowning.

"I mean, I'll meet her," said Tristan. "I don't mean that I'll put her in my harem and only take her out on Tuesdays and Fridays."

"You'd better be serious about this, buddy," said Katie. "My girlfriends are precious. You hurt one of them and it's me you're gonna have to face the next morning."

"I'm more feminist than you are."

"Ha."

"I've got the picture of Barbara," said Julie, passing her phone to Wishnasky. "This was when the three of us went backstage at *A Doll's House*. She was Mrs. Linde. Wonderful portrayal."

Wishnasky saw a photo of a black-haired woman with an unusually triangular face, piercing eyes, and a winning smile.

"Nice," he said. "I think I'll start with her."

"She's an actress," warned Katie. "Needs five hundred people applauding her to feel loved. No offense, Julie."

"None taken."

"I can talk literature with an actress," said Wishnasky. "Shakespeare. Chekhov. Arrange a meeting. Dinner for the four of us. Or take me to the play she's in. Yes, I'm intrigued."

"What about the other two?" said Quentin.

"Put them on hold," said Wishnasky. "I like Barbara. How soon can we do this?"

27.

IT WAS A RED BRICK BUILDING, two stories, not in good condition. There was a battered wooden sign saying "Horn of Plenty" in faded blue letters, and when the rabbi drove through an opening in a chain link fence beside it, Wishnasky, in the passenger seat, saw a group of what looked like vagrants—shabby, unshaven—smoking and talking by a dumpster. Farther into the parking area he saw a clump of old bicycles and four parked cars, including an old Jeep and a rusted Chevy Impala. The land was patchy, weedy in some areas, sandy in the rest. The rabbi parked facing a long, uneven weatherworn fence, then got out of the car and led Wishnasky through a tall brown gate. On the other side was an outdoor eating area made of a dozen or so long folding tables with plastic chairs on either side. On each table was a lit candle in a glass semi-globe and a pair of salt and pepper shakers. There were a few tired-looking people—white and African American, male and female—already seated and talking with each other. At a far table, a young Black man sat alone, staring down at the tabletop and beating on it with both fists as he moved his lips. Beyond the paved area of the eating section, some men and women were standing by a heap of bicycle parts, waiting for something.

"These are mostly the homeless," said the rabbi once they passed through the gate. "Not entirely: some of them have beds at the Friend Indeed in South Boston. But most of them live under bridges, in alleyways, anywhere there's shelter. We serve them dinner every Thursday evening. Follow me inside."

She opened a large, mottled red door, and Wishnasky found himself standing in a large kitchen, dominated by a central metal island. On it were three big brown covered bins, as well as rows of plastic glasses, several piles of plastic plates, and a tower of trays. Against one wall were two huge metal sinks. Several youngish people, mostly in tee-shirts and jeans, were hurrying back and forth from the kitchen into a room Wishnasky couldn't see. "These are all volunteers," said the rabbi. "Stay here; I want you to meet Brooke."

She disappeared into the inner room, leaving Wishnasky to look around and back through the door to the eating area. He was uncomfortable and felt unsafe. Some of the faces he glimpsed appeared hostile, or at least unfriendly. He reminded himself that the rabbi didn't seem at all anxious about her surroundings, but still he couldn't relax. What if those three men seated at a near table were strung-out drug addicts, street fighters with guns or knives? And what about that man staring at the table and banging his fists? He remembered reading somewhere that many homeless people were mentally ill, and he wondered if any of the young volunteers in this edifice were trained as counselors. What should he do if assaulted? Why hadn't the rabbi given him more preparation for such company?

"Hi!" said a young Black woman with a smiling round face and what sounded like a British accent. "Are you new here?"

"Yes," he said. "I'm Tristan. Here with Rabbi Diamant."

"I'm Dianabasi," said the woman, putting out her hand for him to shake. "Everyone calls me Dee."

"You have a great accent," said Wishnasky, shaking her hand. "Where are you from?"

"Nigeria. I'm a student at Boston College. How'd you find out about us?"

"The rabbi."

"I'm so glad," said Dee. "We need an extra server tonight. Xavier is out of town."

"Are you here every week?"

"If I can be. It's very special, you know."

Just at that moment, the rabbi came back with a pink-cheeked, brown-haired woman who looked to be about thirty. "Oh, you've met Dee," said the rabbi.

"Thanks for bringing him," said Dee. "We're one short tonight."

"Tristan," said the rabbi, "this is Brooke. She's in charge of the weekly dinners and can answer any question I can't."

Blue-eyed, Nordic-looking Brooke extended her hand. "Nice to meet you," she said. "Deborah tells me you're a novelist. That's so neat. What's the name of one of your novels?"

"There've been three," Wishnasky said, trying to figure which title sounded least self-important. "Maybe you've heard of *No One From Nowhere.*"

"I'm sorry, but no," said Brooke. "I'll have to read it. Do you mind serving tonight?"

"Uh—"

"It's very easy: you put four plates on a tray, start on the tables nearest the fence, dispense the food, go back to the kitchen and get four more, repeat. Eventually, you snake your way back through the middle section, then along the far end. Just do what the other servers do."

"Sure," said Wishnasky.

"Tristan's searching for God," said the rabbi. "I told him this is the place to look."

"God allows us to be His hands and legs in this service," said Brooke. "So now you can be that too."

"Brooke is Christian," said the rabbi, "as is Patrick, her husband, and Vivian, and Kanesha. Dee is Yoruba, Lance is studying to become a Buddhist monk, and of course you and I are Jewish. It's a nice mix, don't you think?"

"Yes. I—are all these people safe?" asked Wishnasky. "For example, there's a guy out there, staring at the table, kind of banging his fists."

"Yeah, that's Giorgio," said Brooke with an apologetic smile. "He's probably on drugs. Does that a lot. And there are always a few who are drunk or stoned, though they try to hide it. It's mostly very peaceful, though. If anyone acts inappropriately, I just ask them to leave. Come see me if there's a problem."

Wishnasky felt ashamed to be more anxious about Giorgio than were Brooke or the rabbi. Still, he didn't feel comfortable. Was the threat he sensed entirely his own invention? Could any of the rather unsavory types gathering in the eating area be carrying weapons?

Now there were several more young men and women in the kitchen, all smiling at Wishnasky when he looked in their direction. "Let's have our prayer," said Brooke. She bowed her head, and the others—Wishnasky included—did as well. "Dear Lord," said Brooke. "Thank you for the opportunity to feed these hungry souls. Thank you for teaching us this method of doing Your will. Please give us inspiration to be a source of hope in the lives of all those we serve tonight. Amen."

"Amen," said all the others—Wishnasky, again, included—and Brooke raised her head and said, "Patrick, Kanesha, and I will be plating, Lance is on fruit punch, and Deborah, Tristan, and Dee will be serving. Let's start."

Three people, including Brooke, opened the large bins—they were stuffed with food—and started ladling some sort of turkey stew, mixed vegetables, and rice onto the plastic plates. The rabbi took the first four plates, put them on a tray and waited for Wishnasky to do the same with the next four. Then, the rabbi led Wishnasky out to the eating area, where all the tables were now filled with the homeless. The rabbi distributed her four plates to the diners at the first table and signaled Wishnasky to do the same with the next four. Wishnasky heard a "thank you" from each of the vagrants—was "customers" a kinder word?—as he laid their plates in front of them, and he said "You're welcome" or "Not at all," still feeling fearful.

The last of the four was a heavyset middle-aged woman in a threadbare dress that was much too low-cut for such an occasion. She said "God bless you," when he served her.

"Thank you," said Wishnasky, and walked back into the kitchen behind the rabbi.

"You're doing fine," she said.

"I don't understand this," said Wishnasky.

"We'll talk about it on the drive home," said the rabbi. "For now, just keep looking for God."

Serving the food to the sixty or so people seated at the long tables took less than fifteen minutes. Wishnasky began to feel not quite so anxious, especially when some of the most forbidding, unshaven faces offered the gentlest "thank yous." Others, he noted, appeared so distracted by personal crises, they hardly noticed the meal that Wishnasky put in front of them.

"Where's my lobster bisque?" said one dapper, bearded man in an old khaki vest. Then he laughed at his joke, and Wishnasky smiled too.

After everyone was served, the volunteers gathered in the kitchen, where they talked and joked among themselves, and asked Wishnasky polite questions about his writing career. When Brooke announced that it was time for seconds, Wishnasky was given a huge glass bowl full of mixed vegetables and instructed to go from table to table asking if anyone was still hungry. His fears further subsided: these diners were for the most part civil, grateful, and occasionally even funny.

He was again reproaching himself when one tall, bald-headed Black man said, "Now I've been coming here for months and I ain't never seen you around. You new?"

"Yeah, first time."

"What's your day job?"

"I'm a writer."

"You don't say. What sort? I'm a poet myself."

"Fiction, mostly. What kind of poetry do you write?"

"Not much, is what. Words cost money. So does paper, last time I looked. Mostly, I spend all day at the library, reading."

"Yeah? Who do you read?"

"Harlem Renaissance: Zora Hurston, Countee Cullen, Claude McKay. Like to feel that I'm trading talk with them at the Savoy Ballroom. You know McKay's poetry?"

"Not really," said Wishnasky. "Should I read it?"

"Oh yeah. Especially from the twenties."

"I'll take a look," said Wishnasky, without the least intention of doing so. "What's your name?"

"Tristan. You?"

"Arthur Winslow" said the man. "This place needs more writers. I'll have a big helpin' of those vegetables, please."

Having dispensed most of the food in his bowl, Wishnasky returned to the kitchen, where the rabbi was scraping unwanted rice into the garbage. She told him that for many of the men and women at this gathering, the meal here was the only one they could depend on all week. The source of the food was the Commonwealth Hunger Alliance near Park Street Station, and some weeks there wasn't enough to go round. But tonight there was a surplus, and that was always a great blessing. She asked how he was feeling.

"I'm still not sure," he answered honestly.

Brooke announced time for cleanup. Wishnasky walked out to the dining area and, imitating the other volunteers, collected plates and plastic glasses and brought them back into the kitchen. He scraped the dishes into a huge garbage pail, then deposited the dirty ware beside one of the sinks where Patrick, red-haired and bearded, and Kanesha, tall with long dreadlocks, were washing and drying. Then, he went back out and collected more. When the outdoor tables were clear of food and the diners had departed, the other servers and platers folded up tables and chairs. Wishnasky followed their lead, carrying the portable furniture out to a large metal shed at the far end of the parking area.

"Thank you for coming," said Brooke, as Wishnasky and the rabbi were about to drive off. "Do you think you can manage again next Thursday? I don't know how long Xavier will be out."

"I'm not sure," said Tristan. "It depends on my schedule." Of course, his schedule was wide open since progress on the novel had stalled. "I'll tell the rabbi, if you're in touch with her."

"I am," said Brooke. "Have a good evening. Thanks again."

As the rabbi drove him home, Wishnasky was quiet, preoccupied. Finally, he said, "What just happened? Please explain it."

"You heard Brooke," answered the rabbi. "For a few minutes, you and I were God's arms and legs. Distributing nourishment to the Holy One's children."

"But that's pantheism, isn't it? I thought that God was transcendent, and to identify Him with people was sacrilegious."

"We weren't God," said the rabbi. "We were God's instruments. Doing precisely what the Holy One would do if God were here in Boston. But the Deity insists that *we* do it, that we be God's limbs, so to speak. The Almighty wants this very much. It's one of the main things that God wants."

"But He wants lots of stuff, right? 613 commandments?"

"This one gets mentioned more than the others," said the rabbi. "One has to conclude that it's special."

"So the Creator of billions of light years' worth of galaxies has preferred commandments?"

"Look, Tristan," said Rabbi Diamant, as they passed between rows of clothing stores and small restaurants. "I don't know where you got your concepts, but the Holy One isn't some vaguely exploitable Force out of *Star Wars*. The God of *Torah* has a personality, favorite causes, makes specific requests. And this commandment, to look after the poor, is stated so many times, in so many different ways, you have to accept that it matters deeply. Don't take my word for it. Read your Bible. You do have a Bible, don't you?"

"Of course," said Tristan. He still owned the volume of *Torah* that was given to him at his bar mitzvah twenty-some years before. As an adult, he'd hardly looked into it except to find quotes he could refute and mock in his novels.

"It's all in the word 'justice,'" said the rabbi. "Repeatedly, the word 'justice' is defined in the *Torah* as helping the poor and wretched, the orphan and widow. When you first came to see me, you said you were searching for God. Know it or not, that's Who you found tonight: in yourself, doing the feeding. Now the only question is, Will you deepen your acquaintance? Are you willing to come back next week?"

He didn't want to say, *not till I've had some hours to think.* But then he remembered: *You don't have time to waste.* Well, one more visit to feed the hungry wouldn't commit him long-term. He could always bow out later, invent a conflict, a prior obligation. And he *had* felt something, feeding the poor, that was new and worth investigating. But why was it so hard to say what it was?

"All right," he said. "I'm almost sure I can schedule it."

"Good," said Rabbi Diamant and turned the car onto busy Storrow Drive.

An hour later, after his drive from the synagogue back to Newton Corner, Wishnasky unlocked his front door and walked into the darkened living room. For the hundredth time, he reminded himself that Vanessa wouldn't be in the bedroom waiting for him, that he couldn't call her and recount his day, that there was no one to talk to, to counsel him, comfort him. He went over to a table lamp, then thought better of it and sat on his sofa in the dark.

He tried to understand what he'd just experienced. First, he felt ashamed of the worries he'd harbored. Dee, after all, couldn't have weighed more than ninety pounds, Lance was so slight, he looked like a strong wind might overturn him, but these two and all the others seemed entirely unfazed by the roughest and most forbidding-looking of the evening's diners. Was he really so much more cowardly than everyone else? Or had he projected peril onto these hard-pressed homeless, a peril conjured from his ignorance and inexperience? If he did return next week, he would make a greater effort to treat the diners as he'd seen the others do, as deeply valuable individuals well worth knowing. Hadn't he already started on that path with Arthur the poet? Well, good: next time he'd try to learn more about his fellow author. No better cure for paranoia than reality.

And then he remembered something else. While he was serving the evening's meal—each time he'd laid a heaping plate of hot food in front of a hollow-eyed diner—he'd had the most unfamiliar sense that he was actually making a difference in someone's life, affecting the world substantially. Writing in his study, giving a reading at a bookstore, providing interviews to journalists—these all paled to invisibility compared to distributing stew, rice, and mixed vegetables to desperately hungry mouths. The newness of this recognition shamed him: surely a writer of three novels shouldn't be aware now for the first time of something so fundamental. Maybe the problem was that he didn't have children—didn't yet have the experience of providing food, clothing, and shelter on a regular basis to people fully dependent. Or maybe this was what Ion meant when he accused him of not knowing himself. How could he know a self so out of contact with most of the world? But it was true: delivering that plate of food to the large, homeless woman in the faded, inappropriately low-cut dress had felt more consequential than just about anything else he could remember doing.

And *Search for Me*? He didn't know yet. He didn't know precisely what he'd found at the Horn of Plenty. But maybe there was a trace of ...

He rose from the sofa, turned on a light and walked into his bedroom. As he undressed for bed, he felt certain that something important was changing for him.

28.

THE THEATRE WAS IN THE BACK of an old strip shopping center, up a flight of wooden steps, and past a realtor's office.

"Follow me," said Rick, climbing just behind Julie who'd already reached the upper landing. "It's just up here a few steps." They walked along a poorly lighted corridor—it was either gray or looked gray in the twilight—and to a sign that said "The Raft." Julie held the door for Rick and Tristan, then walked in behind them. A few steps ahead in the bright interior, a woman sitting at a small table was dispensing tickets and Xeroxed programs.

"Three for *Happy Days,*" said Rick. "I called ahead. The name is McKenna."

"McKenna," said the ticket taker. "Right. That'll be sixty dollars."

Wishnasky reached for his wallet, took out a twenty and handed it to Rick, who was fishing a debit card out of his own wallet. He took the bill without looking, found his card and handed it to the ticket-taker. A few moments later the three visitors walked into the theatre.

It was small, with about forty wooden chairs placed in six neat rows. There were a few people already seated: a white-bearded elderly man reading his program; three young, laughing women who looked to be college age; a taciturn, suburban couple in their thirties, staring ahead stone-faced. Julie motioned Tristan and Rick to three chairs in the unoccupied second row, and Tristan sat, facing a large blue curtain on a wheeled, movable frame.

"You're going to love her," said Julie, sitting beside him. "She's one of the most talented actresses I know, and it's a shame that she's here and not at the Huntington or American Rep. You'll find out in a moment."

"If you say she's good, I'm sure she is," said Wishnasky.

"We were at the premiere last week," said Rick. "It was so special, it's worth coming again."

"I hate to think that in two weekends it'll be over," said Julie. "I wish someone would record it."

"Union won't let them."

"It's just a shame."

"When she makes it big," said Rick, "we'll be able to say that we caught her performance in this hole-in-the-wall."

A slender young woman with long, wavy brown hair stepped in front of the audience members—were there really only nine of them?—and thanked everyone for coming. "I also want to remind you," she said, looking from face to face, "that The Raft is a nonprofit theatre and we could use your donations. Anything at all helps: just notice the collection box on the way out." She peered into Wishnasky's eyes for a moment, then shifted her gaze to someone else. "And now I present you with Samuel Beckett's *Happy Days*."

She turned, grabbed hold of one side of the curtain frame, and swung the whole apparatus to the side of the stage area. Wishnasky and the others saw a smiling brunette buried to her waist in a mound of dirt. This was Barbara, and Wishnasky immediately found her attractive. He settled into his chair, pleased to think that he could stare at this lovely woman for two full acts without seeming improper.

The play began. Barbara was Winnie, who didn't seem to be aware that she was half-interred as she prattled, chattered, mused, and sang. She spoke occasionally to her husband Willie, who lived near the mound and still had some mobility. The more she jabbered, the happier she tried to seem, the more one was aware of her self-delusion. The earth was swallowing her up, and she didn't even notice.

There was a fifteen-minute intermission. "She's excellent," Wishnasky said as they bought drinks from the makeshift bar. "And she's clearly a fine actress."

"I told you," said Julie.

"Do they have cider?" said Rick.

"You know they don't," said Julie. "Get a Coke."

"Great, I'll have a Coke."

"How old is she?" asked Wishnasky.

"I think thirty-five," said Julie. "Is that okay?"

"That's great," said Wishnasky.

"I'm in the mood for cider," said Rick.

Act Two: the curtain opened on Barbara/Winnie now up to her neck in dirt. Once again, she blabbered, warbled, and passed the time as if unconscious that soon enough she would be fully buried. Remembering (from his college reading) that nothing more in the way of a plot was going to unfold, Wishnasky began to feel slightly bored. But then he reminded himself that soon he'd be meeting this stunning actress and he should be ready to compliment her on the details of her performance. So, he focused on Barbara's eyebrows, how they suggested all the subtleties the buried parts of her couldn't, on her bright eyes and how just occasionally they communicated a heroically-repressed anxiety, on her thin lips with their wistful smiles and emphatic frowns. When the play ended, Barbara maneuvered out from behind the mound, bowed for applause—Wishnasky clapped loudest of all nine spectators—and, with seeming reluctance, took her exit.

They waited near the ticket table for the actress to join them. The other audience members had left the building. "I guess that's your kind of play," said Rick. "All doom and gloom."

"I'm not sure that I buy it anymore," said Tristan. "I'm experimenting with other colors."

"Well, that's unexpected," said Julie. "What's happened?"

"Listen, Tristan," whispered Rick. "I didn't tell you that Barbara's really political. And she tends to get upset at anything right-wing, if you know what I mean."

"No warning necessary," said Wishnasky. "I'm a card-carrying liberal."

"It's just that it's the one thing that can make her a little crazy."

"I'll quote Marx, Engels, and Gramsci."

"Shh," said Julie. "She's coming."

Barbara Ormandy, dressed in a shimmering white blouse and beltless gray pants, appeared with a wide grin. "Wonderful!" said Julie and hugged her. "Wonderful performance!"

"You did it again," exclaimed Rick, taking both her hands. "I don't know where you get the inspiration."

"This is Tristan Wishnasky," said Julie, putting the palm of her hand on Tristan's back.

"Splendid acting," said Wishnasky.

Barbara smiled again, said "No, it wasn't," and they all walked out of the theatre together.

The club they went to was downstairs and around to the front of the strip mall. It was a former clothes shop that had been converted into a jazz space, with a dozen small round tables and a long narrow bar running down its length, and high metal stools in front of it. At the far end was the bandstand, which at the moment was vacant. Most of the tables were taken. The four friends chose one near the entrance, with terrible sightlines—and sat.

"I've read one of your novels," said Barbara to Wishnasky. "I really liked it."

"Thank you. Which one was it?"

"*Potholes of the Spirit*?"

"*Craters of the Spirit*. Yeah, that was my most recent."

"I'm surprised you're not all dressed in black and sporting a hypodermic syringe."

"Well, I've grown up a little since then," said Tristan. "Are you the same actress you were ten years ago?"

"I hope not," beamed Barbara. "I don't think the world could take it." She laughed merrily. "But I'm still impressed that you write novels," she said. "I wish I could. Hey, do you want to teach me?" There was a pause; then she laughed again, as if it were a great joke.

The four of them chatted, drank, discussed Beckett, the Boston theatre scene, Barbara's hope that she'd be cast in Brecht's *Mahogany* that was scheduled to play at the American Repertory Theatre in a few months. Barbara turned out to be a charming interlocutor, joking and bantering, underplaying her talent, making no effort to hide her admiration of writers generally, Wishnasky in particular. Then she named her favorite: Pinter, whose *The Collection* wasn't widely known, she said, but was as brilliant as anything else in his repertoire, including *The Birthday Party* and *The Homecoming*.

"You're Jewish, aren't you?" said Barbara. "Just like Pinter."

"I don't know," said Wishnasky. "How was he Jewish?"

"What are your feelings about Israel? And the Palestinians?"

"I think there should be peace," said Wishnasky. "How about you?"

"I went to Palestine," said Barbara.

"That's right," said Julie. "Barbara spent two weeks in the Occupied Territories last summer."

"How was it?" asked Tristan.

"You're probably a Zionist," said Barbara, pouting a little. "You probably think the Jews had a right to colonize the area."

"I'm glad there's a Jewish home," said Wishnasky, "if that's what you mean. But I'd prefer that the Israelis could live comfortably there, without having to worry about their neighbors." He wondered if this counted as the sort of politics that he was supposed to avoid.

"The poor Palestinians," said Barbara. "Thrown off their own land."

Julie sensed trouble and tried to divert the conversation. "Did you see any theatre when you were in Israel?" she asked. "Is it all in Hebrew or do they have English-speaking plays also?"

Barbara took the bait. "I did go to the Sherover in Jerusalem to see *Henry IV, Part One* in Hebrew. I didn't understand a word of it, but it was glorious, so moving! And to see a big old Jewish Falstaff!" She laughed heartily.

The conversation continued on the subject of Shakespeare. There were drinks and the jazz combo—a trio of guitar, clarinet, and bass—played, and then there were more drinks, and finally the four paid their tab and walked outside.

"My car's out back," said Barbara.

"Ours too," said Julie. "We'll walk with you."

They started off toward the parking lot. Julie and Rick made a deliberate effort to lag behind so Wishnasky and Barbara could stroll together in front of them.

Wishnasky didn't waste a moment. "I'd like to see you again," he said. "Maybe we could have dinner sometime soon."

"I'm onstage Friday and Saturday nights," said Barbara. "And afterwards I'm sort of worn out. But I could do Sunday, early evening. There's only a matinee."

"Sunday would be great. Let me get your number and address."

She entered her information on his phone.

When she finished, he said, "I'm honestly impressed. You're an extraordinary actress."

"Hey, anyone can act buried up to her neck."

"Maybe one day I'll see you in something where you can swing your arms."

She laughed. "That would be glorious."

They reached Barbara's green Honda Civic. "Okay, I'll see you next Sunday, five o'clock," she said. There was a brief, awkward pause, and then she made a sudden move and kissed Wishnasky's cheek. He was surprised. Barbara waved at the two others, climbed into her Honda and started the engine.

After she drove off, Rick said, "Well, what did you think?"

"She's great!" said Tristan. "The total opposite of Vanessa. Just what I need. Thank you, dear friends."

"She's complicated," said Julie. "Don't be too sure yet. Spend a little time with her first."

"Of course," said Tristan, wishing Barbara was going home with him now.

"Good night," said Rick.

"Good night," said Tristan, still feeling Barbara's kiss on his skin. Then, unexpectedly, he felt a pang of pain over lost Vanessa. Why should he kid himself? He'd lost the perfect woman and no one, surely not this Barbara, would ever surpass her. What was his chance of finding another Vanessa?

He drove home suspecting that he'd ruined his future.

29.

HE HAD TO FINISH *TRAVELER*. The deadline was approaching and people were depending on him. No more procrastinating.

One major challenge: to be true to himself, he had to grant Edward Ozono, sad wretch that he was, the merest possibility of something to hope for besides a cold grave. It didn't have to be much more—after all, Wishnasky was still wavering on this God thing and wouldn't insist on a certainty he himself didn't possess. But he'd never published a word that didn't represent his feelings, and his honest opinion at this juncture was that maybe God was possible. To avoid scandalizing his fans, he might have to whisper it, but it still had to be stated. And then this troublesome opus would be complete.

He pondered his method. He would conserve everything already written, pull out the props from Ozono as before, lay him low and make him miserable. But then another force would providentially intervene and the prospect of a return to his feet would appear. There would have to be a woman (who would eventually become a lover) and she would teach broken Ozono a theory of healing beyond anything he'd dared contemplate. She would tell him of the chance—the merest possibility—of a Higher Power, and he wouldn't completely reject it. The novel would end on this ambiguous note, and the reader would understand that Tristan Wishnasky, the celebrated nihilist, was now ready to, well, entertain a somewhat different paradigm. And then, through cyberspace, to Darryl Kamfort.

He sat down at his computer and opened the *Traveler* document. He scrolled to the last rewrite—amazing how long it had been since he had made progress—and hit the enter key a few times. Then he began to write:

It was a terrible Saturday. Famished and despising himself, Ozono stalked through Santa Monica like a ghost. He knew he was walking toward the Pacific, and had an idea of what he might do once he got there. The ocean, at least, would welcome him.

The ocean, at least, would not disdain knowing him.

He crossed a street to its beach side and faced a condominium building beside a Mexican-style hacienda. The path between the two structures would be his conduit to deliverance. He paused a moment and asked himself if this solution was indeed the desired one. When he felt certain of the answer, he took a first step toward his last ecstasy.

"Ed, is that you?"

The voice was female, unfamiliar, and he couldn't tell where it was coming from. Then he saw the blue Buick with the open window on the driver side, and a woman he almost recognized calling to him worriedly.

"Who's that?" he said, irked to be deterred from the end he now craved.

"Yvonne Pardoner. From a thousand years ago, from grade school and Hebrew School. Aren't you the Ed Ozono who was bar mitzvahed when the synagogue was on Hammond Street? The smart kid?'

"Yvonne. Yes, I remember. Look, keep driving. You've got somewhere important to go."

"I'm worried about you, Ed. I've heard you had some bad times."

"A few. Nothing I can't fix. Drive on, please, Yvonne."

"I can't; I need to talk with you. We were good friends a thousand years ago. Would you be so good as to let me talk with you?"

"I don't know why you'd want to."

"Are you on foot? Nobody's on foot here—the police could pick you up. Get in my car."

"I have something to do, Yvonne. Leave me your number. I'll call in an hour."

"No, Ed. I'm not moving. Not till you get in."

He looked into her face as if it were an asteroid from another solar system. He couldn't remember the last time anyone had shown him anything like solicitude. Well, someone to mislead. He guessed he could bear it. The Pacific would wait.

"All right," he said. "I'm coming in."

■

Wishnasky sat back from his computer and read what he'd written. Yes, this was the new approach: after the climb down, a way up. Or at least the potential.

He moved back to his keyboard and resumed typing. The words came as fast as they ever had because he knew, for the first time in months, how to bring *Traveler* to a close.

30.

"SHE WAS A SNOB AND A COMPLAINER, and you're lucky to be rid of her," said Mia Wishnasky as she removed the brisket from the convection oven. "Of all your girlfriends, she's the one I liked least."

Wishnasky was visiting his parents. He was seated at the bar that separated their living room from their kitchen, and he was watching his mother put the last touches on dinner. His father stood by the refrigerator with hands in pockets.

"You know, I liked her," said Morris. "She had a way about her—an energy, verve. I always enjoyed it when you brought her here."

"Vanessa was complex," said Wishnasky, wondering why everyone was using the past tense. "She didn't hide her feelings and some people interpreted that to mean that she was belligerent. But the fact is, deep down, she was tender and vulnerable. I saw that any number of times."

"I liked Sandra," said Mia, slicing the brisket with a long, serrated knife. "You were wrong to divorce her. Not a single woman you've dated since then has been half as good for you."

"You carped about Sandra from the first day you met her!" said Wishnasky. "And now you pretend that you liked her?"

"I also appreciated Sandra," said Morris Wishnasky. "She was a deeply appealing woman. And she wouldn't have challenged you on your Jewish interests. Maybe you two shouldn't have divorced."

"It's been almost ten years," said Wishnasky. "Let's agree to put that particular subject to rest."

"My mother's father was religious," said Mia. "My grandmother begged him to stop studying *Torah* long enough to make a living for the five of them, but he found God so intoxicating, he couldn't get around to making money. So they went through life poor." She was putting the brisket on plates and adding

121

ears of corn plucked from the microwave. "Are you going to turn out like him? Give up writing novels?"

"You know, I'm sorry I told you what Vanessa and I quarreled about. Now, all I'm going to hear is cautionary hokum about people who became religious."

"If you want to be religious, be religious," said Morris. "Only you know what makes you happy."

"New subject," said Wishnasky. "Where are you traveling come December? Let me guess: somewhere in Colorado."

"We're going to Florida," said Mia, serving dinner. "The West Coast this time: Tampa, St. Petersburg. We've rented a condo on Clearwater Beach."

"What's there to do in Clearwater?"

"There's a museum nearby that's only work by Salvador Dali. There's Busch Gardens in Tampa and the Asolo Repertory Theatre in Sarasota. And lots of lovely architecture."

"There's sun," said Morris.

"But finish about Vanessa," said Mia, beckoning for all to move to the dinner table. "After you had your little spat. Did you try to make up? You had what, two more days still on vacation?"

"We hardly spoke," said Wishnasky. "It was extremely uncomfortable. I was glad to get back to the States."

"You might still salvage the relationship," said Morris. "Nothing's final when two people love each other. Call her and say you want to discuss further."

"Don't you dare," said Mia. All three were now seated. "That ill-natured, cold-hearted woman, not wanting to give me grandchildren."

"She was always polite to me," said Morris.

"Let's talk about your vacation," said Wishnasky. "Why not Miami or Palm Beach?"

"With women, no conversation is final," said Morris. "I say this as a compliment."

"I had an uncle who became obsessively Jewish," said Mia. "Stopped shaving his beard, wore a fedora at all times, wouldn't eat in anyone's house if they didn't keep kosher. Finally, he moved to Williamsburg in Brooklyn and joined the ultra-orthodox. Stopped speaking to the rest of us. Is that where you're heading?"

"I'm just investigating, Ma," said Wishnasky. He was realizing painfully that Vanessa's usual place at the table beside him was empty. "And there's no chance of me becoming ultra-Orthodox. The Conservative movement is progressive on everything: women's equality, gay marriage, you name it."

"You should have seen his beard," said Mia. "There could have been crows living in it, or a family of chinchillas. It was so long and thick, you couldn't be sure."

"There's a fine performing arts center in Tampa," said Morris, still thinking about the winter. "We'll see Broadway touring companies for half the price we'd pay in the city. We've already got tickets to *Wicked.* Unfortunately, we won't be there when *Hamilton* passes through again."

"I saw *Hamilton* in New York with Vanessa," said Wishnasky. "Brilliant idea: people of color singing hip-hop all about the founding of America. Mind-blowing. Best thing in decades."

"Speaking of Vanessa," said Mia, "I never told you this story, but now I feel free. A few months ago, when you had left the table to go to the bathroom, I said, 'Vanessa, you never mention your parents. Tell me about them.' And she said, 'I do my best not to think of them and certainly not to speak of them.' And then she went mum. Later, I thought: if she marries Tristan, we'll never see him again. Another good reason for breaking up with her."

"Ma, not to find fault, but are you aware that you laid into her just about every time she visited?"

"It's possible I asked her to explain her peculiar attitudes," said Mia. "I never 'laid into' her."

"Are you joking?"

"I'm serious. But getting back to your Jewish kick: Do you know what happens to men who wear a hat all day and night? Putting constant pressure on the hair follicles?"

"This brisket is *outstanding*," said Morris."

"They lose all their hair. Even young; it's a fact. I had a cousin who many years ago became fanatically Jewish. One day the cap went on; a month later, the hair fell out. I'm only warning you because I love you."

"I wanted tickets to *Dear Evan Hansen*," said Morris to his son. "But it starts the day we fly back."

"So lose your hair," said Mia. "That's the style these days, anyway. Wear a hat even to bed and you'll be right on the cutting edge."

"Call Vanessa," said Morris. "Tell her you want to make up."

"We have ice cream for dessert," said Mia. "Better eat it now before you stop mixing milk and meat. And goodbye cheeseburgers."

"Let's change the subject," said Wishnasky.

"Send her an email," said Morris. "*Want to chat. All things negotiable. Am reconsidering our discussion.*"

"Dad, I don't think Vanessa and I are getting back together."

"The worse for you, then. Mia, darling, is there any more brisket? I could eat this all night."

31.

IT WAS EARLY EVENING, and Rabbi Diamant was driving them back to the Horn of Plenty. There was more than a threat of winter in the autumn air; hurrying along the sidewalks were people already in ski parkas and down vests. Traffic was congested—in Boston, most hours were rush hours—and every few moments someone sounded a horn to express frustration with the slow crawl. In the bay windows of the apartments along the route, Wishnasky could see people eating or watching TV, and for the first time in his life, he wondered how the homeless dealt with the autumn chill—or far worse, the Boston winter with lows in the twenties or worse. In the car, the heat was comfortable; outside, the pedestrians seemed harried and anxious to get where they were going. Where did one go when one didn't have a home?

"Rabbi," said Wishnasky. "You told me once before that you didn't mind me asking difficult questions. May I ask you one now?"

"Of course. I expect you to."

"Why do I have the feeling that Judaism is about an excessive number of laws? Reams of them, bushels of them."

"Is that your assumption?"

"I think so. Don't the law books go on for volume after volume?"

"You told me that your message said to search for God, right? Well, for most Jews over the last two thousand years, following the commandments and prohibitions of Jewish law was the primary method of seeking the Holy One. The Hebrew word that's usually translated as law—*halachah*—literally means 'the way' or 'the road,' and when one performs a commandment, one is walking on the Royal Road—God's prescribed path. Walking on that road, one comes, inevitably, to discover its Engineer. For example, going to the Horn of Plenty tonight puts you on God's road and helps you to understand the Almighty better. Keeping *Sabbath*, eating kosher, all the commandments do the same. I can show you a section of the *Talmud*ic tractate *Baba Metzia* in which the great rabbis argue over the correct method of fulfilling God's instruction on the subject of when to pay a hired laborer. When you walk the road on this question and pay a day laborer by the end of the following evening and not later, you come to see the Holy One with just a little more accuracy. Multiply this by everything else in the Jewish codebooks and what you acquire is a remarkably sharp portrait of the Lawgiver. Since it's your will to search for the Holy One, you could hardly do better than taking on the *mitzvot* little by little."

"And is that possible? Aren't there too many?"

"Lots of Jews do it, and without feeling burdened. I do it, and so do a small but enthusiastic group in my synagogue."

Wishnasky thought for a few seconds about whether he was ready to take on more obligations. Then he said, "There's something else that's always bothered me."

"All right. What is it?"

"Well," he said, "there's that whole 'chosen people' idea. It's always made me uncomfortable. It sounds elitist at best. At worst, it sounds like Jews think they're better than others."

The rabbi nodded. "You're not alone. In theological debate it's called 'the scandal of

chosenness.' It makes everybody nervous."

"And what do you think of it?"

"Depends on how you define 'chosen.' Does it mean Jews are better, smarter, superior? Absolutely not. Does it mean that we somehow were picked to introduce ethical monotheism into the world? Absolutely, yes. Why? According to *Torah*, because God loved our forefathers. Not us: Abraham, Isaac, and Jacob. No other explanation given."

"It still bothers me. It still sounds like we're making a special case for ourselves."

"I also find the term worrisome. But consider this, then: two possible worlds. In one, everybody, no matter their nation or religion, gets contacted by God on the day they turn thirteen. Male and female, straight and gay, Russian and Mexican, the minute they turn thirteen, God comes to them in a vision and says, 'I'm the only God, there's no one but Me, and here are My rules.' You got that?"

"Got it."

"Now imagine another world altogether. In this one, everybody believes in multiple deities with hundreds of different names, some swimming in coral reefs, some hiding in wheat fields or perching in apricot trees. Then, one day a little group in a tiny sliver of the Middle East gets a message: there's only one universal God and it's their job to tell everyone. So, in the face of nearly worldwide hostility, this miniscule group spreads word of God and *Torah*. After a while the Christians sign on, with a few novelties of their own, and after that the Muslims take up membership, also with certain innovations, and by this morning, more than half the world believes in one God and at least Ten Commandments. All starting with this one, microscopically small people. You got that?"

"Got it."

"Okay, which scenario feels more comfortable?"

"Example one."

"Precisely. And which one is true?"

Wishnasky said nothing. Even if she was right, it didn't make things easier. "I would think," he said finally, "that the little group in Example Two might evoke a little resentment in the big, bad world full of other people."

"And we did. And still do. So, tell God to change tactics."

They drove past a small park; it was mostly empty, but Wishnasky wondered how many homeless would sleep there on this cold night, or along the sidewalks of Charles Street. Was there someone in government whose job was to look after people who had no shelter? If you didn't have a home, did you even exist politically? He made a note to himself to research the question, then wondered what he would do with the results. Why was he so ill-informed on these subjects?

After another twenty minutes negotiating heavy traffic, they drove through the chain link fence and into the parking lot of the Horn of Plenty. Once again, there were a dozen or so men and women standing around, wearing ill-fitting trench coats, misshapen sweaters, and insubstantial-looking vests. They were talking and smoking and hardly seemed to notice the rabbi's car.

After parking, the two visitors walked through the wooden gate to the eating area, and Wishnasky saw some of the homeless already seated at the folding tables. He worried about the chill in the air.

"Isn't there somewhere inside where they can be served?" he asked.

"There's a sort of lobby at the front of the building, but it can only fit maybe eighteen or twenty. While the weather's still tolerable, this is the best anyone can do."

In the kitchen, Brooke and Patrick, Dee and Lance and an older, gray-haired woman Wishnasky didn't recognize were already opening the food bins, stacking plates, setting out drinking glasses, and wrapping plastic forks in napkins. When Brooke saw Wishnasky, her face brightened.

"I'm so glad you came back," she said. "Would you mind setting the salt and pepper shakers on the tables? They're in that closet, on the metal shelf in the back."

Wishnasky went into the closet, found the salt and pepper shakers and took a few outside to place on the tables. He looked around for Arthur but didn't see him; what he did notice was how *cheerful* most of the people waiting for a meal in the cold seemed to be. Apparently, living outdoors and depending on the largesse of strangers didn't inevitably dampen one's spirits. And then he thought of the characters in his three published novels, despairing and desolate because they couldn't find Meaning in their middle-class, comfortable worlds. What a luxury such hopelessness was when considered next to this singular panorama. He thought of his character Nigel Zimmerberg, disconsolate over life's vacuity, and then of these paupers, grinning and joking with each other in the bitter cold. Was it possible that the Nigel Zimmerbergs he knew found their air to be so thin only because they were sitting on top of the world?

Back in the kitchen, Brooke announced the time for prayer. Wishnasky and the others bowed their heads as Brooke asked God to bless the receivers of the food along with the givers and thanked God for the opportunity to serve Him on yet another occasion. Then, the assignments were made: this time Wishnasky would be handing out a dinner of sausages, creamed corn, and sweet potatoes along with the rabbi and the stranger, whose name he now knew to be Eleanor. Wishnasky felt proud not to have to ask how to proceed: behind the rabbi and Eleanor, he placed four plates on a tray and walked out to the dining area.

He was handing out his fourth plate when he saw Arthur the poet arrive and slip into a seat at a far table; he was dressed in a large green military jacket and a black wool cap. A few minutes passed before Wishnasky reached the indigent student of literature and laid a plate in front of him.

"So," Arthur said. "The writer comes back."

"Good to see you."

"Did you read Claude McKay?"

"No, I'm sorry, I didn't get around to it. I promise I'll try before next week." This time he meant it.

"Too bad, you've been missing something. Who do you like instead? Who are your top poets?"

"Dead white males, I guess: Yeats and Eliot, Wallace Stevens. A little William Blake. All in the late, lamented Western canon."

"And let me guess: you adore Hemingway and Fitzgerald."

"I admit to owning a healthy respect for them."

"All the Great Blind Men," said Arthur. "Couldn't be bothered to look right in front of them."

"What do you mean?"

"You know what was happening to Southern Blacks in the 1920s when T.S. Eliot was getting teary-eyed over tea and cakes? These brothers were lynched, murdered, and mutilated and their bodies strung up on trees. You know how much good it might have done if Pope Eliot had said one word against racism? Or Wallace Stevens? Or Francis Scott Key Fitzgerald?"

"I never thought about it that way."

"Eliot was King, man, the Commander-in-Chief of all literature, and a word from him would have radicalized thousands of people. But just like the rest of them, he was blind. And deaf and dumb. And it wasn't just the poets. Instead of writin' about cool white Americans getting jazzed in Paris, Mr. Ernest Hemingway might have put in one word, one single word, in defense of the black folk gettin' terrorized in Mississippi. But I guess, among Caucasians, the cosmic blues were a lot more appetizing."

As a relatively recent purveyor of the cosmic blues, Wishnasky felt a reflexive need to defend his favorite Modernists.

"All that was post-World War One," he said. "Those guys had lived through a lot of horror. It's not surprising they felt strung out."

"One word from our loquacious Great Writers and maybe a few hundred black families might have been spared an even longer war. Then, there'd be lots of time left over for regrettin' the lost paradise. Man, silence kills when you're that big."

"I'd better keep serving food," said Wishnasky, wondering if he also might be accused of culpable silence. "Let's continue this discussion at a later date."

"You know where you can find me."

Wishnasky went back into the kitchen, put another four plates on his tray, and returned to the dining area to distribute them. As before, he had the feeling that these minutes serving the hungry were more consequential than most other things he could remember doing. When one diner—a scruffy-looking, shriveled man—said "thank you" to him, he replied, "No, thank *you*."

Back in the kitchen after the serving, Wishnasky walked over to the rabbi. "Are you feeling it tonight?" she asked. "That you're the Holy One's arms and legs here?"

"I don't know. That's a little beyond my way of sensing things."

"The Jewish word for God's presence on earth is the *Shekhina*. And many sages have ruled that whenever a human being does a *mitzvah*, the *Shekhina* rests on that person. I think at this moment, the *Shekhina* rests on you."

"Thank you. But I have to admit, I still find it unlikely that God would depend on someone like me to do a job as crucial as feeding the hungry. It seems too chancy. Undependable. When He could rain manna from heaven in just the right amount."

"Human freedom," said the rabbi. "The Holy One tells us how to make the earth habitable, but if we don't listen, it won't get done. That applies to almost everything. Most religious puzzles dissolve when you realize how much God insists on our liberty. It's enormously important."

"The 'Holy One,'" said Wishnasky. "I notice that you never say 'Him.' It's always 'the Holy One,' or 'the Almighty' and now 'the *Shekhina*.' Is that conscious? Is that a deliberate policy?"

"It is. I'm very careful about it."

"Is it a feminist thing?"

"When most people thought women to be inferior beings, they naturally avoided feminine pronouns for the Deity. Now that there's more equality, we can begin to solve the problem of so many ancient texts using the masculine. To be fair, I avoid 'He' and 'She' altogether."

"Are you insulted when I talk about God as 'Him?'"

"Not at all. Most people still do. But you know, in Hebrew there are feminine and masculine nouns. And the Hebrew for 'The Merciful One' comes from the root *rechem*: 'womb.' And the word *Shechina*, 'God's Presence,' is also feminine. Finally, the name *El Shaddai*, which is usually translated as 'the Almighty,' comes from a root meaning 'breasts.' So, as usual, the *Torah* is centuries ahead of us."

Brooke announced seconds. Eleanor was assigned to carry out a bowl of sausages, the rabbi's portion was creamed corn, and Wishnasky was given sweet potatoes. "I'll tell you a secret," said the rabbi as they headed out. "I still feel anxious about serving sausages. Not that anyone here's kosher. But Brooke tries to accommodate me."

Wishnasky scooped out sweet potatoes for a dozen hungry faces before he worked his way up to Arthur. Seeing his new friend, the tall poet said, "When you read Claude McKay, start with his book, *Harlem Shadows,* from 1922."

"Twenty-two," said Wishnasky. "That's the year Eliot published *The Wasteland.*"

"Well, don't expect some dried-up bellyaching from McKay. You got to be born into the St. Louis aristocracy to feel desperate like Mr. Eliot."

"Didn't McKay ever feel desperate?"

"About racism, sure. And then there was the time W.E.B. DuBois said one of his novels was bad propaganda. Yeah, McKay had his low moments. But he loved life, man, he loved life."

"And you do, too, don't you?"

"Wouldn't miss it for anything."

On the drive back to the synagogue, Wishnasky was feeling strangely happy. "You know," he told the rabbi, "I think I'm enjoying this. It's working for me on some level I didn't even know about."

"That's right," said Rabbi Diamant. "That's what I tell people who ask me: this isn't something I *have* to do, this is something I *get* to do. If I miss a week, I feel bereft."

"I want to confess something, though. When you first brought me here, I assumed all these diners were street fighters and worse. I'm shocked to discover they're so … gentle."

"Don't jump to conclusions," said the rabbi. "Since I've been coming here, I've seen a few fights and near-fights. These people are human—and they're under enormous pressure. But we servers stick together. And there's always the police. I think it's largely safe."

This silenced Wishnasky; it violated the rosy picture of the diners he'd been so happy to cultivate. As the rabbi merged her car into traffic onto Storrow Drive, he contemplated a world that kept contradicting his view of it.

"Anyway," said Rabbi Diamant after some moments had passed. "We need to talk about your search for God. I'm ready to give you your next assignment."

"I thought feeding the hungry was my assignment."

"I told you a while ago that *Talmud* says three things support the world: study of *Torah*, ritual service, and acts of lovingkindness. There's one ritual that you might as well face now that you're building momentum."

"All right. What is it?"

'*Sabbath*. Have you ever kept *Sabbath*?"

"Not really. You mean not working for a day?"

"That's right. You can still read and watch TV and socialize and study *Torah*. But no work, which in your case means writing. And if you do read, it should be nothing about literature, novels, and the latest bestseller. Does that sound simple enough?"

"Almost too simple."

"You'll be surprised, then. The habit of labor goes very deep; it takes some effort to forgo it. But look at *Sabbath* as a day to thank God for so many blessings and to meditate on the miracle of existence. Spend part of it with friends or family, if you like. And start this Friday night."

"Should I come to synagogue?"

"I'd like that, at least on Saturday morning. It's a good way to meet others who are aiming to know God. And to say certain prayers that require a minyan of ten."

"Done."

"Saturday morning, then."

They drove for a few minutes along the highway, and Wishnasky thought that even if there *wasn't* a God, the belief in Him—It—moved people to do some fine things. In thirty-six years on the Earth, it had never occurred to him to lend a hand to the hungry. But the transit from the words in the Camus book to the gravel drive of the Horn of Plenty had been direct. And so he was making a real difference in someone's life—in several people's lives. That was satisfying.

As they approached the synagogue, one last question occurred to Wishnasky. "Rabbi," he said, "you've convinced me that my search means taking these trips with you on Thursday evenings. But when I looked around the Horn of Plenty tonight, there were only a few us of there, plating and serving. If this teaching of yours is so central to Judaism—"

"And most other major religions."

"And most other major religions, why aren't more people doing something about it? Why were there just seven of us?"

"I'll throw the question back to you: What's the opposite of doing evil?"

"Doing good, of course."

"A lot of people disagree. A lot think that the opposite of doing evil is doing nothing. I can't tell you how hard I've worked to persuade my congregation that sitting back and feeling virtuous is *not* at all virtuous, that it contributes exactly nothing to the combat between good and evil on this planet. But apparently, this is a difficult teaching."

"Well, you've got me believing. I'll be back next Thursday. I like making a difference."

"I'm glad to hear it. And let me risk a prediction: the more the God of *Torah* is real to you, the more you'll do things like this. And the less that God is real to you, the less you'll feel any such call."

They pulled into the synagogue parking lot. After she parked, the rabbi said, "Remember, this coming *Shabbat*: no novel writing, no research, no book reviews or literary essays. If you drive, it's only to synagogue. Read the *Torah* for a time, then read anything else that doesn't suggest work. Watch a sports channel if it amuses you. Eat and drink and try to understand who you are when you're not a machine that churns out product."

On the drive back to Newton Corner, Wishnasky's thoughts roamed widely. He thought of the people he'd served that night, and how grateful he was to discover *their* gratitude. He resolved to find and read some of the poems of Claude McKay. And he thought of his coming date with Barbara and wondered if she could comfort him for the loss of Vanessa. Wouldn't that be something, to be able to think of Vanessa without distress? Well, stranger things had happened.

Most reassuring of all: he could now see the end of *Traveler*.

32.

THE NOVEL MOVED AHEAD with astonishing velocity. Ordinarily Wishnasky wrote four pages a day, but in this case he was writing twelve or thirteen. And a lot was happening: he was making Ozono come to trust Yvonne, holding back on Yvonne's religious teaching until Ozono was healed enough to calmly consider it. Still, certain attitudes that the rabbi had communicated were turning up: no human being is really alone, troubles and challenges are features even of a religious life, and one can at least direct one's energies toward alleviating the suffering of others. He had Ozono fighting these notions just as he'd fought them himself, but he also had him opening himself to Yvonne's view just enough to suggest he could be reached. And meanwhile Ozono was falling in love, almost imperceptibly, with this caring, affirming woman. Wishnasky worried at times that his plot was becoming predictable, but he figured this was nothing but the usual authorial self-doubt. Didn't Henry James say that all writers work in the dark? Suggesting in a novel that there was goodness in the world was a great departure for him; naturally it made him nervous.

It was late Friday afternoon and he was making his last preparations for *Sabbath*. He'd been to the grocery and stocked up on food: salmon, Brussels sprouts, cole slaw, pound cake. He'd gone to Barnes & Noble and bought the latest issue of *Vanity Fair*—he'd had to deny himself *Poets & Writers* because it was manifestly work-related—and he'd even cleaned his house, putting manuscript pages and research materials in his study, which he intended to avoid for twenty-four hours. It occurred to him that the rabbi was going easy on him—she hadn't insisted that he light candles, refrain from cooking, from spending money. But he liked this easy introduction to the day of rest and wasn't about to complain. He'd even gone to the Israel Bookstore in Brookline and picked up a *Guide to Shabbat*. That's how good a student he was.

He looked at the clock: 5:34. According to his phone, sundown was in three minutes. Good. He'd skip synagogue this evening, say the evening prayer at home as he'd been doing for the last few days. But how should he start this special day of retreat? Music: over the years, he'd given up his love of orchestral melody in favor of reading and writing and crafting a novelist's life—now for once, he could sit back and listen to his favorite compositions. He'd start with Schubert's "Unfinished Symphony," a piece he'd long cherished.

He searched for its CD case, found it, put it in his player and sat back on the living room couch. There were those mysterious opening phrases in the cellos and basses, the lovely, heartbreaking melody in the oboes and clarinets, the crash of violins followed by the second theme with its unearthly beauty ... He really should make Edward Ozono a music lover, he could describe him at a concert, as E. M. Forster did with his characters in *Howard's End*—

But wait: Wasn't that a work thought? The whole point was *not* to think of work. All right, he'd put it out of mind. Anyway, now the spectral theme that quietly opened the symphony was loud and out in the open, now one was assaulted by Schubert's anguished, tormented outcries, as if the composer couldn't keep the distress inside him from overpowering the gentleness he'd tried to convey instead. What a mélange of emotions! Clever how Schubert presented so many disparate moods in just the first minutes, how much dimension he created right at the start. Had he made Edward Ozono as fully dimensional as he should be? No, he'd failed; he'd suggested his pathos but left the magnitude, the vociferousness of his despair, he'd have to go back and revise the character in Chapter One and then again in—

Work again. Got to stop. Listen peacefully to Schubert.

All right, here came the second movement, when the violins took up a pastoral main theme and stated it so lyrically, there seemed no possibility of storm or stress ever again. It wasn't unlike the rather pleasant opening of *Moby Dick*, when Ishmael speaks of his need for occasional seagoing, then takes us along as he discovers the *Pequod*, never once letting on that the novel will become a thunderous meditation on God and human destiny ... He'd like to try that himself one day: start a novel so innocently, with such an upbeat, even comic tone, that the reader would never suspect all the shocking, life-shattering heights that the later chapters would—

Stop. He had to stop this. No work thoughts. Just for one day, remember?

He arose from his sofa, turned off the CD player and made a beeline to the dinner table, on which he had deposited the new *Guide to Shabbat*. He took it out of its bag, went back to the sofa and turned to page one. Yes, this was what he needed. The author began with reflections on how unprecedented in the ancient world was a weekly day of rest, especially one in which masters had to let even slaves and field animals cease their labors. This led to a discussion of the many places in *Torah* where the *Sabbath* was commanded, and made special note of the fact that it was the only holiday mentioned in the Ten Commandments. The language of the various commands to keep the *Sabbath* were analyzed, the near-total absence in *Torah* of specific instructions as to what did and did not count as work was remarked on, and then there were some paragraphs on how the rabbis of *Talmud* took all of the details of the construction of the Holy Tabernacle as their guide to what was forbidden labor on the seventh day ...

■

He opened his eyes. The book was lying in his lap, the room was dark, and the clock on the wall said 8:39. He'd fallen asleep reading. Strange, he hadn't known he was tired. He reached over, turned on a lamp and stood up, yawning as he did. Well, that was almost two hours without anything like work. Excellent! Now he could pray the evening service, make dinner, watch CNN while he ate, sit back and read *Vanity Fair* or watch a film on Netflix. To be honest, though, he wasn't hungry. When he was so well rested and calm, he could write a couple of dozen pages of the new novel, maybe even more. Of course, he wasn't supposed to labor on this one day, but how often did he feel so lucid, so sure of the unfolding of the plot, the development of the characters, the rhythm and music of the English language? He could still keep *Sabbath*, he would just begin a little later than he'd intended, work till ten p.m. or so, and then log off his computer, find a movie on pay-per-view, put his feet up on his trusty hassock ...

But that would be cheating.

Twenty-four hours: he had to go twenty-four hours without working.

The prospect made him miserable. He was a novelist head to toe. Not to write when he felt so utterly inspired was wretchedness. Would he ever think so clearly again? This *Sabbath* thing was intolerable!

He decided to make dinner. He cleaned the salmon he'd purchased the day before, put lemon salt and butter on it, placed it in the oven, all the time trying not to think about the next chapter in Edward Ozono's life. He assembled a salad, trying, as he chopped a cucumber into sections, not to remember the biography of Arthur Rimbaud that Annie Lubbock at *Ploughshares* had asked him to review. Was it really so difficult to get one's mind off work? Well, why shouldn't it be? What was a man according to Freud if not work and love, and there was no love in his life tonight, so naturally he was focused on his job. Anyway, why would God want people not to labor for one day? Maybe that was a commandment one didn't have to follow in the modern world, maybe it once had a purpose but had become obsolete. He'd be a lot more comfortable if he could write a few pages. Was that the point of *Sabbath*: to make its observers feel unpleasant?

The salmon was cooked, the salad was chopped, he'd put a slice of pound cake on a small plate to make a dessert. He took the food over to the coffee table and turned on the TV. The news was all about the latest Republican attempt to scuttle a Democrat-inspired prescription drug bill. Well, that was interesting. Took his mind off work, anyway. When the commercial came on, he switched channels to HBO, watched Robert DeNiro in some sort of crime movie, then switched to the Tennis Channel and watched a historic match between John McEnroe and Jimmy Connors. Hey, that was a fine way to spend one's precious time: watching old, dead, meaningless, irrelevant tennis matches from prehistoric epochs.

When one could be writing.

All right, then; he'd pray. He put on a yarmulke he'd borrowed from the synagogue, and found the prayer book the rabbi had given him. He flipped to the section called "*Kabbalat Shabbat*"—"Welcoming the *Sabbath*"—and began reading a series of psalms in English. They were all about rejoicing before the Lord, doing righteousness, ascribing to the Lord Glory and might ... What had the rabbi said about this sort of prayer? That the point was to place oneself in appropriate humility before God. All right, that was sensible. Certainly if he'd entered the presence of the President of the United States, or the secretary-general of the UN, or the head of the Nobel Prize committee, he'd want to show the appropriate humility ... One didn't speak much about humility in American culture. What had Ion said to him about developing a sense of humility? Mental note: write an essay on humility as a missing virtue in consumer society—no, stop. Stop. Keep praying.

Now the *Shema*. God is One. Well, who said otherwise? Certainly, his Christian neighbors believed that a single God created the universe, and the Muslims agreed. Where were the polytheists from whom he was distinguishing himself? India? He didn't know anyone from India, and was in any case not very likely to worship Vishnu and Shiva at this late date. If there were no polytheists trying to prevail on him, wasn't it unnecessary to make the attestation of God's unity? Still, it was by reputation the pivotal prayer and he said it, even while doubting its urgency. Then the *Amidah*: the one place where he was allowed to enter his personal supplications. But the rabbi had said one didn't petition on the *Sabbath*, even God got a rest from people's requests on that one day. All right, that made a certain sense.

He finished the evening prayer; it had taken about twenty minutes. Now he was supposed to make *Kiddush* over the wine—and he'd forgotten to buy kosher wine. Well, he had a very nice Australian Cabernet that he'd use instead—no problem with this part of *Sabbath*. He found the wine bottle, pulled out the cork, poured himself a tall glass, said the blessing in the book, and took a long draught. Oh, that was good. He drank again. That was very nice. He poured more into his glass. Well, now, this was one use of the *Sabbath* he hadn't contemplated. And after all he'd been through recently: the message in the Camus book, the break-up with Vanessa, the trips to the Horn of Plenty, the changes in his novel. Oh yes, he needed this *Sabbath* wine. He poured some potato chips into a bowl, took the bottle and his glass and sat down on the sofa. Rest? Oh yeah, he'd rest. With this fine Cabernet, he'd take a much-neglected rest. He filled his glass nearly to the top. All right: here's how he would keep the *Sabbath*.

▪

The phone was ringing. Was it a dream? No, it was real: he opened his eyes, reached into his shirt pocket and clicked on "receive." His mother was on the line.

"Come to Brigham and Women's Hospital. Your father's had a heart attack."

"What?"

"Go to the Emergency Ward. They're operating on him right now."

"What? Yes. Yes, I'm coming—"

Suddenly his mother was sobbing. "I can't bear it! I'm going to lose him! I want to die!"

"Look, just hold on, I'll be there in a few minutes."

"I can't endure it!"

"Look, Ma—just hold on till I get there."

He clicked off, looked around him, realized that he was drunk and shouldn't drive. But a taxi at this time of night—he'd have to wait forever. No, he'd just have to chance it, and if he was stopped he'd explain to the officer about his father ...

He grabbed his car keys and hurried out the door.

33.

HE HAD TROUBLE FINDING PARKING in the Emergency area of the hospital, so he pulled up along a curb and trusted he wouldn't be towed. Then he half-ran to the entrance, passed through an automatic glass door and found himself in a brightly modern space bounded on one side by plastic chairs in which at least a dozen people were seated. Opposite was a glassed-in nurse's station occupied now by a young African American woman with closely shorn hair. He asked her the whereabouts of Morris Wishnasky and was directed to a curtained room just through a corridor to his left. He hurried there and found his mother in a plaid housedress, her dyed-blonde hair disheveled, her eyes so red from crying that she didn't see him immediately.

"Ma!"

"This is going to kill me! I can't live without him!"

"He'll be fine. Tell me what happened."

"He could be dead already! We could have lost him already!"

"We're not going to lose him. Heart attacks happen all the time; doctors know just what to do about them. Now, tell me from the beginning."

Weeping, she did. They had gone to bed around eleven, and Morris had complained about a burning feeling in his upper abdomen, as well as some nausea. They assumed it would dissipate, but shortly after midnight he'd awakened in great pain. He couldn't breathe, he was in a cold sweat, and there was a rhythmic cutting sensation in his chest as if someone were repeatedly hitting him with a small axe. He said, "I'm very sick, I think," and passed out. Mia frantically dialed 911, and after a long fifteen minutes the ambulance arrived. She followed behind in her car and was only told by the intake nurse at the emergency ward that Mr. Wishnasky was being rushed to the cardiac catheterization lab. She was given forms to fill out, but had heard nothing since then.

Wishnasky tried to comfort her. "Look," he said. "Heart attacks are why emergency wards exist. Lots of people have them, lots of people live through them. He'll be fine."

"Why do you stink of wine? Are you drunk? While you father was dying were you getting drunk?"

"My father isn't dying and I'm not drunk. I had a little wine with dinner, that's all. I was actually trying to keep *Sabbath*."

"Since when?"

"Since tonight. Now, how about if I go find out what's happening with Dad?"

"They won't tell you. No one will say."

"Let me try."

But she was right. All the intake nurse would declare was that the emergency technicians had established that Morris had suffered a heart attack and that he was immediately brought to the cath lab for treatment. The specialist on duty was a Dr. Ellman and, yes, he'd operated on multiple cardiac victims over the months since he arrived from his previous post at Yale/New Haven Hospital. As soon as there was word, the Wishnaskys would be alerted to Morris's condition. It could be minutes or hours.

He went back to the room where his mother sat. She had a stunned look now and her voice was strangely steady. "I have no one, only him. I gave up everyone else. My own sisters I stopped seeing. My lovely sisters, their children, their grandchildren, I wasn't interested. I have nothing if he's gone. I might as well go with him."

"He's not going anywhere and neither are you. He's going to be fine."

"It's all my fault. I should have taken him to the hospital when he said he felt nauseous. But we waited two hours. Now, no one can help."

"They'll help him just fine."

"I'm not afraid to die. If he goes, I'll go too."

"A doctor will be here any minute to tell us he's complaining that the hospital smells curiously like disinfectant."

"You don't know. You don't know what it is to love."

"I object to that comment."

"A love like I have with your father you can't even imagine."

"Does it occur to you that I was married once?"

"You've got no idea what it is to give yourself to another person. And in a way you're lucky. In a way I envy you."

She fell silent and stared blankly in front of her. Wishnasky, embarrassed to still feel intoxicated, took this moment to remember the other people he'd noticed in the waiting room on the way in. There had been a young Hispanic-looking woman with two children of toddler age, trying with not much success to keep them quiet and orderly. There was a crew-cut young man dressed in chinos and a collarless shirt, looking like he'd just come from prep school at Exeter or Andover, and there was a middle-aged woman with her arm in a makeshift sling talking to a younger version of herself in a paisley blouse and light blue skirt. What united them, he mused, was trouble: it was what they all had in common. and soon some would find tragedy and others would be spared. He wondered to which group he and his mother belonged. He wondered if he'd ever see his father alive again.

He looked up at a TV screen perched high on the wall. It was turned to a cable news program, and there was a captioned newsfeed running along the bottom of the picture. He half expected to come upon the headline "Drunk *Sabbath*-Breaker Ineffectual as Father Struggles for Survival." Maybe a little coffee would help. Assuring his mother he'd be right back, he walked to the intake nurse and asked where he might get something to drink. She pointed him toward some vending machines in an alcove along a corridor. He walked to the area, passed under an arch, swiped his credit card and pushed a button: a cup descended and black coffee poured into it. When he tasted it, he almost gagged. He poured the coffee down the drain, threw out the cup, and returned to Mia's side.

Now, there was a man with his mother, a tall, black-haired, Asian-American doctor in his forties, with a kind face and name pin on his white coat: Dr. Ryo Okada. "Oh, there you are," he said in a silky, calm voice. "I was just telling your mother about Mr. Wishnasky's condition. I'll repeat it for you. He had a sizable blood clot in the left main artery and probably had the first attack hours before we got to him. We've placed a stent in the artery—it's a sort of tube to facilitate blood flow—but he hasn't regained consciousness and we're worried that during the time his heart wasn't receiving oxygen, his brain function may have been damaged."

"So what are you saying? When will he revive?" asked Wishnasky.

"We don't know. We've moved him into a room in Cardiac Care and you can visit him there in about an hour. When we feel it's safe, we'll run more tests. But I have to warn you, we can't predict the long-term effect of this sort of trauma."

"Is it possible he could still be normal? Mentally? When he wakes up?"

"That's one of the possibilities."

Wishnasky's mother said nothing, but her haunted look was expressive enough. Wishnasky thanked the doctor and put his arm around his mother's shoulder. "In an hour we'll see him," he said. "We'll be there when he revives."

"He's not going to. I've lost him."

"Don't be ridiculous. He'll be splendid."

"I know this. Like I knew that I would marry him the day I met him. Like I knew my only child would be a boy. He won't wake up."

"He'll wake up. Let me get you some soda."

"I don't want anything. I want my lover back. They're going to take away my lover."

"They're not going to do any such thing."

"I don't want you. I want my lover."

She looked away from him, and Wishnasky privately considered the possibility that his mother might be right. So, this was how it happened: a phone call in the night, a rush to the hospital and then the man who gave you half your life, who taught you how to chew with your mouth closed, to ride a bike and to drive, sank into the unknown. He looked up at the TV screen and saw war in East Africa, epidemic in Central America, an epidemic of muggings in Chicago. So, this was what could happen in a world of divinely-ordained freedom. And then you merited a news item: soldiers in El Salvador mutiny and are court-martialed. A prime minister in Nigeria is deposed for corruption. Morris Wishnasky has a heart attack and dies. He looked at the TV anchor: What did she feel, purveying so many calamities? Apparently, nothing. She was unruffled, even vivacious. When would *she* merit a news bulletin?

An hour and a half passed. His mother sat mute, and the news played steadily with its doomy sameness. Then, a male nurse in blue scrubs appeared, and said, "Mr. Wishnasky is in Room 418. You can go up there now." He advised them to get identification bracelets from the intake nurse and explained how to find the elevator.

Wishnasky put his arm around his mother and walked her up the corridor. She was trembling. They came to the elevator, waited for it in silence, stepped in and rode to the fourth floor. A sign said "Cardiac Care," and then they were in a wide hallway peopled by nurses and technicians, and lit brightly by overhead fluorescent lamps. There was a central nurse's station where a man and two women were monitoring several video screens and other electronic equipment. The Wishnaskys showed one of the women their bracelets and were directed to Morris's room.

The door was half-open. Inside, Morris Wishnasky was lying, eyes closed, on his back, with oxygen tubing going into his nostrils and an IV in his arm. He was dressed in a thin smock and was deathly pale; one could only just see his chest moving as he breathed. Behind him were all sorts and sizes of electronic gadgets, including one that was clearly a heart monitor. A nurse—this one a tall, redheaded woman—stood by his bed. She said, "Are you the family?"

"This is his wife," said Wishnasky. "I'm the son."

"He could come to at any time," said the nurse. "Don't give up. But just in case, has anyone talked to you about a DNR?"

"What's that?"

"A do-not-revive. If he dies, do you want us to try to shock him awake?"

"Of course. Why wouldn't we want that?"

"Then no DNR. Take a seat. You may be here awhile."

There was a single vinyl-and-wood chair beside the bed and a beige two-seater vinyl sofa against a window. Wishnasky guided his mother to the sofa and they sat together. His mother looked as ashen as her husband.

"He'll never revive," she said. "He'll be a vegetable and then he'll die. I know this like I know my own name. And it's all my fault."

"It's not your fault. And he'll wake up at any minute."

"My lover," she said. "My only love. My heart. You can't understand."

This time he didn't object, just kept his arm around Mia's bony shoulder and watched the slow rise and fall of his father's chest. The effects of the alcohol were gone. He felt more sober than he'd ever been.

■

Another hour passed, then another. Morris Wishnasky didn't awake. Nurses came by on several occasions, and a Dr. Resnick stepped in to check Morris's vitals and remind the two Wishnaskys not to lose hope. Mia, unmoving, sat back on the sofa seeing nothing, and Wishnasky repeatedly searched his father's face for the merest indication that he was coming awake. There was no such indication.

And then he thought: What if I were to pray?

Another impulse warned him not to.

The first thought said, *yes, pray, and if there's a merciful, loving God, the possibility exists that your father will regain consciousness, your mother will rejoice, all three of you will come together again in felicity. Yes, do it: urgently. With all your soul.*

The other thought said: *pray and then He's got you. Forever. Your father might revive just by coincidence, but you'll never know, you'll have to assume that mighty old God must have heard you and now you owe Him big time. And then you're locked in: to belief, to credulity, to accepting as real what no one in five thousand years of human history has been able to prove. Unfree ever again to enjoy the opportunities available when the sky is conveniently empty. Not free but unfree. A debtor for as long as you live.*

Wishnasky looked at his mother. She hadn't called any other family members, no one but he and she and the hospital staff even knew Morris's condition. If he didn't pray for his father, no one would. No one in the world.

Feeling the risk he was taking, he bowed his head. Then, just under his breath, he said, "Dear God, I've never asked you for anything like this before. And I ... know I don't deserve your compassion when I've done so few of your commandments. But if You would be so forgiving ... Please let my father live. If not for my sake, for my mother, who's in such peril now that I fear for her life too. Please let my dad come awake and be normal." Then came the hardest part: "I will ... always be grateful."

There: he'd said it. He was either the greatest fool who ever lived or the newest recruit in a much-fabled, much-derided army. He felt an intense sense of loss. He felt he'd surrendered something secret and precious, some contraband he loved carrying. But there was no alternative.

■

A half hour later, Morris Wishnasky coughed and opened his eyes. He looked around the room and coughed again.

"Where am I?" he said. "Where's Mia?"

Wishnasky's mother rushed to the bed and embraced him as best she could, crying noisily and kissing his face. "Are you there?" she said. "Are you all right?"

"That was such a strange dream," he said. "I was on an airplane. It couldn't land. Did we land yet? Everyone was so anxious."

Mia blubbered on. Wishnasky watched and felt the tears rise in his own eyes, just enough to reach the outer world and descend his cheek.

"That was bad heartburn," said Morris. "All the time on the plane I wanted to find the flight attendant to bring me some Mylanta. Or Pepto-Bismol. Milk of Magnesia. But all anyone cared about is that we couldn't land the plane."

He and Mia hugged more tightly, and Wishnasky thought: *okay, Lord. You've got me. You saw your chance and You took it. Now I'm yours. No way out.*

"Stop your crying and get me out of here," Morris Wishnasky was saying. "So I had a bad dream. Big deal! Who goes to the hospital for indigestion and a bad dream?"

34.

THE DOCTOR WANTED Morris Wishnasky to stay at Brigham and Women's at least another three days for observation, so Sunday morning, Wishnasky called Barbara and explained he'd have to put off their date. She was understanding, and they agreed to meet the next evening in a restaurant near her Somerville apartment.

He spent most of Sunday and Sunday evening in the hospital with his parents. At nine, he returned to his home and worked on *Traveler*. The book was coming along so well, he began to think that he might beat his deadline by many days. His prayer and the answer it had received—or was that just coincidence?—seemed to liberate him to write about Ozono's religious progress with an ease he'd lacked previously. In fact, the part of the novel that detailed Ozono's religious awakening was becoming more and more lengthy, in spite of the fact that he'd originally intended it as no more than an extended epilogue. Well, he knew how to follow an inspiration, and that's what he'd do. If the novel changed even further, so be it.

He spent Monday morning and afternoon in his father's hospital room, then drove on to the restaurant in Somerville to meet Barbara. She had suggested they rendezvous there —she wanted to know him better before letting him into her living space, he supposed—and he easily found parking along the street. Inside, everything was about fishing and the sea: fish trophies, ship's wheels, paintings of the turbulent Atlantic off Cape Ann. Barbara was a few minutes late, but he was delighted to see her walk toward his table in jeans, a maroon top, and a cocky beret. Her unusually-shaped face was even more enthralling than he'd remembered.

They kissed each other on the cheek and fell happily into a recap of the last few days' events: his father's heart attack and recovery, her crisis over whether to join Actors' Equity.

"I don't dare get a union card, because then all the small theatres that can't afford Equity wages won't hire me," she said. "But if you're not an Equity actor, a lot of artistic directors think you're an amateur. And of course the non-Equity theatres in the area only pay a pittance, so I'm basically stuck in my job at the law office."

"Do you like the law office?"

"Not really," she said and laughed. Wishnasky liked her laugh. He liked the blouse she was wearing, and the tight blue jeans, and the beret she'd placed on the table. He wanted to go to bed with her, and he wondered how many days, weeks, or months it would take before he had his first chance. "What do you do for the attorneys?" he asked.

"Nothing special," she said. "A lot of filing. Typing up letters on the computer. Answering phones. I should probably get paralegal training as long as I'm doing this. I'd make twice the salary."

"I admire any artist who works a second job to support her art."

"That's sweet. But you don't have to do that, do you?"

"My third novel sold well," said Wishnasky. "And then the movies bought it. But I can't live on that windfall forever. Have to make a hit with the next one if I want to keep up on my mortgage."

"What's the new one about?"

"It used to be about a man who had everything taken from him and then had to live with the bare remainder. But recently I've become aware of the ... possibility of some sort of Higher Power or something." He was doing his best not to sound fanatical. "So the very bottom doesn't feel like the right stopping place anymore. Maybe just where you need to be in order to propel yourself upward."

"You really believe in God?" said Barbara. "That's neat. I believe in all sorts of things: tarot cards and crystals and the lines on people's hands. For all I know, it's all true."

Wishnasky wasn't sure how he felt about his Judaism being compared to tarot cards. But Barbara was so lovely, he was happy to overlook it. "I'm glad you're open to things," he said. "You have any hesitation about going out with a Jewish believer?"

"Not if he's paying," laughed Barbara. "I have so little money, it's showstopping!" She laughed again. "Wait till you see my apartment!"

"Am I going to see your apartment tonight?"

She looked at him cannily. "Play your cards right and maybe you will."

For the rest of the dinner, Wishnasky was awash in hormones. Before Barbara had mentioned her apartment, he'd tried to keep his expectations sensibly moderate. Now, he felt the most intense longing to be lying with her, touching her, kissing her prominent breasts, slipping inside her. So maybe there would be a sexual life after Vanessa, after all. And it would be with this luscious creature, an artist like himself, attractive—no, sort of beautiful—and not a bit judgmental about his religious quest. He could barely taste his cod, once the prospect occurred to him. His conversation was automatic: on the surface he was explaining his childhood, his upbringing, forces that had made him the sort of writer he was. But on the inside all he was saying was, "I want you, I want you, I want you ..."

After he'd paid the bill and risen from his chair, he said to Barbara, "Let's go to your place."

"Not yet, Road Runner" she said, laughing again. "Let's take a walk first." She rose, hooked her arm in his and they walked out of the restaurant together, then on to the street, heading into Davis Square. They passed a movie theatre, a candlepin bowling alley, several restaurants and finally the 1940s-style Rosebud Diner, which always made Wishnasky think about his grandfather, whose favorite restaurant had been a diner in Needham Center. It was cold outside—Wishnasky guessed the forties—and when he put his arm around Barbara, she didn't recoil. He wished there were an open bookstore in the area so he could say, "Let's see if there's one of my novels that I can buy for you," and then they'd step into a shop and Wishnasky would show her his work, and then she'd surely go to bed with him. Wasn't this somewhere near the adolescent core of his ambition, the thought that girls would want to have sex with a published writer? And then he'd be at peace. Goodbye, Vanessa, I'm wrapped around another woman. And she's done me the honor of taking me to her apartment. And this pain I still feel at the thought of you is—well, will be—gone soon.

They were looking in the window of a clothing store—it hardly registered to Wishnasky that he was staring at women's shoes—and Barbara said, "Now, I have to warn you. My apartment is tiny."

"We could go to my house then."

"Not for the first time. I'll feel safer at my own place."

"I don't mind that it's small. I've lived in some breadboxes."

"You talk that way now. But wait till you see."

"Let's go. Or I'm going to try to have my way with you right here."

"All right. Come with me."

She turned him around and they walked back toward the far eastern end of the square, then up a side street. After a couple more minutes, she stopped in front of a mid-sized house with double-screened doors. "I have a second-floor apartment," she said. She found her key, opened the door, and led him up a flight of stairs. At a door painted forest green, she inserted another key and led him in.

The first room he saw was miniscule and drab. It consisted of a small metal table against a window looking out on an alley, a couch made out of the mattress of a single bed and two accent pillows, and a four-shelf bookshelf on which there were more green plants than books. One could walk the whole length of the room in a few large steps. "This is the living room," said Barbara. "Pretty much misnamed, huh?"

"It's charming. Home of a starving artist."

"Wait till you see the kitchen. It's even worse."

She led him down a corridor to a remarkably narrow rectangular space. On the right, there were a stove and oven and sink. On the left, just a wall. At the end of the kitchen, a refrigerator backed against a pitiful excuse for a window. There was hardly area enough for the two of them to stand together.

"Still charmed?"

"I don't think I'd hold a reading here."

She laughed her lovely laugh. "It's good training if I become an astronaut." She pointed toward a door between the living room and kitchen. "In there's the one-step bathroom. Step right to the sink, or step left into the shower. Step straight and you're at the toilet." She took his hand and led him back to the living room. "Here's the only room of any size," she said. They walked into the bedroom.

It was beautiful. An inviting king-size bed covered with a lovely blue-and-green plaid comforter faced a bay window on which were various plants, hanging or sitting on a built-in bench. There was a beige carpet with an abstract design under the bed, and against the wall was a large CD player, with several jewel-box CD cases piled beside it. A gold standing lamp against the far wall gave light to a comfortable-looking chair and its hassock. "What do you think?" said Barbara.

"It's a little paradise," said Wishnasky. "All the other rooms exist so that you'll appreciate this one."

"You just like the bed."

"The bed does look inviting."

"You just want me to invite you into my bed."

"I wish you would."

"You've got to pay the price first."

"What's the price?"

"A really warm kiss. One persuasive, exclusive, romantic bedtime kiss."

"I think I can manage that."

He leaned in to kiss her. Immediately, she threw her arms around him and thrust her tongue into his mouth. Wishnasky responded eagerly. It was wonderful to be with a woman not Vanessa, it was wonderful to feel Barbara's ample breasts against his chest; he was so sexually stimulated he felt like a teenaged boy anticipating his first lover. They clinched and together fell onto the bed. Before he knew it, she was unbuttoning his shirt, pulling it over his head when it was only half undone, then loosening his belt and pulling his pants down. Dressed only in his briefs, bulging with excitement, he pulled her blouse above her head, then unhooked her bra and let her sizable breasts free. Now, she was pulling down his briefs, taking his erection in her mouth, letting it out, taking it back, pulling down her jeans and panties together, climbing on top and straddling him. Any intention to ask her about contraception disappeared as he found her and penetrated her. Not only were their sex organs joined but their mouths and their arms. He felt a great burden lifted from him. He thrust himself into her and felt a profound, much-needed relief.

■

It was 6:30 a.m. Wishnasky opened his eyes and saw Barbara, nude, awake, one leg wrapped around one of his, staring at him, smiling. A little light trickled through the bay window with the rising sun. In its illumination Barbara's face looked graceful, poetic. She said, "Are you awake now?"

"Yeah," he said. "Is it already morning?"

"We slept this way," she said. "Interlocked. You're a nice man to interlock with."

"From this moment on, it's my favorite thing."

"You want some coffee?"

"After we make love again."

They did. This time it was slower, more sincere. As miraculous as the night before, but also meditative, gentle.

Afterward, she got up and threw a pale blue shift on and went into the kitchen. "You want some help?" he asked.

"There's not enough room for help," she called back, laughing. "Coffee black or with cream?"

"With cream, please." He put on his clothes and walked into the microscopic living room. Sitting at the small metal table, he was conscious of how much the assessment of one's surroundings had to do with one's mood. Euphoric as he felt, this little room seemed delightfully cozy.

She brought in two coffees, sat down beside him and they drank. He asked her about her childhood, and she told him the story of growing up in Minnesota, acting in school plays and pageants, and then enrolling in the theatre program at the University of Michigan. She'd played Rosalind in *As You Like It,* Cecily in *The Importance of Being Earnest,* and half a dozen other roles that convinced her she loved acting. Out of school, she'd moved to New York City, but after three years of constant auditioning—and working at a car rental agency—she hadn't been cast in one play. When a friend told her the theatre scene in Boston was much easier to break into, she moved to Somerville; sure enough, she immediately got some jobs in the smaller houses. One of the plays she acted in was written by a Palestinian woman about the Israeli occupation of the West Bank. She and the author became close friends, and eventually the latter—Sharmila—invited her to accompany her on a visit home. She'd scraped together the money and spent two weeks in Nablus, living with Sharmila's family and facing, she said, all the indignities regularly forced upon the Palestinians by the Israeli soldiers. That was last summer. Now, she was thinking of writing a play of her own about the brave Palestinian people and their heroic endurance.

"But you're a Zionist, aren't you?" she asked Wishnasky. "You probably support the Occupation."

"I'm glad there's a Jewish state," said Wishnasky. "But I'd rather that it thrived on peace and fairness. I don't know enough to say more, really."

"There's no peace for the Palestinians," said Barbara. "They're constantly subject to searches by the Israeli military, checkpoints they can't pass through, jobs suddenly lost because of the encroachment of the settlements. Sometimes their own lands are taken away and turned into Jewish housing."

"Like I said, I don't know much about it."

"The Jews should never have moved there. The Jews had no right to take Palestinian land."

"Are you talking about the territories or are you talking about all of Israel?"

"All of Israel. They had no right to it."

"Now wait," said Wishnasky, trying to sound as reasonable as possible, and vaguely remembering some warning about Barbara's politics. "Israel was, after all, the Jewish homeland for more than a thousand years. It's not entirely accurate to say they had no right to it."

"Because the Germans were obsessed with exterminating Jews, the poor Palestinians had to pay the price and lose their country? Where's the justice in that?"

It had been years since Wishnasky had thought deeply about Israel, but he felt so sure his attitudes were moderate, he didn't assume anyone could take umbrage at them. "I wasn't just referring to the Holocaust," he said. "Yes, that provided an urgent reason for European Jews to migrate. But if I remember correctly, Jewish resettlement in Israel began long before both World Wars. I have relatives, a great-uncle and aunt, who moved to that area in, I don't know, 1910. It's not all about the Holocaust."

"But you're defending the Zionists."

Wishnasky now remembered precisely what Julie had warned him about. And watching Barbara's breasts heave under her thin shift as she spoke, he had no other desire than to get back into bed with her. He smiled at her warmly.

"Look, you're too lovely and I'm too horny to let world politics intrude on our breakfast," he said. "Are you through with your coffee? Let's go back to bed."

"Are you defending the theft of Palestine by Polish and Russian Jews? Are you saying they had more rights than some poor Arab families that had been living on the land for centuries?"

"The Jews also had been there for centuries."

"Yeah, in the year 6000 BC!"

"More like 1000 BCE," said Wishnasky, trying not to sound supercilious. "And a thousand years after that. Look, darling Barbara, I don't want to argue with you about this or anything. I'm feeling too enamored."

Barbara's face darkened. "I spent two weeks in Nablus seeing firsthand what the European colony in Palestine has done to its innocent victims. I'm not going to fuck a man who can defend that sort of injustice."

"You did twenty minutes ago."

"Meaning what?"

"Meaning nothing. Meaning I'm the same caring human being I was twenty minutes ago when you were lovely enough to take me in your arms and—"

"Imperialist!" growled Barbara.

"Dear, sweet Barbara," said Wishnasky. "We can't either of us do anything about what's going on in the Middle East. Let's make love, let's beautifully establish our separate peace and leave history for the prime ministers and presidents and—"

"Occupier!" spat Barbara. "Colonizer! Murderer!"

"Now wait a minute—"

"Get out, get out of my apartment! I can't believe I just let you fuck me! Why didn't you tell me this over dinner?"

"Who wants to talk politics when the attraction is so—"

"Zionist! Get out!" She stood up and pointed toward the door. Wishnasky could hardly believe that she was throwing him out of her apartment so soon after inviting him into her bed, into her arms. He paused, waiting for her to come to her senses. She didn't.

"Allow me to retrieve my coat," he said quietly.

He walked back into the bedroom, found the coat and returned to the living room. She was still standing there, pointing to the door like a statue.

"I'll call you later tonight," he said. "I'm sure we can get past this."

"Out," she said. He went.

35.

"I'VE TALKED TO HER SEVERAL TIMES," said Julie. "It seems you offended her on a lot of levels."

Wishnasky was at Rick and Julie's spacious, modern loft on the Boston waterfront. They'd agreed to see him on short notice after hearing—from both Barbara and him—about the fiasco the previous night. Now they were seated in the large living/dining room, drinking coffee (Julie), fruit juice (Rick), and club soda (Wishnasky). Outside the large picture windows was another former warehouse that had been turned into living quarters.

"She says you made it clear to her after a few minutes in the restaurant that if she didn't sleep with you, there wouldn't be any second date."

"She what?" said Wishnasky. "That's just false. I never said that."

"She said you insisted on going to her place after dinner, when all she wanted was a pleasant walk and to get to know you. She said you invited yourself up and then jumped her bones."

"That's incredibly inaccurate!"

"Then after you had your way with her in bed, you started preaching about Zionism. You said that you thought the Palestinian people had no right to exist."

"I didn't say anything of the kind!"

"Palestinian children, you opined, weren't fully human. And she can't be with such a man. Not to mention a sexual predator who more or less raped her."

"I object to this whole thing! I never said or did anything faintly resembling those items!"

"Look," said Rick. "We don't want to get into a he-said she-said sort of thing."

"We absolutely have to get into it!" said Wishnasky. "After such an utterly mendacious *she-said*, you've got to allow me my exculpatory *he-said*!"

"I will admit that what she described doesn't sound very much like you," said Julie. "At least, not the you we think we know."

"That's me: the one you think you know! Not her version, your version!"

"Although, you have to realize that for ages men have managed to push sex on unwilling women through a whole grab-bag of insidious techniques."

"I never pulled from that grab-bag. She was the one to suggest I come to her apartment! She was the one who showed me her bed like it was dessert she'd been looking forward to from the moment they served the salad! It was she who told me, virtually in so many words, that she wanted to go to bed with me!"

"What *are* your opinions about Israelis and Palestinians?" said Rick. "What is it she misinterpreted?"

"I have a very peaceable view! I think the two should live side by side in two separate nations and they should respect each other's rights. And I don't think the question should be a litmus test for love affairs!"

"I warned you she was political," said Julie. "If you'd been smart, you would have avoided the whole subject."

"*She* brought it up! Like *she* brought up going to her apartment and viewing her bedroom! Now, can you get her to let up on me? I liked her! I liked everything about her! I'd be happy to see her again and put this squabble behind us!"

"Forget it," said Julie. "If I know Barbara, there's only one way she'd even consider seeing you again."

"What's that?"

"Very simple: you sign on to her political opinions. You come out against Zionism."

"You know I can't do that! I'm *proud* that Israel exists! It's been good for the Jews; it's been good for *me* as a Jewish American! The Greeks have Greece, the Russians have Russia, why should the Jews be any different, why shouldn't Israel be Jewish? This is disguised anti-Semitism!"

"Oh, you'll definitely get right with her by calling her an anti-Semite."

"I said I thought Israel should live happily with its neighbors! Is that such a shocking sentiment?"

"Look, Tristan," said Rick, balancing his fruit juice on the arm of his easy chair, "You're thirty-six years old, intelligent, you read the newspaper and watch CNN, are you telling us that it's a surprise to you that some American leftists find Israel an illegitimate state?"

"It's a surprise to me when they throw me out of their houses after a splendid fish dinner and a night of romantic lovemaking!"

"All the result of incessant pressure from you," said Julie. "According to Barbara."

"I thought you bought *my* side of that story."

"I honestly don't know which one of you to trust."

"You know, it's possible they're both right," said Rick, looking philosophical. "What she sent out as mere politeness, he saw as an invitation. What he sent out as a sincere compliment, she saw as an ultimatum."

"Darling, how does that help here?" said Julie.

"It fits what Dr. Latimer says," said Rick. Dr. Latimer was his psychotherapist, whom he'd been seeing even longer than Tristan had been seeing Ion. "Conscious intention is at best twenty percent of action. What's really motivating us is the unconscious eighty percent. So Barbara unconsciously enticed Tristan into bed after Tristan unconsciously closed off all other options. As to what was going on in the unimportant surface level, they were just discussing the difference between cod and schrod."

"Tristan," said Julie, "is there any chance you could modify your position about Israel such that Barbara might welcome you back for a second date?"

"You mean, could I lie?"

"How important is your feeling on the subject?"

"I like Israel! That's not negotiable!"

"Then your departure from the life of one Barbara Ormandy is final."

"Fine! I don't want her! I already lost Vanessa because I wouldn't stop being Jewish, it's only right that I lose Barbara over refusing to give up Israel! And the next woman I date is not only going to be Jewish and a Zionist, but actually a blood relation of Golda Meir! What about that architect you mentioned before? The Orthodox Jew! I want you to set me up with her for next weekend!"

Rick and Julie exchanged anxious glances.

"Tristan,' said Julie. "I think you need a rest. You're careening from woman to woman like a pinball, and I don't think that's healthy. For you *or* the woman. Give yourself a vacation from romance for a while, and then we might talk about Andrea."

"I don't want a vacation! I want to meet one pleasant, good-natured female who isn't against God, Zionism, or me!"

"Look," said Rick. "We'll be happy to introduce you to Andrea and anyone else—after you've had a little breather. When you're not so hyped up. When you've had a chance to unwind."

"Unwind? Unwind?" He couldn't think of a better retort.

"Yes, you've got to get a hold of yourself," said Julie. "We value you too much to humor you in this state."

"Humor me? Humor me?"

"Drink your club soda," said Rick. "And let's talk of other things. There'll be lot of time for meeting wonderful women."

36.

JULIE WAS RIGHT ABOUT BARBARA making the break permanent. Wishnasky called her: she wouldn't pick up. He emailed her: no reply. He messaged her and as a last resort sent her flowers and appended a note: "Please contact me." She didn't. He decided that maybe his friends were wise in thinking it too soon for him to meet another woman, and he turned his efforts toward his new novel.

The "epilogue" of *Traveler in the Abyss* kept growing. Yvonne had become Ozono's lover and even suggested to him that her appearance in his life might have been ordained, a deliberate step in the cosmic drama. Ozono had learned that there might be a God out there and it might behoove him to trust Him for the first time in his life. Most of what the rabbi had taught Wishnasky ended up in Yvonne's teaching, including the idea that the world stood firm because of *Torah*, ritual observance, and deeds of lovingkindness.

Roland called one afternoon and asked about his progress.

"I think I might have something soon," said Wishnasky. "But I have to warn you, this is a very different novel from the one I described to you a few years ago. I've had a great inspiration."

"Inspiration is for amateurs, and it appalls me to hear you speak of it," said Roland. "Just send in the pages as soon as you can."

"Don't you want to hear my new ideas?"

"Will it make the work go faster?"

"It might."

"Fine, thrill me with your brilliance. I can hardly bear the suspense."

Wishnasky summarized his main character's new trajectory. When he finished, there was a long, uncharacteristic pause on Roland's side of the line.

"So, you're writing a religious book," he said, sounding like a man who'd just been offered scorpions for dinner.

"I wouldn't call it that. Or maybe I would. I don't know exactly what to call it."

"Do you know how meager the market is for religious books? Graham Greene is dead. C. S. Lewis is dead. Religious books are now sold on wire racks in supermarket pharmacies. You purchase your prescription, and then, in fear for your life, you buy a religious book."

"This one is different. This one is mainstream."

"Do you know what happened to Ernie Stillman's sales when he became a Southern Baptist? Have you heard of Wilma Womack since she became a Mormon? Their books are remaindered on the date of publication. Their publishers are suing for fraud."

"This'll be different. The world loves Jewish writers these days."

"Jewish secular writers, yes. Sex with Philip Roth. Superheroes with Michael Chabon. Nobody wants a Jew actually writing about Judaism. Bernard Malamud is deceased. Isaac Bashevis Singer has passed on."

"You'll see. This thing will sell."

"I have been studying the book market since I departed from the military," said Roland, "and I'm telling you your novel will *tank*. It will be a *disaster*. You will *never* recover."

"You know, Roland," said Wishnasky. "For the first time in my life, I think you're misreading what the public wants."

"I'm going to go get drunk on the most potent Russian vodka, delivered neat," said Roland. "Finish your garbage and send it to Darryl Kamfort wrapped in yesterday's newspaper. Then we'll talk about how to rehabilitate you. Better yet, forget all this religion and go back to despair. There's an established market for despair."

"I'll call you when I'm done, Roland."

"Write about incest," said Roland "Psychological abuse, greed, murder, pederasty, gluttony. Nobody's interested in religion."

"Goodbye, Roland."

"You've ruined my day. And your career. Goodbye."

37.

He sat in the rabbi's office, telling her about his father's heart attack and recovery. He included everything he could remember, including the prayer that preceded his father's return to consciousness. "Do you think God heard me?" he asked. "Is that what I should assume?"

"It's possible. And of course, it's also possibly coincidence. But when you've prayed long enough for quite enough things, you'll eventually come to think that so many coincidences can't all be coincidental. A praying person learns lessons that those who don't pray never suspect."

"I must admit I feel uncomfortable," said Wishnasky. "To be in God's debt. Which I can't possibly pay."

"That's wrong: you *can* pay. By helping out at the Horn of Plenty. By practicing goodness. By giving charity. There's a famous section in the *Talmud* where one rabbi asks another, How can we worship now that the Temple's been destroyed? And the answer is, it's very easy: by doing deeds of lovingkindness."

"It doesn't seem enough."

"It's not in heaven," said the rabbi. "What the *Torah* requires is perfectly achievable right here on Earth. It's neither too distant nor too difficult."

"So, what's next? What do I do now?"

"You've yet to sit in on one complete Saturday morning service."

"That's easy to remedy. Presuming that my father doesn't have another heart attack."

"Beyond synagogue, there's still a lot that you'll want to take on eventually. Spending a few minutes each day studying the *Torah*. Learning Biblical Hebrew so you're not subject to some tendentious translation. Making a routine of giving ten percent of your weekly income to *tzedakah*. You scared yet?"

"That's a lot."

"I know. But many people manage it, and without feeling burdened. Finally, keeping kosher—at least enough where you're not eating the forbidden foods. And oh yes, extending your good deeds a little further, so they take up, let's say, four hours a week: ten percent of your work time. In short, raising your behavior to the level of your values."

"I don't know that I'm ready for such a transformation."

"All these are *mitzvot*, commandments. And in Judaism, we express our love of God by doing God's will. You certainly shouldn't try to take on everything at once. But is there anything I mentioned that sounds attractive right now?"

Wishnasky's eyes traveled to the tall bookshelves lining the walls of the rabbi's office. "I love languages," he said. "Had French and German in college, read lots of literature in the original. I guess learning Hebrew sounds slightly interesting."

"Excellent. Biblical Hebrew is a poetic language that's far more expressive than any translation. To read the Holy One's words in the original—it's stunning, it's a great way of obtaining real closeness with God. And then to pray to the Holy One in Hebrew and know what you're saying—there's nothing else remotely like it."

"How should I start?"

"Cantor Kazen offers a beginner's class on Tuesday evenings. The current class started a few weeks ago, so you'll have to play catch-up. But as a student of languages, it shouldn't be too difficult."

"This is becoming a full-time occupation."

"Have you read Goethe in the original?"

"Yes, as a matter of fact."

"Balzac? Flaubert?"

"Yes. And really loved them."

"Now, you can read God in the original. And believe me, the Holy One's got a way with words."

It was an unbeatable argument. "All right, done," said Wishnasky. "How do I say 'thank you' in Hebrew?

"*Todah Rabbah.*" She stood up. "Ready to help the homeless?"

"I guess. But I'm worried about all my new commitments."

"You're doing fine. But I want to tell you, if it ever feels too much, just take a rest. Better to do a few *mitzvot* well than to be so frightened off, you give up everything."

He stood up. "Does there ever get to a point where you've basically achieved everything, where you've pleased God? Do you ever get to a point where you've done the job and can simply coast?"

"Yes and no. Human beings live in time, so it's in time that we have to act. Which means one day's accomplishments don't preclude the next. On the other hand, some days we get it right. Then you can almost feel the Holy One's pleasure."

"And you've felt that? The approval?"

"I think I have, yes."

"Okay. Let's go."

■

At the Horn of Plenty, there was a group of volunteers from a Medford church, and Wishnasky was one of six servers who efficiently distributed all the plates of baked chicken, green beans, and white rice to the homeless. He was beginning to remember faces now and had a good sense of who was a regular and who was new. Some of the diners even greeted him as they would a friend, and he felt embarrassed to have imagined their hostility on his first day. On the other hand, some of the assembled were clearly stoned or drunk, and he overheard one slender young tattooed man tell another, "If he comes near her again, I'll break every bone in his body." So it was a mix, as he should have guessed. Why wouldn't a group of seventy homeless people represent an inevitable variety?

When he laid a plate in front of the poet Arthur, he called out, "My writer friend! Good to see you! Did you read any Claude McKay like you promised?"

"Actually, I did," said Wishnasky, who had looked up the poet on the internet back home. "I read some sonnets—really angry ones. It felt strange to see that much passion enclosed in the strictures of sixteenth-century prosody."

"Yeah, white folk didn't like that much—Black rage in Shakespeare's English. Which poems did you read?"

"'If We Must Die.' And 'The White House' and 'The Harlem Dancer.'"

"Those are good ones all right. 'If We Must Die' was the first Black-power anthem in the history of these United States. Did you know, it was quoted during World War II by Mr. Winston Churchill? And when the prisoners at Attica rose up in '71 that was their battle hymn."

"I didn't know that."

"You go to college?"

"Yes."

"What'd you study?"

"History and Literature."

"They teach Claude McKay in History and Literature at—where'd you go?"

"One of the universities around Boston."

"Here's a man who literally started the Harlem Renaissance, who turned the white sonnet into a mighty weapon against white racism, who wrote the first Black bestsellin' novel of the 20th century—they teach *Home to Harlem* at your university?"

"Not that I know of."

"Right. Funny thing about that. How they happened to miss it."

"I guess my education was pretty skimpy."

"When white F. Scott Fitzgerald goes to Paris and hobnobs with white Ernest Hemingway, that's literary *news* all over town. But when Black Claude McKay goes to England and teaches economics to Mr. George Bernard Shaw, well, that's not worth rememberin'."

"I guess I need to read more about McKay."

"Read his FBI files—how they tried to keep him from comin' back to America after his Grand Tour. And the British Secret Service wasn't none too friendly either."

"Sounds more and more fascinating. But I have to go on serving dinner."

"Most fascinating American success story you never heard. You think about that next time you pick up a book of poetry."

Wishnasky moved on to other diners. With so many servers, the work went quickly, and soon he was back in the kitchen waiting for seconds to be called. As he half-listened to Dee talk about the church she'd just joined in Jamaica Plain, he thought of the figures he'd studied at Harvard—Balzac, Baudelaire, Rimbaud, Gide, all from the storied halls of Dead White Frenchmen. Or Holderlin, Brecht, Mann, Grass—from the luxurious mausoleums of Dead German Caucasians. It had felt comfortable enough from his white male view to be told that these men stood tall at the Temple of Great Literature. But how must it look from Black or Brown eyes, from a skirt or a scarf, to open a college catalogue and see so few women or people of color? Was it dispiriting, challenging, or just plain sad? Why, before meeting Arthur, had he never heard of Claude McKay?

Second helpings were announced, and Wishnasky brought an oversize bowl of rice out to the diners, ladling large portions to the many who asked. Then he was back in the kitchen helping scrape dirty dishes when a short Black woman ran in and cried, "Call 9-1-1, Jimbo's collapsed! Someone call an ambulance!"

Brooke and Patrick rushed outside, and the other servers, Wishnasky among them, followed behind. They saw a blond, bearded young man in torn brown corduroys lying on the pavement by one of the tables, surrounded by a group of the homeless. Brooke jabbed at her phone and spoke into it anxiously, and a middle-aged woman knelt beside the fallen man, trying to get him to talk. Wishnasky turned to the person closest to him, an orange-haired hippie with a ring in each ear, and said, "What happened? Do you know?"

"He was smoking spice, man. That stuff'll kill you."

"Spice?"

"Yeah, that's right. I won't touch that shit."

Brooke, off the phone, asked everyone to step back and give the fallen man air. She looked in Wishnasky's general direction and said, "Please, would the staff go back to cleaning up?" Taking one last glance at the figure supine on the ground, Wishnasky returned, with half a dozen others, to the kitchen. There was talk about the victim—"He's always high on something," said one of the regulars—and within minutes the wail of an approaching siren. Wishnasky tried to focus on scraping food off dirty dishes but noticed that the rabbi was at the door staring out. For a moment, he thought he saw her lips move. Then he heard the emergency technicians shouting everyone out of the way as they put Jimbo on a stretcher.

A few moments later, the excitement dissipated. Wishnasky and Rabbi Diamant helped fold up chairs and tables, and carried them to the large shed. Goodbyes were said to the other servers—all the homeless had departed—and a chastened Wishnasky climbed into the front seat of the rabbi's car.

"You think he'll be all right?" said Wishnasky as they merged into traffic.

"I think so," said the rabbi. "Something like this has happened three or four times in the year-and-a-half that I've been coming here. Nobody's died yet."

"Is it always drugs?"

"It's always drugs."

"So how do you feel about that? Knowing that some of the people you're serving are probably too stoned to even feel grateful?"

The rabbi thought for a moment. Then she said, "Not everyone has a comfortable job like I do, in an air-conditioned office, with a secretary, three weeks of vacation, and restaurant meals every Saturday evening." She paused again. "Not everyone gets to go to St. Lucia when they need escape."

"I understand."

"I don't mean to sound glib. Always I have to ask myself, where would *I* find my release if I were homeless and penniless? Can I say without hypocrisy that I'd turn down the chance to feel elated on this or that narcotic? It's not shocking that some do drugs. What's shocking is how many can stand to stay sober."

They drove on in silence, and Wishnasky reflected on the image of Jimbo face-up on the ground while a crowd of the dispossessed looked on in solicitude. He'd been concerned too: not judgmental, not reproachful, but worried for this stranger who only a few minutes before had accepted his offer of more rice. Would the blond, bearded man survive the evening? Would his desire for a piece of paradise send him young to his grave or would he be back next Thursday evening, barely fazed by what would seem to him a necessary hazard of the "good" life?

He looked at the rabbi. "You told me that if I came to the Horn of Plenty, I'd find God there," he said. "Where was God when Jimbo was laid out on the concrete? What sort of sense do you make of it?"

"Were you genuinely worried when you saw him lying there motionless?"

"Yes, very much."

"Then God was in you. Do you find that idea difficult?"

"Yes, to be honest."

"Work on it. Try out the thought. Heschel says God is wherever we let God in. Try doing that more consciously."

All the way back to the synagogue, Wishnasky pondered the concept of a Deity whose insistence on human freedom allowed for the coexistence of believers and atheists, the super-rich and the homeless, celebrities and vagrants. Why was this so hard to accept? Why was he holding out for a different image, a childhood image, when so much experience demonstrated otherwise?

38.

HIS FATHER WAS TO BE RELEASED from the hospital in the afternoon. When Wishnasky walked into his room, his mother was already there packing up assorted items in a purple and red suitcase more appropriate for an airport.

"Congratulations," said Wishnasky. "According to the floor nurse, you're escaping a day earlier than most heart patients. You must have had the best sort of heart attack."

"The best is the one you don't have," said his father. "I would have left here the first night if they'd let me."

"Your father has been given a list of rules by his physician," said Wishnasky's mother. "He's not to overexert himself in any way, he's not to pick up any heavy packages, get involved in demanding housecleaning, or have sexual relations."

"That's too bad," said Wishnasky. "Since he's always liked interrupting a good day of housecleaning by having sex with large packages."

"Very funny," said his father. "You didn't go through this, so you make jokes."

"He's also not allowed to get angry or express high emotion."

"It's either act like a corpse or turn into one," said his father. "Well, good. For the next few weeks I'll have the emotional life of a fig newton. No, figs are too excitable. A Lorna Doone. A vanilla wafer."

"No CNN," said his mother.

"We'll watch your favorite, PBS," said his father. "They act like they're *all* recovering from heart attacks."

They walked out to the hospital parking lot, Wishnasky carrying the bag. He helped his father into his mother's car, put the suitcase in the trunk, and then climbed into his own car and followed behind them. His mother was an extremely cautious driver: she stayed in the far right lane, drove at half the speed limit, and turned on her directional lights almost a full block before she turned. Wishnasky wished he'd given her a twenty-minute head start.

At his parents' house, his mother made coffee—decaffeinated for the outpatient, regular for her son and herself—and brought out a store-bought cinnamon cake that she cut into rectangles and served on little white china plates. They sat in the living room, his father and mother together on a couch, Wishnasky opposite in a velvet-upholstered chair.

"So, tell me something about you," said his father. "And don't ask me about my heart or anything even near to it. I'm tired of talking about such things"

"There's lots to tell. For example, I'm making great progress on my new book."

"Good. It's about time."

"What about girlfriends?" said Mia. "Have you found someone to replace that nauseating Vanessa?"

"Funny you should ask. I'm just waiting for some buddies to set me up with an Orthodox woman."

"Now that's a good joke," said his father. "That's even funnier than *my* story."

"All those rules," said his mother.

"Yeah," said Morris. "Are you going to tell her you're not kosher? Are you going to tell her you love scallops?"

"I intend to be entirely honest."

"At least the Orthodox have lots of babies," said his mother. "You marry this girl and I'll have all the grandchildren I ever wanted. So, come to think of it, I like the idea. Go out with her, marry her, and bring me infants in yarmulkes. Soon, so I can enjoy it."

"Tell her you eat lobster," said Morris. "Oysters. Sometimes clams. What's so terrible about a clam that God doesn't want me eating one? If He didn't want me eating one, why'd He make them so appetizing?"

"It's good to hear you inquiring about religion, Pop. That's something new."

"I never had time for it. Too many commandments. As a man recovering from a heart attack, let me tell you, it's pleasure in life that matters, not tying yourself up in knots over what's permissible or not."

"Bring this Orthodox woman to dinner, I want to see her," said Mia. "Or will she eat at a house that's not kosher? Find out."

"The trouble with you," said Morris, "is too much time on your hands. If you hadn't made all that money from your last book, you'd be too busy working a forty-hour week to indulge in all these experiments. So, this year it's Judaism, the next year ballroom dancing, the year after that playing the xylophone. A man with no work, no wife, and no children. No wonder you've got time for so many distractions."

"I work every day. Or at least—" he caught himself, then went on. "Six days a week. On my new novel. It's work, believe it or not."

"And on the seventh day you're actually keeping *Shabbos?*" said his mother.

"I'm trying."

"Well, look at that," said his mother. "You're serious. You're really doing this?"

"Of course he's doing it," said Morris. "He has no obligations."

"Since you're so Jewish, now you can explain the Holocaust." said his mother. "I can understand everything, even earthquakes and volcanoes. But how could God let a million Jewish children be murdered? Answer me that and I'll become more *frum* than you. I'll go to synagogue every week for a year if you answer that one question."

"It's about freedom," said Wishnasky. "It's about God wanting human creatures to exercise free will, even if they use it horribly."

"He should have intervened," said his mother.

"Maybe He did,' said Wishnasky. "Maybe He made sure that after Hitler was defeated, Israel came to be."

"Not good enough," said Mia. "A million babies thrown into the crematoria. Into the electrified fences, gassed in 'showers.' He shouldn't have permitted it."

"I think," said Wishnasky, "that we're supposed to make this a world where such things are impossible. Instead of waiting for Someone Else to do it for us." He got up. "I gotta run" he said. "I'll come back to check up on the heart patient in a few days. And I'll call every evening." He kissed his mother on the cheek and his father on the forehead. "I'm glad you're feeling better," he said. "You're too amusing to lose."

"Lots of babies," said his mother. "All in tallises and tefillin."

"I'll do my best."

"To make up for some of the lost ones," said his mother. "Thrown into the fire."

"I'll keep it in mind," said Wishnasky and left.

On the way back to Newton Corner, he wondered when Rick and Julie would introduce him to Andrea. Andrea: imagine a lover with whom he could talk theology as casually as he could great literature or politics. Someone who wouldn't cringe when he thanked God for some turn of fortune, who wouldn't misunderstand his trying to keep the *Sabbath* or perform other *mitzvot*. From the moment that the message had appeared in the Camus book, he'd been fighting the derision of most of the people he knew. What a relief it would be to date a woman to whom he could speak honestly about his quest, who wouldn't see it as a capitulation to fantasy.

Andrea! He could hardly wait.

39.

THE SO-CALLED "EPILOGUE" of *Traveler*—now filling a third of his total pages—was coming along so quickly, it scared him and thrilled him and made it so nervously exciting sitting at his computer that he felt like a fighter pilot in a tailwind. Surely this was inspiration: to have all the right words pouring out of you; the ideas marching in one big, noisy parade for you; the characters begging you to bring them back for another telling flight of meaningful dialogue. Never, in two decades of serious writing, had his work gone so swiftly, with so few obstacles along the way. He wondered if he were now writing from a deeper, truer place than he'd ever accessed in his three novels of despair. Was this how the gold miner felt when he sifted the dirt and discovered those first gleaming nuggets? Maybe he'd never truly been a writer until this moment. The word "breakthrough" caromed around his psyche deliriously.

Yvonne and Ozono had become lovers. But first, she had taught him to look at his fall from grace as a necessary lesson in humility, and to respect the God who loved him enough to bless him with this education. Yvonne taught him to pray, to accompany her to the Square Meal Café, where together they fed the homeless, and previously self-adulating Ozono acquired a refreshing perspective on what really mattered on this troubled planet. Above all, Yvonne taught him that life came with a curriculum: that he was born with a mission, to heal the world, to heal himself, to love and to grow. And lest he feel himself too much an object of her pity, Yvonne made him aware of all her own failures, the sexual adventurism she was still recovering from, the scars from her marriage, the vitriol of her divorce, and the lasting damage she'd done to her family out of arrogance and insensitivity. All this and then paradise in each other's arms. Yes, fulfillment was possible. People were put on Earth not to flounder but to strive for and achieve mastery. And mastery meant learning to make the world livable: to go about the serious, unselfish business of improving the universe.

He contemplated the last pages: How better to end than to show Ozono finding a new position in a computer company, a position that would restore to him his dignity, his sense of purpose, his genius? Was such a finish too perfect? Well, sometimes people *did* get back on their feet after adversity; it would be dishonest to ignore all the stories in the world about fighters who managed not only to stand up after a knockdown but who prevailed, who even won. Simplistic or not, that's what would happen to Ozono. And if the critics attacked him, still the readers—that lovely mass also made up of some-time losers—would thrill at such a blatant affirmation of faith in the triumph of the human spirit.

Wishnasky pushed his keyboard away from him and glanced at the clock: it was shortly after midnight. He wished he had someone to contact with the news that this draft was near complete and he honestly didn't think it would need much rewriting. But the one woman he'd spent years with, Vanessa, despised his new faithfulness, and Barbara despised his Zionism, and Andrea was nothing more than a tantalizing possibility. He thought of calling one of his college friends, but figured they were peacefully asleep with their wives and wouldn't like to be shocked awake for such a reason. That left Roland: Well, why not an email at least? He wrote: "Great News: almost done, roughly 70,000 words. Think I'll have the revision at least a week before deadline. Don't prejudge this: it's going to explode."

He went into the kitchen, found some white wine in the refrigerator, opened the bottle after a brief struggle and sat down with his glass. He'd come a long way since writing *No One From Nowhere*. His fans would be shocked by the spirituality of the new novel, but some would come along with him, of that he was sure. And Roland had to be wrong: people still read Claudel and Mauriac and Singer somewhere, in some corner of the earth untouched by Netflix and video games. So, now he had left Camus and Sartre behind, but he'd entered the company of Evelyn Waugh, Flannery O'Connor, Marilynne Robinson and lots of other successful writers-of-faith. Oh yeah, he'd disappoint some critics, but weren't his critics as human as he? Didn't they also wrestle with angels? Wouldn't some of them greet this new departure? No doubt there'd be a few who'd hold out for the old doom-and-gloom, but that was only to be expected. Literary modernism, from *Les Fleurs du Mal* to *The Wasteland* to *Krapp's Last Tape* was history. In the new dispensation, anything was possible: even God.

As he drank down the wine, he could hear the crowds cheering.

40.

WISHNASKY WALKED THROUGH the Boston Center for Contemporary Art, a guest at a party marking the opening of a new exhibit. The exhibit was called "Atrocities" and featured two dozen mobiles illustrating various examples of human cruelty, sadism, wanton destruction. The artist was Sidney Echevarria, a much-ballyhooed wunderkind whose previous work had earned him the sobriquet "Goya of the VisArt Brat Pack." Only twenty-six years old, he'd already won several top honors, and his work was housed everywhere from the Getty in California to MOMA in New York and the Pompidou in France. Rumor had it that his oeuvre had already made him many times a millionaire.

The gallery was crowded with sixty or seventy invited guests, drinking liquor from the open bar and munching on crackers and pâté de fois gras. Wishnasky recognized Lloyd Cobb, whose holes in the floor were all the rage for home-owners who could afford them; Francesca Inclamata, the sculptor of aborted fetuses; Nancy and Victor Drib, the famous Send-Us-Cocaine Twins; and Robinson McCarter, whose photographs of celebrities vomiting had caused such a sensation at the previous year's Venice Biennale. But it was Echevarria's art that dominated Wishnasky's attention at this moment: one mobile seemed to represent SS men at a concentration camp pistol-whipping prisoners, another showed the people of Hiroshima running from the atom bomb, a third showed Chinese soldiers firing on unarmed protestors in Tiananmen Square. What was particularly disturbing about these already disquieting scenes was their representation in pink- and blue-painted metal such as one might find in an infant's bedroom, hanging above a crib. Wishnasky thought he understood Echevarria's message—that great atrocity had become so commonplace in the modern world, it was now every toddler's inheritance—but he also felt there was something indecent about treating human agony so ironically. Or was he thinking like a philistine?

"Tristan," said a voice, and then Stella Lombardo, the painter of severed heads, was walking toward him and away from a clump of distinguished guests. Her dark brown face registered joy at seeing her friend. "Well, what do you think? Are you shocked?"

"Stella," said Wishnasky, and they kissed, once on each cheek. "I don't know. I have a complex reaction."

"That's because it's the real thing, dear," said Stella, looking around her. "I have to hand it to Izzy: just when we thought that art's capacity to outrage was utterly exhausted, he found an untapped gusher. Brilliant. I'm jealous."

"There's something ... not right about that mobile," said Wishnasky, pointing at an artwork that showed an ISIS terrorist mowing down a line of blindfolded Iraqi soldiers. "What it depicts is too terrible to be represented as a kind of child's toy."

"That's the point," said Stella. "That's how you know it's genuine art."

"Because it vulgarizes something horrific?"

"Because it upsets you, darling. Let's be honest: that's the only way anyone in my world can separate art from kitsch anymore. If it makes you say, no, that's absolutely not art, then it's truly, demonstrably, unquestionably art. If you say: not only is that not art, it's obscene, then not only is it art, it's a classic. And believe me, it's hard to find a subject matter anymore that's not only infelicitous but objectionable. And dear Izzy's done it. These mobiles are ingenious. I wish I'd thought of them before he did."

Wishnasky looked around: there was a mobile of Japanese soldiers torturing American prisoners in World War II, and just a few feet beyond it were Rwandan Hutus murdering Tutsi women and children in the 1990s. And all dangling from the ceiling like playthings, like toys.

"Is this what we've come to?" he said to Stella. "Are we so parched for indignation?"

"What *we've* come to, yes," said Stella. "We visual artists. Meanwhile, in your neck of the woods, naïve realism is still credible. *You've* got it easy."

Wishnasky looked into the next room, where there was a mobile of a 19th-century American soldier shooting a Navajo Indian in the back. "Is this why you paint severed heads?" he asked. "Because everyone's so numb, you've got to assault them just to make the barest contact?"

"Listen," said Stella, her gray eyes sending lasers through his head. "Think about the work that's made headlines over the years. Lovely Carl Andre puts a pile of bricks on the floor and sells them to the Tate for $12,000 dollars. So many people object, it instantly becomes True Art. Or enchanting Andres Serrano makes a photo of a crucifix submerged in a tank of urine. So many people protest, the photo instantaneously becomes an icon. Of course, we owe it all to Duchamp, taking a urinal and displaying it as a sculpture; that was prescient. Meanwhile, you novelists get a pass. Tell a good story in ordinary language, and critics call you a genius and give you a Pulitzer. We have to work."

A very short man whom Tristan didn't know walked over. "Stella," he said, "isn't this mind-blowing? Isn't it spectacular?"

"Tristan Wishnasky, Gavin Wurnicker. Tristan's the novelist, darling, whose books are all about the terrible Nothingness we're ensconced in. Gavin's a composer, Tristan. His last work premiered in Hong Kong and consisted of an entire symphony orchestra recreating the howling of a pack of coyotes in Utah. The critics were unanimous: if Beethoven were alive today, he'd be Gavin Wurnicker."

"Pleased to meet you," said Wishnasky. "So you like this exhibit?"

"Adore it," said Gavin, who had the crouch of a jockey. "What an imagination Izzy has! Did you see the one of Christopher Columbus slaughtering the Arawaks? Did you see the one of Catholic Crusaders putting the torch to a crowd of Cathars? What a wide-ranging mind! I'm dazzled! Aren't you dazzled?"

"I'm not sure," said Wishnasky. "Something's bothering me here."

"If it worries you, it's true art," said Stella. "That's the only test."

"I guess I wonder," said Wishnasky, trying out a new thought, "if all this excess is the result of … exhaustion somehow. Sort of like a drug addict who's lost his ability to feel the dope and has to take triple the amount just to get a little buzz. I think maybe … after the Impressionists, Cubists, Surrealists, and so on, the Abstract Expressionists, all those heroic painters and limit-testing canvases … there's nothing left. There's nothing left but to shoot up as much junk as you can find and hope for a twinge of feeling. Art's reached a concrete wall, and all that's left is to throw oneself against that wall with such violence as to leave a fresco of blood and bone."

"Oh, it's much worse than that," said Stella, smiling as if she were remembering something charming. "Ever heard of Piero Manzoni?"

"I'm not sure. The name sounds familiar."

"1961, darling. He collected his own poop in ninety tin cans and sold it as *Merda d'Artista: 'Artist's Shit.'* A few years ago, a tin sold for €275,000."

"Seriously?"

"Aren't you jealous?"

"And you're saying this is good?"

"I'm saying it passes the test brilliantly: it's definitely not art and it's utterly obscene. Which means that it's really, really, really art. I'll go even further: it's perhaps the greatest work of art of our time. I'm serious: there's more in play there than in everything from *Water Lilies* to *Guernica* to *The Persistence of Memory.* If one of my paintings had a tenth the ramifications, I could be mentioned in the same breath as Praxiteles and Michelangelo."

Wishnasky tried to understand. True, there was nothing more personal than one's own excrement. And after all the confessional poems and tell-all memoirs, after the nude self-portraits and endless displays of filthy laundry, maybe *Artist's Shit* was simply inevitable. Just as Romanticism had found its peak in the operas of Wagner, modernism and postmodernism might have reached their summit with *Artist's Shit.* The concept was unbeatable.

"I need to look around," said Wishnasky. "See you, Stella. Good to meet you, Gavin." He walked into another room in which a group of mobiles were hanging, one representing Genghis Khan disemboweling Germanic infants, another showing Aztec warriors plucking the hearts from still-living human sacrifices. *Artist's Shit*, he thought; yes, that was the extreme that no one could surpass. Urgently personal, indubitably hostile, it was at once better than Dada, performance art, Plath and Lowell, Charles Bukowski, Laurie Anderson, Mapplethorpe and a hundred others. *Artist's Shit*; yes, that was the standard to beat. He'd somehow known it when he started his career as a novelist, and on a subconscious level, he'd been working toward it tirelessly. And only now, only after the strange encounter with the Camus book, had he dared to change direction …

He opened the door to the outside. The last thing he saw on his way out was a pink and yellow mobile, hanging like a toy, of Belgian colonists working Congolese laborers to death. Disturbing, but following certain logic one couldn't object. He walked out into the sun and the clear blue-green day.

41.

THIS TIME RICK AND JULIE had insisted on conditions: he was to make it clear to Andrea from the outset that he had only weeks before broken up with a long-time lover, and he had to promise he wouldn't try to initiate sex after the first date. Julie also reminded him that as the child of Orthodox parents, Andrea might be a little more sensitive than other people to some of the obscenities so prominent in modern life. He was to respect her personal borders and proceed with caution. Julie hastened to add that she'd find it a major affront if Andrea sent her a report that sounded anything like Barbara's.

He called her at 7:30 on a Wednesday evening, figuring she'd be back from work but still wide awake. When she picked up the phone, he immediately said, "Hi, Andrea? This is Tristan Wishnasky, Rick and Julie's friend. Is this an okay time to talk?"

"Hi, Tristan," said a warm soprano voice. "This is a fine time. Julie's been telling me all about you over the phone and I have a particular version of you in mind. Do you look like a novelist? Very preppy, but thoughtful, with pink-rimmed glasses?"

"I have contact lenses."

"Pink-rimmed?"

"Of course. How about you: What don't *you* look like?"

"Well, I'm not short and blonde," she said. "I'm not mustachioed or bearded."

"That's a relief."

"I guess I look like an architect. What about you?"

"I'd say the same thing: I'm not short or blond, or mustachioed or bearded. And Rick is the only architect I know, so I also don't look like an architect."

"That's a relief: I need to meet people from other professions. The fact that you're a novelist makes you so exotic, I feel like I'm on holiday just talking to you. Are you working on a novel now?"

"Yes, and I'm almost finished, so I'm kind of intoxicated. You couldn't have met me at a happier time."

"Oh, good. What's it about?"

"About a man who gets to the bottom and then starts swimming upward."

"So it's hopeful."

"Very. Now you: tell me what you do as an architect."

"Not enough. I'm in the wrong place probably. When I got out of architecture school, I thought I'd devote myself to building postmodern monuments with lots of ornament and color cleverly quoting earlier styles. Instead, I'm redesigning interiors for people with lofts in the South End and along the Boston waterfront. My main claim to distinction is that I do it for Dan Hibbert. Have you heard of him?"

"Not really."

"He's a big name: to have your bedroom designed by him is the urban equivalent of wearing the royal jewels. And he's so successful he's got about thirty of us no-names doing his grunt work while he goes around getting photographed for the *Times* Style Section. It's not at all where I should be."

"Is it difficult to find a different job?"

"It's difficult to give up a dependable salary and the prestige of the Hibbert name. But once I get the courage, I'm going to. Anyway, that's what I tell myself. What about you?"

Wishnasky recounted his life as a novelist, emphasizing his change from the despair and nihilism of his first three books to the high hopes of the new one. He found it pleasing to be able to say that he'd changed course and was relocating his sense of the holy from literature to religion.

"I think I know what you mean about finding literature holy," said Andrea. "That's how I feel about certain music. I'm sort of obsessed with Joni Mitchell, the early albums especially. Are you familiar with her work?"

"Not very well. I know "Woodstock" and "Free Man in Paris."

"I've read every biography of her available. I can tell you how she got her first album contract, who she wrote her best songs for, all her lovers and her three marriages. You're going to be shocked at how much she means to me."

"Maybe you'll play me some of your favorite tracks sometime."

"I might do that. My life has unfolded to the soundtrack of *Blue*. And I'm not speaking from ignorance: I also own most of the albums of Bonnie Raitt, Linda Ronstadt, Nancy Griffith and a bunch of others. And still there's nothing even close to *Blue*."

"So you understand when I say I used to think great literature was holy."

"Probably I do. Why did you change?"

"I suppose I began to suspect that God and the *Torah* were even more sacred than Flaubert and *Madame Bovary*. Not to mention good works, deeds of lovingkindness ... am I embarrassing myself?"

"No, why would you think so?"

"You have to understand, almost everyone I know would have hung up the phone by now. Talk of God is strictly off-limits in my milieu. And I understand: for most of my life, the artist as surly, disrespectful rebel against authority was my ego ideal. I'm still shocked by my change. To be honest, I'm still not comfortable with it."

"At least you're working it out. It seems most Jewish men I know take their religion for granted. It's refreshing to meet someone for whom these issues are alive."

"That's not what I thought you'd say. I figured the Orthodox were always dealing with questions of religious propriety."

"A few are. The rest just go through the motions—not insincerely, but without a great deal of thought. It's how they were raised, so they just accept it."

"Is it how you were raised?"

"That's right. I'm the furthest thing from a rebel."

"You keep kosher? Keep the *Sabbath*?"

"From Friday sundown to Saturday nightfall, I don't answer the phone, don't turn on the TV, don't cook, and don't drive. Just like my parents. And their parents."

"Is it difficult?"

"Not at all. To do otherwise would be difficult. It's also my favorite day for catching up on books and magazines."

"What sort of reading do you do?"

"No literary fiction, I'm sorry to say. I like detective stories and thrillers written by women: Sara Paretsky for example, or Janet Evanovich, or Gillian Flynn. I like reading to escape."

"Escape what?"

"You know: work and everything. I like *People* Magazine and sometimes even *Vogue*. I'm afraid you're going to despise me for the sorts of things I like."

"Not if you'll excuse me for having devoured all the deliberately transgressive novels of Georges Bataille."

"Excused. Now you."

"Excused."

"That's a relief."

"But not the *Enquirer*."

"Wouldn't touch it."

"Then we're on the same wavelength."

"Wasn't that simple?"

"I have a feeling," said Wishnasky, "that things that weren't simple at all
with other people are going to be very easy with you. When's a good time for
us to see each other? Just this talk has already made me want to meet you."

"Well, that's a problem. I'm kind of booked up for a while—unless you don't
mind going on a date with my parents along. They're flying in from a vacation
in London on Friday, and we were planning on going to the movies Saturday
night—a revival of Hitchcock's *Rebecca*. Would that be okay with you? They're
really nice people, and they'll be impressed you're a novelist. And about your
Jewish evolution."

"This isn't some Orthodox custom is it—on the first date one meets the
parents?"

She laughed. "No, it's not, I promise. But if you find the idea too weird, I
fully understand. We can wait till the weekend after."

"Why wait?" he said. "I'll date you *and* your parents Saturday night."

"Oh, thank you. I'll do my best not to make it strange."

"I'm sure you will. But now, tell me where to meet you. The three of you, I
mean."

She did.

42.

THE BEGINNING HEBREW class met at night in the synagogue sanctuary. Someone had placed a long rectangular table just past the entrance to the massive room, and when Wishnasky arrived, there were already six other adults seated around it, with Cantor Kazen, round-faced and carrot-haired, at the head. Wishnasky said a general "hello," then took the only empty seat, between two middle-aged women, one heavyset with dyed red hair, the other short and slender with black-and-gray. The cantor smiled at him and cleared his throat.

"Tristan?" he said.

"Yes. That's me."

"Good," said the cantor. "We welcome a new student: Tristan Wishnasky. Over the phone he's told me that he's an expert at modern languages and decided it was time to know his mother tongue. Let's wish him hello."

All around the table people greeted him.

"We were just beginning to learn some masculine nouns and verbs," said the cantor. "As I mentioned at the last lesson, you only need ten nouns to read the sentences in Chapter Three, and only six verbs. Let's start very simply on page thirty-one." Everyone, Wishnasky included, opened their books. "*Mo-sheh* is Moses, *Dah-veed* is David, *za-char* is remembered, *mah-lach* is ruled. All right, somebody say in Hebrew: 'Moses remembered.'"

"*Mosheh zachar,*" said the bespectacled man opposite Wishnasky.

"Good. Now 'David ruled.'"

"*Dahveed mahlach,*" said the petite woman on Wishnasky's right.

"Excellent. Now 'David remembered Moses.'"

"*Dahveed zachar Mosheh.*"

"Very good work. Now let's add more verbs."

The class lasted just short of an hour and Wishnasky was pleased to find Hebrew easier to follow than French or German had been when he'd first studied them. He learned that most Hebrew verbs were based around a root of three letters, and that if you learned the word for "teach," you were just moments from knowing the terms for "instructor," "student," and "*Talmud.*" He learned that, as in French and German, there were both masculine and feminine nouns, and one had to adjust the verb form for each gender. At the end of the class, the cantor read a short Hebrew section from Genesis—the Hebrew name of which was *Bereishit,* he explained—and then translated it into English. The Hebrew went "*B'tselem Elohim bara oto, zachar u'nekayva, bara otam.*" In English, the cantor said, it meant "In the image of God He created him, male and female He created them." Then he explained that these Hebrew words were the basis for the *Talmud*ic assertion that the first "Adam" was both male and female, and was eventually split into two people when God willed it. "This is the sort of overtone that you can't get from a translation," the cantor said. "And so much of the Hebrew of the *Tanakh* is like that: poetic and resonant with many different levels of meaning. I applaud you all for choosing now to learn this."

Once the session ended, the redheaded woman to Wishnasky's left turned to him and said, "Are you any relation to the novelist Tristan Wishnasky?"

"I'm extremely related to him. I *am* him."

"Oh, I'm so delighted. My name is Bernice Chaite. I think I've read all your novels."

"Uh-oh. I'm surprised you'd still want to talk to me."

"Don't be silly. I found them moving. I'm delighted to meet you."

"Well, those books were pretty bleak," he said. "Are you a regular synagogue-goer?"

"Every *Shabbat* morning, yes."

"Then you probably found my novels too despairing."

"Not at all. I don't see how one can live this life without moments of despair. There are so many reasons to lose hope."

"You're not religious?"

"I'm very religious. Why would you assume otherwise?"

"I suppose I thought that if a person really trusted in God, she'd have faith that everything would work out in the end."

"In the end, maybe it will. But we don't live at the end, do we?"

"I suppose not."

"And meanwhile, history has been calamitous, hasn't it? And maybe the Messiah is going to come one day, but till then, how not to mourn over the diseases and disasters and the murders? And Jewish sources don't teach mindless optimism. Have you read the Book of Lamentations? Do you fast on *Tisha b'Av?*"

"I'm not even sure what it is."

"It's the day the ancient Temple in Jerusalem was destroyed. Every *Tisha b'Av* we mourn, as if the devastation had just occurred. And for a lot of people around the globe, every day is *Tisha b'Av*, isn't it?"

"I guess so. So when you say you enjoyed my novels..."

"I recognized the sadness as something I've felt myself. Many times. Over terrible losses, real tragedies. And I don't think that God gave us tears so that we'd never use them. Fortunately, I can feel enough about the world where I can still cry."

Wishnasky suddenly had a feeling that the optimistic novel he had almost finished revising was based on an immense misunderstanding. Cautiously, he asked, "But do you also agree that there are good things in life also: people who heal, for example?"

"Of course. I depend on it."

"I've decided to write about that side of things for a change," he said. "But I don't want it to be facile or naïve."

"My husband," said Bernice, "was orphaned at age six, grew up in foster homes, and was abused on several occasions by his so-called foster parents. He's now a wonderful family man, successful in business, and so deeply loving, I could eat him." She gave Wishnasky a big smile. "Of course, there are success stories. But we have both: laughter and tears. And any adult has reason to employ both, if you understand me." She paused for a moment as if considering something important. "May I make a small request to you?"

"Of course."

"If you're coming back to this Hebrew class—"

"I plan to."

"May I bring one of your books? And ask you to inscribe it with a wish for my husband? He's even a bigger fan of yours than I am."

"If he's gone through what you said, and he's a healthy, much-loved family man, I should be asking for *his* autograph."

She laughed delightedly. "I'll tell him you said so. That'll make him feel dandy."

"You know," said Wishnasky, "those earlier books ... To be honest, I didn't want to look at the mix of things, the good and the evil. I wanted to write as if the whole story were trouble and nothing but."

"Well, that's not true, is it?"

The cantor, who had been talking with the bespectacled man since finishing the class, now walked over to Wishnasky and Bernice. "So," he said to Wishnasky. "How does Biblical Hebrew compare with French and German?"

"Cantor," said Wishnasky. "Is it acceptably Jewish to despair at times?"

"'Even when the sword is at your throat,'" said the cantor, "don't give up on God's help. That's in the *Talmud*. So no, never despair of God. But other things? Well, 'a time to embrace and a time to refrain from embracing.' God willing, we'll get from the bad to the good."

"I used to write novels that made the whole enterprise look a failure. Life itself. Human life."

"*Weltschmerz*," said the cantor. "A young man's affliction. And now you've gotten over it. But tell me, how do you like the sound of Hebrew?"

"It's beautiful."

"Exactly the right attitude. Did you follow everything we covered today?"

"Yes, very well."

"I'm not going to suggest that it's all this simple. In a few weeks, we'll get to some of the more complicated verb forms. And the vocabulary of *Prophets*, for example, is much more difficult than that of the Pentateuch. But stay with us on a regular basis and you'll get the hang of it."

"Thank you. That's what I'll do."

He left the synagogue and thought about his conversation with Bernice Chaite. Of course she was right: there was good and evil in human life and to focus only on one or the other was misleading. But had he erred in the new novel by making too much of the good? He thought of the trajectory he'd given to Ozono, from despair to hope, from isolation to companionship. Well, he hadn't, after all, claimed that was the only story. Some lives *did* end happily, some wounded *did* heal. There was, after all, a time for embracing. Then Roland's words came back to him: there was no market for religious books, he would lose the audience he'd built over a decade's work. Would he?

Or was that the inevitable judgment of a mind so cynical it couldn't sense the human longing for encouragement, for success stories?

Well, the public would decide. And till then, the important thing was to remain true to his inspiration. And that inspiration said that life was too precious to regret. As he walked out to his car, he noticed the mysterious, waving oaks and firs just beyond the synagogue parking lot, the half-moon soaring overhead, the light clouds swimming effortlessly across the dark sky. How had he missed this land- and skyscape in his first three books? Damn the naysayers! He wouldn't miss them again.

43.

TRAVELER IN THE ABYSS was complete. The book was short—clearly, it would end up fewer than 200 pages when published—but it was efficient, intense, the focus staying on Ozono and Yvonne's rescue of him, and incorporating, in broadly suggestive ways, much of the Jewish learning Wishnasky himself had absorbed. He'd cut most of the story of Ozono's fall so that his hero was near bottom when the novel commenced. What followed was simple: a quasi-medical application, a kind of moral and religious salve that Yvonne applied to Ozono's wounded soul until it was strong enough to breathe on its own. And there was an excitement in the prose of the book, a *frisson* that Wishnasky attributed to the fact that what he was writing about was something he felt firsthand, not at a couple of removes from an existentialist model. Yet he still felt misgivings about abandoning his heroes. What would atheist Flaubert think of him now, what would atheist Joyce say, what about atheist Brecht? If he had styled himself a rebel when writing his nihilist early works, he felt doubly that now, sinning against his literary parentage, spitting in their eyes, refusing their astringent legacy. In choosing faith, he was being faithless to them.

He scrolled through the completed manuscript, rereading sections at random. And as he did, he became aware of another surprising fact: this was a novel about *redemption,* and writing it made him feel like a redeemer himself, if not of poor Ozono, then of those anonymous readers who themselves might feel trapped at the sea bottom, searching for a way up. Imagine if someone was dissuaded from despair by his novel, rescued from misery, maybe from suicide? It was just possible—it made him nervous to consider it—that just as he'd provided food for the hungry at the Horn of Plenty, he'd be providing psychological sustenance to some of the more spiritually homeless, comfortless readers in his audience. Doing so, wasn't that one way of serving God? So many *mitzvot* to do. Wouldn't it be something if his novel itself was a *mitzvah*?

He looked again at a random page. There was a meaning to all this, to so many paragraphs he didn't want to change, didn't need to because they expressed his intention so precisely. Another few days just for safety's sake and he'd send the manuscript to Darryl Kamfort—not late but early. And then the noise this thing would make. Some would call him a renegade, some would call him an apostate, but some would say: this book gave me strength to persist, to prevail. Some would thank him, not for revealing yet another dead end but for illuminating a highway out of trouble and fear.

He turned the pages and thought: *all right, Sovereign of the Universe, now my search for You is about to go public.*

44.

AT THE HORN OF PLENTY, the dinner was meat loaf, yellow rice, and a quinoa salad, and there were so many diners, little would be left over for second helpings. Wishnasky noted that Jimbo was back at his favorite table, appearing animated if not robust, and that Arthur, whom he'd been looking forward to seeing, seemed somber and out of sorts. Still, the poet invited Wishnasky to come back and talk with him when he had a chance, and he agreed before turning his attention to delivering more food. Several of the diners said "God bless you" when he served them, and he practiced saying "God bless you too" when they did. Time for seconds came and went, and afterwards Wishnasky wandered over to Arthur's table. He found an empty chair and pulled it up beside the homeless poet.

"Are you all right?" Wishnasky asked after he sat. "You seem troubled or something."

"Oh yeah, I've been ill," said Arthur. "I've got Crohn's Disease, and it comes and goes. That's how I lost my job, that's how I lost my savings: big bad America makes you pay for getting sick. You gonna get sick, move to Canada. Move to Europe, there they take care of each other. Big bad America ain't got the same attitude."

"I don't know much about Crohn's Disease."

"You don't want to know, either. You don't want to know the bad cramps, the fatigue, and the runs. The way it saps your energy. And there's no cure, you don't want to know that either. It's mean and it's stubborn."

"Then, you sure you want to talk now or would you rather put it off?"

"Put it off till when? I don't put anything off! I could put off my whole life!" He slapped the table with his open palm, then paused and drank a little water. "But that's not your fault, Mr. Writer. I just thought since we're getting to be acquaintances these Thursdays, I should know more about you. And why it is you come out here to tend to us casualties."

"Casualties?"

"That's right. That's exactly what we are."

"Casualties of what?"

"Of the war. You know which one. With a few big winners and a lot of little losers like us. You know how many of us there are? I looked it up once: forty-five million, forty-five million in America, wounded, sidelined, can't afford breakfast. You hear how the army in Afghanistan wouldn't let reporters take pictures of soldiers coming home in coffins? Same with us: we're not supposed to exist. Which makes me wonder how you happened to notice."

Wishnasky pondered his answer. Even now it wasn't easy to just blurt out the news of his religious growth. But maybe Arthur would sympathize.

"A while ago, I began studying my religion," he said. "And the rabbi who comes here alerted me to all the commandments in the Bible about feeding the hungry. So, I guess that's what I'm doing."

"Yeah, they can't cut us from the Bible. All them prophets talkin' about ending people's misery, Jesus himself sayin' that when you feed them, it's feedin' him. They've removed word of us everywhere, from the newspapers and the television, but they're stuck with that pesky Bible. No matter how much it embarrasses 'em." He smiled as if the memory of Scripture were a personal victory. "So you're here servin' God."

"Well, I'm trying," said Wishnasky. "I guess it doesn't amount to much, me showing up for ninety minutes. But I feel like it's a start."

"Did you even know this place was here before you started getting religious?"

"No, I didn't."

"Just what I'm sayin'; they keep us under wraps. Gotta hand it to 'em: it's no easy trick, sweeping forty-five million people under a big rug. Well, anyway, tell me about you. You wrote some novels? What about?"

Wishnasky told him of his first three novels, emphasizing their pessimism and their ignorance of a world like the one Arthur lived in. He then explained about *Traveler,* how it was going to surpass the other books in its message of something to hope for even after disaster. Arthur listened closely, nodding his head from time to time and sipping on his water. Finally, he frowned.

"It's not right," he said. "You have this character, Ozono, lose everything important and then this woman comes along who helps him back on his feet. That's not how it goes. You're tellin' a lie."

"How's that?"

"I informed you I've got Crohn's Disease. So, I can't stay on a job five days at a time, 'cause the disease flares up and I gotta run. 'Course, I lose that job, and the next one and the next. So what does that leave me? My social security money and food stamps, nothing else. Which ain't enough to pay rent *and* electric *and* a real meal *and* the bus. So who's helping me rise up from the bottom of the ocean? Where's this woman you're tellin' me is just waitin' in her car to rescue me?"

"I don't know," said Wishnasky. "I guess every case is special."

"No, it's not," said Arthur. "When there's forty-five million *anything*, it's just crazy to call 'em 'special' or 'unusual' or 'out of the ordinary.' Look around this place, talk to some of the others. You see that woman over there? She was raisin' two infants when her husband walked out on her, she lost his salary, and suddenly she's got three mouths to feed and no job. You tell me: how's she gonna pay for diapers, baby food, and her own food, rent? She can't go out and find work because then there's no one to keep her children, she can't afford daycare 'cause she's broke without a husband. Where's the woman in the car who's gonna come along and rescue her? Look around, and then tell me where that woman is. She ain't nowhere."

Wishnasky accommodatingly looked around for a moment. It was true: there was no Yvonne Pardoner coming to whisk these homeless souls to a warm living room and a new life. But did that make his message invalid?

"Of course, you're right about the poor," he said. "They deserve more than a few encouraging words in someone's fiction. But in the meantime, I want to suggest that where there's faith, there's always a possibility of a turnaround. That's all I'm saying."

"Well, I hope it gets here fast," said Arthur. "I hope it knows my address." He looked away from Wishnasky, who waited a moment, realized that Arthur was through speaking, and returned to the kitchen.

He found the rabbi leaning against the sink, reading something on her phone. When she finished, he told her about the conversation he'd just had. "So Arthur calls them all 'casualties,'" he said.

"And he's right," said Rabbi Diamant. "I can't tell you how many times the homeowners in this neighborhood have tried to get this place closed down. All sorts of excuses, but it's plain what the real problem is: nobody wants to be reminded of the downtrodden every day. They certainly don't want them a block away from where they eat and sleep."

"So you're agreeing with Arthur: there's some sort of conspiracy of silence."

"That's right—and of hypocrisy. If the people who wrote our laws were even slightly religious—and of course they all claim to be religious—this society wouldn't be so unjust. Looking after the poor would be part of the government's mission statement."

After the clearing of tables and the carrying of folded furniture to the old shed in the back of the lot, Wishnasky rode back to the synagogue with the rabbi. It was a chilly night, and a film of frost was beginning to appear on the windows. He looked out through the pane and wondered why it was so easy to hide the poor. He himself wasn't blameless: he'd managed to live in the Boston area most of his life and had never driven through the its most depressed areas. It was remarkably easy to remain unaware, if that's what one preferred.

"These visits are still changing me," he said to the rabbi. "I'm having lots of new thoughts."

"The *Torah* calls it 'having a circumcised heart,'" said Rabbi Diamant. "So don't be surprised if it comes with a twinge of pain."

Wishnasky remembered the discomfort he'd felt on the day he'd prayed for his father's recovery. Was that what it was, the first opening of his heart? He thought how often Vanessa had reproached him for living in a private world, how his mother had accused him repeatedly of a fundamental selfishness. He'd denied it vociferously in both cases. But was it true?

All right, he'd entertain the possibility—the bare possibility—that he was less than the generous, thoughtful citizen he'd long considered himself. But that was changing, wasn't it? Or was it?

45.

As usual, finding a parking space in Boston was trying, but Wishnasky finally left his Camry three-and-a-half blocks from the movie theatre and hurried to meet Andrea and her parents. Andrea had told him that she was tall and brunette, and had also briefly described her parents. So when he reached the Coolidge Corner Cinema and saw a pretty brunette beside a scowling, yarmulke-wearing gray-haired man and a smiling, copper-haired, sixtyish-year-old woman, he knew he had found them.

"Andrea?" he said to the tall woman, whose long hair framed a lovely oval face and dark brown eyes. She was wearing a black dress on which red roses and green leaves twined around each other from knees to collar.

"Tristan?" she said.

"I am if you are."

"Then I am."

"Me too."

They laughed and shook hands. "These are my parents," said Andrea.

"Ben Isaacs," said the still-scowling man as he put his hand out for Tristan to shake.

"And I'm Judy," said Andrea's mother. She and Wishnasky shook hands also, and Ben said, "So, you're a novelist."

"Afraid so," said Wishnasky. "Andrea tells me that you used to own a network of medical diagnostic centers."

"Until one year, three months, and twenty-six days ago, yes. And now I'm a free man."

"And you were CFO of an advertising agency," Wishnasky said to Judy. "That's very impressive."

"We don't always chaperone Andrea on her first dates," said Judy. "Second dates, yes. Third dates, absolutely."

"Just pretend they're not here," said Andrea.

"Don't waste your time," said Judy. "We plan to glom onto you and our daughter like Krazy Glue. If you feel a weight on your shoulders, that's Ben adjusting his seat."

"Mom!" said Andrea, laughing. "My mother is the comedian in the family."

"It was all the spreadsheets I stared at," said Judy. "They would turn anyone into a joker."

"Let's talk after the movie," said Andrea. "If we go in now, we might find four seats together." She herded the others up to the box office and into the theatre. Soon they were ensconced near the back of the crowded house. Andrea was on Wishnasky's right; on Andrea's right was her mother and next to her, Andrea's father. Wishnasky looked at Andrea's face just as the lights dimmed and saw she was untroubled. But he felt anxious.

For the next two hours, *Rebecca* held their attention. Wishnasky was almost sure he'd seen the film in college, but the only segment he remembered was the opening shot in which a camera seemed to pass unobstructed through a closed gate. Then he found himself confusing the plot with *Jane Eyre's* and wondering if the supposedly-deceased Rebecca might turn up, unhinged, behind a door in Manderley's attic. Once Rebecca's real secret was revealed—that she had humiliated Maxim de Winter repeatedly, that he had despised, not loved, her, that she had taunted him mercilessly on the day of her death—Wishnasky felt cheated: the whole tedious movie should have been about that dramatic misalliance. By the end of the film, as de Winter's house burned down, he couldn't help feeling: it's about time. But when he glanced sideways at Andrea and her parents, they seemed entirely absorbed.

After the film, the quartet walked, two by two, in the direction of a patisserie Andrea recommended.

"I was bored," Wishnasky whispered to her. "Until the end, anyway. Did your parents like it?"

"I think they loved it. It's one of their favorites."

"Then I'll keep my thoughts to myself."

"Don't be silly! They love a good argument about the arts. It'll help them bond with you."

"I feel like I'm sixteen years old and they're giving me the once-over."

"Be yourself and I'm sure they'll love you."

He realized that he was afraid of Andrea's father. He had to assume that the man must surely disdain him for walking outdoors without a head covering. He tried to suppress his discomfort. "What did *you* think?" he said. "Too long or just right?"

"Too long," she said. "The dynamic was obvious as soon as Olivier married Joan Fontaine. I would have cut about twenty minutes in the middle."

"Which is not to say Hitchcock's not still the great Hitchcock."

"*Rear Window,*" said Andrea.

"*Vertigo.*"

"*The Birds.*"

"*North by Northwest.* All more ingenious than *Rebecca.*"

"Tell my parents that," said Andrea. "They'll think you're a connoisseur."

"I feel like I'm fourteen," said Wishnasky. "And just about to break their precious Ming vase."

"*Rebecca* is hardly their precious Ming vase."

"I'm not talking about *Rebecca.* I'm talking about you."

The patisserie was small with a long glass counter along the left wall, under which were all varieties of confections made from wheat, fruit, and cream. After the four moviegoers chose their coffee and pastry (an innocent-looking cheese Danish for Wishnasky, *petits fours* for Andrea), they retired to the bright back space of ten or so oak tables. They chose a round one.

"So," said Ben, after sipping his *café Américain,* "what did you two think of the film?"

"Nothing happened in the middle," said Andrea. "Just ratcheting up the suspense when the suspense was already ratcheted."

"You agree, Tristan?"

"I think so. It was a little too long."

"What bothered me," said Judy, gesturing with a *madeleine,* "was how utterly vacuous Joan Fontaine was. Of course she worried that her husband didn't love her—there was nothing to love! Only a pretty face and absolutely no substance behind it. Evil Mrs. Danvers had so much more personality."

"I think that was the point," said Andrea. "Rebecca was complex and there-fore a harridan. Joan Fontaine was a zero and therefore ideal. So the moral is, women should aim to be nobodies. Then, they'll catch Laurence Olivier."

"What did you think, Tristan?" said Judy with a smile.

"I agree with you: all the women with character were either malevolent or ridiculous."

"The story's not entirely irrelevant," said Ben, putting down his cup. "Maxim de Winter marries Rebecca and discovers soon after that she's not at all who he thought she was. If the statistics are right, half of the marriages in America go precisely that way. Hitchcock got *that* part right at least." He looked directly at Andrea, then at Wishnasky, and for a moment he was scowling again.

"You can't really blame people," said Judy, as bright as her husband was sour. "Spouses *do* change during a marriage, oftentimes in ways they themselves couldn't have predicted. So, maybe the good news is that fifty percent of marriages still thrive, in spite of all the alterations." She smiled encouragingly at her daughter.

"That's right," said Wishnasky. "For example, *your* marriage. Andrea tells me you two have been together thirty-four years."

"It's frightening," said Judy. "You've got to wonder how we stay interested."

"I'll tell you how we stay interested," said Ben, putting down his coffee cup. "When I look at this woman"—he gestured at Judy—"all her qualities fall away. The good ones, the bad ones, everything in between, they disappear. And what I feel is pure fascination. Same as the first day I saw her and nearly tripped over my own feet. Why do I feel it? I couldn't begin to tell you. But that's the reason we're still together. Because I can't lose that feeling."

"Thank you, darling," said Judy. "As for me, what I always found compelling in you was your aftershave."

Everyone laughed, and Wishnasky noted privately that Ben was right: as he'd told Ion, what had drawn him to his ex-wife was something intangible, magnetism she'd had, and it lasted a few years and then it left—decisively. But how to keep the attraction forever?

"This is really too intense," said Andrea. "Tell Tristan about your London trip. Tell him about the play you liked so much."

"We saw a drama called *Consent* by a woman named Nina Raine," said Judy. "It started at the National, and then was such a success, it moved to the West End. It was about a group of good friends, including three attorneys, and on the surface it was all about rape, adultery, and truth-telling. But the real subject was how nearly impossible it is to interpret the behavior of even the people closest to you. How anything a person does can be understood in twenty different ways, and how the search for reality is so urgent and never-ending. It was brilliant. I was overwhelmed. Ben's been telling everyone they must see it."

"And as soon as possible."

"Not everyone has plans to fly to London tomorrow, dear," said Judy.

"It'll come to the US," said Ben. "It has to. It's that good."

The conversation turned to other plays and productions, and it occurred to Wishnasky that the subject he was sure Ben and Judy would eventually broach—his fledgling Judaism—was not going to come up. *Too bad*, he thought. He'd been looking forward to the opportunity to show himself worthy of an Orthodox daughter, to flaunt his good deeds at the Horn of Plenty, his saying of daily prayers, his efforts to observe *Shabbat*. But instead, the four discussed a little-known play by Alan Bennett that they'd seen before leaving London, along with Sam Wannamaker's Globe Theatre, which they'd toured and loved, and the Egyptian sarcophagi in the British Museum. Weren't they even a little curious about his religious transformation?

But a few minutes later, when the subject was the massive crowding in Piccadilly Circus, a different thought came to Wishnasky: it was no accident that all the matters Ben and Judy discussed were so far from controversial. It was deliberate policy. These good people were doing their best to keep him comfortable, to steer away from any subject that might possibly embarrass him or create dissonance. The contrast with his own parents—with his mother in particular—was too obvious to be missed. Upon making a new acquaintance, *she* would search for the weaknesses, the problem areas, the secrets; then, through indirections and innuendos, she would test her new "friend" until a break occurred and a hidden rawness would emerge in all its discomfort. Not so Ben and Judy: they wanted Wishnasky to feel at ease, well-liked. So they avoided discussion of the difference in their religious practice, the fact of Wishnasky's divorce, his reputation as a nihilist writer.

"London sounds terrific," he said to Ben and Judy. "I thought I'd seen the best of it when I was there fifteen years ago, but you make me want to go back."

"You would fit in very well," said Judy. "With your literary accomplishments, London would welcome you with open arms."

"You've got to visit the first chance you get," said Ben, who seemed to be scowling less often. "Don't put it off for years like we did."

And so, the rest of the evening passed with cordiality, mutual encouragement, and harmless humor. Wishnasky felt accepted, and Andrea seemed contented and happy.

He had a chance to confirm his intuition once the four of them left the patisserie. "What did they think of me?" he said to Andrea as they walked a few yards ahead of her parents. "Am I good enough for their daughter?"

"They loved you," she said. "You're very smooth and personable. You couldn't have done better."

"That's a relief. Now, what have the three of you got in store for tomorrow?"

"I'm taking a half-day off from work. So the Museum of Fine Arts and the Isabella Stewart Gardner Museum. Then lunch and I drive them to Logan. I'll call you later in the evening and we can arrange a real date."

"Your parents are so engaging," he said. "It makes sense that they turned out a daughter as nice as you."

"They just like that you're Jewish. Don't be surprised when my father tries to make you Orthodox."

"Where do *you* stand on that question?"

"I don't believe in trying to change people fundamentally. A little surface stuff, fine, but basic principles are out of bounds."

"Then it seems that you're not only lovely, you're very wise."

"And you're a flatterer. Incidentally, when my father talked about half of all marriages failing, that was meant for the two of us. To ponder as we consider the second date."

"Did you ponder it?"

"Not for a minute. Now, I've got to go. Talk to you Sunday evening?"

"I can't wait."

"But of course you should say goodbye to my parents now."

"Of course."

"Do it well; so far you've made an impeccable impression."

46.

"AND NOW YOU'RE HAPPY," said Ion Petrescu, wearing a cashmere gray sweater that matched his spiky hair. "You've accepted a deity in your heaven, you're pursuing a woman who makes sense to you, and your novel has changed direction. And all because of a few words in Camus. Or rather, out of Camus."

"I guess so," said Wishnasky. "And I've got to thank you for counseling me to take those words seriously. The way I was feeling at the time, I might have ignored them."

"The Mind wants human flourishing," said bug-eyed Ion. "It wants you developing your potential to the highest degree. I find it personally pleasurable to see yet another example of a human existence rerouted in the direction of its thriving."

"I'm not quite there yet," said Wishnasky. "When I first volunteered at the Horn of Plenty, I didn't recognize half the feelings that place provoked in me, and even now, when I think of going there, or of dating Andrea, or of observing *Shabbat*, I feel displaced, out of sorts, between worlds. Is there a term for this in the literature?"

"There is, and I'll get to it. But first I have more questions about this Orthodox Jewish woman. How is your attitude toward her different than it was toward your actress friend and toward Vanessa?"

"I apparently pushed too hard with the actress, so I'm trying to ease up. And then the knowledge of her ... piety also makes me want to tread softly. Beyond that ... it's too early to tell."

"Are you prepared for the possibility that she may only find sex acceptable within

marriage? Can you tolerate such a delay in your usual timetable?"

"I don't know. I'm just trying not to press it."

"I am not a believer in the prohibition of sexual relations between mutually agreeable adults," said Ion. "Pre-marital, post-marital, straight, gay, or otherwise. But I'm also conscious that something very special has been lost since society became so progressive. Call it 'complicity,' the knowledge that only oneself and one's spouse knew each other carnally. Among millions, billions of others. Imagine what that consciousness once meant to a married couple. The exclusivity. The solidarity. Even the collusion."

"I think I'd be exasperated with a woman who wanted to put off sex till marriage."

"I know that. But I'm trying to prepare you for the possibility that your traditional girlfriend may feel differently."

"I've got to hope you're mistaken."

Ion grimaced, reached forward to pick up a coffee cup from his desk, and drank from it for a few seconds. He set it down, cleared his throat, and squinted his bug eyes. "But that is not today's priority. Today's priority is this conceptual language you've asked for, this new way of understanding yourself." He paused again, examining Wishnasky's face. "Have you ever heard the distinction between Universe and Cosmos?"

"No. I've always assumed the two words were synonymous."

"This is a distinction you need to know. According to it, 'Universe' describes all existing matter—stars and planets, humans and giraffes, protons and neutrons. Everything material, ruled by physics and mathematics, biology and chemistry. The domains of science. All things more or less visible."

"All right."

"'Cosmos' is different. 'Cosmos' includes all of nature but subsumes it within a spiritual reality, ruled over by a God or gods, inhabited above and below by angels and demons, focused in pivotal ways on human beings as mediators between spirit and flesh. That is the realm you are coming to discover."

"I don't know about that angel and demon part."

"Don't interrupt. Now, the Universe is mostly void: for every star or planet, there are many more billion light years of empty space. 'Cosmos' is mostly full: one's deity is everywhere, and there's hardly a square inch of space that's not replete with good and evil spirits, vying for priority. Living in the Universe, one's characteristic pleasure is the feeling of enormous freedom and one's malady is deep loneliness and even despair; living in Cosmos, one's strength is the certainty of significance and purpose, one's malady is a sense of unworthiness and sin. For most of history, humanity lived in the Cosmos, but starting in the 18th century, more and more people have lived in the Universe. You yourself have made a transit in the opposite direction: it was in the Universe, not the Cosmos, that you lived and wrote your first works. Naturally you were subject to fits of confusion, despondency and not least, exaggerated narcissism. After all, ego is one of the few certainties in Universe."

"I'm trying to work on that ego thing."

"Of course you are: in the Universe, the message is 'Every man for himself,' in the Cosmos, the message is "Do unto others as you would have them do to yourself." If, as you say, you're beginning to notice the oppressed and abandoned, it is only because in the Cosmos, this has always been an urgent duty."

"Was I fully in the Universe before the Camus book? Didn't I have tendencies in the other direction?"

"Think for a moment about your novels. When a writer like you believes himself to live in the Universe, he writes *No One From Nowhere* and *Craters of the Spirit*, in which vast spaces loom above and beneath every isolated character and one is always a step away from annihilation. When such a writer changes his domicile to the Cosmos, he writes novels like the one you tell me you are engaged in, where hope, love, and compassion are more to the point. I'm not surprised that you feel off-balance while in the midst of such a transition. The gusts in the Cosmos are not a bit like the gales in the Universe."

"What about you, Ion?" said Wishnasky. "You claim not to believe in God. Is it this enigmatic Mind that allows you to live in the Cosmos?"

"Precisely," said Ion. "Mind functions for me as God does for you. And is quite as demanding that I devote myself to my fellow humans. Please do not now disparage it, as you have shown a tendency to do."

"All right, I'll give it a break. But what happens next? Do I ever get comfortable in the Cosmos, or do I always remain aware that there's an alternative habitation—which, by the way, afforded me not a few pleasures over the years."

"You face three dangers: first, that you will confuse your few, faltering steps toward the Cosmos as having brought you the whole distance. Second, that you will think your new orientation frees you from the shocks and distresses of Fortune. Last, that you will feel yourself superior to those souls still tossed about in a tempestuous Universe. Avoid these errors, and you may enter more happily into your new haven. Fall into one or more, and your deity, whatever you call it, may correct you with a jolt."

"Ion, I've known you for over a decade, ever since my marriage failed, but you've never confided this Universe/Cosmos distinction to me before. Why not? Why'd you hold back?"

"When your problem was your marriage, I focused on your marriage. Now, you're ready for a different teaching, and of course I'm happy to oblige you. As always, the right solution seeks out the right problem."

"Are there other things you're not telling me because you think I'm not ready yet? Are you holding back on all sorts of gems?"

"You would find them irrelevant, if not nonsensical. At such time as you are ready to recognize a jewel as a jewel, I will introduce such into our transactions."

"I want 'em now. All your jewels. I don't want to wait. Sock me another."

"I would no more do so than a medical doctor would waste an antibiotic on a man suffering from a virus. I am not so obtuse."

"Ion, please, one more jewel! Dazzle me! I'm your perfect audience!"

"Either we return to the subject of our therapy or I end the session. What more do you want to say about this woman Andrea? If she's not, as previous women were to you, a conquest to be made, can you go even further to see her as navigating the same currents as you, as a feeling, thinking product of a unique combination of history, biology, parents and peers? Can you respect her not only as a sexual being but as a precious free will testing reality with her every action? In short, can you believe her to be as complex as yourself?"

"That's asking a lot, Ion."

"I know that. But what's your answer? As you've moved toward the Cosmos, have you moved toward this?"

47.

HIS NEXT DATE WITH ANDREA was mostly of her devising. She wanted to walk with him through the Harvard campus where he could tell her about his college years—a big clue to his personality, she said—and she could point out various architectural features he might have missed as an undergraduate. "But I want you to tell me the meal, not the menu," she said. "What it was really like to go to school there, not the glossy brochure stuff. And I'll do the same on the buildings: their real impact, not the adulatory bunk from the tour guides."

On the drive to Brookline, he couldn't help but wonder what her apartment would look like—did the Orthodox decorate differently? So, when she opened the door on the ground floor of a three-story, yellow brick building, he half-expected to find something foreign, Middle Eastern. Of course, he was wrong: inside was a spacious American living room shaped like a hexagon, with a built-in bench at one bay window and lots of plants and flowers along the other walls. Even though the sun was setting, there was still lots of light coming into the apartment, and the effect was magical. In the background, Joni Mitchell was singing—something jazzy that he didn't recognize—and Andrea herself was dressed in a lovely blue-and-white print blouse and a deep blue skirt and low heels, and the smile on her face when she asked him inside was notably genuine.

"Nice place," he said. "As lovely as you."

"That's sweet. Come on in. We have time for wine or coffee."

"Wine, I think. Kosher, I assume?"

"That's right. But not the synagogue stuff. Israeli. And wonderful. And the music on my CD player is one of those albums you ought to know: *Wild Things Run Fast,* by you know who. When she was still in full flight from her folkie past."

She walked into the kitchen and he used the time to look at the art on her living room walls. There was a poster from a Bonnard show at the Museum of Fine Arts, a framed photograph of a zebra nuzzling its child, and on one wall a group of photographs showing Andrea and her family at different ages. He noticed that all the boys and men wore yarmulkes, and her mother almost always had a scarf covering her hair. He inspected the pictures that showed Andrea as a child, and he thought: *she was beautiful even then.*

"Touring the museum, I see." She had walked in with two half-full wineglasses.

"Pretty nice family dynamics."

"Three brothers and me. And my parents trying to keep the apocalypse from breaking out. Not always possible when four siblings have to coexist."

"I'm an only child. I always wondered what it would be like to have brothers and sisters."

"You gain a real respect for privacy."

"I'll bet. Shall we toast?"

"Sure." She handed him his glass. "What should we toast to?"

"To bridges across cultures."

"Are we *that* different, you and I?"

"For the last few months, everything's been different. I'm making so many changes, I'm getting windburn."

"To bridges in general, then," she said. "The Mass. Ave Bridge. The Longfellow Bridge. The Golden Gate and the Brooklyn Bridge."

"*L'chaim.* Right?"

"That's right. *L'chaim.*"

They drank, and Wishnasky thought: *this is a stable, generous woman. Not contentious like Vanessa, not volatile like Barbara.* He worried for a moment that the patriarchal tendencies of Orthodox Judaism might have created an Andrea who was submissive in the old-fashioned way, who saw herself as a helpmeet rather than a full human being. But then he thought of their interactions up to that point and the anxiety dissipated. An architect. A modern female. There was nothing backward about her.

They sat with their kosher wine and tried to get to know each other better. She talked about her job and its constant demands on her patience, and he explained how he was trying to finish his first hopeful, life-affirming novel. They talked about Boston—the beauty of Marlborough Street, the concrete desert of Government Center, the unreality of the South End after a fresh snow, the comforting sight of the Custom House Tower so near to tourist-infested Quincy Market. Andrea told him that she'd chosen the neighborhood of her apartment because it was only a short walk to synagogue—no driving for the Orthodox on *Shabbat*—and he said he'd like her to see his cozy house in Newton Corner. Then it was time to go into Cambridge. They walked out to his car and twenty minutes later found a parking place near Kirkland House and Harvard Square.

"Let's start here," said Andrea as they reached the Out-of-Town Newsstand in the center of the Square. "The menu says it's the pulsing heart of the Harvard experience. So what's the real deal?"

"If your sleeping quarters border this world-renowned neighborhood," said Wishnasky, "as mine happened to do, it means squealing buses at all times of the night and traffic noise so constant that you want to scream for a little quiet. Coming from a tranquil neighborhood in Lexington, I was utterly unprepared. In retrospect, I'm amazed that I lived with it for a full year."

"Architecturally, there's nothing very special here," she said. "Those red brick buildings were constructed in the 1920s, if I remember correctly, and had no point except to mesh with the existing Harvard architecture. Let's walk into the Yard."

They passed through an open gateway and Wishnasky pointed out Straus Hall, where he'd lived freshman year. "Menu and meal," said Andrea.

"Menu: in these ivied halls, one begins a journey that will ultimately lead him into the honored company of Harvard scholars, ready to take on the whole world with sagacity and a sense of history."

"And the meal?"

"Intense, overwhelming sexual loneliness. Pining for women, yearning for them, aching. On the plus side: making friendships to last a lifetime. And smoking a lot of weed. But oh, the loneliness."

"Weren't freshman women available?"

"If they were good-looking, they made sure to hook up with upperclassmen. We first-years were the lowest of the low."

Andrea giggled. "All right, over there is Massachusetts Hall, designed in 1720 by John Leverett and Benjamin Wadsworth. Architecture: Georgian style, symmetrical and modest. I love this building: sober, thinkable, solid. One of those cases where the meal matches the menu. Let's keep walking."

And so it continued: they strolled through the Yard, then out to narrow Quincy Street with its modernist Carpenter Center for the Arts. "Menu:" said Andrea, "the only building in the United States designed by Le Corbusier, and therefore amazingly successful. Meal: it looks like a grand piano that's smashed into a stone wall. It's horrible." At Andrea's urging, Wishnasky recounted his favorite memories of Harvard: friends he'd made, professors who thrilled him, the excitement of meeting great writers and scholars, all the marijuana he'd smoked, and his pride at editing the fabled literary magazine. And also the underside: virtual anonymity in classes with hundreds of students, professors who reiterated their latest bestseller and called it a lecture, and again and again the terrible loneliness of needing a lover and not finding one—at least till senior year, when he started dating the woman who would eventually become his wife. Andrea, meanwhile, disclosed herself through her aesthetic: a healthy interest in the traditional, but a huge respect for the best modern buildings from the massive Gund Hall Graduate School of Design (architect John Andrews) to the high-rise Japanese-inspired William James psychology building (Minoru Yamasaki) and the sprawling, ultra-progressive Science Center (Josep Lluis Sert). Being Orthodox, it seemed, didn't stop her from loving contemporary shapes or recognizing beauty in its most unexpected forms.

When they had walked as far as the Divinity School, Andrea said, "Were you religious at all during your four years here? What did you believe? And how did Harvard affect it?"

"Religion just didn't figure," he said. "And even worse in a way, neither did ethics. What I've learned of Judaism recently, the insistence on righteousness and upright living—I mean, it's ironic that Harvard began as a school to train ministers, and 400 years later it didn't even advise you on how not to slaughter your roommates. It was all Athens and no Jerusalem: what to know, not how to live. If I were designing a curriculum for the future leaders of the planet, certainly ethics would be a requirement, at least for a semester. Or comparative religion, or anything that might suggest that right living is a crucial topic to imbibe. Which one doesn't acquire just from breathing."

Finally, after he and Andrea, heading back to the Square, stepped into a striking, mostly-glass library building on Mt. Auburn Street—interior designed, she said, by Samuel Anderson, one of the more imaginative of contemporary museum architects—they took a breather in a tiny coffee shop.

Over his café Americano and her café au lait, he asked her about women's position in Orthodoxy.

"It's far from ideal," she said. "But on the other hand, you're told so often that the key to Jewish survival is the home, you get a feeling of real importance. Because the woman famously runs the home. It's a curious royalty, but it's royalty."

"But don't you feel yourself a second-class citizen in some ways? I mean, if I understand correctly, Orthodox women can't be rabbis, can't be called to read from the *Torah*, aren't counted toward a *minyan*. Doesn't it bother you at all?"

"It bothers some of my friends, who talk a lot about the need to amend Jewish law. Or who persuaded our rabbi to let us women study the *Talmud* together. But I guess I'm not a firebrand. I'm too tired after work to attend a lecture on Tractate *Ketubot*. I just want to cuddle up on my sofa and read a celebrity memoir, like Sally Field's or Katie Couric's. Does that answer disappoint you?"

"I'm just surprised. If I were a woman, I'd want as much equality religiously as I expected politically."

"You don't realize what you'd be up against. When the Orthodox talk about tradition, they don't mean fifty years ago, they mean 3,000. The woman who breaks through that barrier is going to have to be some kind of genius."

They walked back to Wishnasky's car and headed back to Brookline. After a few minutes, Wishnasky had an impulse to reach over with his right hand and hold Andrea's. She didn't resist. He told her he was enjoying the time with her far more than he had a right to, knowing her so little. She said, "Me too," and squeezed his hand. They drove the rest of the distance that way, and then he was on her street, in front of her apartment.

"Shall I come in?" he asked, not shutting off the engine.

"I don't think so," she said with a look of apology. "But I'd like to see you again. And if you don't mind, I'd like to read one of your novels. Maybe the third one."

"I'll give you a copy next time I see you," he said. "But just remember: the guy who wrote that desperate thing was a lot different from this guy. This guy's trying to follow a better inspiration."

"I'll remember that."

"Good night, then."

"Good night." She squeezed his hand again and popped out of the passenger side.

As she walked alone to her front door, Wishnasky felt embarrassed to have fantasized something more sensual. Maybe Barbara was right: maybe in ways he didn't realize, he had compelled her to think that the evening would have to end with sex. Well, he'd be more circumspect this time. He'd keep his distance until the woman had clearly signaled her desire, and even then he'd move slowly.

He drove home hoping that one day Andrea would desire him.

48.

As usual, a few hours' work had taken days. But this was it: *Traveler in the Abyss* was definitely, decisively finished. Wishnasky looked at the three o'clock sun from his study window and felt relief, pride, satisfaction. He looked on the bottom of his computer monitor and read: Page 190. 74,971 words. He could hardly believe it.

He called Roland. As usual, Roland barked "Hello" as if he were being disturbed by an IRS agent.

"It's Tristan," Wishnasky said. "I've finished the novel. I'm going to send it to Darryl Kamfort in three minutes. And then to you."

"I'm terrified," said Roland. "Did you change your mind about the religious angle?"

"That's the core of the book now."

"Too bad! Awful! Miserable! Kiss goodbye the readership it took you three books to build. I've warned you what the market's like for religious novels."

"I know what you say and I know what I feel. Call it intellectual honesty. And I think people will show themselves hungry for just this sort of thing."

"You're committing literary suicide if this book is what you say it is."

"Look, Roland, are you saying that you want me to find another agent?"

"Don't send it to Darryl yet. Please. Let me read it first. I'll start right away; then we can talk."

"You're not going to change my satisfaction with what I've done here."

"Don't jump to conclusions. Maybe it's not too late for revisions."

"I've already revised it a thousand times."

"Let me read it. Then I'll call you."

Roland clicked off and Wishnasky went to his computer and sent the document. Then he stared at the computer screen. There it was: over 70,000 words in the service of a perspective that to him, at least, was revolutionary. 70,000 words that he hoped would be as palliative as the words in his earlier novels had been caustic. He felt relieved and only slightly apprehensive: Roland couldn't be right.

There was one thing more: he bowed his head and prayed to God that *Traveler* would be a great success, bringing consolation to its readers and proving that it was possible to write an unapologetically religious book that was also an artistic accomplishment. The prayer over, he sat back in his chair and breathed deeply. Finally finished.

It would be right to celebrate. He rose, went to the kitchen cabinet, found an unopened bottle of rum from the St. Lucia visit (so nice to be able to think of Vanessa without pain), opened and poured himself a drink. He sipped a little, then a little more. This was a fine moment—or was supposed to be. He took another drink and walked over to the comfortable armchair in the living room. He sank into it, feeling confident, even smug. *You don't have time to waste.* No, he didn't. So he'd acted. At some personal expense. And the result? A novel he could stand by.

He closed his eyes and basked in the good feeling. Finishing past novels, he'd felt a glorious elevation, as if he'd raised Tristan Wishnasky to a higher level of existential being, of personal *virtu.* But this felt different: for the first time in his life, he'd turned his talent as a writer toward the service of others, of all those in need of affirmation and hope. And the effect was a joy related to the gladness of serving the hungry at the Horn of Plenty, or sending his tithe to UNICEF or Oxfam. Surely, God would reward him for such a change; surely, the life to come would offer more delights, unexpected windfalls, happy coincidences, unexpected triumphs. He'd read the message in the Camus book and he hadn't failed to act. A blessed future was the only possibility.

He called Andrea and proudly announced his good news. She was delighted. She made him promise that she, too, could read it soon.

Life was looking up.

49.

"Either you are inconceivably stupid," said the voice on the phone, "or you are incurably insane. You can't send this to Darryl. You must tear it up and start again."

Wishnasky had been sorting through mail and paying bills when the call came in. He had just written a check for several hundred dollars' worth of electricity, and he'd been daydreaming about the royalties from *Traveler.*

"I'm not retracting anything," he said. "It's what I believe; it's what I had to write. If you don't care for it, too bad, it's what I stand by."

"I know exactly what to tell them," said Roland. "Your father had a heart attack. Your lovely girlfriend, Vanessa, walked out on you and turned you into a thick lump of peanut butter. You were slammed again and again and you were too punch-drunk to write responsibly. I'll get you a new deadline, two years from now. And you can write the book you were born for: about life at the bottom of the Grand Canyon. In the lowest valley of the Marianas Trench."

"This is the book I was born for, Roland."

"You know that I love you. You're an egomaniac, it's true, and your capacity for self-righteousness has been a problem from the start. But still, your work has always spoken to me. *No One From Nowhere* made me cry. *Craters of the Spirit,* despite a certain overly-conscious literary quality, touched me deeply. But this—this is *tripe.* This is wishful thinking, kitsch, and optimistic garbage. You've made a little place for yourself in our literary landscape, but this will blast you into the gutter, into the landfill. Let me do you a favor and ignore that you sent it to me. Let me tell Darryl Kamfort, that jackal, that hyena, that you've suffered tragedies and reversals and with life in the balance, you have no choice but to break deadline. Allow me to save your reputation. The alternative is unthinkable."

Wishnasky heard something in the distance: an ambulance siren. Warning Roland or warning him? He wasn't sure.

"I'm standing by it, Roland."

"The critics will eviscerate you, claw your heart from your chest cavity and leave your bloody, mangled carcass for the buzzards."

"I'm standing by it."

"You will lose half your readers when they see the reviews, another third through word of mouth. Only the crackpots will admire you. The crackpots will believe they are looking in a mirror."

"I gotta go. Roland. Nice talking with you."

"I tried to stop you. I warned you from the start."

"I'll remember that, Roland. Gotta run, gotta send it on to Darryl now."

"You have amputated your career. You have self-mutilated. You desperately need help."

"I'm hanging up."

"It's not too late to turn back."

"You're wrong, Roland. Goodbye."

50.

IT WOULD BE WEEKS before he heard from Darryl Kamfort. So he utilized the interim focused on his next goal: to romance Andrea so successfully that she would want him as a lover. He called her every night, accompanied her to the Boston Lyric Opera, the American Repertory Theatre, and to several kosher restaurants. His pursuit didn't interfere with his hours at the Horn of Plenty or at Hebrew class, but more than anything, the campaign to win Andrea's trust occupied his consciousness. He was becoming used to her lithe form and easy amiability. He had to struggle not to imagine her nude in his bed.

Her Jewish credentials were pristine. She did everything by the book, from the food she ate to the charity she gave to lighting the *Sabbath* candles twenty minutes before sundown every Friday. She attended an Orthodox synagogue in Brookline every Saturday morning, and prayed the prayers in Hebrew, understanding every word. She even took a regular *Shabbat* walk after synagogue and a *Shabbat* nap promptly at 4 p.m. One Sunday he went with her to a kosher supermarket near the synagogue, and he was impressed by how many people there knew her, asked about her parents. She was apparently treasured also by her colleagues at Dan Hibbert's office—except by Hibbert himself, who made a rule of not smiling on any of his employees. Wishnasky visited her at her work desk one afternoon and marveled at her ability to create three-dimensional computer models of condominiums and apartments. Most notably, he respected her refusal to speak ill of people—an offense that she called *lashon ha-ra*, evil tongue—and how she tried to find the best in even the least appealing of her acquaintances.

On the other hand, their sensual life advanced at a snail's pace. They had kissed, finally, but anything beyond that was strictly out-of-bounds, and the one time that Wishnasky tried gently to touch her breast, she'd grabbed his hand at the wrist and sent it back to his side. Julie had said that Andrea wasn't a virgin, but there was nonetheless something virginal in the way she gave him notice that his advances were unwanted. *All right,* he told himself, she was on a special timetable, and he'd just have to wait it out. But deciding was easier than doing. He ached for Andrea. She didn't seem to notice.

One evening, at last, something changed. They had a dinner date at a Hungarian kosher restaurant in Chestnut Hill and Andrea looked ravishing. She was wearing a gray overcoat—it had been raining all day—over a dark blue dress with thin pink stripes and she'd never seemed so magnetic. Once they were seated—they had to wait twenty minutes, even with a reservation—she reached across the table to take his hand.

"When will your novel be published?" she said. "Aren't you impatient?"

"I learned not to be years ago. I learned that anywhere from six months to a year-and-a-half might pass between turning in a manuscript and seeing the book on sale. There's just no point in getting too antsy."

A server came to their table and asked if they'd like drinks. Wishnasky ordered a bottle of Merlot and Andrea smiled affirmatively.

"Now tell me about you," said Wishnasky. "On Thursday when I called you, you said you were in Milton and too busy to talk. What was that all about?"

"We're designing a shopping mall," she said. "My boss wants the mall to be punctuated by decorative rest areas and an indoor playground, but the owner sees every available square foot as purely commercial. I was chosen to speak for the firm because I'm a woman. So yes, a cynical choice. I think the idea was, when a woman says to put playgrounds in a mall, it's instantly more persuasive."

"Did it work? Did you persuade?"

"I don't know. What would you say if the choice were between an extra business paying rent and an indoor playground making mothers and toddlers happy to have a rest from shopping?"

"I'd go with the playground."

"Exactly. By the way, do you *want* kids? I've never asked you your image of a family."

He didn't miss the smooth transition. And what it portended.

"I'd like a couple of kids," he said. "Maybe a boy and a girl. Anything more and I don't think any one of them would get enough attention."

"Older children can be taught to look after younger children," said Andrea. "I'd like at least four kids, two and two. I love the idea of a house with ankle-biters everywhere, lipstick on Barbie and the hamster loose in the kitchen."

"My ex-wife wanted a bunch of kids. We agreed to put it off till we had more money. By the time we got the money, we were divorced. Irony knows best."

"You never talk about your ex-wife. Is that your style or is it too painful?"

"It's not painful in the least. What do you want to know?"

"How it ended. Or maybe you told me."

"I vaguely alluded to it. I loved her at first, wanted to spend every minute with her. But for her, time kind of stopped the moment we said our vows. It was as if marriage sedated her, left her stranded in time. After a couple of years, I was a couple of years older and she was the same age as on our wedding day. Then three years, then four. Eventually, I felt like I had no traveling companion."

"Did you tell her that?"

"You know, I didn't. That's my one regret about that marriage. I was so sure that it was dead, it didn't occur to me to try to save it. And that was wrong. I could have shown more initiative."

"Will you always tell me if we're growing apart, Tristan? You won't just leave me stranded, will you?"

He was surprised at the emotion in her voice. "No, of course not. I've learned better by now."

"Let's look at the menus."

For the rest of the dinner, he was conscious of a change in Andrea's attitude. Had he finally passed some test, shown her enough fidelity, gotten beyond some defenses? If so, he didn't know how. But all through dinner, Andrea was vibrant, vivacious, exuding warmth and satisfaction beyond anything he'd seen before. What had happened?

After dinner, he drove her back to her apartment and slid over the front seat to kiss her goodbye. As always, he said, "Should I come in?"

"Yes," she said, smiling. "Tonight you can come in."

In her apartment, she put on Joni Mitchell's *Ladies of the Canyon* and offered him more wine. They sat together on her sofa and she explained the background to many of the songs: how "Willy'" was written for Mitchell's lover, Graham Nash, and "The Arrangement" was commissioned by a movie director who chose not to use it; how "Rainy Night Man" was written for Leonard Cohen, and "Woodstock" was penned as compensation for the fact that Mitchell couldn't be at that festival. Then, they talked about the things they wanted to do together in the spring. She wanted to drive down to Newport and see the oldest synagogue in the United States; he wanted to drive up to Montreal and practice the French he'd been losing little by little since leaving college. She wanted to investigate the art exhibits at Mass MOCA, the contemporary museum in the western part of the state; he wanted to rent kayaks and discover where the Charles River went after it left Cambridge. "There's one thing else I'd like," she said. "And I don't want to wait till spring."

"Oh yeah? What's that?"

"I'd like to make love with you."

He couldn't believe what he'd heard. But it was true: the change he'd been waiting for had finally come.

He reached for her hand; she gave it. He looked into her eyes, which were wet with emotion and vulnerability and the word "yes."

And then he saw some other things.

He saw that she was offering not her body but her soul.

He saw that she was offering not her now but her future.

He saw that she was offering not just sex but profound, lasting, authentic love.

And he knew that he didn't love her back.

He liked her, admired her, valued her. He wanted her, craved her, saw more goodness in her life than he'd known in most other human beings he'd met, and found that goodness sexually magnetic. Inside and out, everything about her was captivating.

But he also knew that that agreement, that subliminal congruence that had to exist between a man and a woman if their connection were to survive, wasn't there with her. Not at all. On a checklist of personal attributes, she was everything he could ask for. On the deeper, non-rational level, he was unmoved, untransformed. At the restaurant earlier that evening, he'd noticed three or four women who made his pulse quicken; but not Andrea. Yes, he cared for her. But the compulsion, the mysterious urgency just wasn't there.

And now she was looking at him with so much tenderness and vulnerability that to accept her proposal would be the rankest villainy.

"I can't," he said quietly. "I'm not a thief. And I don't love you like that."

"I don't understand," she said, trying to smile. "What's wrong? Tristan, I'm ready."

"I'd like to know you all my life," he said, taking both her hands in his. "I'd like to keep up with your every move from this moment till we're ninety.

But, for some reason, I don't love you and to go to bed with you would be dishonest. I'm sorry. I didn't know till now."

Tears came to her eyes and she removed her hands from his.

"I think you should go," she said. "I don't think you should be here."

"No, you're right." He stood up. "But I'll call you later tonight. When I get home, just to say how much you honestly mean to me."

"Not tonight," she said. "A few days. Please. Please go now. Please, Tristan."

He took one last look, felt an urge to kiss her, decided against it, reasoned that he shouldn't say more—and walked out her front door. He felt a pressure in his chest which he realized was prelude to his own tears.

He climbed into his car, thinking that he didn't recognize himself. All his adult life he'd been a man who would jump at the chance to sleep with a willing woman if he found her sexually interesting. To instead be so honorable struck him as uncharacteristic and oppressive.

But then he remembered the look in Andrea's eyes and understood it wasn't honor at all. It was simple decency. One didn't exploit a person one cared for.

All the way home he was in a daze, crying, then not, then crying again. When he entered his house and sat down in the dark living room, he cried for Andrea, whom he'd let down, and for himself, who was lonelier than ever. When would the learning finally stop, when would he finally reach port? He considered calling Andrea, asking if he might reverse himself. But he knew he couldn't do that, not without the most extreme hypocrisy. Instead, he'd have to live with this new person he was becoming.

Oh, this idol-smashing was rough when the idol was oneself.

PART THREE

51.

PART THREE

EIGHTEEN MONTHS PASSED. The book was published.

And the reviews were withering.

The New York Times couldn't hate the book enough:

> What can you say when a clear-sighted, even visionary author puts on his rose-colored sunglasses and refutes every observation that once made him indispensable? This is the question a reader of Tristan Wishnasky's *Traveler in the Abyss* has to face on almost every page of this feckless, regrettable wish-fulfillment of a novel. Mr. Wishnasky, whose previous work limned the shape and substance of our Western desolation, has apparently suffered too much Reality Fatigue and has withdrawn into a religious bubble wherein all intractable questions are conveniently answered with God, prayer, and the love of a good woman. That the first two of these solutions, at least, are unlikely to persuade many in our post-Nietzschean age is apparently of no importance to a faith-befuddled scribe anxious to trumpet his new devotion. Farewell, then, to our intrepid *No One From Nowhere* (Mr. Wishnasky's first and much more perspicacious novel), and hello to just another Enthusiast behind a pulpit. Those of us still facing the great Nothingness will apparently have to go it alone.

> The subject of this short novel (weighing in at under 200 pages) is Edward Ozono, a former computer mogul whose career hits a desperate low before Chapter One begins, and who has lost his wife to divorce, his family to resentment, his income to unforgiving capitalism, and his hopes to a Silicon Valley so treacherous, there's nowhere to go but deeper degradation. Dazed and unshaven, about to stumble into the Pacific Ocean, Ozono is spotted by Yvonne Pardoner

(get it?), a childhood friend from Hebrew School days who invites him into her car and out to her conveniently congenial bungalow. Once there, she proves herself a veritable (and oh-so-cliché) angel of mercy. She feeds him and washes him, binds up his emotional wounds, and teaches him that a loving God wants him happy and back in the saddle. It's these ultra-religious passages that cloy the most: after all the organized murder of the last two world wars, after the desolation caused by AIDS and the devastating famines in Africa, to be told that a compassionate Deity is superintending the earth is hardly more credible than it was to Voltaire after the earthquake in Lisbon. But Mr. Wishnasky has seen a light, and he's insistent that his readers, too, bask in its effulgence. So, we get page after page on God's will for human happiness, on the earth as a testing-ground with, yes, rewards in the afterlife, and on the free exercise of Good Works as a panacea for all humanity's woes. By novel's end, when Edward Ozono takes on a new position at a fledgling software concern (not a spoiler: no one who gets past the first thirty pages will have any doubt as to the finale), he's rejuvenated, revitalized, and, as the religious would have it, redeemed. We can be sure that he has nowhere to go but to the heaven on earth that all good children enjoy before graduating to the higher paradise.

No doubt we should be forgiving of Mr. Wishnasky's metamorphosis. After all, in his first three novels, he steered closer to the edge than most of his colleagues ever dared, and if finally he was terrified and driven distinctly in reverse, still he had a good run. Now readers will have to turn elsewhere for their glimpses of that debacle Walter Benjamin wrote about, the one that looks to us humans like one tragedy after the next, but to the eternally retreating angel of history as a single, ever-growing conflagration. Yvonne Pardoner may tell Ozono, "There's an all-benevolent God watching over you," but those of us buffeted by modernity's manifold horrors need a more credible fiction than that one. *Traveler in the Abyss* can be tolerated as a genuine *cri de coeur*; but it's a hundred and fifty years too late. After the Somme and Auschwitz and Hiroshima and Rwanda, it's not likely that moderns will find much comfort in an old-fashioned house of worship, of whatever denomination. There's napalm in the air; there's what Nicholson Baker calls "human smoke." It'll take more than a look at Scripture to give us consolation—or direction.

The review in the *Boston Globe* was scathing in a different way:

Hey, Martha, let's see what Tristan Wishnasky is up to in his latest novel, *Traveler in the Abyss*. You remember Wishnasky: he made a huge literary kerfuffle with his nihilist bleakfest *Craters of the Spirit*, and if that didn't drive you to incurable despair, there were always his previous Tomb-y Tomes, *No One From Nowhere* and *The Anguish of the Condemned*. But like post-*Wasteland* T. S. Eliot, Wishnasky has now beat a retreat to the precincts of faith, leaving the rest of us in this indifferent universe even lonelier than yesterday. Can it be? Can *triste* Tristan really be revisioned as a rabbi? Consider the plot: an amoral Jewish computer tycoon, ruined by smarter, hungrier men, abandoned by pitiless wife and ungrateful children, finds himself with just pennies and not even a rusty wristable razor to his defamed name. Before you can say Deus Ex Machina, an old school chum appears and whisks our mopey mogul to her comfortable pad, where she offers an old-fashioned hot meal, a warm body, and not nearly least, some tepid old-time religion. Our exec, in no shape to critique his racy rescuer (beggars and choosers, you know), quickly transforms into an avid student of *Torah*, doer of good deeds, and believer in a deity who has a thing for losers from Geekland. Trading in his pre-collapse ego for a post-collapse soul (yes, Wishnasky several times uses the word "soul"), our prince begins what we're clearly to construe as his climb back to eminence (off Jacob's ladder, you ministering angels: here comes Intel Isaiah). The ending's all too predictable, but by then we're so joyful to be finished with this screed, we welcome it like a revelation.

Earth to Wishnasky: we tried it centuries ago, and the blood's still on our digits. Or wasn't it religion that slaughtered your confreres in the Crusades, thousands of helpless women as witches, 3,000 innocents in the Twin Towers? From your comfortable keyboard, piety may look therapeutic, but in this test tube called Gaia, that chemical's one hundred percent cyanide. Which leads me to muse: What do you foresee for us nonbelievers? Perdition? Eternal torment? If digital man Ozono's hitched himself to the celestial wagon, what about us decent, unfaithful folk who surrender our seats on the T to exhausted old biddies, who give to CARE and Save The Children but still can't manage to believe in a celestial Absentee Landlord and His reign of error? Ninety or so pages into Wishnasky's ardent apologia, he has Yvonne Pardoner inform credulous Ozono, "God wants people to search for Him." Oh yeah? And what about us bozos who've done our best efforts avoiding Him like the plague? We pitched out our Bible the day Galileo recanted reality, the day they incinerated Giordano Bruno, the night they strangled William Tyndale. Now our search is like John Lennon's: to imagine a world free of fanatics. Strip a few believers of their *keffiyas* and maybe their suicide belts will follow.

But back to literature and its discontents: there are problems in your plot, Mr. High Priest Come-Lately. You posit your Jewish genius as a dyed-in-the-wool infidel and then have him transmogrified into a Hebrew-loving Habakkuk before your fantasy is two-thirds finished. Is this his haste or yours? You put not-yet-divorced Ozono in bed with unmarried Yvonne, and not a word about adultery, fornication, or all those other sins your deity surely will slap them with come Judgment Day. Is this kosher? And speaking of judgment, what about all those transgressions which Ozono supposedly devised during his unregenerate top-of-the-heap years? Did he win a Get-Out-Of-Hell card when he rolled his ivories on Pardoner's futon? In other words, your WouldbeGood Book has holes the size of the Sea of Galilee, and even an atheist like this critic can't help but find them unswimmable. You had me—not to mention thousands of others—when your beat was the Great Absence.

In sum: *Traveler in the Abyss* is an ineloquent sermon only the choir could love, and even they might harbor doubts. Glad to know Wishnasky's found God; but no, we don't want to hear about it. We empty sky types have other tasks: like peering through the dark and dressing against the chill.

There were several other reviews of a similar tenor in Chicago, Los Angeles, Washington, and a very few—from small, suburban newspapers—that were cautiously, even respectfully positive. But the journals whose words could sell books were uniformly skeptical, and Wishnasky prepared himself for a drubbing on Amazon, at Barnes & Noble, at Books-A-Million. There would be no Critics Circle Award for this volume. As for sales, well, maybe there were consumers who didn't read book reviews.

Roland called on the morning of the *Times* debacle.

"Well," he said. "Did you see it?"

"I saw it. And I know: you told me so. You don't have to rub it in."

"We're switching into rescue mode. It's possible the religious audience is bigger than I predicted. We're not going to assume the worst."

"Roland, I know you too well to believe you're being authentic. Go on and say it: I'm an idiot. I don't understand publishing."

"If you can imagine me saying it, there's no point in me doing so. Now, here's your strategy for the next few months: I want you to shout out your conversion as if it were the most urgent thing in the world."

"I don't know that I've had a conversion."

"Very charming: you're so drunk, you can't remember picking up the glass. By the way, the grapevine has it that Oona Callahan has been picked by the *New York Review* to do their demolition. Expect the worst. She hates religion."

"So does everybody, it seems."

"Not in Atlanta, or Birmingham, or Baton Rouge for that matter. I expect your sales in the South will lift your spirits. Through the whole Bible Belt in fact. You're going to make a lot of new friends with this book."

"Roland, just say what you mean: I've screwed up royally and my one hope is that a few rednecks will be curious."

"I want you to embrace the religious readers. The *Left Behind* crowd. The zealots who bought *The Shack* and *A Course in Miracles*. Most Jewish readers are too secular for this sort of thing, but the Christian market is huge, add the New Agers, you could be a star. There's even a self-help angle. I'm not giving up on you."

"You mean I've bungled so monumentally, you're sending a Get Well card."

"You've made a small miscalculation."

"I've ruined my career. Go on, this politeness is unbearable."

"I would never kick a man when he's down. I'm not so insensitive."

"You are and you would and I can hear everything you're not accusing me of."

"Then there's no need me saying it. Call me when you get to the city and we'll have lunch at a kosher restaurant. I'm assuming you're strictly kosher these days."

"I've been experimenting with it. It's not total yet."

"All right, I'll keep that in mind. But Tristan, you'll get through this. There will be other novels."

"So this isn't goodbye?"

"One doesn't run from a smash-up. Think of me as your First Responder."

"I stand by it, Roland. Even if the whole world's against me, I stand by that book."

"Wonderful. You take just that tone whenever challenged: desperately obstinate. It should stimulate curiosity."

"Thanks for trying to sound upbeat."

"You're going to survive this."

"I'll call you."

"It's a pothole. You'll get over it. Drive on."

52.

HIS PUBLISHER, tellingly, had not arranged a book tour, so Wishnasky used his own contacts in the Boston area and New York in an effort to publicize his problematic new volume. His first appearance was on WGBH-TV; he arrived at their Brighton studios a half hour early, met the "Book Talk" host, Flora Vittorini, and was cordially guided onto a soundstage. A technician pinned a mic to his lapel, and led him to an easy chair across from matronly Flora as the intro music played and she briefly introduced him. Then the questions began.

He was happy to discover no hostility in her queries, only what seemed like real curiosity. When Flora asked him how he came to return to his Jewish roots, he didn't talk about the words in the Camus book, or the answered prayer for his father. He offered instead something that had recently occurred to him: "I was a success," he said. "I'd had three acclaimed novels, one movie deal, and a great relationship with a woman, I was soaring." Then he paused for effect. "You know, Flora, I think I wanted Someone to thank. It was just the opposite of the hero in my new book: I was on top, I was a winner, and I just knew that pure chance wasn't the force that had brought me there. So I said, 'Thank you.' I said, 'I'm grateful.' And I've been saying it ever since."

The next interview, at WBUR-FM on Commonwealth Avenue, only lasted fifteen minutes before it segued into a long segment for listeners' calls. There were several anti-religious rants, including one from a man who'd been raped by a priest when he was a boy and now assumed that all faiths must be covering up equivalent outrages. But even when fielding the angriest callers—"I loved your first three novels," said one alienated woman. "so you're my greatest disappointment"—Wishnasky maintained his calm *politesse*.

"You apparently want to turn the clock back to the Dark Ages," said one grumpy caller, to which he answered, "Actually, I'd like to think that somehow I'm turning the clock forward."

"Well, it's not happening," said the grouch. "The churches and synagogues are all in the garbage, and your narrow little book isn't getting them out of there."

"None of us knows the direction of history," said Wishnasky, trying to sound unruffled. And then, more hopefully: "Maybe the stereotype of the nihilist artist rehearsing doom from his garret is what's going out of style. Maybe I'm so far forward, you think I'm backward."

Finally, in Worcester he was on TV again, this time live, and the show's host, Elliot Feisenheim, gave him an opportunity to distill some of his feelings about the change he'd undergone. "I'm Jewish," Elliot said, "but I haven't been to synagogue in twenty years. The reason is simple: I never found the prayers in the prayer book very relevant, and I never understood why I was saying things I didn't feel to a God who must have been quite as bored as I was."

"You can't let the set prayers get in the way," said Wishnasky. "I never finish a session without telling the Holy One how things are going for me personally, and what my most urgent needs are. That's how I maintain an ongoing relationship with God."

"I don't know if I *could* pray even if I wanted to," said Elliot. "It's been so long. It would feel very awkward."

"Maybe prayer's an art too. Maybe it's an art that we've lost and have to rediscover."

So the New England dates passed, to be capped by a reading at the Strand Bookstore in New York. At Logan Airport, waiting to board his plane to the city, Wishnasky downloaded *David Copperfield* onto his iPad—it was a novel he remembered as guardedly sanguine, and he needed to be reminded that art could be optimistic. But he found his mind wandering back to the angriest callers on WBUR. What unsettled him was not the irreligion of so many people—he knew the trend over the last decades—but their rancor, their virulence. They spoke as if he'd joined some conspiracy against human happiness, as if the Salem Witch Trials had transpired not centuries but moments ago. Why so much wrath? Was there any other subject that made people so insanely irate?

On the airplane, he started *David Copperfield* for the third time: "Whether I shall turn out to be the hero of my own life, or whether that station will be held by anybody else, these pages must show." Good old Dickens, out to reform society as society's servant. What was so wrong with that? Weren't *Oliver Twist* and *Bleak House* worthy creations? Then he wondered: What was Dickens's religion? He Googled the subject and discovered that Dickens professed a broad, non-denominational Christianity and was particularly impressed by American Unitarianism. This information comforted Wishnasky, and he returned to *David Copperfield* with renewed interest.

So, his mind oscillated all that evening, between excitement and distress, enthusiasm and misgivings. When the plane touched down at Newark Airport, he was as unsure of himself as he'd ever been.

53.

DURING THE CAB RIDE to the Strand, as the skyscrapers of Manhattan rose around him, Wishnasky's anxiety took on a new coloring. He realized he was losing something, something that from his college years had been mammoth, tremendous: a certainty that he was riding the *zeitgeist*, that he was as modern as modern came. Now, looking out at the glass-and-steel towers of Manhattan, he felt antiquated, unfashionable. It was strange to be pledged to a vision born not in the delirious Paris or Berlin of the 1920s but in the sun-drenched Land of Israel thousands of years earlier. Even stranger was the degree to which he felt committed to his vision; he'd become a true believer. How was it possible?

He thought about his most recent Hebrew class with Cantor Kazen. They'd looked at Leviticus 19, and Wishnasky had been struck by the power in the original language of this single chapter, featuring everything from "You shall be holy because I the Lord your God am holy." to commands that one leave part of one's harvest for the poor, not steal or lie, not distort justice, not hate or bear a grudge ... Nothing he'd studied at Harvard about Apollinaire or Hermann Broch had so stunned him with its force or beauty. And then to think that these rules had formed the basis of Western society for over 3,500 years, that his own culture had been brought to birth with these words ... Yes, Gide in French was lovely, and so was Mann in German. But these were secondary figures speaking of subordinate things, not in the same universe as *v'ahavta l'rea'cha k'mocha*: "You shall love your neighbor as yourself." How could he *not* be mesmerized by words of the *Torah*?

So all right: he was ensnared. And he'd written a novel in which his changing worldview was paramount, and as a result he'd been demoted from prophet to dupe. Leaving what options? To accept a role as a minor voice? How could one aspire to be minor? But what was the alternative? To change course again, take up the old nihilism? Disreputable, hypocritical. Maybe there was no solution: maybe one simply wrote as honestly as possible and hoped that at least a small audience would respond. He remembered hearing that Virginia Woolf had never thought her novels would attract readers. Why not work with the same understanding? Embrace an honest obscurity?

He leaned his head back and closed his eyes. At his impending appearance at the Strand, he was supposed to start with a twenty-minute section of *Traveler in the Abyss*. Probably he'd avoid alienating skeptical New Yorkers if he read from the first chapter, when Ozono was still down-and-out and Yvonne hadn't yet spoken of religion. Yes, the first chapter was clearly the least controversial, the one that sounded most like his old self. But wasn't there something craven in putting on such a front? Maybe Roland was right, instead of underplaying his new faith, he should brandish it, trumpet it, shout it to the rafters. No, that would send people flying. He imagined himself back at college, going to a reading at the *Harvard Advocate* and hearing some faith-besotted novelist read not literature but a religious tract, a poorly-disguised homily: Wouldn't he have run for the exit? He would have vaulted back to his room in Adams House and grabbed up a book by an up-to-date skeptic like good old Wallace Stevens. What were those lines he had loved in college, about poetry taking the place of religion? Now that was good modern literature. You could be a great writer if you wrote about "empty heaven." You couldn't get more avant-garde.

He was no longer avant-garde. He wasn't ironic enough to be postmodern. There wasn't a good word for what he was.

He thought of something Rabbi Diamant had said to him a week before at the Horn of Plenty. He had asked if it bothered her that, according to the most recent Pew poll, most Conservative congregations were shrinking. "Of course I'm worried," she said. "But being a rabbi isn't just my job, it's who I am, it's in my bloodstream. What will come of religion, I don't presume to know. But I know myself. And I've got to be true to her." Maybe that was enough: authenticity. No matter how lonely. He thought of the discovery he'd made about *Psalms*, that contrary to logic, they often expressed nothing but trouble, victimization, misfortune. Why had the rabbis who compiled the Bible included those cries of distress? Didn't they realize that people chose religion precisely to get *out* of distress? Sure, the Christians had the crucified Jesus to remind them that even a good life might end in suffering, but wasn't

Judaism different? Apparently not. Apparently, you could honestly work your way toward observant Judaism and still get a bitchy little review in the *Globe*.

"Forgive me, God," he said under his breath. "I'm getting shamelessly trivial."

There was no alternative: he would have to take his punishment, smile and endure it. If he wasn't to be a great innovator, he could still be a fine writer. Still treat the language with meticulous care. A stylist: that's how he could be known. Four thousand years extinct, but of interest as a stylist. Yes, that's what he'd aim for.

But O Kafka! O Beckett!

So hard to leave you.

54.

THE CROWD AT THE STRAND was composed of about fifty people, most of them seated in the rather tight downstairs area set aside for readings. A lectern had been set up on one edge of the space, and beside it Wishnasky, a copy of his new novel in hand, waited to be introduced. He noticed all the people who *weren't* interested in hearing him—browsers in the stacks who preferred absent authors to a live one. Well, maybe they were on to something. Some real authors weren't very important anymore.

The waiting ended; a slender, tawny-haired young man in horn-rimmed glasses walked up to the lectern and welcomed Wishnasky, calling him a writer who'd "shocked the literary world by turning from the signature hopelessness of his first works to what has widely been seen as an embrace of God and religion." He finished with a list of awards Wishnasky had received for those early novels, and then the nervous author was alone at the lectern, thanking the young man and the audience for their support.

He opened his book and read. The section he'd finally chosen was from the third chapter of the book, when Ozono first heard Yvonne's expression of Jewish faith and admitted that faith was something he knew little about.

"It's not that difficult," Yvonne said, pouring herself another cup of tea. "You just decide that what's human is too spectacular to be explained by nothing but Darwinian good luck. You say, yes, I accept that I ascended from the apes, but my reason, my language, my Marriage of Figaro and my Hamlet can't be explained by mere evolution."

"Freud called religion an illusion," said skeptical Ozono.

"Freud's a good example," said Yvonne, smiling as if she were glad to be reminded. "You look at all the theorists of the human mind—Freud and Jung and Rogers and Maslow and all the others in between—put them all together and still they don't

exhaust the complexity of the human psyche. Which is just a little too wonderful to be the random result of lusty amoebas."

"Chance exists," said Ozono. "Unless you're trying to tell me that it was God's will that I lost my job at the computer company."

"I didn't say," said Yvonne. "But I know that God hides Himself and wants you to search and find Him. And sometimes He's not to be found at the heights. Sometimes you have to descend to the lowest valley if you really want a glimpse."

"Well, I'm there," said Ozono, at the point of tears. He put his elbow on the table and rested his forehead in his right hand. "That's just where I am. And I don't notice God here."

"You haven't started looking yet," said Yvonne, sitting beside him. "But I'll help you. I'll take it as a privilege."

He read for another ten minutes, then came to the end of the chapter and put the book down on the lectern. "That's about it," he said apologetically. "I guess I'll take questions now."

Immediately several hands shot upward. He pointed at a middle-aged man with a two-thirds bald pate and what he hoped was a kind face. "Yes, sir," he said. "Yes, you. Your question."

"I can't speak for the others here," said the man, who was wearing a cobalt blue Oxford cloth shirt and jeans, "but I hightailed it out of religion when I was a seventeen-year-old high school kid in Springfield, Illinois, and that and moving to New York were probably the smartest moves I ever made. Don't you think it's a little late to be exhorting people to come back to the fold?"

"That's not why I write," said Wishnasky, groaning inwardly. "I try to express my deepest truth and as for the effect on the reader, if they're satisfied that I've told a good story, that's all I need. So no, I'm not telling you to return to whatever faith you escaped from. That's your private business." He pointed at a small white-haired woman who looked vaguely pious. "Yes, you, ma'am."

She stood up. "I've read all three of your first novels," she said in a low-pitched, throaty voice. "And they've given me the strength to carry on through some honestly terrible times. But I was abused by a religious mother and I've been trying to heal all my life from her fanaticism. Why should I read your new novel if it's all about a God I identify with torture? You know what I feel after hearing your reading? I feel like you're trying to send me right back to the witch who brutalized my youth and nearly killed me!"

From the crowd there was a murmur of what Wishnasky assumed was assent.

"I'm sorry you were mistreated," he said. "But I also know from personal experience that there are a lot of hungry people, a lot of battered people who have been rescued by religion and religious workers. That's the kind of faith my book is about, not the sort that I'm sure was very harmful to you. So let's make that distinction. Next question." He looked around and found an attractive young woman with long straight auburn hair and an encouraging smile. "Yes, you, please."

"I'd like to know if you see your new book as participating in the forward movement of many artists today away from Modernist/Romantic clichés?"

At least she wasn't attacking his faith. "I suppose I do," he said. "Many of the great Modernists were my heroes once, but finally I see their worldviews as too solipsistic, too unconcerned with the battle between good and evil that's playing out in this world. So, I guess I've moved away from them. Not without surprising myself along the way, though."

The questions—mostly censorious, a few more or less grateful—and answers—mostly defensive—went on for another half hour, after which time the young man who had introduced Wishnasky came back to the lectern, thanked the author for reading and the audience for listening. There was a smattering of applause and the ordeal was over. Wishnasky shook the young man's hand and was heading for the staircase when the auburn-haired woman who had asked him about modernism hurried over to his side.

"May I have just a moment with you?" she said.

"Sure. What's your question?"

"It's not a question, really," she said, speaking quickly. "It's an invitation. I'm Aileen Silver, I'm the head of a group called RARE, which stands for Radical Artists Restoring the Earth. We're kind of a nationwide network, with lots of different artists, visual and literary, in many different media, all representing a departure from the old trope of art-as-socially-irrelevant. I've been worrying for a while that we're missing a religious component, and I think your new novel might be just what we're looking for. Would you be willing to meet with me for half an hour some afternoon and let me pitch our organization?"

"I don't live in New York. I live in the Boston area, and I'm on a plane back there in a few hours."

"Could I meet with you now, then? It'll just take a few minutes. You must need coffee or lunch after all the unpleasantness in the Q and A."

Wishnasky thought about his prospects for the next couple of hours and even with no plans, felt an impulse to say "no." But he also remembered that this woman had treated *Traveler* as something progressive, maybe even advanced, and for that he was grateful. How could it hurt to listen to her talk about her organization? She seemed genuine and intelligent. The alternative was to sulk alone.

"Fine," he said. "But you know the city better than I do. Where should we go?"

"Come with me," she said and darted up the stairs. Wishnasky followed, hoping he hadn't made a mistake.

55.

HER GROUP (Wishnasky learned as they sat in the coffee shop, she talking away breathlessly, he trying hard not to be depressed by the memories of his reading) had been in existence for three years and was committed to sloughing off the reputation of artists as concerned with nothing but watching themselves emote. She said that the Modernists and Postmodernists she wanted to repudiate were all really nothing but late Romantics, committed to a concept of the artist as an eccentric genius living at a distance from most of the population, and committed to an egoistic vision that left the needs of the Earth and its inhabitants devalued. Meanwhile the planet—her group, she said, called it "The Artwork"—was reeling from abuse, from climate change and pollution and deforestation and the unstocking of fisheries, and if the mission of the poet had once been to stand up for the rights of the individual consciousness, now she was obligated to turn her gaze to the more imminently threatened globe.

So, with a few painter and sculptor friends—all of whom had been students together at the Rhode Island School of Design—she had started RARE, which was dedicated to the next step after late Romanticism/modernism. RARE found artists all around the US who were working to rescue The Artwork one way or another, and they carefully documented each tree-planting and river clean-up with paintings and essays and photographs displayed in accommodating art galleries and museums. They'd had one such showing just a few months ago, at a gallery in Tribeca, and on his next visit to New York, she could show him her copy of the "remarkably exciting" catalog.

As for herself, she saw RARE as her truest calling; though she'd trained as a painter in oils and acrylics, her art now consisted of collecting documentary accounts of the transformation of abandoned urban land into vegetable gardens. Other recent RARE projects included a campaign to ban plastic drinking straws from Albany restaurants (they weren't biodegradable), the clean-up of an Atlantic coast beach in Connecticut (beer cans, Coke bottles, and Styrofoam cups, mostly), and the promotion of a company making men and women's sportswear from post-consumer waste. The Earth—"The Artwork"—was every RARE member's canvas, and if she and her colleagues didn't boast the charisma of wild-eyed geniuses in an *atelier,* they stood for something else: the certainty that their work was urgently necessary for the planet's survival and, therefore, on the real cutting edge.

As for what she wanted with Wishnasky: she had the sense, listening to his reading (and knowing a little about his past novels), that he also had grown impatient with Modernist tropes of alienation and wanted to be a positive force on earth, not just one more crier of woe. Did he think his new religious turn was consistent with RARE's approach to restoring The Artwork?

"To be honest, I haven't given it much thought," he said. "I would guess that the Jewish attitude is that it can't be right to treat the Holy One's creation as some sort of piñata to be smashed and vandalized. But I haven't elaborated my thoughts much beyond that."

"Do you think you'd be willing to write something on the subject, even just one essay or short story, any time in the next few months? We're really broad-minded—we're all artists and we know how artists cherish their freedom. But there were once groups of Impressionists, Cubists, Futurists, and their being in a group didn't stop them from individual distinction. Would you consider becoming RARE's first religious author?"

"What more would I have to do?"

"Nothing, really, except alert me to your progress, so I can put the details in our blog. And oh yeah, allow us to use your name online in our list of members"

He wasn't the least bit interested, but didn't want to disappoint her to her face. "I'll have to think about it," he lied. "I'm not really one for joining groups."

"No, I'm sure you're not," she said. "But we honestly think we're the next wave in aesthetic history, that one day people will look to our Earth-consciousness as the natural sequel to the conventional paint-and-canvas model everyone favored back in olden times."

Trying to change the subject—at least he thought that was what he was doing—he said, "Tell me more about yourself personally. What's your own training? What's your background?"

"Sure," she said. "Well, I was born in Knoxville, but I grew up in Baltimore, and I was crazy about drawing and painting from earliest childhood. I have two sisters, one's an attorney now, one's a social worker, and since our parents were very Montessori-type former hippies, they indulged our inclinations, meaning I got to take art lessons even before I left primary school and after that it never stopped, middle school, high school, and finally RISD. But that image of the Romantic artist—you know, Frida Kahlo working herself sick in the service of her vision—just seemed so passé to me by the time I graduated, and I sort of agreed with Arthur C. Danto that the visual arts had pretty much reached their terminus by the 1960s. I mean, the field wants an entirely new direction, not just another byway. And then I came upon writers like Suzi Gablik and Richard Shusterman and it was clear to me: it's not a big step to saying the whole earth is the real Artwork, and if it's in danger and needs attention, this is what *has* to follow minimalism and conceptual art and all those other dead ends. And some friends agreed. So, we started RARE." She paused for a moment. "I'm also Jewish, but I don't practice at all. And I'm talking too much. Was that what you wanted to know?"

"In a way," he said. "But how do you support yourself? New York is so expensive."

"I teach painting at a middle school in Brooklyn," she said. "It's really lots of fun, and the kids are so creative."

"Do you live in Brooklyn?"

"Yeah, in an apartment with a married couple. I have a bedroom but we share the kitchen and bathroom. It's a little cramped but that's the price of living in the city."

He had already conceived an image: a third-rate painter sentenced to languish in a public school, anxious to make some sort of name for herself and inventing this ridiculously inconsequential ecological movement. Which no doubt was filled with other third-rate artists. Not the sort of thing one tied one's reputation to—especially not a reputation that was already plummeting. Of course, he couldn't say any of that.

"Are you married?" he said.

She smiled. "Been with my boyfriend so long, we might as well be."

"What does he do? Another artist?"

"Oh no, thank goodness. He's an internet whiz—designs sophisticated websites. I needed one for RARE, and that's how we met."

It was time to get free of this time-killing distraction. "Well, I'll tell you," he said, "RARE sounds like a great organization. But I don't think it's for me."

"Would you at least let me text you some more information? Say, our mission statement and a link to our yearbook?"

"All right. I guess that can't hurt."

"May I have your cell phone number?"

He took a pen from his pocket and wrote it on a napkin. Then, he handed it to her and stood up. "Thanks for the pitch. But at the moment I'm still absorbing the response to my new novel and I don't think I'm ready to make any more life-changing decisions. I admire your ambition, though." He plucked his wallet from his back pocket and put a ten-dollar bill on the table. "I'm glad you introduced yourself. Good luck to you and your group."

"Do you need help getting where you're going?"

"No, I'm fine. Thanks for the chat."

Putting any thought of Aileen Silver from his mind, he walked out into the bright afternoon and headed up the street in the general direction of Midtown. He always enjoyed New York in early afternoon light, and here on Broadway there was the usual stimulating bustle, as if everyone knew precisely his or her mission in life. He thought again about the reading: the fact was, he'd been disparaged by most of his listeners, the main exception being a woman who wanted his name for her artists' collaborative. Well, at least his name was still important to someone. As he waited for the light to change on a busy street corner, he thought of all the people he'd heard from who felt let down by religion, or, at worst, completely violated. How to tell so many people to ignore their own experience?

Well, he was a novelist, not a social scientist. He would stand by his *Traveler*. Even if the whole world was against him.

His phone buzzed. He took it from his pocket and found a message from Aileen Silver: "Great to meet you. Remember RARE and me!"

He could hardly forget either if she was reminding him so soon.

56.

"I'M SORRY YOUR NOVEL hasn't been greeted more favorably," said Rabbi Diamant. "But I'm sure you know better than to take that as a gauge of its value."

She was driving Wishnasky to the Horn of Plenty. It was a warm spring afternoon, the trees starting to look confidently green, and the glow from the setting sun bathing everything in muted gold. The rabbi was dressed in a yellow blouse and a brown skirt, and she seemed to fit into the scenery with remarkable felicity.

"I guess I never realized how many people feel contempt for religion."

"They don't know what they're rejecting," said the rabbi, driving beside the Charles River. "What most people think of as religion is only their childhood experience of being compelled to go to synagogue or church by parents who only went there themselves because *their* parents had gone. Ignorance leading ignorance. I wish more people had taken your lead and looked into it. Come to me and told me their doubts. Learned to read the *siddur* in Hebrew. Learned to pray personal prayers."

"I understand why they're so against it," said Wishnasky. "What I don't understand is the fervor."

"Why wouldn't they be fervent? Forced to go to a somber, humorless house of rote worship just to be told that they were failing a punitive God—who wouldn't rebel against that after years of discomfort? Prescribed prayers and blanket indictments, all the talk about sin and retribution—who wouldn't prefer to spend the time at a Red Sox game?"

"Yet you stay in your job."

"The Jewish view of life is a grand one, about improving life, 'perfecting the earth under the kingship of the Almighty' as the *Aleinu* prayer says. That's all of Judaism right there. But you know what Heschel said? He said the Jews are messengers who've forgotten their message."

"Or they just don't like it."

"I'd be pleased to meet congregants who understood their religion and then had some intelligent objections. But that's almost never the case. The case is they only know what was forced upon them in infancy."

They drove along for a few moments in silence, and Wishnasky, looking out his side window at the students walking and playing on the banks of the Charles, wondered how many of them bothered to think about God or the possibility of cosmic obligation. Then they crossed the river and headed toward East Boston and its less cheery sights. Soon the housing was of two distinct types: rundown working class apartments and bright new construction for the wealthy. Wishnasky had read in the *Globe* about the many Hispanic residents of the neighborhood, worried that soon they'd be priced out of their own long-term homes. The article had seemed irrelevant when he read it, of interest only to those moving out or in. But now he was conscious of gentrification's pitiless despoliation of the low-income. Just one more indignity to add to the others.

"I have a novelist's problem with the planet I live on," he said at last. "Insofar as it's one I didn't create, I have trouble conceptualizing it. But it's where I have to live. So somehow I've got to … think it through."

"And to help fix the broken parts," said the rabbi as they turned into the Horn of Plenty. As they rolled through the gap in the chain-link fence, Wishnasky saw a police car, along with two white, official-looking sedans.

"I want to ask you something else," he said. "It's about the Jewish view on the environment. I met a woman back in New York who made me wonder about the attitude to—"

He was interrupted by the sight of worried-looking Brooke, hurrying out of the back gateway and gesturing to the rabbi. Rabbi Diamant stopped the car and opened her window.

"They're closing us down," said Brooke, near tears. "Maybe they'll listen to you. They say we're in code violation."

The rabbi quickly parked and bounded out of the car; Wishnasky, hurrying behind, passed through the kitchen into the large, frowsy-looking lounge area that he'd seldom entered. Beside the unshapely, weary-looking sofas, he saw a male and female police officer and three men wearing white shirts with the "City of Boston" logo stitched on the pockets. Brooke pointed at one of these—a giant, short-haired and burly, his muscles stretching the fabric of his clothes—and said, "He's the one."

"I'm Rabbi Diamant," said the rabbi. "What's the problem here? We need to feed these people."

"Yes, ma'am," said the giant, looking kindly down at the rabbi. "But we've found sixteen safety violations in this edifice and we're required by law to close it down until such time that it's safe for use. Mr. Spalding has already had two warnings."

Spalding was the man who owned the shelter. Wishnasky had never met him.

"What are the violations?" said the rabbi. "How extreme are they?"

"We found overloaded circuits, damaged wiring with evidence of rat feces, a water line with open electrical wires wrapped around it, and faulty breaker panels. It also seems that the refrigeration unit is illegally set at forty-seven degrees Fahrenheit when forty-one is the legal maximum. Though I wouldn't yet swear to it, I think I've also discovered unstable beams in the kitchen area supporting a hazardous ceiling."

"Can you at least allow the homeless to eat their dinner before you close us? Many of them depend on this meal to last them for days."

"This building's not safe for anyone, ma'am," said the giant. "We're as concerned about them as you are, and right now they're in danger being anywhere near these premises."

The female police officer, a brunette no older than thirty, came over to them and said to the giant, "I'm going to move them out."

"Yes, please," he said. Then, to the rabbi, "I share your sympathy for the poor, ma'am. That's why I don't want them exposed to harm." He followed the police officer out of the lounge and into the kitchen.

"Is there anything else I can do?" the rabbi said to Brooke.

"I don't think so," said Brooke, looking ashen, desolate. "If they'd at least wait till the meal was over ..."

Wishnasky walked through the lounge and back into the kitchen, where several servers were standing, poised to dish out a meal for no one. He went outside to the dining area: the female police officer was there, announcing that the shelter was officially closed and that everyone should leave. Some of the homeless were already on their way through the gateway; others were still sitting at the tables, as if they hadn't heard or didn't understand. Wishnasky saw Arthur at his usual table, watching with curiosity but making no effort to vacate. He walked over to him.

"Hey," said Wishnasky. "Tough luck about dinner."

"You know what's happenin' here?" asked Arthur, his hands in his lap. "You figured it out?"

"I'm concerned that I have."

"It's like I always said: us casualties, our job is to stay invisible. But someone in the neighborhood's seen us hidin' out here, and that breaks the rule. Can't have so many wounded in anyone's face. Might even turn the people 'gainst the war."

"I'm beginning to think you're right," said Wishnasky. He looked around the dining area—more homeless were leaving, more places were emptying—and he had an impulse to help. "Let me give you some money," he said. "So you'll get something to eat tonight."

"I can't turn you down."

Wishnasky reached for his wallet and removed a twenty. He felt instantly ashamed, as if it wasn't enough. But Arthur took the bill without a word and stood up.

"This was a nice place to eat," he said with an ironic smile. "I'm honestly surprised they didn't close us down sooner. We were gettin' to feel looked after."

He turned his back to Wishnasky and walked away from the table, through the tall wooden gate and out of sight.

Wishnasky went back into the kitchen and found the rabbi writing on a small notepad as the burly inspector talked to her. He arrived just in time to hear her say, "I'll be calling them," and then the inspector walked off.

"Can you do anything?" he asked.

"Probably not. This is the third time they've been back here, and the violations still haven't been addressed. Probably Kevin Spalding can't afford that much electrical work."

"Is there a solution?"

"I don't know yet. We've got to find out what it'll cost."

"What about me? Should I be doing anything?"

"There's nothing to do. We might as well go home."

On the drive back to the synagogue, the rabbi was mostly silent, pensive. Wishnasky tried not to disturb her, but a hundred thoughts were prodding him. Finally, he said, "What if fixing the world is too big a job? What if people aren't up to it?"

"There's a *Talmud*ic saying," said the rabbi. "'It is not for you to finish the work; but you have no right to withdraw from it either.' In other words, don't expect too much—but hang in there anyway."

"You don't get discouraged?"

"Disappointed—often. But there's nothing to do but pray and soldier on."

Beyond them, night was falling. Wishnasky was conscious that they were driving in the wrong direction, away from the people who depended on them for sustenance. "I feel cheated," he said finally. "I wanted to make a difference tonight."

"Congratulations," said Rabbi Diamant. "You're coming to feel the privilege of doing a *mitzvah*. Take it away and it leaves an absence."

"Is there some way I can make up for it? Till the place is reopened?"

"I can send you to a website listing all sorts of other volunteer opportunities in the area. There's Big Brothers—a lot of kids need the helping hand of an adult. There's the Marjorie House, a shelter for battered women. There's Amnesty International and The Literacy Project. There are several food pantries at local churches. I'll send you a website."

"All right, thanks. I have the time, and I want to help."

When he was back in his own car and on the way to Newton Center, Wishnasky thought about what Arthur had said. Was there really a war against the losers in the American economy? A conspiracy to keep them invisible? Again he recalled that he had lived most of his life in the Boston area without even knowing the Horn of Plenty existed—or was necessary. How was that possible?

As he pulled into his driveway, he promised himself that he'd quickly choose another group to volunteer with. Then his phone beeped and he saw a message from Aileen Silver: "A word to the wise: ordinary detergent residue discharged into lakes and rivers kills salmon, trout, and frogs. Don't forget RARE and me!"

He was immediately regretful that he'd given her his phone number.

57.

"So," said Ion Petrescu. "You followed your inspiration, and the result is you've been mocked by the reviewers and your fellow mandarins. And you want my opinion."

They were seated in Ion's office, Ion bolt upright in his swivel chair, Wishnasky slumped in the soft armchair opposite him. Ion, in a short-sleeved green shirt and gray pants, was being characteristically smug, but Wishnasky didn't mind; it was a relief to have someone to whom he could confess his full malaise.

"See, I'd read once that Emerson said that if you follow your truest light, the whole world will rush to help you."

"Emerson is America's greatest literary mystery. Weirder than Poe. Bizarre, inexplicable. I wouldn't look to Emerson for anything applicable."

"Well, Joseph Campbell said 'follow your bliss.' Which I thought I did."

"Bank embezzlers follow their bliss. Serial murderers follow their bliss."

"So who should I have listened to, Leonard Bernstein? All right, why don't symphony directors program *Kaddish* in their seasons? Why do they all prefer the suite from *West Side Story*?"

"Are you honestly so surprised?" said Ion. "We live in a secular, scientific age, and any man or woman who chooses to speak loudly about faith will be promptly excoriated by unbelievers. For the next few months, I predict derogation, denigration, contempt and many nasty letters."

"I thought you told me to get religious! I thought you told me the Universal Mind was sending me a directive!"

"That's correct. And I would say so again in the same circumstances."

"But you knew what the response would be?"

"My dear Tristan," said Ion in his most courtly tone. "One does not follow the True Way for public approval. One does not bend toward the Light expecting the cheers of the benighted. You have gone where Mind wants you; take pleasure in that. But also don't be surprised if the rest of the world reviles you. Or burns you at the stake."

"If you knew this is what I was heading for, why didn't you warn me?"

"Because the alternative was far worse."

"And the alternative was?"

"To live in denial of the Mind and its insistence on growth. I encouraged you for the sake of what used to be called your soul."

"My soul was doing fine! My soul was enjoying interviews in the *Times* and the money from a movie deal! My soul felt at home in its cute little house in Newton Corner that now it's going to lose! Is the Mind so dead set against money, fame, and creature comforts?"

"You already know the answer. You know that living authentically in the Cosmos is far more important than the sales figures on your latest artifact. Instead of flogging yourself for a few bad reviews and the inevitable loss of income, exult in the fact that with your good works and your charity, you are beginning to achieve the only distinction that really matters."

"Did you see my review in the *Globe*?"

"I'm sorry to admit that I did."

"And I should exult? I should be overjoyed?"

"For the very last time: what matters is entering into harmony with Mind. You need further validation? I validate you. I admire you. Not today's tantrum but the choices that led to it. Keep to the path you're on. You're faring beautifully."

"I don't like being a pariah, Ion."

"It is a shame that in our time, the righteous feel themselves pariahs. If it were up to me, things would be otherwise."

"You know, maybe I'm done with literature. Finished. I'm going to write best-selling novels about sex acts, clinically described! Or about serial murderers, that get turned into serial television!"

"You know better than that. Keep to your path."

"My path is strewn with daggers."

"Then thicken the soles of your feet. And stop complaining."

58.

"MUST BE IN BOSTON this weekend. Urgent to see you. When can we meet? Remember RARE and me!"

The text had been sent late the previous night, but Wishnasky didn't see it till the morning at breakfast. Sitting at the round maple table in his kitchen, buttered bread and a cup of coffee in front of him, he felt irked by the repeated appeals from this exigent woman. He messaged back:

"Can't make meeting. Slammed with work. Many regrets."

He sat back and resumed reading the editorial page of the *Globe*. There was a controversy over the official spending of a state senator, and the newspaper was calling for her resignation. She had promised to reimburse the Commonwealth of Massachusetts out of her own private bank account, but the *Globe* said this was an insufficient expiation. The future was, as yet, unclear.

His phone beeped and he looked at it. "Will disclose subject when I see you. Top secret. Please trust me." He wrote back, "Sorry. Work overwhelming. And *Sabbath* for rest." She wrote back, "Involves you personally. Most crucial matter. Please please short meeting."

He felt displeased, even surly. The possibility that a meeting with this wannabe artist could possibly be "crucial" was little to none. He'd had lots of experience over the years with pushy fans who felt the right to attach themselves to a televised author, and he'd developed sturdy reflexes with which to keep them at bay. This was clearly such a case. So after a moment, he wrote: "If urgent, send text. No time for confab." Then he picked up his *Globe* and resumed reading.

Moments later, his phone beeped. Increasingly annoyed, he read, "Please please please: thirty minutes together. Won't waste time. Won't bother you again." He was about to write back, "No time and goodbye," when he had second thoughts.

Aileen Silver wasn't bad-looking; she was apparently intelligent, and she had been so flattering back in New York, it might be good for his ego to humor her for half an hour. He decided to name an urban cafe so busy, he could hear her out for a brief time, and then, after a quick thanks, wish her well and get lost in a crowd. He wrote, "All right: Sunday 3 p.m., the Itinerant Coffee Bean in Harvard Square." The ICB was an indoor/outdoor establishment from which he could disappear into the mob on Mass. Ave. in half a moment. Yes, that was the solution.

But her next message surprised him. "3 p.m. good but not coffee place. The Chalk Rooster in Arlington. Essential to discussion."

This was ludicrous: why in the world was this stranger naming the meeting place when he was doing *her* the favor? And Arlington was out of the way (so was Harvard Square, but nostalgically it was closer). He'd squelch this bid immediately. "Can't make Arlington," he wrote. "Will be near H. Square Sunday. Sorry, but final." There was a thirty-second pause, during which time he smirked at his phone, daring it to contradict him.

It did. "Please Please Please The Chalk Rooster," he read. "Will pay your lunch and gas. Promise you'll be glad." He'd be glad? She'd buy his lunch? He sat back, stupefied, and tried to conceive an answer. He'd say, forget it, can't make Cambridge *or* Arlington. He'd say, don't overplay your hand, Ms. Silver. He'd say, be grateful that I'm willing to meet with you *anywhere*.

But then he re-read the string of messages. And he remembered talking with Aileen in New York. She'd been so deferential, so solicitous, treating him not as a novelist in freefall but as a much-adored success ... If she had some crazy idea that she needed to talk to him, and at some favorite restaurant, why not give in to her silly entreaties and take the drive over to Arlington? Even at this mysterious Chalk Rooster, he could get up and leave if she became too bizarre.

Feeling superior, he wrote, "Will pay own way. But Chalk Rooster fine. See you 3 p.m." He waited a few minutes for her to respond, but she didn't. He wondered why he felt that he'd just lost an important argument. Furrowing his brow, he put his phone back in his pocket, picked up his coffee cup, and walked to his study.

A bigger question than how to treat Aileen Silver had been pestering him: what to write now that *Traveler* was published. He'd been able to put it off all through the eighteen months between turning the novel in to Darryl Kamfort and seeing its publication. But at last it was inescapable: he had to move on. Another novel was the obvious answer, or, as a stopgap, a few short stories. But on what subject? Becoming a faithful Jew? He had no desire to revisit that particular theme. Well, then what? What did he care about deeply enough to spend months and maybe years writing? He remembered the days when his sense of the Gaping Canyon of the Void had been so capacious, there seemed always another crevasse to excavate, another cave to explore. Well, those days were gone. Perhaps he could write about some Biblical figure, as Thomas Mann had done in *Joseph and his Brothers*. No, he had nothing to add about Joseph or Jacob or Moses, for that matter.

Wait: what about himself, his present situation? He could write about a one-time hero, now abandoned by his devotees, taken for dead. Or what about that essay Aileen had asked for in New York, the thing about Earth-consciousness? No, the subject was *her idée fixe*, not his. Damn it: all that was clear as he stared into his computer monitor was that he had a mortgage to pay, and a dwindling heap of money from a movie sale. If *Traveler* didn't sell well, he'd be in trouble in just a few months. He got up from the desk, walked into his kitchen and looked out the window at the familiar firs, oaks, and maples. He had gotten used to this arbor, loved the long green lawns and quiet streets of his cozy neighborhood. He didn't want to give it up.

He walked over to the bookshelf in his living room and found the Hebrew/English Bible he'd bought at Cantor Kazen's suggestion. He turned to *Psalms*, leafed through them randomly, and then stopped at Psalm 56: "Be gracious to me, O God, for people long to swallow me up; all day long they oppress me." Well, things weren't *that* bad: none of his critics had threatened cannibalism. Yet. So far. He turned a few pages more. Was there a psalm for smug authors who ignored their seasoned literary agents? On the other hand, maybe Roland was also right about the Bible Belt: his sales might soar in Alabama. In Mississippi.

He decided to pray. He sat back at the kitchen table, folded his hands and closed his eyes. "Dear God," he said, "I've tried to do what You said. I've searched for You, and I've done my utmost to convey my discovery to the people around me. But the result seems to be that I'm taken as an oddity, an object of derision polite and otherwise, and if the book critics are right, I'm a self-righteous hack. I'm honestly happy about my spiritual growth, and I don't think anyone can deflect me from Your service, but You know, it's a little lonely. I mean, the big fish who are spurning me are the ones I used to swim with. So, please help me navigate. Please help me make sense of it. And thank You for Your patience as I lurch ahead stupidly."

He opened his eyes and sighed. Maybe he could distract himself with TV news. He trudged into his living room, found the remote, turned on CNN, and lost himself in the latest national scandals.

59.

THE FIRST CLUE to his new book's subject—though he didn't recognize it at the time—came in his Biblical Hebrew class, where the cantor had moved on from the five books of *Torah* to the more difficult language of Amos, Hosea, and Isaiah. As usual, when Wishnasky entered the synagogue, he found the long table set up just inside the sanctuary, and several people sitting round it: Bernice Chaite, looking business-like in a black pantsuit; bespectacled Ed Troopman, white-haired and almost always grinning; young Wallace Shertz, who regularly attended the class without speaking; perfectly coiffed Elaine Oster; and typically unshaven George Firestone, in his thirties. Wishnasky was just saying hello when the cantor, looking healthy and well-fed, cleared his throat and the class began.

For the evening's meeting, the Hebrew students had been asked to study Isaiah 58, in which God explains why He doesn't seem to be answering the prayers of His worshippers. Simple enough, says the Holy One: what you call a "fast" (*tzom* in Hebrew) just isn't good enough. But:

Is not this the fast that I have chosen?
To loose the shackles of wickedness,
To undo the bands of the yoke,
And to let the oppressed go free ...
Is it not to deal thy bread to the hungry,
And that thou bring the poor that are afflicted to thy house?
When thou seest the naked, that thou cover him,
And that thou hide not thyself from thine own flesh?
Then shall thy light break forth as the morning ...
Then shalt thou call, and the Lord will answer;
Thou shalt cry, and He shall say, "Here I am."

The members of the class agreed that the vocabulary was relatively straight-forward—though the Hebrew for "shackles" (*hartzubot*) and "oppressed" (*retzutzim*) was unfamiliar—and that it made sense that this section was read every Yom Kippur in traditional synagogues. But at least one student—Elaine Oster—had a problem with the chapter's message.

"God seems to be saying that if I want my prayers answered, I have to jump through certain hoops. But what about His mercy? If God is merciful, as He says repeatedly in the *Torah*, why shouldn't He hear me on a slow day, when I haven't lifted up any oppressed or fed any hungry?"

"Does anyone want to answer?" said the cantor, his round face so open and inviting, one knew he'd never criticize or judge.

"Didn't we study a few weeks ago in Exodus," said Ed Troopman, holding his eyeglasses in his right hand, "that God says to Moses, 'I will be gracious to whom I will be gracious?' So He does occasionally answer the prayers of people who don't deserve it. I mean, as far as I know, that's the definition of 'grace.'"

"In Hebrew, *chayn*," said the cantor. "Unearned reward."

"But are we saying that we have to earn God's attention?" continued Elaine. "I thought we'd agreed that the Holy One was a loving Parent, *Avinu Malkeinu*, 'Our Father, Our King?' But a loving parent doesn't reserve his love for only those moments when you earn it. It pleases me when my children do good, but I love them whatever they do, or, for that matter, don't do. I want God to be at least as loving as an ordinary mother."

"Tristan, you look contemplative. What are you thinking?"

In fact, Wishnasky was straining to keep his mind on the discussion and not on his novel. Still, he joined the discussion. "Well, those are three very different subjects," he said. "Love, grace, and availability. If I understand the *Torah*, God is always loving, regardless of whether you've deserved it, and even when He punishes. That's like a parent. And 'grace' is what you said: undeserved blessing. But this thing in the *Isaiah* quote—this offer to be there right beside us when we relieve the oppressed ... That's something special. That's like a contract. If you do this, I'll do that. And if it's true ... then it's remarkable. We're being offered a bargain. And it's not out of our pay grade."

"It's too mechanical," said Bernice, her red-framed face wrinkled in thought. "I believe that God is beyond anything so automatic. That's genie-in-the-bottle stuff: *say the right words and I'll do your will.* My concept of divinity is so much loftier."

"He doesn't say He'll do your will," said Wishnasky. "Only that He'll listen, He'll give you a chance. After that, of course, it's anybody's guess."

The discussion returned to the verb forms in the chapter, especially the reflexive verb *titalam,* "to hide oneself." Wishnasky was still focused on the thought he'd just articulated. It *was* a contract. God so much hated injustice, He was willing to offer His nearness to anyone who acted against it. Couldn't Wishnasky's next novel live up to that contract? He listened again to his fellow students: they were arguing over the meaning of "thy own flesh"—Hebrew *basarcha*—in the phrase "hide not thyself from thy own flesh."

"I think He's talking about your own family," said Bernice. "We all know people who treat distant strangers more decently than they treat their spouses or children. This is a necessary reminder: look after your own."

"It means everyone," said George Firestone, the newest member of the group. "God, who's incorporeal, is reminding us that we humans all share material being. We're all the same in having flesh. So there's no one unrelated."

"Does anyone remember a verse in Genesis in which the phrase 'one flesh' is mentioned?" said the cantor.

"Of course," said Ed, wearing a baseball cap instead of a yarmulke. "It's about marriage: 'Therefore a man leaves his father and mother and cleaves to his wife, and they become one flesh.' *Basar echad,* I think."

"That's right," said the cantor. "Now what can the *Torah* mean by *basar,* flesh, if a married couple can share a *basar*? Or if you're commanded not to turn from your own? Tristan, what do you think?"

"I don't know," said Wishnasky. "When we were reading Genesis, I thought that the word might refer to some spiritual essence running parallel to the physical world. But as to 'hiding' oneself from one's own flesh, I don't think I understand."

"Let me add yet another way of looking at it," said the cantor. "In Ezekiel 36, God asserts that He will transform a cold, hard sinner by giving him a 'heart of flesh'—*lev basar.* In that case, 'flesh' seems to mean the ability to sympathize, to feel compassion for others. If that's the meaning, then what would it mean not to hide from your own flesh?"

Bernice spoke up immediately. "Don't hide from your own compassion. Don't hide from your own mercy."

"Excellent," said the cantor. "Yes, it's possible that 'flesh' here means 'goodness, generosity.' It's possible that God knows how sometimes people are embarrassed by their own kindheartedness and try to lie to themselves about it."

Wishnasky listened carefully. He was sure this discussion was relevant to him, but he didn't know precisely how. Why did he feel that "hiding from his own flesh" was so germane? Was it about his relationship to his parents? To the way he'd treated Andrea?

"Let's move on in *Isaiah*," said the cantor. "'*V'zarach ba chosech orecha, v'afehlatcha ka-tsaharayim'*—'Then shall your light shine in darkness and your gloom be as the noon day.' The word *zarach* for 'shine,' does anyone remember it from last week's discussion?"

And so the class continued. And Wishnasky increasingly felt that a certain question was being answered for him, but in a language he didn't understand. And until he recognized that language, he'd continue in the dark, missing everything right in front of him.

How was he hiding from his own flesh?

60.

AT FIVE O'CLOCK the next day he was at a party for Wanda Pulaski, a sharp observer of urban sophisticates altered by cocaine, LSD, easy sex, anything even remotely intoxicating. Her latest *roman à clef, The Square Root of Oblivion*, was already a bestseller, and she had appeared on late-night television with Jimmy Kimmel and Stephen Colbert, delighting them and their audiences with her dazed reports from the delirious Glittersphere. Wishnasky had first met her ten or twelve years ago, when they both had been invited to take part in a symposium on the Crisis in Modern Consciousness. But that was before the public embarrassment of *Traveler in the Abyss*, and now he crept into the hotel ballroom that her publisher had reserved for her with the furtiveness of a man who'd been invited by mistake.

He'd hardly entered when a voice said, "Tristan! How good to see you! Come here, so we can chat!!" It was Stella Lombardo, the fashionable painter of severed heads. Wishnasky walked over to a group that included her and two men he didn't recognize. They were standing by a long white table over-flowing with food—meats and cheeses and multi-colored fruits.

"Tristan Wishnasky, this is Victor Estephan and Xavier Loop." Wishnasky nodded at the two men and they nodded back. "Tristan is a wonderful novelist who just scandalized everyone by making God one of his characters. Tell me it's all true, Tristan. Tell me you've gone to the other side."

"The other side?"

"You know what I mean: the pious, the devoted. Tell me you mean every word of it and you're not just being ironic!"

"I haven't gone to any other side," said Wishnasky. "I've introduced the possibility that one might be a believer and find that belief healing. I really haven't changed that much."

"Nobody in Europe goes to church," said tall, suave Victor Estephan with a distinct Spanish accent. "It's only in America that people still believe."

"My great-aunt is religious," said Xavier Loop, whose lips were strangely puckered, as if he were tasting the air around him and finding it sour. "Goes to Mass every morning, makes confession, invites her priest over for sandwiches. The last time she asked me my opinion of her observance, I told her an anecdote about Hitchcock. He was driving his car on a rural road when he saw a priest and a boy walking along the shoulder talking. He immediately pulled up beside them, rolled down his window, and whispered, 'Little boy, little boy, run for your life!'"

All but Wishnasky laughed uproariously.

"But honestly, Tristan," said Lombardo after her laughter had subsided, "whatever persuaded you to make the change? Did someone get to you? Was it a family member, a lover?"

"Call it my conscience."

"Oh, that sounds serious. But tell me how you've changed, then. Do you pray? Do you give everything to charity? I gave a hundred dollars once to Save the Children or something like that, and for the next five *years* I was inundated by requests for money from every open pocket in America. That's the last time I make *that* mistake."

Boris Bulovich, the film director, walked over to the group, Scotch whiskey in hand. He took one look at Wishnasky and said, "You've got a lot of nerve coming to this shindig!"

"What do you mean?" said Wishnasky, preparing for an onslaught.

"You novelists are supposed to be sworn enemies of one another! And not only does Wanda have the balls to invite you here, *you* have the cheek to take her up on it! Remarkable!"

Relief washed over him. "Boris, long time. What are you working on these days?"

Boris brought his lips to Wishnasky's ear conspiratorially. "I almost have the funding," he whispered. "It's called *Dead, Deader, Deadest*. It's about zombies who invade a post-World War Four dystopia. I have a commitment from Regis Imhof: he'll be the madman who becomes *de facto* leader of the undead. If everything goes well, knock on wood, we'll start filming in September."

Wishnasky backed up a few steps to put some space between Boris and him. "But you've got a new book," said Boris, closing in in response. "With a religious angle: brilliant. Worked for Dylan, worked for Madonna; first we play red, then we play black. Oh, I know what you're doing. Until the next novel, yes? Which will also upend them! Clever, my friend, shrewdly calculating that the fickle public wants surprise, variety, the unpredictable!"

Before he could reply, a woman's voice said, "Tristan! I thought it was you! Come here and tell us your news!" It was Irene Gerber, the magazine editor, and she was standing with men and women whom he guessed were employees. She walked over to him, vodka in hand, and kissed him on the lips.

"Oh, Boris, you won't mind if we borrow Tristan for a moment? He's just the man we need to figure out this awful conundrum." Boris smiled bravely, and she herded Tristan over to her group. "Thank goodness you're here," said Gerber. "You've heard the gossip about Sherry Ostriker?"

"No," said Wishnasky. Ostriker was a famous newscaster on a cable channel. "I guess I missed it."

"You're going to be stunned," said a short, young man with a mustache. "Last Saturday morning, 8:30, she was photographed leaving the condo of Eddie Velasco." Velasco, Wishnasky knew, was a celebrated baseball player. "On the next morning—Sunday at 7—the paparazzi found her leaving Charles Walliston's cottage in Georgetown." Walliston was the junior senator from Kansas, and an up-and-coming figure in the Republican Party. "Two men, two mornings. And Walliston's only recently divorced."

"Legally separated," said Gerber. "And there was hope of a reconciliation."

"You're all Puritans," said a futuristic-looking woman with long metallic hair who suddenly appeared out of nowhere. "If she wants a different man each night, I say go for it. Damn the torpedoes. And I'll deck any busybody who calls her a slut."

"I'm not condemning her," said Gerber. "I'm just marveling at her ability to service herself with the *crème de la crème*. Especially when Eddie Velasco's been virtually camping out in Uma Slotkin's pelvis. But this woman takes what she wants."

"Sex is too precious to be entrusted to *homo sapiens*," said the metallic woman with a coy smile. "I much prefer the style of bonobo culture, where females are dominant and any potentially dangerous rivalry is defused with some convenient genital-to-genital rubbing."

"Sherry Ostriker has had her share of genital-to-genital rubbing," said the short, intense young man.

"The real story here is Eddie Velasco," said Gerber. "This is a man who has so many children from so many celebs, it would take an umpire to keep them straight. Soon enough, he'll be able to fill Fenway Park with nothing but sons and daughters."

Wishnasky was wondering how to extricate himself from the group when Boris Bulovich came back over, put his arm around him, said "Excuse me" to the others, and led him away.

"I have to ask you, Tristan," said Boris in a whisper. "Something that's worrying me, oppressing me, keeping me up at night: Do I have the stuff to make a worthy zombie movie? Maybe it's a young man's domain, maybe I lack the guts or the vision. Tell me, and don't mince words, my good friend, from what you know of me, do I have it? The prowess? The virtuosity?"

Wishnasky looked into Boris's tender, imploring eyes and could hardly believe that just a few short months before he had considered the company of these people a reward for his literary efforts.

"I gotta go, Boris," he said, and slipped out of the film director's grip.

As he hurried to the exit, he overheard a British-sounding middle-aged man say to a Eurasian-looking twenty-something-year-old woman, "Of course, he knows next to nothing about the restaurants in Denver, or for that matter, in Tahoe. Just because you've eaten at the Four Seasons, you can hardly claim to be an adult." The woman opened her mouth to reply, but Wishnasky was gone before he could hear her.

61.

THE INTERIOR OF THE CHALK ROOSTER was tasteful and elegant, with nothing bucolic about it except a blackboard featuring a chalk drawing of a rooster, under which the day's specials—mostly salads—were noted. Of the twenty or so bleached-pine tables arranged around the large space, only half were taken, and there was no sign of Aileen at any of them. Wishnasky walked up to the L-shaped maître d's desk and told a smiling strawberry blonde, "I'm meeting someone for a late lunch." She asked if he preferred to wait at one of the upholstered benches against the wall or to go directly to a table. He chose the table and was led to a four-seater mid-restaurant.

He was just looking at a menu when Aileen rushed in. She was wearing a white pinstripe blouse and a blue skirt that ended at her knees. "Hey!" she beamed at Wishnasky, and it suddenly occurred to him that she was much more attractive than he'd remembered, from her long, straight brown hair to her concise figure and slender ankles above white spaghetti-strap shoes. She glided into the seat opposite him and said, "I'm sorry I'm late. I still don't understand the traffic around here."

"It's easy," said Wishnasky. "In Boston you can't tell the drunk drivers from the sober ones."

She laughed. "I think you're right. And all the one-way streets that never go in the direction you want."

"Ancient cow paths," he said. "Devised for badly deranged cows."

She picked up the menu but didn't look at it. "I'm really glad I finally made it, though," she said. "And I have a surprise for you: I read your new book over the weekend."

"You're joking. And you still consent to dine with me? In public?"

"I thought it was lovely," she said. "I thought it was moving and wonderfully hopeful."

"It's a pity you don't work for a major newspaper."

"RARE's opinion counts for more than the newspapers'. If you've got our seal of approval, that's all you need. What do you think of this restaurant?"

"Seems nice enough. Is it special in some way?"

"Just wait till you hear," she said, and gestured to a young, mustached waiter who had just finished serving nearby diners. When he reached them, she said, "Would you please tell Scott Finster that Aileen Silver would like to see him?" The waiter moved off without a word. "We're starting to assert our influence," Aileen said. "We imagine a time when RARE's imprimatur can really affect a business's growth."

"Are we affecting this restaurant's growth?"

"You'd better believe it. All the thousands of gin joints in Greater Casablanca, and I came all the way from New York to just this one. And you came too, from ... where do you live?"

"Newton Corner."

"Newton Corner. To bring our commerce and the good chance that we'll go and recommend them to others. That's one of the great things about RARE: we know how deeply important dollars and cents are to everyone. Just because we're artists doesn't mean we're idiots. And if we've chosen a life that doesn't translate into giant payoffs, still we can strengthen our fellow travelers—"

She was interrupted by the appearance of a narrow-faced, fortyish man wearing a navy blue blazer and a thin black tie. "I'm Scott Finster," he said.

"Scott!" said Aileen happily, and jumped to her feet to shake his hand. "I'm Aileen, Willem Leggett's friend from RARE. And this is Tristan Wishnasky." Tristan waved in greeting. "We're doing what Willem told you, frequenting your business because you have RARE's recommendation." She sat again. "My friend Tristan is a famous novelist. If he mentions you in his next novel, it could mean thousands of new customers."

Scott looked pleasantly at Wishnasky, then turned back to Aileen.

"We're grateful for your patronage," he said. "We've had a few other visitors who also mentioned your group. Thanks for the heads-up."

"Tell Tristan about the restaurant. The reason we list you."

"All our food is locally grown," Scott said to Wishnasky. "We have a direct relationship with the Waverly Farm in Acton as well as connections with local farmers from here to Western Mass. We're totally committed to organic, sustainable farming and won't partner with any supplier we haven't personally inspected. Since we only serve what's seasonal, the menu changes a lot from week to week—that's the point of the chalkboard."

"I'm impressed," said Wishnasky, though he didn't know what "sustainable farming" meant. "You must be very conscientious."

"They get all their cheeses from a wonderful creamery near Braintree and all their wine from a vineyard in Westport," said Aileen. "Think what it means to the air quality that they don't rely on long-distance trucking. They even try to persuade customers to visit their source farms, free-roaming chickens and all. That's so advanced!"

Feeling increasingly uncomfortable at being the target of a sales pitch, Wishnasky asked Scott, "So, what do you recommend today?" he said. "What's really fresh?"

"I'd suggest the Sun-Lover's Salad," said Scott. "Romaine and red-leaf lettuce, Marcona almonds, radish, feta cheese, and citrus vinaigrette. The spinach in the spinach salad was actually biked in this morning. And our grilled Portobello Mushroom features Concord-crafted cheese and a local walnut vinaigrette dressing."

"Tell him how RARE found out about you," said Aileen.

"It was through the artist Willem Leggett," said Scott. "He came in here one evening and told us about his group, and we invited him to the Waverly Farm to see where it all starts. What he discovered was that they're thirty percent solar energy, they use the heat from their refrigeration system to raise the temperature of their hot water, they practice drip irrigation and do all their gardening with a bare minimum of herbicides—"

"Willem said this should be the first RARE-approved restaurant in the whole Boston area," said Aileen. "They're doing in a business sense just what we're doing as artists: tending to The Artwork. It's so exciting."

The door to the restaurant opened and a group of college students—three female, two male—walked up to the maître d's desk—but the maître d' wasn't there. "Excuse me," said Scott to Aileen and Wishnasky. "I should look after this. But thank you for coming from such a long way." He nodded to both of them and walked off toward the students, who were looking around confusedly.

"Do you understand now why I said we had to meet here?" said Aileen. "Why it couldn't be anywhere else?"

"Sure: you're growing your organization. Every move has to fit policy."

"No no no! That's much too bureaucratic! We're *supportive.* We're *committed* to helping one another. Do you know how the first Surrealists did it, wrote manifestos for the movement, exchanged ideas in the same journals? What André Breton and Man Ray did for each other, that's what RARE's artists are doing! This is a really exciting time for you to get to know us!"

Wishnasky didn't feel much excitement about RARE, but he was increasingly appreciative of the woman who was commending it. Then he remembered her lover—whom she'd compared to a husband—back in New York, and he told himself to stop dreaming.

"Anyway," he said, "I guess I'm curious as to what was so important about us seeing each other. Your text messages were so insistent."

Aileen sat back for a moment and Wishnasky saw she was blushing. Then, much less confidently than before, she said, "All right, I'll tell you. But I want you to think about it, yes? You won't just blurt out an answer before you've had time to mull it over?"

"I'll mull for hours and hours."

"For days, if that's what it takes. Because I want you to say 'yes.' It's really important to me."

"So important you couldn't just tell me over the phone?"

"The best things happen in person. Not in e-mails, text messages, phone calls, or on Facebook. The impact of two human beings actually encountering each other always makes an enormous difference. Anyway, that's what I've found."

"Well, here we are. Having an encounter."

"Exactly: so listen. Because this is something I deeply want."

It all had to do (she explained) with the latest RARE project in the Boston area. It was taking place in the suburb of Sudbury, a few miles away from Concord and Walden Pond, but in a mostly ill-off area that had none of Concord's wealth or exalted history. More precisely, there was a rundown middle school in South Sudbury surrounded by many acres of abandoned, desolate land, and one of RARE's operatives—the same Willem Leggett whom Scott had mentioned—had obtained the approval of the school authorities to turn some of this wasteland into a robust community vegetable garden, thus reclaiming a piece of The Artwork from years of abuse and neglect. Willem had already enlisted a dozen volunteers in the Metropolitan Boston Area who would pay a nominal fee to own a small plot in the new garden, and those same volunteers were ready to dig up the earth, replace it with more fertile soil (donated by a Bedford garden company), fence off the various plots, and install (under the direction of an amenable Charlestown landscape gardener) the irrigation. From spring to mid-autumn—before the first frost—this abandoned stretch of The Artwork would flourish with red beets and orange carrots and white cauliflower. Work on the garden was to begin in a few weeks, and it was projected that everything would be up and running a month-and-a-half later.

As to Wishnasky's contribution (Aileen continued) he would accompany her and her digital camera to the site several times over the course of the garden's creation. After observing the metamorphosis from chaos to order, he would write a 2000-word essay to back up Aileen's photos for a gallery on Staten Island. Wishnasky would write his piece *gratis*; it would be published in the catalogue, and the effort would win him a coveted membership in RARE.

When she was finished, Aileen sat back, a light radiating from her smiling face. "Do you have any questions?" she said.

"I do, as a matter of fact."

"Of course. Ask anything."

"Well, to start, why me? Especially after the tepid reception of my new novel, what makes you think anyone would want my take on your project?"

"I don't understand why you're so obsessed with your critics. You wrote what you believed, right?"

"That's right."

"Then that's all that matters. You're an artist, you take chances. To have an essay by you in our volume would be tremendous."

"I'm not really an essayist. I've pretty much devoted myself to fiction all my life."

"All the better. People will be surprised, and they'll want to read you."

This was getting nowhere. So, to be more practical: "How many visits to the garden?"

"Let's guess four. And of course, you can pay a call any time you like, even when I'm not with you. But if we can harmonize your words with my photos, all the better."

Wishnasky reasoned: saying "yes" would put him repeatedly in the presence of this rather alluring woman (who had a boyfriend, who had a boyfriend, who had a boyfriend) and give him a subject when a subject was precisely what he was lacking. On the other hand, he felt he should be focusing on his next major project, not distracting himself with something of no personal significance. Still, the size of the commitment—2,000 words—was next to nothing: a few pages on his computer, about the equivalent of a half a day's novel writing. Sure, it was feasible. But an instinct told him not to say so too immediately.

"All right, give me a few days and I'll get back to you," he said. "I can at least assert that I'm not definitely opposed."

"Wonderful," said Aileen, and smiled so broadly, he felt embarrassed not to have committed himself at once. "I knew when I saw you in the city that you'd be right for us. And I felt it even more when I read your novel."

"Ow. That old thing."

"That beautiful ode to healing and hope. You'll be perfect in RARE."

A waiter came by—not the one who had fetched Scott Finster—and they ordered their salads. For the rest of the meeting, they talked about the vicissitudes of living in New York and Boston. When he could cautiously do so, Wishnasky tried to learn more about Aileen's personal life, particularly that inconvenient boyfriend. But his subtle prompts were either missed or deliberately ignored, and he finished the lunch as uninformed as before.

As they were leaving the restaurant (he offered to take the check but she insisted on paying for her own meal), he asked where she was staying the night. "With a friend in Medford," she said, and he couldn't help wondering if that friend was male or female. Then, walking her to her car, he had the strange feeling that there was something else he should be saying. What was it? Something important ... But all that came to mind was, *Did you really like my novel?* No, that couldn't be it. He resolved to stay quiet.

At her car—a rented Dodge Charger—she put out her hand to shake his. "Don't be too slow to join us," she said. "I really think you belong in RARE."

"I'll let you know in a few days," he repeated. She got into her car, maneuvered out of the parking space and drove off into the distance.

As she disappeared, he felt a pang of regret. What had he forgotten to say to her?

All the way home he failed to imagine it.

62.

THE HORN OF PLENTY had not reopened. When Wishnasky called the rabbi to confirm that once again they wouldn't be driving to East Boston together, she asked if he had decided upon an alternate group with which to look after society's downtrodden. Hearing that he hadn't, she said she *would* like to meet with him, even if only for a half-hour. She seemed unusually businesslike, and Wishnasky wondered whether she was tiring of their consultations.

All the way to Lexington, he felt curiously unmotivated. Everything was on his mind except the homeless who, no doubt, had found food and shelter elsewhere. When he pulled into the synagogue parking lot, he felt sullen, impatient. When he walked into the rabbi's office and saw that the door to the inner room was, unusually, closed, he felt no disappointment. "She's in a meeting," said her secretary. "It wasn't on her schedule and it's very important, so she's asked you to wait. She apologizes, but it was an emergency."

He sat on one of the upholstered wooden chairs against the wall, pulled his phone from his pocket, and read the news feed: the fight over Brexit in England, the threat of more Russian interference in American elections, a trade war with China, an electoral battle in Colombia. But none of it touched him: what he really wanted was to go back to his home, stare at a blank computer screen, and imagine his next opus. If only he could imagine it!

The door to the inner office opened and there was Rabbi Diamant walking behind a middle-aged couple and a teenaged girl. Both adults looked like they'd been crying; the girl, perhaps sixteen, stared ahead grimly, didn't once look left or right during her entire transit out to the hallway. Wishnasky heard the rabbi say, "I'll see you again on Monday," and then the three were gone.

The rabbi, looking somber, nodded to Wishnasky and said, "Come in."

In her office, she gestured to the round table where they usually talked, and Wishnasky chose a chair and sat. The rabbi, stone-faced, sat down opposite.

She said, "I apologize for the delay. Part of my job is being available in crises, and this was precisely that. Now, let's talk about your work pursuing *chesed,* deeds of lovingkindness."

"Are you sure that this is the best time for it?" said Wishnasky, restive. "I can come back another day."

"The love of parents for children is so deep and desperate," said the rabbi, "it is chastening to be reminded of how overpowering it can be. I've just had that reminder. In response, I feel very small." She inhaled sharply, as if to reinvigorate herself. "But that's not why you're here. Let's talk about your Jewish practice."

"You said that the Horn of Plenty was still closed."

"And will never reopen. Kevin Spalding doesn't have the money to pay for the needed electrical and structural work. He could still salvage a few dollars by selling the place, which would thrill the shelter's neighbors, who for a long time have wanted it gone. So, that's probably going to happen." There was a pause. "Don't you want to know how all those people you used to feed are getting their meals?"

"Yes, of course. Please tell me."

"Some of them are probably using the free pantry at the Commonwealth Hunger Alliance—it's a long trek, but not too different from the Horn. As for the rest, begging for dollars on street corners and maybe eating one meal every other day. I see a few of them sometimes when I'm driving through the city, and I try to leave them with something."

Wishnasky thought about Arthur and his contention that the system didn't want its "casualties" in public view. "I never see them," he said. "How many are there—homeless people—in this area, I mean?"

"About ten thousand," said the rabbi. "And possibly more that haven't been counted."

"That's maybe ten thousand people who are somehow there and not there."

"Yes, curious, isn't it?"

He was about to apprise her of Arthur's theory, but before he could pursue it, the rabbi moved on. "Let's talk about your personal journey," she said. "I'm concerned that it's stalled. The night they closed down the Horn of Plenty, I named several other places where you could continue your search for God. Apparently, you haven't looked into any of them. Why not? Are you losing your momentum? Are you falling back into old patterns?"

"No," said Wishnasky. "I've just been … alerted to some other issues. When I can, I promise you I'll volunteer elsewhere."

"I'm not convinced," said the rabbi. "And I distrust good intentions. I told you before that I intended to teach you the adult version of Judaism, and in that version you're either climbing or you're falling. You had persuaded me you intended to seek God like a Jew, but now you're acting like you're ready to throw it over and be done with it. Or do you feel that your months at the Horn of Plenty exempted you from other commitments?"

"No—not at all," said Wishnasky, surprised at the rabbi's vehemence. "Please remind me of your suggestions."

"Big Brothers/Big Sisters, Amnesty International, or the battered woman's shelter in Revere. I can name others, if you like."

"I don't know. I guess I'm most intrigued by Amnesty. What can you tell me about it?"

"They do exceedingly good work. They'll put you in touch with a *mitzvah* we haven't ever talked about, *pidyon ha-shevouim*, redeeming the captives. You may not be aware of it, but there are thousands of innocent people around the world suffering from abominable conditions in prisons they were thrown into for professing political freedom or practicing their faith. You can learn more from the Amnesty chapter head in Cambridge. Shall I give you his email?"

"What would I have to do for him?"

"Not for him: for the mistreated. Write letters to ministers of state and prison directors, organize petition drives, contact legislators, and maybe even write some op-eds about particularly egregious cases."

"I don't know that I'm right for that."

"Why not? Attend a meeting and you'll hear about beautiful and courageous human beings, many of them desperately in need of your help. These are people in dungeons because of one remark in a newspaper, men and women being tortured because they spoke up for democracy in China or Saudi Arabia or the Congo. How could you better use your time than in trying to obtain their release?"

"And if I write a letter for a political prisoner in Africa, I'll be searching for God the same as I was at the Horn of Plenty?"

"Precisely the same. A different struggle requiring different methods, but the Holy One hates injustice and wants all of it rectified. So yes, this well qualifies."

He felt uncertain. Was he in fact trying to shirk his responsibility? He managed to say, "Rabbi, I admit I'm feeling some resistance. I realize I also felt scruples about the Horn of Plenty initially, so maybe I just have a phobia about new projects. But for the record, I'm uncomfortable."

"I understand. But try to think why."

He labored to name precisely what was bothering him; then it came in a rush. "Look," he said. "Ever since I saw that message in the Camus book, I've been turning into someone new. With your help and encouragement, I've started giving ten percent of my royalty checks to charity, I've been feeding the homeless, observing *Shabbat*, I've even changed the subject matter of my fiction ... And you know, maybe I'm worried that I don't recognize myself. Maybe the man I've become is a better man, but is he me? Is he authentic? Aren't I losing something also with all these transformations, one after the next? When it's over, will I even know myself?"

The rabbi peered at him as if she were trying to decipher a code. "You'll know yourself," she said finally. "And it'll make sense—I promise you."

"How can you be sure?" he said. "I feel conflicted right now, schizophrenic, divided against myself. I'm still getting over the bad reviews of my novel, and I'm still baffled a little. Who wrote it? Was that really me? And now, you want me to take things further."

The rabbi, tight-lipped, grave, nodded. "I'll tell you a story," she said. "A Hasidic tale from an earlier century. A king tells his son: there's a tower a short way from here. In front of the tower is a great boulder. I want you to take that boulder and carry it to the top of the tower." She paused. "Are you following this?"

"Yes. Of course."

"Good. So, the prince goes to the tower and sees the boulder he's been asked to lift. He tries to hoist it: it's too heavy. He tries to push it: it won't budge. For hours he does everything possible to follow the king his father's command. But he can't raise the boulder." She searched Wishnasky's face again, as if for signs of understanding. "Anyway, after a while the king approaches his son and says, 'have you done what I asked you?' And the son says, 'I can't. I've tried and it's impossible.' At which point the king produces an enormous hammer. And he says, 'Go now, smash the boulder. And by the way, that boulder is your heart.'"

The rabbi waited for Wishnasky to react; he didn't. "Do you see?" she said. "No," said Wishnasky.

"The prince's heart, all of it at once, was too heavy to lift. But smashed in pieces, one after the next, it can be carried to the top of the tower. One after the next. Maybe it's a slow way of doing things. And maybe one piece isn't quite congruent with the next, or with the one before. But I guarantee you, that when the last of the pieces is at the top of the tower, you'll find they all fit. They fit back together. And they are your heart. And yes, you'll recognize it."

Wishnasky cocked his head to one side and closed his eyes. Was it possible he was getting tired of lifting? He opened his eyes again. "So it has to be this way?" he asked. "One piece at a time? Couldn't I have raised the boulder all at once?"

"Impossible," said the rabbi. "Much too massive and unwieldy. But let me give you the email of David Hammond at Amnesty. And then try to lift another fragment of your recalcitrant heart."

The rabbi rose, walked over to her desk, checked an address book and wrote something on a small yellow pad. She tore the note off the pad and handed it to Wishnasky. He took the note, stood up, said "Thank you," and was about to leave when RARE came to mind. "Rabbi," he said, "if you don't mind me asking: What's the Jewish attitude toward environmentalism? Is there a specific doctrine?"

"Oh yes, *Bal Tashlit*: 'Do not destroy'. It's based on two verses in Deuteronomy and forbids the wasteful consumption of anything, natural resources included. Why? Are you thinking of working for the planet?"

"Is it a *mitzvah*?"

"Absolutely. As Rabbi Samson Raphael Hirsch said, humans beings are 'given to the earth, to respect it as divine soil' and to be 'the administrator of the whole divine estate.' That's entirely consistent with the *Torah* and *Talmud*."

"I thought that the first humans were told to rule over all creation."

"Rule over it, not blast it to kingdom come. And Adam is told to 'work the earth and guard it.' Jewish environmentalism is all about guarding it."

"Good to know," said Wishnasky, feeling a twinge of pleasure. "All right, I'll call your contact at Amnesty. And attend a meeting. Thanks for the push."

"Tell David that I send my best. And that I'm sorry my schedule doesn't allow for more time with him."

"I will," said Wishnasky, and walked out of the office, clutching the note.

63.

HE LAY IN BED LATE that evening and tried to make sense of the feelings buffeting him about. The rabbi's remonstrance still made him uncomfortable, as if he were a student whose teacher had accused him of indolence. Then, there was his anger at Ion for not warning him what sort of reception he could expect for his new novel. Which led him to worry that that novel would be his last—that, unlike nothingness, God was a subject you could broach only once.

And then there was Aileen—Aileen who had a lover! She'd said as much, and there was no reason not to think that she was delighted with the guy, enjoying his caresses every night and morning, and thinking of Wishnasky—if she deigned to think of him at all—as nothing more than the latest addition to her ecological group. But then he thought of her text messages: "Remember RARE and me." Wasn't that something more than an appeal to his comradeship? Or was he deluding himself? Maybe she sent those notes everywhere, to every potential activist, man, woman, and schoolchild. "Remember RARE and me." Why also "me"? Why not just "RARE?" "Remember" what? Her straight brown hair? Her trim body? *Everything really important happens in a face-to-face encounter*, she had said. That was obviously untrue—it had to be a ruse she was deploying in order to seduce him. But then why had she been so careful to do nothing, not one thing, suggesting a romantic intention? She wanted his name in her catalogue, that's what she'd said.

She imagined four meetings in Sudbury, at the site of the new garden. She couldn't have been more clinical. It was safest to expect nothing. To be really safe, he should turn down her writing request and put her out of mind completely. Out of mind: Was she in his mind? This was bad; this was regressive. Aileen had a lover: she was probably going to marry her handsome, dashing website designer tomorrow. What more did he need to know?

Well, he would call her in a few days. Probably her man would answer (would hear her phone dinging on the night table), and when he asked to speak to Aileen, the jerk would say, "She's just coming out of the shower now. Aileen darling, phone call, honey." That's all he needed: first the bad reviews, then the rabbi's impatience, then attraction to a woman two hundred miles away who had a longtime paramour with whom she practiced every sexual position.

He thought back to the girls who had broken his heart when he was much younger. There was Cathy Cartwright in high school, whom he'd yearned for, pined for, and finally confronted head-on with his profound devotion. On a Friday afternoon she'd said "yes," she'd go steady with him. On the following Monday, she'd stood him up and then refused to take his calls, till on Tuesday she told him that she was in love with Mitch Jorgensen and that Mitch, under pressure, had finally admitted he loved her too. Oh the pain of that loss: and then to see them, Mitch and Cathy, arm in arm for the rest of the year, laughing and frolicking in the school hallways, each unasked-for sighting another turn of the knife, another assault on his whole being so painful he took to walking the corridors with his eyes lowered. Hadn't that taught him? And then, five years later, Donna Quayle, whom he'd fallen for when she moved into the large house he was sharing with six other post-collegiates. Donna Quayle who went to bed with him every night for a month and then told him, with casual disdain, that she'd lost interest and her friend, Pancho, would be staying the weekend. And after Pancho, there was Kit and Andy and Rusty and so many more, and each new man was a fresh cut on his thin skin—humiliation by a thousand cuts! Hadn't Donna taught him once and for all to keep his heart to himself until he was sure, absolutely sure, that the woman he gave it to could be trusted with the merchandise? In all the years since Donna, he'd prided himself on his caution, and now here he was, in his mid-thirties, beginning to fall for a woman who was already committed elsewhere. Was he insane? Did experience mean nothing?

Well, he would call her and tell her he wasn't going to write for her silly group. No, wrong: just the opposite. He would tell her yes, of course, he'd be delighted to write for her. And then he'd ask her when was the next time the two of them could get together—why was his stomach feeling so raw?—and they'd make a date and until then, he'd play it cool, glad to have a new friend, nothing more, nothing extra.

Yes, right, he'd play it aloof—why was his stomach rumbling? Was he going to be sick? He felt half a breath away from vomiting! Aileen, The Artwork, Sudbury—but his stomach, this terrible weakness—what was happening to him? Didn't he know better than to fall in love? But how not to fall for such a lovely, intelligent, funny, compassionate, exquisitely enlightened woman? He was going to be sick!

64.

He called Aileen at 4:15 the next afternoon, dreading the possibility that her lover would answer. But it was she who picked up.

"Tristan? I'm so glad it's you."

"Good to hear it. Well, I've thought about your offer."

"Oh, please don't turn us down. We really need you. We need your talent."

"I guess I still have some questions. If I were to do this, I'd need to know a lot more about RARE, your other projects, and your program for the future. I'd want to do a sort of interview. How available are you?"

"By phone? Just about any evening. I could manage it tonight if you wanted."

"No, you've convinced me that people need to be with each other physically if they want true understanding. I'd like to get this done face to face."

"Okay, good. How do you want to meet?"

"Well, I need to talk to my agent in New York anyway. I could rendezvous with you in the city."

"Oh, I'd love to. When can you be here?"

"I could fly up on Friday, see Roland if he's available, and then keep the *Sabbath* at my hotel. What are you doing Saturday evening?"

"I was supposed to go out with Gerry, but he'll understand if I have to cancel. Saturday night would be fine."

This was going suspiciously well. "Cool," he said. "Let's say Saturday night. I can message you with more details of place and time before we meet."

"Oh, this is so great," said Aileen. "It sounds like you're going to help us!"

"I guess I am. I'm in."

"Hooray! I can't wait to tell Willem! How'd I persuade you? I'm so happy!"

"Well, this rabbi I meet with has been telling me that the obligation to look after nature is mentioned in Deuteronomy. So, I guess I should be on it. The *mitzvah*, I mean."

"That's right. We do good deeds! Oh, Tristan, I have to say it: you're going to love RARE. We really make a difference."

"I suspect you're right. Thanks for thinking of me."

"See you next Saturday."

"Yeah. See you."

He put the phone away: he was going after her, boyfriend or not. Life was an obstacle course. Life was a battle. He was setting his sights on Aileen Silver. The feeling he had for her, that non-rational, inexplicable gut reaction he couldn't help but recognize—it was all the convincing he needed. There was no law obstructing him: she wasn't married, after all. Two hundred miles was a short distance, a single step if one was willing. Yes, he'd come to New York and she'd fall into his arms. He'd exhibit his environmental conscience and she'd fall into his arms. He'd write her 2,000-word essay and—

He took his cell phone out of his pocket and looked up "drip irrigation."

65.

THE APARTMENT WAS NEAR MIT in East Cambridge, and Wishnasky had so much trouble finding street parking, he finally pulled into a lot and forked out fifteen dollars. Then he had to walk four blocks to the wooden house that in the twilight looked indistinguishable from all the others. He saw several names on the post next to the door, pushed the button under "Hammond," and was buzzed in a few moments later. He climbed a wide, worn stairway to the second floor landing, then looked around till he saw a half-opened door with the number 21.

Once inside, he found himself among a group of about a dozen people, most of them in their twenties, standing and chatting. There were coffee cups in their hands, and on the CD player he recognized John Coltrane's *Giant Steps.* Off to one side there was a bright kitchen from which he could smell the distinct scent of mint tea. A small, pleasant-looking woman with dark brown hair and a welcoming smile noticed his uncertainty and walked up to him.

"Are you a new member?" she said. "I don't remember you from last time."

"I'm sort of investigating," said Wishnasky. "My name's Tristan. I'm one of the congregants in Rabbi Diamant's synagogue."

"Oh right, I think there are a couple of others like that here. I'm Joan. Nice to meet you. Shall I introduce you to the head of the group?"

"If you don't mind."

She led Wishnasky into the kitchen where he saw two African American men—one tall and no older than twenty-eight or twenty-nine, the other short and gray-haired, perhaps in his sixties. Joan waited until there was a pause in their discussion and said, "David, this is Tristan, he's one of Rabbi Diamant's finds. Tristan, this is David Hammond and his father, Jonas. David's head of the section."

273

"Hey, Tristan," said the younger Hammond, shaking Wishnasky's hand. "Welcome to our meeting. Have you belonged to any other Amnesty group?"

"No. This is my first."

"Terrific. Do you have any special interest? Prisoners of conscience, women's reproductive rights, death penalty, gay and lesbian rights?"

"I think prisoners of conscience. People who are being mistreated."

"There are enough of them," said the other, older man in a gravelly whisper. "Middle East, Russian Federation, West Africa, Southeast Asia. Where's your main interest?"

"I don't know yet."

"The worst offender is China," said the elder Hammond. He was wearing a red and green flannel shirt and baggy black trousers. "When I started this group, it was the Soviet Union. Since the fall of Soviet communism, it's China, and after that the Arab countries. Some of the former Soviet republics also have their bad characters. Kazakhstan and Tajikistan."

"I'll be interested to learn more about it," said Wishnasky.

"Would you like some tea?" asked the younger Hammond.

"No, I'm fine, thanks. When does the actual meeting start?"

"It's time now. Take a seat in the living room and we'll get going." The younger man clapped Wishnasky on the back, then moved into the darkish living room and turned off the Coltrane. "We're going to begin," he said loudly, and in just a few seconds, people moved to the chairs already set up in a rough oval. Looking around, Wishnasky noticed a slight preponderance of females, and that half the group members were Black or Brown-skinned. Besides Jonas Hammond, he was the oldest person in the room.

The meeting followed in what, to Wishnasky, seemed a haphazard sort of order. First, the younger Hammond asked a woman named Bonita to speak about the group's adopted prisoner of conscience—a Thai human rights defender named Udom who had been imprisoned without charge after criticizing the military government in what he thought was a private email. She spoke of the efforts being made at Amnesty headquarters in London to get a lawyer in to see the activist, and of the failure of that effort so far. She asked who in the room had written a letter that month for Udom, and almost everyone raised their hands. She thanked them, then reminded them to keep the pressure on the Judge Advocate General in Bangkok and the Thai Ambassador in Washington. "Every letter you send—even if you never get a reply—may keep Udom alive," she said. "He's a brave and greathearted man, and we're not going to give up."

Then it was time for reports from other members of the group representing distinct regions of the world. One spoke of an imprisoned court secretary in Uzbekistan who had made the mistake of reporting violations of justice to what he thought was an impartial oversight committee. Others spoke about an incarcerated political cartoonist in Angola, a Colombian activist jailed for supporting the property rights of indigenous peoples, and three young Chinese pro-democracy activists who had been sentenced to ten years in prison each for the standard Chinese charge of "picking quarrels and provoking trouble." Next came the Amnesty member whose specialty was anti-death penalty work: she spoke of death row inmates in Nebraska and Texas, of their latest appeals, and, in one case, of the strong possibility of a commuted sentence. This was followed by the specialist on gay and lesbian rights: his report was on the Russian Federation, and the attempts by the family of one recently incarcerated man to visit the prison where their son and brother was being held. Finally, a tall African American young woman spoke of what she called a "major Amnesty action" to free seven Turkish human rights defenders sentenced to fifteen years imprisonment for their activism on social media. She passed a petition around the room and asked for signatures and addresses. The petition would be sent to Amnesty USA headquarters in New York and combined with hundreds of others in an ultimate mailing to Ankara.

After the meeting ended, Wishnasky approached David Hammond and thanked him for allowing him to sit in.

"Hey, my pleasure," said David. "Hope you don't mind that I didn't introduce you just yet. I figure prospective members prefer anonymity, at least till they officially join. Did you learn what you needed to?"

"I don't know," said Wishnasky. "Does all this letter writing work? Your prisoner in Thailand—do you really think you can get him released?"

"Ask my father," said David. "Dad," he called out to the older man who was sipping his tea a few feet away from them as he examined a petition. Jonas Hammond walked over to them. "Tristan wants to know if we've ever been effective. Tell him about Sonia."

"1985," said the elder Hammond. "The Soviet Union was still in existence, and I was a member in my first Amnesty group, working out of Natick. Our prisoner of conscience was a Ukrainian woman, Sonia Mirichenko, who'd been convicted of teaching the Ukrainian language to schoolchildren, which the Soviet authorities had forbidden. She was placed in a psychiatric hospital, force-fed psychotropic drugs because you had to be insane, see, to reject Soviet law.

"Well, we wrote for her every month. We wrote the head of the mental hospital, the mayor of the city, the premier, the ambassador to the US and the US ambassador. And it worked—something did. One day, Amnesty in London sent us word she'd been released. Before that moment, not a one of us got a letter back from anyone, not from the lowest abuser on the totem pole. But she told Amnesty, on her release, that once her jailer had said to her, 'You have a lot of friends in the United States.' And she thought we spared her from being tortured to death. She said we'd mattered."

Jonas Hammond reached into his pants pocket, fished out a handkerchief and coughed into it. Wishnasky wondered if the difficulty he had speaking was the result of a recent illness.

"I eventually came to lead Amnesty Natick," Jonas continued. "And during the years that I ran that group, I heard of a hundred prisoner releases. Failures too: more often than not. But even one woman in Myanmar redeemed from hell makes it worthwhile. By the way, do you know the name of the worst prison in Myanmar? 'Insein prison.'" He spelled it out. "How's that for coincidence?"

"Do you want to join us?" asked David Hammond. "We get together like this once a month, but there's lots you can do between meetings. Should I give you the case file on Udom so you can start to write for him? It'll tell you the addresses to send to, the sort of things you might say, and the appropriate forms of salutation for each official. And if it's all right, I'll contact you when it's time to send a delegation to Congressman Flannery when he's in Boston."

"Yes," said Wishnasky. "I'd be happy to help."

"Just leave me your phone number, said the younger Hammond. Meanwhile, I'll get you the materials." He walked away and Wishnasky was left with Hammond Sr., who coughed and then smiled at him over his cup of tea.

"What's your interest?" said the older man. "How'd you decide to come to our meeting?"

"I'm trying to live up to my obligations," said Wishnasky. "Religious ones. Jewish ones. I'm learning that I have those. Obligations, that is."

"I've seen a lot of religious people in my Amnesty groups," said the elder Hammond. "Jewish and Christian, Catholic and Protestant. Also Muslim. Also atheists. You don't have to believe in order to feel the injustice of what the Chinese are doing to their activists every day. Lately, they've been arresting attorneys who've taken human rights cases. And they don't just go after the activists: they harass the families, send thugs to beat up friends and spouses. I must have written fifty letters for Liu Xiaobo before they killed him. Even the Nobel Prize couldn't save his life with those rotten sadists."

"I was volunteering at a soup kitchen," said Wishnasky, "where I could see the people I helped. I don't know how I'll feel writing dozens of letters into outer space."

"You gotta use your imagination," said the elder Hammond. "You gotta imagine what those jackals feel when they see your name on another envelope."

David Hammond returned with a manila file folder in hand.

"Here's everything you need to start writing for Udom," he said. "Don't be afraid to personalize your letters—we don't want the recipients to feel they're getting a form. And dues for the group are fifty dollars a year. We use it for postage and herbal tea and snacks. Meetings are every third Wednesday of the month, seven to nine, usually here. When I'm out of town, one of the other members volunteers her apartment."

"What do you do when you're not working for Amnesty?" said Wishnasky.

"I'm an associate professor on a tenure track at MIT. Teaching statistics."

"I'm a novelist," said Wishnasky. "Live in Newton Corner. Glad to meet you."

"What's your name again? Maybe I know your work."

Wishnasky hoped not, and it turned out that he was right. Neither son nor father had ever heard of him or his first, doomy novels. Or the latest one, the failure.

Feeling some relief, Wishnasky gave his cell phone number to David, said his goodbyes and headed back to his car. On the way to the parking lot, he thought about the fact that while he relaxed in his Newton Corner home, watching cable television or contemplating his new novel, there were people—good people—being starved, beaten, tortured with cattle prods for wanting democracy, liberty, free speech. He thought how he'd passed thirty-six years on the Earth knowing next to nothing about such people.

And it struck him more sharply—more sharply even than he'd felt at the Horn of Plenty—that he had written three novels about philosophical despair, about the meaninglessness of life, while not-so-cynical men and women around the planet were risking everything they possessed for some items that did, after all, have meaning—the right to speak freely, to elect their leaders, to be treated with dignity. And it occurred to him again that his nihilism—the condition he'd written about in three heartfelt novels—had been a luxury of the very complacent, the relatively rich and comfortable. Meanwhile, there was a broken world crying out if anyone deigned to listen. A world that, according to Isaiah and his fellow prophets, God wanted him to repair.

Once back in his car, his thoughts turned to Aileen and her project of restoring "The Artwork." At least her efforts addressed a genuine problem and offered real solutions. How could he not admire her? And he thought of his own next work—how far he was from imagining it. Was he losing interest in literature? Why was it so hard to conceive his next step?

66.

THE NEXT CLUE to his new book came when he met his parents at their house in the suburbs and drove them to Boston Harbor. It was a clear spring day, temperatures in the low seventies, and a walk along the breezy waterfront seemed the perfect pastime. Soon they were strolling past trendy hotels, chichi stores, upscale groceries, and warehouses that had been converted to condominiums. Ahead and behind them were dozens of other pedestrians also excited by lovely spring.

"How's the Jewish kick?" asked his father, who was walking with a cane now. The physical therapy had been working, but he got tired more easily than before the heart attack and found the support good for his balance and self-confidence. "I see you're not wearing a yarmulke yet."

"I wear a yarmulke when I pray," said Wishnasky. "Or when I'm in a synagogue. It's only the Orthodox who say you have to wear it everywhere else."

"We're waiting for you to become Orthodox," said his mother. "If you're going to go three-quarters of the way, why not go the whole distance?" She smiled at a baby in a stroller, then at the man pushing it. "When you were dating that Orthodox girl, we thought she'd make the difference. You realize, you've never told us what went wrong between the two of you."

"I didn't love her," said Wishnasky.

"They never measure up," said his mother. "And now you're in your thirties, no wife and no children. Maybe the real problem is that you're holding out for the impossible. A nice human being isn't enough for you."

He considered telling them about Aileen, then thought better of it: they'd only lump her with all the others.

"I just want to find someone that I'll still care for over the long haul," he said. "Like you and Dad, for example."

"So you claim. In any case: we're giving up. The only reason we put up with the New England winters over the last few years was so we'd be near when you brought us grandchildren. But it's more and more clear that's not going to happen. So congratulations: we're moving."

"What? Moving where?"

"There's an area of St. Petersburg which is only a few blocks from the water in one direction, and from downtown in another. When we were there last February, we talked with a realtor who showed us some lovely condominiums. We've been in touch with him recently, and he found us a good deal. It's a little pricier than we wanted, but for twelve months of sun, maybe it makes sense. We're planning to fly down later this month and, if we're satisfied, sign a contract. So. thank you. For staying single."

"When would you move?"

"I'd say July. We'll put the house on the market sooner, but we don't expect a quick sale. That's one thing you can do for us: drive by a couple of times a month and make sure everything's hunky-dory. Do you think you can manage that?"

"Of course. But this is big news. When did you decide?"

"What difference does it make? We had one reason to stay and it turns out we were deceiving ourselves. So, great: have lots of girlfriends, and don't settle down with any of them. You don't even have to visit. You're freer than ever."

Wishnasky was conscious of his father's silence. "Dad, are you okay with this?"

"Over the years," said his father, "your mother has shown a lot of foresight. This sounds like a good choice." His words lacked enthusiasm.

"Last February he strolled through St. Petersburg in a polo shirt," said Mia Wishnasky. "Shorts and a knit shirt. In mid-winter. And sandals. He knows this is the right thing."

There was a crowd up ahead, and the three walkers approached it to see what the attraction was.

"Look," said his father. "A juggler. I like jugglers." And in fact, on a broad grassy plaza backed by the harbor, a thin, dark-haired young man was juggling bowling pins in front of a score of spectators.

"All right, we'll look," said Wishnasky's mother. They joined the semicircle of people watching the performer, beside whom sat an open suitcase for donations. He was dressed in white pants and a rainbow shirt, and he smiled broadly as he spun the rotating pins over his head.

"This guy's good," said Wishnasky's father. "I wish I could do that."

"You could, Dad," said Wishnasky. "There are a hundred things you could do with your time aside from sitting at home all day watching the History Channel."

"I had a heart attack," said his father. "You want me to sign up to play football with the Patriots? Go for fullback? Defensive end?"

"You could join a book club or take courses at Harvard Extension."

"In what subject would I take these courses?"

"Whatever interests you."

"What interests me is enjoying this juggler. Leave me alone."

Wishnasky watched the juggler reach down quickly and add a fourth bowling pin to his airborne collection. So his parents were moving. He felt half-sorry, half-relieved. Four fewer eyes scrutinizing and judging his every move. On the other hand, those eyes had been part of his world for so long, it felt odd to think of going on without them. Had he really failed them by not producing grandchildren?

"When I get married," he said. "I'll fly my wife and our babies to St. Petersburg for endless vacations. We'll visit so long, you'll beg us to leave. Strained food and pacifiers and dirty diapers all over your condo, everywhere you look. A big crib and Barney the dinosaur on your TV."

"Big talk," said his mother. "We're no longer waiting. You fooled us too many years."

Now the juggler had added a soccer ball to his collection, and the crowd was applauding his increasingly challenging feat. Wishnasky wondered again whether he should tell his parents about Aileen, then decided they would accuse him of wanting her only because she lived so far away.

So instead, he said, "By the way, I'm thinking of joining Amnesty International. They do a good job looking after political and religious prisoners. I'm kind of excited to think about it."

"Who put you up to that?" said his mother.

"Rabbi Diamant. We had a long talk after the soup kitchen closed, and that's the result. I'm full of enthusiasm. This is outside anything I've done before."

"They are not friends of Israel," said his father.

"No?"

"No."

"Maybe I can change their attitude," said Wishnasky. "At least the ones in my Boston group."

"You know," said Wishnasky's mother, "when you were a boy you had all sorts of odd ideas about people. About trusting them too much. About sacrificing your own interests to theirs. You should be careful or you'll fall right back into that pattern."

"I don't remember being particularly altruistic as a kid," said Wishnasky. "I think I was approximately as self-serving as the next infant."

"You've forgotten," said Mia. "I had to stop you at times from giving your toys away, emptying your lunch box to other children. If one of your kindergarten friends was crying, you'd stop anything to run over and help her."

"That's strange: I don't have the first memory of any of that."

"I trained you out of it," said Mia. "I saw how you were allowing the other children to exploit you, and I came down hard, taught you to be tough. This attitude you've struck since becoming a novelist—thick-skinned, couldn't care less, interested in yourself and nobody else: I put that in you. I created that. And I had a good reason, too. Now you're undoing all my hard work."

Wishnasky searched his memory, but had no recall of ever being unusually unselfish. Well, there was one vague memory ... "I can think back to one thing," he said. "Whenever I came home from school excited about some accomplishment of one of my friends, you would say, 'Why are you crowing about someone else's successes? It's *your* successes you should be talking about. Let the other children run home to tell their parents about *you*!' I do remember you saying that. But nothing else of the kind."

"You were such an easy mark," said Mia. "Just about anyone could take advantage. I worked hard to make sure you didn't turn into the world's victim."

With one last flourish, the juggler caught everything in his arms and bowed to the crowd. There was laughter and applause, and Morris Wishnasky said, "Let's keep walking."

"First I want to give him a little money," said Wishnasky.

"Don't be a fool," said his mother.

"I'm becoming that kid again," said Wishnasky, reaching into his back pocket for his wallet. "I'm sharing my lunchbox." He found a bill, walked over to the juggler's open suitcase, and tossed it in.

"You're a boob," said Mia Wishnasky. "You treat money like that and soon you won't have any."

"Tip of the iceberg," said Wishnasky, feeling strangely willful. "I'm already tithing my income, and do you know, I enjoy it? Sitting down Friday afternoon, wondering to whom to write a check, for what poor people or sick people in Appalachia or Tibet? Do you know it's become one of the high points of my week?"

"When you open your checkbook one morning and there's nothing for *you*, then you'll understand what I'm saying," said Mia Wishnasky.

"You know what I look forward to?" said Wishnasky, defiant. "What that kid in me looks forward to? To writing letters for political prisoners. To the moment when the soup kitchen reopens and I can get back to feeding the homeless. Or maybe I'll volunteer at a battered woman's shelter or a children's hospital or the free clinic in Cambridgeport."

"Stop showing off and let's walk," said Morris.

"You'll be sorry," said Mia. "When the world sees a pushover, it pushes. It lays him flat. There's an old Yiddish saying: If you act like a goat, wolves will devour you. That's what you're asking for."

"What else have I forgotten about my childhood?" said Wishnasky. "What else did you train me out of?"

"Bedwetting. Fear of the dark. You're being obnoxious."

But he was feeling joyful.

67.

ON FRIDAY MORNING he flew to New York, took a cab from LaGuardia Airport and was at his hotel by 1 p.m. It was a narrow blue modern building wedged between two tall brownstones, and was so out of harmony, it seemed that the indignant, older edifices on its flanks might at any moment squeeze the interloper out of existence. He left his one suitcase in his compact room on the sixth floor, then set out to meet Roland.

The walk to Chelsea was exhilarating. Unlike the crowds in his part of Boston, the New York throng was, as always, in a terrible hurry. This was a city where one *got things done*, and if you happened to be on the way to the doing, you let nothing slow you down. As for the great skyscrapers everywhere—a thousandfold more than in downtown Boston—they peremptorily let you know that the real world was *in them*, that until you found yourself in an elevator going up, up, up, you were no one, a dwarf, a squirt, a cipher. Wishnasky had many times thought about moving to Manhattan, getting closer to his agent, his editor, his publisher. But he worried that whatever competitiveness drove him in Newton Corner would become elephantine in Times Square, and he'd come to despise himself for not appearing on electric billboards like the latest Broadway blockbuster. Boston was provincial compared to Manhattan, but the pressure was off there—that was the keyword, *pressure*—and one could afford a little serendipity. As he surged across a city street with fifty other urgent pedestrians, all of them capable of trampling a straggler under foot, he marveled that New Yorkers could live at such a pitch. What self-possession it must require!

When he reached Roland's office/apartment in a row house on 23rd Street, he climbed the few steps to the front door, buzzed and waited. Then he heard a gruff voice say, "Who is it?" and he replied, "It's me, Tristan. Buzz me up." A moment later the intercom whirred and Wishnasky pulled the door open.

He walked up a wide staircase to the second floor and knocked at number 2A. Moments later, Roland was glaring at him.

"So the prince condescends to visit his lowly subjects," he said, and gestured with his right hand. Wishnasky walked forward.

It was a likably bright apartment, with a spacious, peach-colored living room, a kitchen directly through one doorway, and a brief hallway leading to a bedroom on one side and Roland's business office on the other. Usually, Roland invited Wishnasky into the office; today he gestured at the living room sofa and said, "Sit." He offered coffee or water—Wishnasky demurred—and then said with a quizzical look, "So how do I deserve this extraordinary attention?"

"You know I try to see you every time I'm in the City."

"You should have moved here after *No One From Nowhere.* The opportunities you've squandered, hiding out in New England. You could be ten times as well-known, a celebrity of the stature of a Salman Rushdie, a Margaret Atwood, what Philip Roth was for forty years. Instead, you're afraid to cut the umbilical cord to Mother Harvard, so you stay in that backwater. And you're a fraction of what you could be."

"I always wanted my books to be famous," said Wishnasky, as soothingly as possible. "As for myself, I could take it or leave it."

"That's an ignorant attitude. What do you imagine is the point of publicity: to build an author's ego? It sells books, my suburban friend. One TV appearance sells thousands of novels, a profile in the *Times* thousands more, you honestly think Rebecca Mallory cares one iota about your self-image? She sells *product,* she reports to the *stockholders,* if you'd take your eye off God for ten seconds, you'd see why living in Newton Corner is just bad business. But after the mess you made with *Traveler,* maybe bad business is your specialty. Or have you learned your lesson?"

Wishnasky peered at Roland and tried to remember why he'd kept this curmudgeon as his agent for fourteen years. The fact was, he's sent out fifty copies of *No One From Nowhere* to agents when that first novel was finished, and only Roland had had the acumen to see the book's viability. Even then, Wishnasky had cringed at Roland's combativeness. But he'd reasoned that it was likely just the same attitude that won him such generous contracts from publishers. And later, when Wishnasky was much more successful and other agents tried to poach him from Roland, Wishnasky'd felt an obligation to stay with Roland, who'd taken a gamble on him after his time as a Marine and his start as an agent.

"I haven't changed, Roland," he said. "I got interested in my religion, and that interest continues."

"At least tell me you're through writing about it."

"I don't know. I'm only sure that I don't intend to repeat myself. Beyond that, I can't say. Let's assume the next novel's percolating."

"Well, percolate it more judiciously than the last. Some of your readers won't have given up on you. But two books in a row on a religious theme and you'll lose them forever. Take my advice this time; you know what happens when you don't."

Wishnasky looked around Roland's living room. On the walls were posters advertising books that Roland had represented with glorious results. He realized that his new convictions had most probably removed his work from their company. Then he recalled a distant memory: *Search for Me.*

"I'm sorry, Roland. I can't be who you want me to be."

"So you're going to write another flop."

"I don't know what I'll do next. I can't say for certain."

"Then I have a prediction to make: you're going to give up writing entirely."

"I very much think that's not true."

"You're going to realize you want to spend all year praying and studying God's word, and you're going to close up your laptop. That's all I can see if this religious jag is serious."

"I think that you're wrong."

"Have you started the next novel?"

"I've given it a few passes."

"And you came up empty, am I right?"

"I'm just waiting for the right subject."

"No, I'm sure of it: you may not know it yet, but you're becoming a monk. The time is fast approaching when the *Torah* will be your morning newspaper, your afternoon talk show, and your evening movie. I see this as clearly as I see you sitting in front of me."

Wishnasky thought about the difficulty he had had imagining his next work, and worried that Roland might be right. But of course he couldn't say so. "I'm a writer, Roland," he said. "It keeps me breathing."

"I'll tell you again: what drove you to be an author was lust, pure and simple. Women-fame-money, the usual trio. One day soon you're going to know it, and religious Tristan will be scandalized. Then goodbye to every novel inside you. I wish I were wrong. But you'll see."

"I don't think you know me as well as you imagine, Roland."

"I was right about *Traveler.*"

"About its sales figures, yes."

"And I'm right about this—you're going to throw over literature entirely."

"I don't know that."

"Well, I do. Still I harbor a last hope: that you'll face some trauma, some shock to your infatuation with God and the Bible so powerful that it will turn you back to your original vision. Which was harsh, astringent and *true.*"

"I don't know, Roland. Looking back, I think my gloom was pretty smug."

"Then get smug again or you're lost forever. Which I would truly hate to witness."

68.

Back on the outside, Wishnasky tried to forget Roland's predictions and instead enjoy spring in New York. He pointed himself northward, toward his beloved Central Park. He imagined basking in the luxurious foliage there awhile, then walking back to 38th Street on Park or Fifth, perhaps stopping for a sandwich along the way. After he'd traveled the few more blocks to the hotel, he'd rest on the queen-sized bed, read more of Heschel's *God in Search of Man* on his iPad Mini, and finally go to synagogue for *Shabbat* evening services. And then back to his hotel room and anticipation of Aileen.

The walk was a relief after the tension of the talk with Roland. The air was fresh, the temperature around seventy by the time he got to the park, and he was almost at peace. Central Park was the anti-city: it was crowded, of course, but beneath the miles of trees there were seemingly unhurried people lounging on the grass, picnicking, schmoozing, and taking the sun. He bought a lemon-flavored Italian ice from an elderly vendor, wandered randomly, only trying to stay relatively close to the park's periphery. Ambling among the thinkable, good-hearted elms and cherries, he could muse on his love object: what she was doing at this moment, whether she was even conscious that he was strolling only a few miles from her, whether he figured in her imagination at all. A blonde mother with her small blond children, one in a stroller, one waddling beside her, passed him on one side, and he was cognizant of his own mother's insistence that he was missing out on his chance to have children. He saw a group of schoolboys carousing together, punching each other's shoulders and making wisecracks, and he was aware that his closest friends, Rick, Chet, and Quentin, had families already, possessed a joy he'd denied himself. Was *anybody* going to be the solution to this? He thought back to Andrea and her desire for a large brood; he could almost understand it.

After most of an hour, he left the park, headed to Fifth and started the long walk through the crowds back to his hotel. He stopped for a fruit plate and coffee at a bright, modern restaurant in the sixties, then braved the mobs in the forties and returned to his room. He took a shower, changed into a crisp white shirt and black pants, downloaded Heschel on his iPad, and read for a while. When he began to lose interest, he turned on TV and watched a local news channel. At 6:15, he put on a gray sports coat and took the elevator to street level. The synagogue he had discovered on the internet the day before was just a few blocks from his hotel, and he was looking forward to the service: he wanted to thank God for the series of events leading to this moment, just in case Aileen's appearance in his life was no accident. It was so odd, the unfolding of events: if he hadn't ever seen the words in the Camus book, he wouldn't have changed the subject of his novel, wouldn't have arranged a reading at the Strand, wouldn't have fielded a question from the lovely woman with the auburn hair ... In his previous incarnation, he would have thought this one accident after another. But now ... was there a shape to it?

Minutes after leaving the hotel, he found the synagogue. It was a squarish brick building fronted by three white columns, its large double doors open and a crowd just visible inside. He stepped in and saw perhaps forty people who had preceded him, the men in coats and ties, the women in sober dresses, a few impatient children earning their parents' remonstrances. Wishnasky stepped from the anteroom into the sanctuary, found a space in a long upholstered pew, picked up the prayer book in the holder in front of him, and turned to the "Welcoming the *Sabbath*" section. He was pleased to discover that he felt at home in the familiar pages. A few minutes later, the last congregants sat down—there were many empty seats, though—and the rabbi, a smiling, middle-aged man with a friendly, Russian-looking face, ascended the bimah along with the short, energetic cantor, announced the page number and the service began.

It was over in exactly one hour, and was entirely a pleasure. Many of the tunes that the cantor sang were the same ones Wishnasky knew from his *shul* in Lexington, and the stirring call of the *Shema* was as potent in New York as it always was in Massachusetts. There was a brief sermon—about the *Torah* portion *Shemini,* in which the clean and unclean animals were distinguished from one another—and a reminder to the congregation that in three weeks the synagogue social hall would be the site of an Israeli Film Festival. During the

Amidah prayer, Wishnasky thanked God for bringing him to New York and Aileen, and prayed—though he feared he shouldn't—for success romancing her. When the service was over, he filed out onto the street, saying *Shabbat Shalom* several times to congregants who greeted him with the same words. He felt a strange validation, as if he belonged to an alliance with branches all over the world, and he'd just been welcomed into one of them. Would he have felt just as snug in a synagogue in Montreal or Marseilles or Madrid? It was a warming thought.

He walked toward his hotel and stopped at a restaurant—he'd taken on a lot of *Sabbath mitzvot* over the preceding year, but not yet the one that said to refrain from making purchases on the holy day—and enjoyed a broccoli stir fry with a salad and soda. Then he returned to his room, changed clothes, found his Hebrew textbook, propped up some pillows on the bed and tried to study. But he was soon discouraged: the easy, early days of learning Hebrew had long passed, and now he was challenged by bizarre verb conjugations—the jussive, the cohortative—that too closely resembled other bizarre verb conjugations with which he'd struggled. Feeling stymied, he laid the book aside and thought about Aileen: no doubt the image of a grown man spending his Friday night reading abstruse Hebrew phrases would appall her, remind her of how glad she was to be committed instead to her debonair basketball-flinging, football-heaving, hockey-puck-slamming lover and the wild heartbeat-quickening punk-rock concerts to which he always took her on Friday evenings. What in the world made him think he should come to New York? He turned on the TV with the remote on the night-table and watched a few minutes of insipid crime drama. Well, he wasn't sorry he had no time for *that.* He surfed through the cable networks till he found a Discovery Channel program on *The Voyage of the Beagle: Charles Darwin in his Time.*

Now this was interesting: if all truth was in harmony with all other truth, then Biblical religion had to find a way to harmonize with Darwin's discoveries. After all, the evidence for evolution was decisive—the fossil record alone could convince an honest skeptic. So how to reconcile the one picture of creation with the other? When the *Torah* said humans were made in God's image—a statement offered about no other species—was this a sign that the purely human things—language, reason, creativity, free will—were given *outside* evolution, by God Himself? Could Stephen Hawking's existence be explained by blind natural forces? The program flashed a portrait of Darwin in the 1860s, along with a quote: "A man who dares to waste one hour of time has not discovered the value of life." Darwin himself, with his scruples, ambitions, elegance—certainly he was something more than a randomly evolved trilobite. He'd have to explore this further: Charles Darwin's existence as an argument for the uniqueness of God's gift to humans. Wishnasky closed his eyes and imagined white-bearded Darwin giving a talk at the Royal Academy of Something or Other ...

He woke up with a start. Where was he? Yes, the hotel. He looked at the clock radio on the night table beside him: 7:23 a.m. He'd been asleep for eight-and-a-half hours. He washed up in the bathroom, put on his jacket and took the elevator to the first floor. A block and a half from the hotel he found a twenty-four-hour restaurant, stepped into it and sat at the counter with seven other breakfasters. Coffee and pancakes later, he wandered back into the New York morning and the noisy trucks and buses thundering along the streets with moving vans and speeding taxicabs. An hour till *Sabbath* morning services: he returned to his hotel room, watched a morning news program, then left again and walked to the synagogue.

This time the place was packed. The reason became immediately clear: there was a bar mitzvah going on and a great crowd had gathered to welcome a young man into adulthood, Jewish style. When Wishnasky stepped into the sanctuary (after donning a *tallit* and skullcap in the anteroom), he saw an awkward-looking, black-haired adolescent already up on the bimah talking to the rabbi, while among the pews the horde of congregants was chattering noisily. He found an empty space at the far end of one pew, picked up a prayer book, and waited for the service to begin. It didn't—the jabbering crowd didn't quiet, and the rabbi was conferring not only with the young celebrant but with the cantor and a stranger. Wishnasky was beginning to think that he could pray instead in his hotel room when the cantor approached the pulpit, cleared his throat at the microphone, and started singing *"Mah Tovu."* The chatter of the congregants faded away and soon some of them were singing along.

What followed were two-and-a-half hours of *Shabbat* morning service, with the diminutive bar mitzvah boy looking anxious but sincere in his black suit and black-rimmed glasses, alternating with the rabbi in leading the prayers. Wishnasky followed along, said in Hebrew and English all the requisite sections, and observed, as innocuously as possible, the many congregants who were too busy murmuring to each other to join in praise or supplication. How many of these apparently upper-middle-class folk attended synagogue when there were no parents of a thirteen-year-old to require their presence? How many understood even a word of the Hebrew hymns they were ignoring?

Realizing guiltily that he was criticizing strangers for the same lack of Jewish education that he himself once possessed, he resolved not to think ill of them and turned his thoughts instead to the young man whose occasion this was. This nervous youth was doing his level best to sound decisive as he sang out the paragraph beginning "*Nishmat kal chai*"—"the soul of all that lives." Peering into those large, frightened eyes behind the heavy glasses, Wishnasky remembered his own bar mitzvah more than twenty years before. Tristan Wishnasky at age thirteen, after seven years of Hebrew School, had understood next to nothing about Judaism, the *mitzvot*, the call to social action. He had learned how to read Hebrew characters, but not how to translate them. Yes, he had been told that upon his thirteenth birthday he would become a man, but no one, neither his childhood rabbi nor his parents, had tried to persuade him that he would in fact now be fully, personally responsible for performing God's commandments. No, he now realized, he hadn't become a man at his bar mitzvah, and neither, for that matter, had any of his school friends. Just the opposite: after a year of learning to lead the services, to don *tallit* and *tefillin*, to give to charity and keep *Shabbat*, the boys in his bar mitzvah class had come, on that special occasion, to the end, not the beginning, of their Jewish practice. After his bar mitzvah, Wishnasky, like all of his friends, had *stopped* doing *mitzvot, stopped* saying prayers, had promptly dropped everything, to no one's objections. What the boy on the bimah should have been saying on this occasion was not, "Today I become a man," but "Today I put all evidence of manhood behind me. It was there for a year, thanks to the requirements of this ordeal, but today I cast it off. The next time you can expect to see me in synagogue is thirty years from now, when my own son gets bar mitzvahed—and then casts off the commandments as precipitously as I did."

The service was near over. In his closing remarks, the rabbi reminded the congregants that they were invited to lunch in the social hall in honor of the new "man," but Wishnasky stayed only for the closing song of *Adon Olam*—"Lord of the Universe." Then, smiling at all the well-wishers who took him for the bar mitzvah boy's relative, he made his way back out to the bright New York afternoon. He felt like a stroll.

In the pleasant Saturday afternoon breeze, he tried to understand his emotions. He was certain now that for him, Judaism was a fine thing: a deep and meaningful call to action, to the recognition of God's sovereignty, the obligation of social justice, and the full employment of the intellect on texts more profound than any great novel. But he'd learned this lesson late, and he regretted the time wasted—twenty-four years, to be exact—from his bar mitzvah till now. Even a lackadaisical young person might have spent some of those years making a difference in a troubled world. When he thought of all the good he hadn't done, the charity he hadn't given, the consolation he hadn't spread, he felt ashamed and repentant. Could one play catch-up after such a bad start? Could he ever compensate for the time he'd wasted?

Wishnasky bought a *New Yorker* at a newsstand and checked the listings as he walked in no particular direction. He had to decide how to spend the time before seeing Aileen. His first impulse was to go to the Museum of Modern Art and enjoy the new Rauschenberg exhibit, but a few hours viewing art might too easily lead him into thoughts about his writing—not in the *Sabbath* spirit. Then he saw that the Museum of Natural History was offering exhibits that had nothing to do with the literary life—investigations of bird flight, of the human sense organs, of dark energy in the cosmos. At that institution, at least, he could muse on the mystery and wonder of God's creation. Then, he'd wander back at leisure to his Midtown hotel, shower, say the Afternoon Prayer, and dress to see Aileen. Lovely Aileen—only a few miles away from him. What was *she* thinking at this moment?

He stopped searching for his next stopping place and enjoyed the breeze against his face. And his mind returned to the synagogue service he'd recently left. He was irked with himself for having felt so judgmental. Maybe he was wrong about the trajectory the young man at the bimah was traveling on. Maybe he'd become a religious Jew of the most authentic, observant type. Maybe he'd heal his part of the world more successfully than any other. One thing Wishnasky knew—when he bothered to remember it—was that you couldn't know anyone from just a few hours with them—people were so deep and complex, histories were so wide and unexpected, it took months or even years to begin to understand them. So instead of condemning the bar mitzvah boy to a life of thoughtlessness, why not imagine him setting out on the road to greatness, to dazzling accomplishment, as a Jew, as a thinker, as a doer of *mitzvot*? Yes, that too was possible: that he'd just witnessed an important step in the path of a great personage. As long as one was guessing, why not guess the very best? Wasn't this one of the interpretations of that line in the *Talmud* the rabbi had apprised him of: "Judge everyone on the scale of merit?"

He came to a street corner and waited for the WALK signal with a few other pedestrians. Why go to any museum or gallery when all the sights were right here out in the open? The light changed and he crossed over to nowhere in particular.

69.

I<small>T WAS</small> 7:20 P.M. and he was sitting at the Kenyon Deli, waiting for his date. The restaurant's wide interior was divided into two large spaces, and there was a constant bustle of diners and servers, a cacophony of excited voices mixing in the air with the pungent aroma of sauerkraut. On the walls were photographs of theatre and film stars with inscriptions: *best to Nate Kenyon; love you, Nate Kenyon; kisses to Nate Kenyon.* Wishnasky was huddled in a centrally located booth nursing a Rolling Rock and wondering how he'd react if Aileen never showed up. Every time a new body appeared in the doorway, he craned his neck to see if it was her, and each time it wasn't, he mentally kicked himself for feeling so needy. He had to remind himself: it was dangerous to want anything too much.

And then, there she was.

She looked gorgeous in a pink and white checkered blouse and black skirt. Her hair had been recently cut and fell halfway to her shoulders, and she was wearing just a minimum of makeup. She walked in, looked around worriedly, saw Wishnasky waving and, with a huge smile, glided over to his table and sat. She held out her hand.

"The subways in this city have gotten painfully antiquated," she said as they shook hands. "And they're off schedule more often than on. I'd have arrived here more quickly if I'd walked all the way from Brooklyn."

"Not a problem," said Wishnasky. "I'm just glad to see you. Ever been to this place?"

"I know less and less about Manhattan every year," she said. She looked around for a waiter. "May I have a sip of your beer?"

"Of course." He handed her his glass, she took it and drank. As she did, Wishnasky remembered something from the *Torah*: Avram saying to Sarai,

"I know that you are a woman of beautiful appearance.'" He thought he understood it now. "You keep that and I'll order another one for myself," he said.

"Can't we share?"

"All right, we'll share. You know, next time I'll make a point of coming to Brooklyn. I wasn't thinking about the distance when I said we should meet here."

"I'm so glad you're joining RARE, I would have met you in Wyoming."

"Actually, I've come to the conclusion that your organization is refreshing, not to mention innovative. I want to hear more about it."

"In a minute," she said. "After I've calmed down from the subway. Where are you staying?"

"Three blocks away. A little hotel between two behemoths."

"Walking distance. Pretty clever. Which one's our waiter?"

"The one talking to the bartender."

"I'll be right back," she said and slipped out of the booth. As Wishnasky watched her approach and talk to the waiter, he had to recall that in her mind she had come to discuss business, business only, and that he was insane to allow himself to become so enamored. The woman had a lover!

She returned and sat. "I've ordered a bottle of wine," she said. "A Sauvignon Blanc. Is that all right? I probably should have asked you first."

"No, that's fine. Do you want to look at the menu?"

"After the wine. Now tell me about your flight from Boston. And what you've been doing since you got here."

Wishnasky did his best to answer her questions as if he weren't completely enchanted by her proximity. Entrancing, too, was her scent: just barely like gardenias, too sweet to be soap and too subtle to be perfume. Flustered by his rush of feelings, he found it easier to turn the conversation toward her—her work in the public schools, her living arrangements in Brooklyn, her parents—both in Santa Fe, where the air was good for her father's asthma—and how she visited them every summer while her other siblings—a sister and a brother—dropped by on Thanksgiving or for Chanukah.

"Are they religious?" he asked when she mentioned the winter holiday.

"Not much," she said. "But they like the trappings. Menorah in the window. And they have a Passover Seder, but the next day they eat bread. And they're not kosher at all: they eat pork and lobster and oysters and clams."

"Sounds like my parents."

"So, how did you get all observant, if that's the case? Are you the rebel for doing so? The black sheep?"

He explained without mentioning the message in the Camus book. He talked instead about deciding that the time had come to investigate his religion, his conferences with Rabbi Diamant, his study of the *Torah* and Hebrew, finally his volunteering at the Horn of Plenty. Trying his best not to sound over-zealous, he said he was satisfied with the changes in his life, even if they'd led him to write a novel no one wanted to read.

"So, you've become a *mensch*," she said, smiling. "You're trying to live your beliefs. And it's cost you some popularity."

"Yeah, the *zeitgeist* and I have a rocky relationship."

"I told you I loved your book."

"That's kind. You're in a small coterie."

She laughed. She had a lovely laugh. And a boyfriend. Life was hell. Wishnasky stared at her lovely face and tried to feel brave.

70.

THE WINE WAS SERVED, and a toast was offered to RARE and its artists. Which led Aileen to announce that finally she was ready to answer any questions Wishnasky might have about her group.

What he wanted to say was: How can I persuade you to leave your lover? Instead, he offered: "Doesn't it bother you, as an artist, that you've given up your canvas and easel? I mean, theoretically, it's great to save the planet, but don't you find it dispiriting that you're no longer producing paintings?"

"Look," she said with great seriousness, "what better canvas can there be than the Earth itself? If you can organize colors on a flat white surface, why not organize them instead on a black garden bed, or a gray mountainside, or a green lake? Conventional art is exhausted, everyone knows it, everything from the most obscene photographic realism to the most abstract all-white canvas has been spit out a million times, there's no room for progress there; every breakthrough broke through decades ago. But realize that Earth is The Artwork, and immediately it's clear that we've hardly started: parts of the canvas are, yes, beautiful, but elsewhere they're fouled, blasted, crying out for painters and sculptors. What's the real cutting-edge: to paint an oil of East Rutherford or to paint East Rutherford? To redesign it, sculpt it, add color and texture."

"It sounds like the work of a landscape architect."

"Landscape architects are our allies, but mostly they deal with private property. RARE aims at public spaces: rivers and oceans and parklands and grasslands. We envision a river as it could be at its most aesthetic, and then we organize a clean-up all along the shore, send boaters to fish the crud out of the water, finally we photograph the result and it's not a simulacrum of beauty but beauty itself. What could be better?"

"The Earth's enormous," said Wishnasky. "How can you hope to sculpt and paint more than a few bits of it?"

"We love that challenge. It means there's enough for a whole generation of artists, it means the movement needn't worry about outliving its usefulness after a very few years, like Fauvism or Cubism."

"And you're sure it's art you're doing and not some sort of civil engineering?"

He immediately regretted saying it when he saw her indignation. "Of course it's art. And it has precedents. Have you read any essays by de Kooning or Motherwell or especially Barnett Newman? You should read some of the interviews that Newman gave about his zip paintings. Are you familiar with those?"

"Great fields of color interrupted by ultra-thin vertical lines."

"Exactly. And he said, if people understood them, it would mean the end of totalitarianism! Here were these dedicated, sincere figures who honestly thought that their abstractions could save the world! Which just *has* to make you ask, why not do the job directly? If that's what making art's about, why not recognize that the real canvas is right there under your feet?"

Wishnasky thought of the cocktail party for Wanda several days before—the triviality, the waste of spirit—and compared it to Aileen's passionate advocacy for her vision. Maybe her program wasn't as improbable as it seemed. It was certainly more attractive than the gossip and mean-spiritedness of the art crowd with which he was most familiar.

"So what do you want from this essay you've asked of me?"

"In your wonderful prose, detail the transformation of a sorry little parcel of dirt in sleepy Sudbury into a red, green, and orange vegetable garden. Produce the literary version of the photographs I take."

She smiled at him hopefully, but Wishnasky was remembering all the people in his life who had in one way or another scorned his turn to religion. He had to know if Aileen was another. "I agree that the Earth is an artwork," he said. "But I'm convinced God is the original artist. Am I going to step on any toes saying so?"

"Step on them, please! Step on as many toes as you can reach!"

He was about to say, "You don't know what you're asking for," but before he could, their waiter appeared and asked for their order. Aileen chose a salad with chicken; Wishnasky settled on baked salmon and potato. The waiter made a few brief marks on his pad, then walked off.

For the rest of the evening, they discussed their daily routines: Wishnasky's as a novelist between books and in search of a subject, Aileen's as an art teacher in the public schools, working with children of every level of talent. She said she'd never met a student who wasn't artistic, but some found their skills spontaneously, while others needed a great deal of coaching—which she was delighted to offer. That led to a discussion of their favorite painters— for Wishnasky, Matisse and Klee and Dubuffet, for Aileen, Thomas Cole, Frederick Church, Albert Bierstadt—the great American landscape painters of the 19th century. "Before RARE got started, I was exactly like you: all about Kandinsky and Mondrian, all that once-revolutionary abstraction. But now RARE has led me back to some figures who deserve a new look. They're progenitors, they showed on canvas what we're aiming for on the real Artwork, and they turn out to be wonderfully worth studying."

When dinner was over, Aileen, with an unhappy look, declared that she had to go; Wishnasky didn't ask why, for fear she would say that her lover was waiting up for her. He offered to find her a cab, but she insisted on the subway. They paid the bill—once again, she preferred to go Dutch—and walked out into the cool night.

For a time, they strolled in silence. Then Wishnasky blurted out, "So tell me more about your boyfriend. I never hear you speak of him."

"There's not much to say on that particular subject."

"Why not?"

"It's not working. We've been divorcing for months. I've tried to end it, but he won't let me. He's terribly attached."

His heart leapt. Trumpets sounded.

"That's too bad," he said. "Or maybe not. If it's a bad relationship, then it's appropriate that it expire. Naturally or otherwise."

"What about you? I guess you've got lots of floozies."

"Not really. I was going with an Orthodox Jewish woman for a time, but it didn't come to anything. Haven't been dating much since then."

"That's hard to believe. A famous author."

"Not as famous as all that. Plus Boston's full of famous writers. Most of them teaching at Harvard or MIT. Maybe I'd stand out in Des Moines."

"Hard to believe you've never been married."

"I have been married. Almost ten years ago. It didn't last long."

"Her fault or yours?"

"It just fizzled. First we knew each other, then we became strangers."

They walked along in silence again, Aileen letting him know with brief gestures which streets led to her subway entrance, Wishnasky wondering if she was wooing him, had been doing so all along. Or was it all his imagination? The last thing he wanted was to make a play for her and discover that he'd misread all the signals. So, he said nothing and felt miserable.

When they reached the stairs leading down to the subway, Aileen said, "Let's tell each other goodbye here. I've had a lovely time."

Wishnasky felt desperate. "Would you like to meet for breakfast? I could come into Brooklyn this time. My flight out isn't till three."

Her face lit up. "Not breakfast," she said. "But to show you something astonishing. Have you ever been to Brooklyn Bridge Park?"

"I don't think so. I assume it's at the foot of its namesake."

"Yes, but on my side of the river. It's undulant and green and strewn with flowers, and just a few decades ago, it was the ugliest eyesore in the world. A terrible wreck of a place: rotting warehouses, decrepit wharves; that something beautiful might arise from it was almost unthinkable. But it did. You see it and you'll understand RARE even better than you do now. Let's meet at nine."

"Another example of you only making moves that reflect on your organization?"

She blushed. "Maybe you're right. Maybe I didn't realize that about myself."

"Don't be embarrassed. It's kind of charming."

She told him how to get to the area of the park called Pier One, but he barely could hear as he contemplated kissing her. After an awkward pause, he said, "See you in the morning."

"See you," she said, and put out her hand for him to shake. Then, he watched her turn and climb down the stairs till she was out of sight.

He stood alone for a moment, in rapture. She was romancing him—maybe. She was leaving her lover—maybe. There were no coincidences in this life—maybe.

How in the world could he wait for the morning?

71.

NOTHING THAT EVENING could quiet his hopes or calm his anxieties. He tried watching cable news, making a journal entry on his laptop, reading *God in Search of Man,* staring out his window at the New York cityscape; all in vain. Finally, he lay in bed in the near-dark, stared at the ceiling and felt the seconds pass in the cadence of his breathing, the rhythm of his heartbeat, the nervous tapping of his right hand against the bed covers. He wanted to sleep in order that it might already be morning, he wanted to sleep so he wouldn't look haggard when Aileen next saw him; he wanted to sleep just so his noisy, worried, fanciful thoughts would kindly cease. And when he saw on the clock radio that it was 4:16 a.m., he resigned himself to staying up the night—at which point he dozed off.

He was up at 6:30, after a series of alarming dreams, had coffee and a shower, and then attempted to reconnoiter the territory. All the delirium of the previous night had disappeared: he felt a cold, fatalistic calm, as if his destiny had already been determined for him long ago and all he had to do was to go through certain motions until the verdict—reciprocity or not—was rendered. A *Times* had been left outside his door; he tried reading it without success, then turned on cable news and watched the pundits declaim on trade negotiations with Mexico, a shooting in Missouri, forest fires in Japan. At 8:15, he turned off the TV, put on *tallit* and *tefillin,* and said the Morning Prayer. When he got to the section where personal supplications could be added, he said, "Please, Lord, please make that woman feel toward me even a little of what I feel toward her. And if that's not appropriate, if I shouldn't ask You to interfere with her free choice, please at least give me the wisdom to find a way to her heart." He said the *Aleinu,* the psalm of the day, placed his *tallit* and *tefillin* back in their velvet bags, and took an elevator to the lobby, found a cab, and rode to Brooklyn Bridge Park.

He found himself on a sweeping green lawn with breathtaking views of the bridge and the towers of Manhattan. There were already many other park visitors, some sitting on blankets, others ambling on the paved perimeter. On the grass closest to the East River, there were shade trees and multicolored flowers. Near the tip of the pier, shrieking children raced around a playground.

And there was Aileen: in white jeans and a navy blue shirt. She was smiling so broadly, it made him uneasy. What did she know?

"Hey!" she called out.

"Hey," he said.

"Isn't it stunning? And to think that only a few years ago, it was decaying, disintegrating, abandoned. Do you see those flowers?"

He looked at a clump of yellow and blue blossoms.

"They're nice," he said.

"You'll find everything here: Spanish bluebells, Southern Magnolias, Korean Spice Viburnum, and don't miss the water gardens. We've got butterflies and bumblebees and turtles. Can you believe that we're standing in New York City?"

He was feeling it again—that dispassionate stillness, as if his life was all mapped out for him and he had no choice but to speak words that were written for him eons ago.

"Let's sit," he said.

"Sure. We can look out at the harbor."

They walked downhill to a bench and sat facing the water. Wishnasky stared blankly ahead and then heard himself speak.

"Look," he said, "let's get this over with."

"Huh?"

He felt as if he were floating weightlessly, an astronaut in his spaceship. "I don't know what you feel, but I'm really attracted to you. I'd like to spend time with you, and not just as a colleague. I'm romantically interested is what I'm saying, and I want to know if you are too. I have to know if that's possible." He turned and looked intently into her eyes.

There was a long pause as she stared back. Then she sighed.

"That took long enough," she said.

"What did?"

"I've been pursuing you since the reading in New York and you didn't even notice! I message you, no reply. I manage to come up with an unlikely reason to drive all the way to the suburbs of Boston, and all you can talk about the whole time is business, business, business. And then last night, focusing on nothing but work when I gave you every opportunity to get personal. Phooey! You almost lost your last chance!"

"What?"

"You think it's no gamble for me to chase you so shamelessly? What about *my* dignity if you're not interested? What about the humiliation *I* face?"

He stared at her moronically, unable to process the information. "The first time I asked, you said you had a boyfriend," he said. "What was I supposed to infer from that?"

"What should I have said: hey, I like you, and I'm available, so take me to bed? And anyway, I *do* have a boyfriend, and yes I'm *ending* that relationship, and no, I *didn't* want to do it until you promised you'd be there for me."

"You were waiting on me before you broke up with your lover?"

"Is there something wrong with that?"

"Is there something—why didn't you say so? How was I supposed to know? Do I understand anything about you?"

"Sure you do, "she said, smiling. "It's me: Aileen. The woman who fell for you the minute she saw you at the Strand. And whom you're going to love immeasurably."

The weightless feeling changed into a sensation of mild vertigo. "The woman I'm going to—Are you sure you know what you're getting into?" he said.

"I think so," she said. "You're smart and you're serious and you're only recently religious. You desperately need a practical side, which is one reason you need me. And you're an artist confused about his art, which is another reason I showed up at just the right time. And by the way, you'll want to marry me, I can tell you that right now."

"I will?"

"You can count on it."

This was too much. Who was this woman? "I don't think I understand your certainty about things," he said.

"Obviously."

"Do you want to explain?"

"We're at a park where they've rescued the Earth from desolation. In a few more minutes, you're going to take a plane back to Boston, and I'm going to break up with Gerry. Once I pull off that stunt, you and I are going to spend some quality time together."

"You want to skip breakfast and go back to my hotel?"

"Not this trip. Next one."

"How do you know we'll be compatible?"

"Sexually? Not a problem. But I won't jump from one man's bed to another. Wait till the breakup, then we can think about making love. Is that hard for you to do?"

"I don't think so."

"Good, I'm worth it. But now, answer this question: how do you feel about going with a Reform Jew who eats shrimp? Is that a problem for you?"

"Not at all, if you don't mind that I'm kosher."

"Not a deal-breaker. And if that's the only big difference between us, this is going to go even more smoothly than I thought. Why are you staring at me in that way?"

"All that stuff about RARE—that was just so we'd spend time together?"

"Absolutely not! RARE is real, and I'm completely devoted to it! Didn't you see my emails: 'Remember RARE and me?' Both of us, not one or the other."

"Just for the record, I'm not confused about my art. I'm just going through a fallow period while I try to figure out what's next."

"All right, I take it back. You don't need my assistance."

"That's not to say I don't welcome your suggestions."

"You're squeezing my hand a little hard."

"Oh. Sorry."

He withdrew his hand and stared at the woman sitting beside him. So she'd been waiting all this time for him to declare his intentions? But there had been *no* intentions on the day that he met her; it was weeks before it even occurred to him that she was, after all, attractive. And now she was telling him that he'd inevitably want to marry her? Who thought this way? Who confessed such thoughts?

"But listen," said Aileen, her tone now sober. "For the next few days I'll need to focus on my art classes. But next Sunday, Willem's organizing a major push on the Sudbury garden. I've got to be in Providence Friday late, talking to some RISD seniors about joining RARE when they graduate, but I can fly to Boston Saturday morning and meet you at your home by afternoon. We can spend the time together and the next day, go to the garden and do our work."

Did she always have everything so precisely spelled out? "I hate to leave you now," he said.

"Me too. But there's no point in our talking further till I've split with Gerry. Still, I want something to remember that's better than talking. Let's just circle Pier One. And hold hands. Only not too tight."

"We're going to walk and hold hands?"

"You're sounding goofy. Get up."

Wishnasky rose—still disoriented—and Aileen rose beside him, reached for his hand, and they circumambulated Pier One. Repeatedly, Wishnasky felt an impulse to speak, then thought better of it and held back. It was so bizarre to be with this disconcerting companion. He felt as if he were sixteen again, with everything to learn about the opposite sex. Was this good or bad? Why did she make him feel so mystified?

Finally, Aileen said, "I've got to go. That'll have to do."

"I'll walk you to your subway stop."

"I'd rather you didn't."

"I'd at least like to kiss you."

"I'd like that too. You've been so hard to work on. A kiss would be a relief."

They kissed, and Wishnasky felt her sink into his arms. That felt better; that was something he could understand: a couple, a matched set, fitting together comfortably.

She stepped away from him and said, "I'll call you later in the week. Leave next weekend to me."

"I'll be thinking of you."

"I'll think of you, too. Bye, Tristan"

"Bye."

72.

THE FLIGHT BACK TO BOSTON hardly touched Wishnasky's imagination, and the taxi ride from Logan Airport passed in a dream. Once he was back in Newton Corner, he attempted to throw himself into his routine as if the activity would distract him from thoughts of Aileen, but no such luck. He wrote a few meaningless paragraphs of what was clearly *not* his next novel, tried to sift through personal mail (keeping the few letters that praised *Traveler*), tried to study Hebrew, but gradually felt his will dissolve into excitement, even giddiness. Every few hours, he thanked God for Aileen's existence ("I don't know how much You had to do with it, to be honest, but I'm guessing You were involved") and to convince himself of his productivity, he wrote entries in his journal ("If I remember correctly, she likes the poetry of Robert Lowell, the memoirs of Mary Karr, and the fiction of Toni Morrison. Must investigate further"). By the time he showed up at Ion's office, he could barely think of anything besides Aileen and their—potential—life together.

He waltzed into Ion's chamber as if high on antidepressants and proceeded to tell the therapist that he was joyously, formidably, mentally *well*.

"I'm here out of my sense of compassion, Ion. I figure at this point you need me more than I need you."

"I'm glad that your love object has shown a reciprocal feeling for you. I can only recommend that you enjoy the pleasure of this eventuality as long as it lasts."

"It's going to last a lifetime. Remember, I told you so."

"The love, perhaps. The phantasmagoria, no."

"Oh aren't we pessimistic. What's-a-matter, doesn't your wife make you cuckoo anymore?"

"Love, as several contemporary musicians have noted, is a drug, and one's first experience of it is, of course, intoxication. But once the metabolism adjusts, something deeply spiritual often comes to replace it: *Eros*, to its own surprise, transforms into *agape*. I am happy for you, not because of your present lightheadedness but because it may eventually lead to that higher state. Perhaps then you will find yourself in a previously unaccomplished harmony with Mind, and all I have told you on the subject will finally make sense."

"It's not Mind, Ion, it's God that put Aileen in my life, and I'm beginning to think that you need a little therapy of your own."

"I am satisfied to hear you admit that there is something greater than human will behind one's mortal transit. I haven't forgotten that when we inaugurated analysis, you saw nothing behind nature but a void."

"But enough about me," said Wishnasky, feeling mischievous. "Tell me about Ion. Tell me *your* stance on how I'm going to feel about Aileen thirty years from this morning."

"If your love is real?"

"No ifs, Chucky."

"Chucky?"

"Lay it on me, Renfroe. Thirty years of Aileen: what am I feeling?"

"That she is part of yourself. That you would defend her no differently than you would defend your own ego. That your life and hers are outward symptoms of a single essence."

"Right out of the Bible, Norman. 'Flesh of my flesh, bone of my bone.'"

"Even Plato believed that the first humans were a united thing, male and female."

"Those Greeks thought the highest thing in life was reason, Ion. And they were wrong, wrong, wrong. It's love. She and me. Me and she."

"Are you conscious of the distance you've traveled in this analysis? Do you remember the days when you considered suicide an option?"

"Not me, Carruthers. Not when my sweetheart's gonna be calling in a few days."

"I'm pleased to once again witness the generosity of Mind. I wish you well with your new *amour*."

"Yeah, God is generous. God is merciful. Try saying it, it won't hurt you."

"Call the Benevolence what you will, I'm glad to see you rewarded."

"Not half as glad as I am, Engelbert. Drummond."

"Do you know that at this moment you are indistinguishable from a lunatic?"

"And loving it, Stanley. Loving every moment."

73.

THE THIRD CLUE to Wishnasky's next book came up in conversation with Chet just before they faced each other in tennis. Chet had seemed distracted when Wishnasky met him at their sports club, and though he welcomed his friend's news about Aileen and their coming rendezvous, there was clearly some other issue weighing on him. As the two men dressed for tennis in the locker room, Wishnasky asked Chet what was troubling him.

"It's an exasperating case," he said, pulling a knit shirt over his head. "Consider a thirty-four-year-old Salvadorian woman and her fifteen-year-old son. She and the boy both say that they were threatened by gangs with death if Enrique didn't join up. But American Immigration wants proof that their lives are really in danger, and the only people who can prove it are the gangs themselves. I don't have to tell you that they're not planning on helping out."

"So, what can you do?" said Wishnasky, seated and pulling on his socks.

"I've got to find someone who can corroborate their stories. And I can't; everything I've tried fails. The best I've been able to do so far is to discover other refugees who've been granted asylum and who know these same gangs and the sorts of threats that they make. If the stories match up, it's possible a judge will overlook the fact that this particular ultimatum was witnessed by no one but my two clients."

"Is that a probability?" said Wishnasky. "Have judges accepted that sort of evidence before?"

"Almost never. It's a long shot. But I've got to work with what's available."

They were dressed. Taking racquet bags, they walked past row after row of green lockers where other men were dressing or undressing. They passed through a door, walked through a room with windows on the courts, then went through one more door and out onto the playing area. Two women were still hitting on the court they'd reserved. "Is it that time?" called the blonde, thirtyish one after winning a point. The other was tall and gray-haired.

"Afraid so," said Chet.

"All right if we finish the set?"

"Of course."

Chet and Wishnasky walked out to the bench between their court and the next one over. As they did, Wishnasky watched the women play. They were both skillful, sending long topspin forehands crosscourt back and forth, each waiting for a misstep before she slammed the ball down the line for a winner.

"You know, I've got a problem of my own," Wishnasky told Chet. "I'm completely stymied by the question of what I should be writing, what's in me to do now. I have no interest at all in duplicating the last book, and all the subjects I might focus on have been handled resoundingly by others. I've seldom felt so useless."

"Do you want a suggestion?" said Chet.

"Sure, if you've got one."

"I'll tell you how I think," said Chet. "There's work that anyone can pull off and there's work that only I can do. I try to keep the two distinct in my mind always and attempt to narrow my efforts to the stuff where I'm actually personally necessary."

"Give me an example."

"Well, the obvious one is wife and family—only I can be there as husband and father, and if I don't get it right, no one else is going to take up the slack."

"Now apply that to work."

"All right: to begin where I'm *not* essential, there are any number of other law professors who can take my place in front of a class. My personal experience is unique, I suppose, so I can offer some special incidental remarks and comments. But the law's the same, whoever's teaching it. So, I don't fool myself that I'm indispensable at the university."

"Then where's your importance?"

"My refugee work: there I really matter. What most would-be immigrants are saddled with these days are court-appointed lawyers who are undertrained, overworked, and trying their best to get as quickly as possible through an overwhelming number of ever-multiplying cases. I'm better prepared, better connected, and I can afford to devote myself to just a few clients. So, yes, I think I'm justified in saying that in the few cases I'm able to take, if I don't do the job, no one else will. Which gets me energized and convinces me that the time is well spent."

"All right. That's your case. Now how about mine?"

"There must be something," said Chet, "that you and only you can write. A novel such that, if you don't compose it, no one else will."

"I don't think there is," said Wishnasky. "Or maybe I should say, I already wrote it and the reviews were devastating."

"Maybe you're just not thinking," said Chet. "You must have some experience that no one else has had, that requires *your* talent."

Wishnasky watched the gray-haired woman prepare for an overhead smash, then drive a high lob with sizzling speed into the blonde's backhand. There was no chance of return and the game was over. The two women came to the net, shook hands, and fanned out to retrieve their tennis balls.

"I don't think so," he said. "When I wrote my first three novels, I thought I understood the absolute meaninglessness of things in a special, even exclusive way. I don't feel that way about anything now."

The two women came up to the bench, thanked the men for waiting, and Wishnasky and Chet walked out to opposite sides of the court. As Wishnasky waited for Chet to drive a tennis ball toward him, he was still thinking about his next novel. What was it he could write that nobody else could? About Judaism? The rabbi's overstocked shelves were evidence enough that there was no shortage of such volumes. About love, writing, sex, God? There must be thousands of such books. What was the book that would never get written if he didn't write it? On what subject was he indispensable?

Chet slammed a ball to his backhand and he put the subject out of mind.

74.

DEAR ADMIRAL MANAYING (Wishnasky wrote some hours later):

I'm writing to you about Udom Latawan, a human rights activist who is currently in Chiang Mai Prison because he spoke up for a democratic Thailand. I'm concerned that he'll be tortured while in prison, and he apparently has not been allowed contact with his family or an attorney. Nor have any charges against him been formally brought.

General, I know that American credibility on such matters has been weakened by our operation of a rogue military prison camp at Guantanamo, and I'm also aware that the American government has not always lived up to its human rights ideals. But, surely, you know that it is not right that a young Thai citizen (only twenty-three, according to my sources) should be jailed and abused because he expressed the simple desire to see his country a democracy. No doubt you're a student of history and are aware that the great wars for human liberation began more than two centuries ago. That's more than 200 years during which humanity has shown that the love of freedom and democracy is no passing fashion, that it's a constant throughout the world, as much in North America as in South, as much in Vietnam as in Thailand. What Udom Latawan has done, in other words, is to lend his voice to a conversation that's been going on since 1776, not to mention 1789, 1830, 1848, and 1989. History, to be succinct, is with him. And your job, as a powerful leader, is to recognize that he stands with Thomas Jefferson, Jean-Jacques Rousseau, Ho Chi Minh and Nelson Mandela. That's whom you're imprisoning when you put Udom in confinement. Those are the ones whose voices you're trying to stifle.

I know that you want better for your country and yourself.

Please release Udom Latawan. He deserves a medal, not torture.

Sincerely,

Tristan Wishnasky

He folded the letter, placed it in an envelope, wrote the address and added international airmail postage. As he did so, he wondered if maybe the rabbi was right. Maybe if the decision had been left to him alone, he would have treated the closing of the Horn of Plenty as the terminus to his efforts of lovingkindness. There was something selfish in him—if he were honest enough to notice it—that was ready to spend seventy-two sleepless hours working on a difficult stretch of novel, but felt thirty minutes devoted to helping a stranger an imposition and a drain on his time. Deep down, was he so egocentric? Did other people mean so little to him?

Well, he was back—would send David Hammond his dues, would start looking for other prisoners to support. He was back searching for God in the manner the rabbi had taught him: by performing the commandments.

He opened a new screen on his computer and started a second letter.

Dear Ambassador Chittsawangdee:

I'm writing to you about Udom Latawan, a human rights activist who is currently in Chiang Mai Prison because he spoke up for a democratic Thailand. I know that as Thai ambassador to the US, your influence is limited and you're hardly the first person to whom your head of state turns for advice. Nonetheless, I'm writing to ask you to urge the Thai government to free Udom Latawan, whose only crime was to use God's gift of speech to promote the only form of government which assumes everyone's equal dignity: democracy. I won't bore you with the details of the religious doctrines I subscribe to, but I'll insist on just one of them: that Udom Latawan possesses the divine image as much as does Admiral Manaying, Ambassador Chittsawangdee, and Tristan Wishnasky. Instead of incarcerating the divine image and possibly subjecting it to torture, surely your task is to honor it and stand up for its God-given rights. If the shoe were on the other foot, if it were you now in Chiang Mai Prison, wouldn't you want your ambassador to believe in your holy essence? Show your courage then, and urge the Thai government to release Udom Latawan. His soul is as sacred as yours or mine, and as deserving of the blessing of freedom.

Sincerely,

Tristan Wishnasky

He folded the letter, placed it in an envelope and affixed a stamp. As he did so he noticed the same emotion he had experienced at the Horn of Plenty: the feeling of mattering, of doing something substantial. He rose and walked out of his house to put the letters in the mailbox. He was seeking justice again. It was how one ought to spend one's time.

75.

THE BREAKUP, Aileen told him by phone, had gone as smoothly as it could, given Gerry's reluctance to believe he was anything other than every woman's dream. Anyway, now she could move on to her rendezvous with Wishnasky. Her flight out of Kennedy was scheduled to arrive at 12:30, and since Wishnasky would be observing *Shabbat* at that time, no, he didn't have to meet her at Logan Airport. But would he be home from the synagogue by, oh, 1:45? Then, good, she would arrive in an Uber at approximately that time and they could share a little wine and maybe walk through the neighborhood. She felt so glad that they'd be together in just a day. Did he feel the same? Then have a good evening and *Shabbat Shalom*. And would he please think of her when he went to sleep that night?

He was back from the synagogue on Saturday at 12:35, removed his coat and tie, organized the kitchen and bedroom for the fourth time, and finally rushed to the door to embrace Aileen when she arrived. They held each other closely until she said, "Let's go in." He put her suitcase and carry-on in his bedroom, offered her the choice of Pinot Noir or Cabernet, and then sat down on the sofa beside her. And they talked.

They talked as if it were necessary to say everything: most of her life story from childhood in Baltimore to art school at RISD, then the move to Brooklyn and the creation of RARE. For his part, there was the tale of the despairing adolescent, the aspiring writer at Harvard, and then the success of his first novels. She spoke at length about her enthusiasm for restoring the Earth; he spoke with fervor about his rediscovery of Judaism. She spoke ruefully about her fellow artists who thought her a dropout from real art work; he told her how his agent assumed his literary life was over. Twilight came and there was still more to talk about: he suggested they order out and they agreed on pizza. Soon after, they devoured a large garden pizza with mushrooms, green peppers, and olives, and more wine.

As they ate, they compared their feelings about the arts. Aileen talked about moving from landscape painting to landscape planting; Wishnasky spoke of the need for a religious viewpoint in contemporary literature. He recalled that the Enlightenment dream of Reason had crushed the religious worldview of Dante and Milton, that in turn Reason was discredited by the savage massacres of World War I, and that Modernists like Yeats and Joyce had tried to find a new center for Western culture, but the only center they could find was the fetish of the artwork, the holy *Wasteland,* or *Mrs. Dalloway* or *Ulysses.* Yes, she concurred, when she'd started out at art school, the most spiritual entity was Picasso's *Guernica* or Barnett Newman's *Vir Heroicus Sublimis,* and when a single Matisse sold for thirty-four million dollars, wasn't that saying that, in fact, the thing was divine? Precisely, he agreed, the arts had become a temple for people who didn't go to temple; yes, she confirmed, the only Higher Power that her artist friends recognized was Diego Rivera or Georgia O'Keeffe or that holiest of holies, Jackson Pollock. So, didn't something have to change? And wasn't the first step away from this idolatry of the artifact the realization that beauty began not in a museum but in a forest, a mountain range, or on the shore of the Gulf of Mexico? Absolutely, he insisted, and wasn't the first talk of Beauty in Western discourse the moment when Eve recognized that the Tree of Knowledge was "a delight to the eye"—*ta-avah l'aynayim*—wasn't *that* the beginning of the category of the aesthetic, a tree, a natural object? Yes, yes, yes, she concurred, and wasn't it right that aesthetic appreciation return to its source, the Earth itself? Yes, yes, and yes. Yes again!

It was ten o'clock. "I'm really tired," Aileen said. "I don't know if I can continue. Let's go to bed."

"It's so lovely to be with you. I feel like I've been waiting for this moment my entire life."

"C'mon, we can sleep now and make love tomorrow. Here, take my hand."

He did. They walked into the bedroom, and Aileen fell fully dressed onto the comforter, saying, "I'll brush my teeth in the morning."

"Me too," said Wishnasky, and fell beside her. And they slept.

76.

WISHNASKY, IN JEANS AND A TEE-SHIRT, was making coffee when Aileen, still in the clothes she'd slept in, wandered into the kitchen.

"Hey," he said. "I've got toast and butter and jelly. I've also got breakfast cereal and lots of milk. Or we can go out, if you prefer."

"No," said Aileen and yawned. "What time is it?"

"Around 9:45. I've only been up a half hour."

"Work at the Sudbury site begins at noon," she said. "Let me clean up and then I'll join you."

She walked back into the bedroom, opened her suitcase, removed some items and took them with her into the bathroom. Wishnasky heard the shower and, after a time, she reemerged in black jeans and a pastel green knit shirt.

"I'll make some toast," she said. "Where's the bread?"

"I'll do it," said Wishnasky, and put two slices of bread in the toaster, fetched a plate on which he set a stick of butter, and pulled a jar of raspberry preserves from the refrigerator. A few moments later the toaster *dinged* and he put the toast on the plate.

"That was some confab we had," Aileen said as she took her first bites.

"I know. I think we solved all the problems of artistic theory for the next couple of centuries."

"Decades would be better. If it only takes forty years to save the earth, everyone can go back to old-fashioned still lives the next day."

"How's the toast?"

"Good. Have you eaten?"

"Yeah. I was so hungry, I couldn't stop myself. But I'll pour myself more coffee."

They discussed their plans. There was a lot of work, said Aileen, to be done at the Sudbury garden site. Depending on how many RARE members were there, they might get everything accomplished by two or three o'clock. That would give Wishnasky and Aileen time to go back to his house and clean up. Then her flight back to LaGuardia left at 6:15.

"I thought we agreed we'd have some unrushed private time together," said Wishnasky, trying not to sound too disappointed.

"Me too. It's possible. Let's just see how the dig goes."

While she was finishing her breakfast, Wishnasky shaved and put on an old pair of tennis shoes. Aileen took her Nikon camera out of her carry-on, and the two set out for Sudbury.

They were on Route 2 passing through Concord. Around them were the turquoise hills and lush forests of the area where the Revolutionary War had begun and where, decades later, Emerson and Thoreau and Louisa May Alcott had held forth. Gazing at the verdant land, Wishnasky was reminded that indeed the first knowledge of beauty was knowledge of the Earth, and that all human artifice only came afterward, a pale copy. But these thoughts dissipated when he glanced at the woman beside him and became conscious of being in love, of being in the presence of the beloved, of being loved in return. Sometimes, it seemed, miracles happened, and the puzzle pieces fit. Or was that judgment based on ignorance?

They were a few minutes late getting to the school, and what Wishnasky saw first was a series of nearly-identical beige brick buildings fronted by a sign that announced "Franklin Pierce Middle School. Home of the Panthers!" Off to one side of the school was a large expanse of empty brown field, punctuated occasionally by pathetic-looking tufts of grass (or were those weeds?). Some distance down the field were half-a-dozen cars and two trucks—one yellow, one green—and a group of people, standing and watching a man pushing some sort of misshapen machine.

"Park up there with the others," said Aileen.

"They don't mind me driving on their field?"

"They're grateful we're here. You'll see. Just drive up."

It only took a few seconds to pass over the field and reach the parked cars, and when Wishnasky pulled up he saw a tall white-haired man pushing what looked like two lawn mowers in head-on collision up one side of a not-very-large rectangle cut into the ground.

"What's he doing?" he asked as he cut the engine.

"That's a gas-powered tiller," she said. "The ground's so tightly packed, there's no way we could break it up ourselves. That's Nate; he's contributing his time and equipment." Out of the car, she and Wishnasky joined the crowd watching Nate proceed.

"Willem," she called to a short, brown-haired man with long sideburns and wide shoulders. The man looked at her, smiled, and went over to embrace her. "This is my friend Tristan," she said, gesturing at Wishnasky. "He's writing the essay for our book."

"Thanks for your interest," Willem said as they shook hands. "Tristan Wishnasky? Aren't you a novelist?"

"Guilty as charged."

"Have a look at our garden," said Willem. "Been working on the school board to let me plant it for almost a year. Finally, they figured it wouldn't hurt if their kids knew something besides computers."

"It looks good. Smaller than I would have guessed, though."

"Yeah, it had to be or else the school wouldn't have paid for the irrigation. And we don't have that many subscribers to the plots. But hey, anything's a start. Are you here just to observe or you want to take part in the muscle-work?"

"My rabbi tells me that mending the world is a religious obligation. So, I guess I'll take part."

"Terrific. When the time comes, the shovels are over there."

Willem moved off to talk with a slender African American woman, and Wishnasky and Aileen watched Nate push the heavy tiller up and down the garden-in-the-making. The strange-looking machine made a loud, grinding noise as it dug into the earth, then spat out the churned soil back onto the garden floor.

"What are the shovels for?" Wishnasky asked Aileen.

"Once the ground is loose enough, we're going to get rid of the old soil. Next, we'll measure out individual plots and put wood framing around them, fill in the plots with enriched earth that's much better for growing vegetables. That's what all those packages in the back of the yellow pickup are."

Wishnasky tried his best to think of this landscaping as art but found it difficult to make the leap. Then, he remembered Aileen's commitment to the original "Artwork," and he resolved to swallow his doubts. After all, hadn't the great Modernist writers been told what they were doing wasn't genuine literature? Weren't they accused of producing something that was too great a departure from the accepted canon?

Aileen was taking photos of Nate breaking ground, and Wishnasky didn't want to interrupt, so he stood apart and watched quietly. Then Willem called out, "Let's start the dig, everyone." Aileen gestured to Wishnasky, and the two of them walked together to the area where the shovels lay; Aileen picked one up and handed it to him.

"How good are you at digging?" she said with a smile.

"Had great training as a child. Earthworms and anthills. Haven't practiced much since."

"Childhood experience is all you need. Follow me." She started toward the nascent garden.

For the next thirty minutes, a dozen RARE members dug out the bed of the garden, tossing the unwanted soil onto a large pile that grew steadily into a respectable-looking hill. Occasionally, Aileen stopped to walk around the area and take photos, then returned to the digging alongside the others. Finally, just as Wishnasky was beginning to tire, Willem called out that it was time to frame individual plots. As Wishnasky watched, several RARE members, with the help of Nate and his measuring tape, inserted wooden planks edgewise into the flattened dirt, turning the garden bed in minutes into a matrix of small rectangles. Then, it was time to unload the enriched soil from the yellow truck and spread it in the garden. Wishnasky joined the others lugging great unwieldy sacks to the garden-in-the-making, and poured the dark black soil where directed by Willem.

Forty minutes later, the exhausted Wishnasky trudged to his car. He leaned against it and tried to catch his breath. Aileen walked up beside him and said, "Had enough?"

"What's left to do?"

"Nate's going to help them lay the irrigation pipes. I don't need to be here for that. We can go."

"This is more demanding than I'd guessed."

"Wait a couple of weeks till the vegetables are planted. Then, you'll see how worthwhile it was. Did you get material for your writing?"

"I'm sure I must have. When I recover, I'll think about it."

"These authors," said Aileen. "A little honest labor and they're exhausted. Let me tell Willem we're going."

She walked over to Willem, spoke with him briefly and they embraced. Then, she came back to Wishnasky's car.

∎

On the drive back to Newton Corner, Wishnasky could only think about Aileen's impending departure. Nothing was as he'd intended: his original plan had been to welcome her to his home, share wine and food, have a brief chat, and then wander into the bedroom and make love night and morning. But now it was late Sunday afternoon, she had a plane to catch in a few hours, and they were sweaty and, in his case at least, tired and grimy. He thought he might offer to catch a plane to New York, meet her at her apartment and consummate the relationship there. He thought to convince her to stay in Newton Corner till 9 or so, spend all that time in bed, and then let him drive her to Brooklyn overnight. Why had they spent so much time at the dig? Why was nothing ever the way he imagined it?

Nearing Newton Corner, they talked about what they'd just experienced. Aileen was exhilarated, thought every step of the dig had gone superbly, and again assured Wishnasky that once the vegetables were planted, the little piece of earth they'd labored over would show its gratitude in a rainbow of colors. She reminded him that there were other RARE gardens, in New York, Connecticut, even New Hampshire, and all these little reclamations would ultimately add up to something important. He should wait till he'd eaten a cucumber or a head of lettuce from the new garden before underestimating their efforts. Then he'd know what it meant to be a Radical Artist Restoring the Earth.

They pulled into his driveway and walked to the front door. Wishnasky was distraught, rueful that his weekend with Aileen was almost over and he'd hardly touched her face, hardly run his hands through her hair. But when they walked into the kitchen, she said, "Do you want to wash off?"

"No, you first," he said.

"I mean together, silly. Let's get naked. Right?"

She reached down and pulled her blouse over her head. She was wearing a flesh-colored bra which she quickly unsnapped and removed. Wishnasky found her breasts beautiful and moved forward to kiss them.

"Not yet. First let's get clean together."

He hurriedly unbuttoned his shirt as she removed her jeans and panties. He pulled down his trousers and his underwear, revealing his erection, and she turned and, laughing, rushed into his bedroom and, from there, to the bathroom. He followed, got past her and turned on the shower. The water coursed loudly through the nozzle and after a few moments, it was warm enough and he said, "Get in." She did. He followed behind her and pulled the curtain closed.

"Soap me," she said.

He took the white bar of soap from the rack hanging on the showerhead and slid it over her skin, starting at the neck, descending to the breasts, then down to her loins, which he rubbed softly and repeatedly till she began to groan. "Now you," he said, handing her the soap. She soaped his chest and his back and then began running her hand up and down the shaft of his erection. The feeling was so intense, he was afraid he'd come too soon.

"Stop," he said. "It's too much. I want you too much."

"Do me then," she said. "Use your mouth. I'll tell you when I'm about to climax."

He fell to his knees and ran his tongue along the groove of her vagina while the water splashed on his head. His tongue moved up and back, all around, in and out, and his hands gripped her buttocks from behind as she groaned more and more until she said, "Put yourself in me. I'm almost there."

He stood up and placed his hand on his penis, guiding it into her vagina which was slippery and warm. Then he grasped her shoulders as he thrust back and forth. She moaned, and when she said, "Yes, I'm coming. Now," he moved more quickly and harder until he felt the start of his own orgasm. She embraced him so tightly he felt as if she were trying to merge into him, and then she let out a deep sigh and relaxed her hold. They kissed deeply and he lowered his head to kiss each nipple.

Then, they laughed with childish joy.

And they let the shower water wash off everything they didn't need.

■

On the drive to Logan Airport, they tried to schedule their next meeting. Passover was coming in the middle of the week, but Wishnasky was willing to miss the Seder at the rabbi's house if he could spend the time instead with Aileen. Aileen insisted that it made no sense to visit her during the week, when her bedtime was early (had to be up by 5:30 to get to school by 7) and the arrangement at her apartment made privacy nearly impossible. But on the following weekend, she would come up on Friday and go to synagogue with him for the evening *Shabbat* service. Then, they'd have nearly three days together. Wouldn't that be lovely?

Wishnasky pulled his Toyota into short-term parking at the airport, took a ticket from a buzzing machine, and found an empty parking space. Once inside the terminal, they headed directly to the automated ticket machines; Aileen punched in her information and was rewarded with a boarding pass. Then, they joined a long line of people waiting to check their bags. Half an hour later, they continued to the departure area.

They walked as far as a uniformed woman beside a sign that announced ONLY TRAVELERS WITH TICKETS BEYOND THIS POINT. "We've got forty-five minutes," said Wishnasky. "Let's get a drink before we say goodbye."

"I'd rather not. I'd rather leave you now and have some time to reacquaint myself with myself. I hope you don't mind."

"No, not at all. There's a lot of think about."

"I'll be back in just a few days. That'll give us time to savor what we just enjoyed. And to savor what's to come."

"I already miss you."

They kissed, deeply and long. Aileen flashed him a smile and turned to show her ticket and driver's license to the airport official. She looked back one last time and nodded lovingly to her sorrowing lover. Then, she walked away.

Wishnasky felt terrible: he wanted to be with his lover! Miserable, he walked to the exit.

77.

THE FINAL CLUE to his new book came at the Passover Seder to which the rabbi had invited him. He'd never been to a Seder before: his parents certainly hadn't celebrated the holiday, and even in his bar mitzvah year he'd managed to ignore the festive meal at his synagogue. So, when he reached the rabbi's address—a ranch house in white brick on an attractive lane in Bedford—he didn't know what to expect. But the rabbi had assured him that he wouldn't be the only first-timer there that evening, and she was particularly happy that now he could finally meet her husband. As for swearing off bread for eight days—well, if Wishnasky could manage it, he'd be doing a new *mitzvah*. And if not, then maybe he'd get to it next year: one must always be improving.

He walked into the rabbi's house—the front door was half-open—and saw about ten people—strangers to him, all—seated at or standing around a large, long table. There were two middle-aged women, a (married?) couple in their thirties, an uncomfortable-looking man in his fifties, standing alone, and two young people, one a boy of about seventeen and the other a nine- or ten-year-old girl, all talking away happily. Closer inspection showed that the long table was actually made of two smaller ones that had been placed together and covered by a single white tablecloth. On it were twelve place settings, six bottles of wine, and several unopened boxes of matzo. Wishnasky didn't see the rabbi and felt awkward around so many strangers, so he made his way through the crowd—smiling at everyone as he did—and walked into the kitchen where a dark-haired, bearded man of about thirty was stirring a big pot, and the rabbi, a few feet from him, was carving a turkey.

"Hello, Rabbi," said Wishnasky. "Can I do anything to help?" Looking around, he saw that there were no empty surfaces—food and dishes were everywhere.

"Tristan." said the rabbi. "I want you to meet my husband. Caleb." The bearded man turned from his pot of soup. "This is Tristan Wishnasky who's been studying Judaism with me. This is his first Seder ever."

Caleb Diamant stuck out his hand for Wishnasky to shake, and said, "*Hag sameach.*"

"That's 'happy festival,'" said the rabbi. "Or did you already learn that in Hebrew class?"

"I don't think so," said Wishnasky. "But *hag sameach* to the both of you. Is there anything I can do? Any foods or dishes you need brought to the table?"

"No, everything's where it should be. But introduce yourself to the other guests. I'll bet some of them know your novels. Sweetheart, do you want to introduce Tristan to the others?"

"Give me five minutes," said Caleb. "I'm almost done here and then I can oblige you."

"Not necessary," said Wishnasky. "I'll do it myself. You keep to your preparations." He turned around and walked back to the large dining area where the uncomfortable-looking fiftyish-year-old man seemed the right person with whom to begin.

"Hi," he said to the man, who was a few inches taller than he, and whose graying hair was parted on one side. "Tristan Wishnasky. Glad to meet you."

"Stan Dolgin," said the man with a grateful look as they shook hands. "Are you in the congregation? I have to admit, I don't know any of these people besides the rabbi."

"My status also," said Wishnasky. "How'd you happen to get invited?"

"I'm new to Boston. My company transferred me just a few weeks ago, and when I dropped by the synagogue in Lexington, the rabbi asked if I had a Seder to go to. I didn't and she was kind enough to invite me to hers."

"I'm in a comparable situation," said Wishnasky. "I've spent the last year-and-a-half acquainting myself with Jewish practice, and this is a new observance for me—my parents aren't observant. I doubt I'll understand half of what happens here this evening."

"The Seder I know," said Stan. "Passover is just about the only Jewish holiday that my family back in Seattle ever observed. So feel free to ask any questions."

"Thanks. I may do that."

"Wishnasky," said Stan. "I think I knew some Wishnaskys back at home. What do you do when you're not here keeping the holiday?"

"I'm a writer. What about you?"

"Investment analyst for Merrill Lynch. Divorced, which is why I'm here on my own. Three grown children, all of whom are right now celebrating with my ex back in Washington state. You ever been out to that part of the country?"

"Actually, no. Hey, do you mind if we sit together? You can help when I'm baffled by the progress of the service."

"Not a problem. It's good to know someone."

Wishnasky introduced himself to a few other guests, and then the rabbi came out of the kitchen and announced, "Please take your seats. It's time." He found a place such that Stan was on his right side and an attractive blonde woman in her mid-forties was on his left. Opposite him was a tall and athletic-looking man and his partner, who was almost as tall and wore his hair back in a ponytail. Wishnasky imagined that the one was a football player, the other a golf star. Neither of them looked particularly Jewish.

The rabbi stood up at the head of the table beside her husband. "We're going to start with *Kiddush*," she said. "There should be wine in everyone's cup. Pick up your *haggadot* and turn to page four." Wishnasky picked up the booklet in front of him and found the page. "Now with your wine glass in your right hand, say the second, third, and fifth paragraphs together with me in Hebrew: '*Baruch atta Adonai Eloheinu ...*'"

For the next forty minutes, Wishnasky followed the service according to the rabbi's instructions, enjoying her explanations of each section, and eating when told to. The meal was unlike any other he'd ever had: parsley dipped in saltwater one moment (the green vegetable signifying rebirth, the saltwater the tears of the enslaved Israelites), bitter herbs and apple/nut/cinnamon mix (the herbs for the bitterness of slavery, the mix for the mortar used by Israelite brick-makers), and of course, matzo (the "bread of affliction"). He was fascinated to learn that ten drops of wine were removed from the second cup of wine to express sympathy for the Egyptians who'd had to suffer ten plagues before they released the Israelites from bondage. But he was moved most of all by what the rabbi said extemporaneously just before the complete meal began:

"Before we eat," she said, "I want to point out one essential fact about the Exodus that this holiday commemorates. As you all know, it was on Passover that God intervened in human history in an unprecedented way: to rescue a whole people—whom *Torah* says numbered 600,000—and to bring them out to the desert to receive the Holy One's commandments. So, who were these people that the Almighty chose to notice? Were they elite, the best of the best, the achievers who stood higher than any of their neighbors? No: just the opposite. They were slaves, the dregs of society, impoverished, oppressed, aliens in a land that despised them, outcasts. *That's* who God noticed when all around them were happier people, more successful, more prominent, winners not losers. That's the message of this holiday: before anyone else, before the kings and the celebrities and the wealthy and the powerful, we're to notice the oppressed, side with the wretched, sympathize with the subjugated. *That* is why Jews have typically been found in every liberation movement in Western history, *that* is why Jews have often ignored their own financial interests to side with the victims of inequality, *that's* what the Jewish obligation is at every moment: to be liberators themselves, to imitate the Holy One. And on this Passover eve, that's what we're all called on to remember—and do."

Then it was time for the festive meal, and Wishnasky was able to learn more about the other guests at the Seder. The couple opposite him was comprised up of a pharmaceutical representative (the husky one) and the concierge of a Boston hotel (with the ponytail); the blonde woman on his left was an advertising executive at an FM radio station and was converting to Judaism; and the seventeen-year-old next to her was her son, a high school wrestler. The half-dozen others remained unknown to him, but that didn't seem to matter much. Stan, sitting on his right, was always ready to talk about his divorce or ask Wishnasky questions about the writing business.

After dinner, the rabbi announced the long grace after the meal, the drinking of a third glass of wine (you only had to sip a few drops, Stan explained), and then the praises of God called *Hallel.* There was a fourth cup (sip) of wine and everyone said *L'shanah ha-ba'ah b'rushalayim*—"Next year may we be in Jerusalem." The rabbi announced the end of the Seder, thanked everyone for coming, and reminded all to drive carefully. Wishnasky exchanged goodbyes with the few people he'd talked to, traded phone numbers with Stan, and walked over to the rabbi to thank her for inviting him.

"Did you enjoy yourself?" she asked after saying goodbye to the nine-year-old girl who had recited the "Four Questions," traditionally sung by the youngest participant.

"I liked your little sermon," said Wishnasky. "To have this reminder of the Exodus every year—that's pretty powerful."

"In Latin America there's something called 'liberation theology,'" said Rabbi Diamant. "But from a Jewish standpoint, all theology is liberation theology. It's been that way for 3,500 years. And it's shaped—or should have shaped—all Jewish behavior."

"I don't think it shaped mine," said Wishnasky. "For most of my life I pretty much ignored the poor and the put-upon. Should I feel guilty about that? Should I pray to God to pardon so much callousness?"

"It can't ever hurt to ask the Holy One for forgiveness. But the real test of repentance is how the penitent acts *after* the apologies. Now that you've had some Jewish learning, you're aware that your responsibility is to what the *Torah* calls 'the orphan and the widow,' meaning the wretched, the miserable, what your friend at the Horn of Plenty called 'the casualties.' Now that you know that, you can act."

The casualties.

"You made a good start at the Horn of Plenty," said the rabbi. "And now taking on the business of Amnesty International. Eventually, you'll see that looking after the downtrodden is a necessary part of a good life. And there's so much to do, of course."

Wishnasky was hardly listening. He was hearing, instead, what Chet had suggested: the book that wouldn't get written if *he* didn't write it. And what the cantor had taught: don't hide from your own flesh. Flesh as compassion. Flesh as mercy. One's own mercy, however suppressed.

"Tristan?" said the rabbi. "Are you all right? You're looking distant."

And what Ion had said over a year ago, when he'd tried to understand why he felt so ashamed to give money to a beggar in front of Roland. No, his agent wasn't the problem: it was himself, the wise child who'd learned to quash his kindest instincts, not to be generous, not to be compassionate, to take every naïve, loving impulse and twist it into something callous and cold. To suppress a child's natural, lovely magnanimity when he saw another being in pain.

"I'm all right," he said to the rabbi. "I'm very much all right. I think I've just found something I was looking for."

And so he had. And he could already turn the pages.

78.

HE MADE THE DRIVE over the bridge to South Boston in under an hour, but even hewing close to the railroad tracks, he couldn't find anything called the Friend Indeed. So he pulled up beside a young, suntanned blond man with a cardboard sign saying "Homeless. Please Help," and, after giving him a few dollars, asked for directions. It turned out he'd passed the place a few moments earlier. Back in his car and knowing what to look for, he saw a nondescript, dusty-looking white building with a thin white plank in front of it, on which was written "Friend Indeed. Rooms for Rent." He parked across the street—the whole area looked abandoned—and walked up the rickety wooden stairs to the porch on which a couple of middle-aged men were playing cards.

"Excuse me," said Wishnasky. "I'm a friend of Arthur Winslow."

"Ain't never heard of him," said one of the men. "You a cop?"

"No, I'm not a cop. Thanks." He walked through the open door and found himself in a large lobby-like area, furnished with tattered, mismatched sofas on which a dozen or so people were lounging and chatting. Wishnasky strolled over to a small, hunched-over woman eating potato chips out of a small bag and asked, "Excuse me, do you know if Arthur Winslow's here?"

"Don't know him," she said, not looking him in his eyes.

"Can you tell me who's in charge of this facility, then?"

"Yeah, Muriel, she's in her office." Still avoiding his gaze, she pointed to a hallway with doors on either side. "Third door on the right."

Muriel turned out to be a friendly, elderly Black woman wearing a blue scarf around her hair and a long checkered shift. She told him that there was no one named Arthur Winslow registered, and that no one but the registered had a right to live on the premises. Wishnasky knew better than to suggest that Arthur might be dwelling there illicitly. He thanked her and walked back to the lobby, feeling perplexed.

Just then a tall, pot-bellied Black man walked up to him, scowling.

"I hear you're looking for Arthur," he said.

"That's right? Do you know where I can find him?"

"Maybe, maybe not. Who would *you* be?"

"Tristan Wishnasky. I used to serve food at the Horn of Plenty. We used to talk about things—politics, literature. We talked about Hemingway and Fitzgerald. Tell him it's his writer friend."

"You stay there," said the man. "I'll see what I can find out." Then, he turned away and lumbered up a wide, mottled staircase. Wishnasky watched him disappear and mused on the complex network of supports required when one lived outside conventional society. A few minutes later the man returned. "Can you keep your mouth shut?" he said.

"Of course."

"Then do it," he growled, turned back to the staircase and started climbing. After a moment, Wishnasky followed.

The pot-bellied man led Wishnasky up the stairs and down a musty-smelling, uncarpeted corridor till he came to a door marked 19C. He knocked once and they entered.

It was a small, mostly bare room with a window looking out on a wasteland of dirt and grass. There was a table and battered easy chair some inches from it, and against the opposite wall, a single bed—on which Arthur was sitting with a newspaper in his lap. There was also an air conditioning unit jammed into one window, but Wishnasky could feel that the air it was sending out into the room was tepid at best.

"Well, if it ain't the famous writer," said Arthur with a smile. "Come out all this way just to see me."

"How are you?"

"Not too bad. How'd you find out I was staying here?"

"A woman named Gladys, keeping court underneath the Longfellow Bridge. Rabbi Diamant thought she'd know what you were up to. How is it staying at this place?"

"Well, officially I'm not here. According to the rules, I don't exist. But I got friends who don't have much respect for the rules." He looked to the pot-bellied man who had accompanied Wishnasky. "I remember him, all right. You can go."

The man took one last, mistrustful glance at Wishnasky and, without a word, walked out the door. After he did, Arthur said, "Now that is a fine human being. One of the few. Like the saying says, you never know till the shit comes down."

"Are you hiding here?"

"You could call it that. There's a rule against overnight guests, you understand, but the Good Lord makes a man need to sleep sometimes, anyway. So we put a bedspread on the floor, and I'm accommodated."

"How are you eating?"

"At the soup kitchen near Park Street Station."

"They serve all week?"

"Twice a week. But Thursdays there's a free market: one at a time, we get to fill a paper bag with canned goods, beans and some fruits. Why you asking?"

"I have an idea that I'd like you to consider. It might make you some money. Make some of your friends a little money too. Would you be interested in earning some cash?"

"Man, ain't nobody wants to hire an old Black poet with Crohn's Disease. I learned that good and well."

"Then listen to my proposal," said Wishnasky. "I want to edit a book: it'll be called *The Casualties,* and it'll be first-person testimonies by you and maybe a dozen other men and women who are living out in the open, or under bridges, or maybe in rooming houses like this one. I'll interview each of you and turn your answers into separate chapters, a different person in each chapter. I'll write the introduction and add personal commentary at the start and finish of each testimony, and when the book starts to earn money, I'll divide it up among everyone I interviewed and take an equal portion for myself. What do you think?"

"Mister, what makes you think that anyone cares to read my story?"

"I've given that some thought. The fact is, I've still got a reputation because of my first three books. So my name still means something. And this could be important: people are afraid of vagrants, fearful of the homeless, but with this volume they could safely settle into their cozy living rooms and find out just how human you are, and what a shame it is that we live in a system that spits out thousands of men and women and leaves them on the streets or hiding out like you've been doing. Maybe we could even persuade people to make some changes."

"You'd print what I say? All of it? Even the angry?"

"That's right. And everything else you've told me. How you used to make a living until you came down with your ailment, and how America's been trying to dispense with you ever since. How no one can live on only food stamps and Social Security, how you're taught to keep out of sight from the rest of us and the police. Aren't you the one who said the public doesn't want to see the casualties of the system? Well, let's make them see you. And let's find out how it affects them."

Arthur stared down into his hands as if they were what would be interviewed. Then he looked up. "Nobody's gonna read it," he said. "No one wants to know. That what I've learned."

"I think you're wrong."

Arthur took the newspaper off his lap and put it beside him on the narrow bed. He ran his hand over the top page and then put it back in his lap.

Finally, he said, "How much money you imagine I'd get from this book?"

"I don't want to overestimate it. Hundreds, certainly, maybe even a few thousand. For being as forthright and crotchety as you could possibly want."

Arthur rubbed his wrinkled forehead with his hand. "I don't know if I trust you," he said. "Wouldn't want you twisting my words."

"Wouldn't think of it. And by the way: I would need your help deciding who else to interview. You do that and you'll get even more of the book's proceeds."

"All right, man, though I think you're crazy. When do you want to start?"

"As soon as possible. Tomorrow morning, if you like. I've got a digital recorder that I can set on the table there and we can let loose. Then, even before I interview anyone else, I'll write up your chapter. As a test run, so to speak. I may even show it to my publisher."

"If we start tomorrow, you'll bring me that money?"

"A little of it, okay, but the rest won't come for months, maybe more than a year. But here's what I'll do: I'll give you a two hundred dollar advance when I come in tomorrow. We'll count it against your payment when the book's eventually published. I'll also write up a memo of agreement you can sign."

"Don't you write me a check," said Arthur. "No one's going to trust me with a check. I'd need cash if you're serious."

"I'll get you cash. And what you can do for me is talk as honestly as you've ever done. That's what people need to hear."

"They're not gonna like it."

"Excellent. I'm already fascinated."

79.

It was almost 11 p.m. Wishnasky sat back on the pillows he'd propped up against the headboard. He was wearing jeans and a tee-shirt, and his laptop computer, supported by his crossed legs, shone its steely light into the otherwise dark bedroom. Outside his window, the gentle rustling of tree limbs in the breeze was comfortingly familiar. He scrolled through the pages of Arthur's testimony, looking for areas that needed cutting or reshaping. This time he didn't find any. He scrolled to a section toward the end and read:

I don't blame anyone for the fact that I can't keep a job. It's not their fault I have Crohn's and can't be depended on to show up at work. I wouldn't myself want an employee who called in sick every week-and-a-half. If I got a business to run, then I want dependable workers.

But what I do blame is the system that didn't protect me from all the worry of not having money, not being able to buy food or clothes, or rent an apartment to lay my head in. You'd think that with all the smart people in this big country, someone would have figured by now how to help a man in my situation.

You want to know what really bothers me? It bothers me when someone says, Arthur, you've just had a bad run of luck. Bad luck: That's crazy. It's about money, man, money, about not having enough money to buy yourself some good luck! Even the Crohn's wouldn't be that important if I had enough dollars. One thing leads to another, man. If my folks hadn't been under the everyday stress of being so poor, would my momma have gone on the drugs eventually? If my dad could have found a better job to support her, you think she still would've walked out on him, lookin' for a better life? And if the USA had made sure I got to go to college, would I be sitting here now and talking to you? You see what I'm saying, the only hard luck that I ever had is that I couldn't afford the good luck. I spend my days at the library, don't you forget that. I know all about those other countries where they don't let you be poor, how they're looking after everyone, not just the cats with the cash. You know how many poor people there are in this country? I looked it up: forty-five million. Are you telling me forty-five million people in this place had a run of hard luck? Man, that ain't luck: that's policy.

This was good, expressive, usable. Wishnasky scrolled further ahead so that he was near the conclusion. Yes, there was the section where Arthur compared himself to others:

And you can't brush me off by saying I'm special, or one of a kind. I know a woman who had a good job in an auto parts store. Then they went out of business and suddenly she can't afford breakfast. She applies to twenty other jobs, nobody wants a middle-aged Hispanic lady whose only strength she can tell them is that for twenty years she sold cans of transmission fluid and antifreeze. She gets a few dollars from Social Security, without it she'd starve. You tell me, who's looking out for her? If she ends up living on the street, who are you going to blame for it? And I know a bunch of people in even worse trouble than her. I know a white man who fought in Iraq back in 2003. When he came home, he wasn't the same: had the frights day and night, couldn't hold a job so he took instead a monthly check from the VA. But he's got a wife and a kid, and then his mother dies and his pop moves in with him, and how're they gonna find food for four mouths and also pay nine hundred a month rent, and electricity and water and car payments and food? How's he gonna get his pop to the doctor if he can't afford a car and the gasoline? Here he fought for his country, and it repays him by sending him to the churches for free clothes and the soup kitchens for a little meat or chicken. You think there ain't people who starve to death in this country? Yeah, I know people who died of starvation. It never says so in the paper, they like to say it was a drug overdose. But that drug hit a weak body, a body that didn't have any resistance left, and of course the cat died. Of hunger, not drugs.

That also was publishable, not too repetitive, though he'd have to be careful that each testimony had a unique perspective. And he'd have to find witnesses who represented a cross-section of the poor: white, Black, Hispanic, male, female, children. What about Arthur's conclusion—was it informative enough? He scrolled to the final section:

So how do I see myself? That's easy enough: I'm just one of the casualties. According to the newspaper, I'm one of about forty-five million walking wounded in this country. forty-five million ignored Americans, not sure if they'll get another meal before they die. And you know how the government didn't want any reporters taking photos of dead bodies coming back from Afghanistan? Well, it don't want photos of us, either: the ones that the system leaves bankrupt and starving. If we make too much noise, they put us in jail where we're even further out of the picture. If we line up outside to get free food from a soup kitchen, they tell us we're stinking up the neighborhood and they close it down. You understand: there's forty-five million of us, and most people don't see even one. But you know what I know? They're going to see us one day. Somehow, someday, a change is going to come and all us hidden casualties are going to come into the light. And the people of that time—they're going to look back at the old days and they're going to say, man, wasn't America cruel in those times? Wasn't it heartless and mean—I'd be ashamed if I was part of it. I'm glad I live now where we don't have to feel that shame.

This was so useful, he had to consider putting it in a preface to the book: something to get the reader's mind working. On the other hand, he didn't yet know what his other interlocutors would say, so he'd better put off that decision for a while. He made a mental note: one interview done. Next, he'd have to decide whether to send it on to Darryl Kamfort as a taste of the volume he'd projected.

He folded up his laptop, placed it on the night table beside his bed, and lay down, still in his jeans. It was strange, focusing on someone else's words, someone else's vision. But he was happy with the progress he'd made already with Arthur, and he was convinced that *The Casualties* was the book he should be composing. He'd have to show this opening chapter to Aileen when she came up tomorrow. If she liked it, he would know with more certainty that he was on the right track.

Aileen, Aileen … she was right after all: the current crisis was too dire for the usual sort of art. When things changed, then they could return to the beautiful and the well-said. Aileen: in less than twenty-four hours, she would be beside him, they would be wrapped in each other's arms, and they would find peace in each other … How fortunate he was. How good that all had turned out as it did …

He slept. A deep sleep.

■

And then a few hours later, when the clock said 3:41, he suddenly awoke. And was profoundly afraid.

The thoughts came all at once, all in a piece, with devastating clarity. He was living a lie. There was no benevolent God watching over him in heaven, there was only matter, brute, mindless matter, and even more than matter, emptiness. There was no future for which he could hope, there was only aging and infirmity and loss of function leading up to death. If Aileen was precious to him now, well, so had been Vanessa and every other woman he once thought he had loved. In time he'd see through Aileen also, see through to the vain wanton who was flying from man to man, who'd given her body to dozens of so-called lovers before him, and would someday tire of him too and go on to the next naïf. He saw that the religion he'd taken on over more than a year was just a wish-fulfillment blithely propagated by others with the same delusions that he'd bought into, a vision that was bankrupt and moribund. He saw that the book he was composing would make a difference to no one, that poverty like Arthur's would continue and proliferate and not a politician in America would ever do anything to stop it. He saw that he'd given up a successful career as a novelist, only to replace it with common journalism of the sort that was tossed every day into garbage cans and gutters. He saw that he'd been right in his first three books: he was No One From Nowhere and overlooking it at all was the vast nothing.

And then his phone beeped: he had a text message.

Which was strange at three in the morning.

He picked it up from the night table beside his laptop—where it was charging—and looked at the screen. It glowed with the words: *Your soul not your mind.*

He froze. It was happening again. It had been so long, he'd assumed that there'd never be another such contact. But there it was on his cell phone. In bright words against darkness.

Then the words disappeared. And replacing them on the small screen, as the beeping continued, was a new sentence: *The bush burned but was not consumed.*

Confusion. He failed to understand. Surely if he were smarter, he would know how to respond. Would know what he should be thinking.

But then the message vanished once more, and in its place came the words: *Never stop searching.* And he whispered, "I won't. I'll never stop searching." The phone's screen went blank and the beeping ceased.

He stared into the dark for a few minutes, listening to nothing in particular, just trying to organize his emotions. He had to see Aileen as soon as possible. He had to work on his new book, *The Casualties.* He had to study Hebrew with the cantor and work harder for Amnesty. He had to write an essay about reclaiming and restoring God's Earth.

He lay down and closed his eyes. Did he have the strength for the pursuit that the messages demanded? Was it in him—lazy, egoistic Tristan Wishnasky—to live a good life?

He looked at his cell phone screen: nothing. No more messages. And he was tired.

He thought: I can do it. With God's help. Not abandon any of it.

And he fell into a deep sleep.

80.

THE DRIVE TO THE GARDEN was mostly filled with the conversation of Aileen and Rabbi Diamant, to which Wishnasky occasionally added an insight. Aileen, riding in the back, wanted to know all about the difficulties the rabbi had faced in her efforts to assume what for most of history had been a man's job, and the rabbi wanted to know all the details of Aileen's upbringing in a family that ignored most Jewish themes from *Shabbat* to eating kosher.

"I had no other desire than to lead a congregation," said Rabbi Diamant. "From the time I entered my first synagogue as a little girl, it's what I wanted. I loved Hebrew, the holidays, the idea of *Shabbat*, the learned arguments in the *Talmud*."

"I'm so impressed," said Aileen. Even though she wasn't to be the official photographer for the new garden, she'd brought her camera with her—its strap was around her neck.

"No, *I'm* impressed with you. Tell me a little more about your upbringing."

"My parents didn't have any environmental conscience, at least none I ever noticed. My father was a patent attorney before he retired, and my mother had a store for children in a strip mall that was always months from going under. They never talked to us about the Jewish religion, except to give us gifts on Chanukah and say good things about Israel. I guess you'd call them ninety-nine-percent secular."

"Your mother didn't even light Friday night candles?" asked the rabbi. "Were your folks aware of the commandments?"

"Not at all. Now, all my great-grandparents were supposed to have been religious, back in the forties, but it didn't rub off on the next generation, I guess. I never even had a taste of *matzo* till I went to college and visited the Hillel House."

"Tristan, that's more or less how you grew up too, isn't it?"

"In a way," said Wishnasky. "But my parents wouldn't know a *mitzvah* from a mango. And I can't remember one time when either one wrote out a check to charity."

"There's the school," said Aileen. "Rabbi, I have to warn you, the size of the garden isn't very impressive. I don't want you to feel we misled you about the significance of getting it planted."

"I had no preconceived notions of it."

"It's all a part of reclaiming The Artwork," said Aileen. "We have to go a little at a time. Every victory matters."

"I won't criticize your garden for being too small."

Wishnasky drove into the school parking lot and then onto the long, mostly brown field leading up to the garden plot.

"That's Willem's car," said Aileen, excited. "And that truck is Polly's. Look, there's Oscar and Angie."

Wishnasky pulled his car up alongside a black Nissan Sentra and cut the engine. Aileen popped out of the backseat and ran to embrace Willem, who was leaning on a shovel and talking with two other men. Wishnasky and the rabbi left the car and headed for the garden, neatly divided into separate plots. There were plants growing in most of them.

"We'll have to ask Aileen what these are," said Wishnasky. "I can't tell one vegetable from another."

"I think that's lettuce," said the rabbi, pointing at one of the plots. "And that next to it—I don't know, maybe mustard greens."

"Isn't it beautiful?" said Aileen, walking back to them with a big smile. "It's probably been a hundred years since there was vegetation growing out of this land. But the earth wasn't meant to be ignored and abandoned: it was meant to grow food and take CO_2 out of the atmosphere, and bend its children toward the sun. Do you know that this is the third garden RARE's planted this year? Oh, excuse me, there's Rebecca: I have to talk to her before I forget." She hurried off in the direction of a pleasant-looking, slender middle-aged woman.

"Rabbi," said Wishnasky, "is there a blessing over a vegetable garden?"

"Well, God told the first humans to "work and guard" their garden. So, I'd say something similar: may it be the Lord's will that these people work and guard their garden."

"Thank you," said Wishnasky. Just then, Willem walked over to them and shook Tristan's hand. Tristan introduced the rabbi.

"Thanks for coming," Willem said to her. "Do you have any questions?"

"Just which plants are which," said the rabbi.

"That's easy enough. Over there, in the right corner, are tomatoes and radishes. In the next plot just beside it are lettuce, eggplant, and kale. The next one's also lettuce, but with cucumbers and tomatoes. There's more radishes, some carrots, and at the far end zucchini. I see more of the same all along the other side, especially cucumbers, but no, that's broccoli in the third plot on the left."

"Which one is your plot?" asked Tristan.

"Next to the last on the left. Cucumbers and radishes."

Wishnasky scanned all the effort going on around him. The growing garden was worryingly small: if this was how The Artwork was going to be reclaimed, it would take centuries. But then he thought of his own work: recording the witness of a few human casualties out of millions. He remembered the verse from *Talmud*: "It is not for you to finish the work; but you have no right to withdraw from it either."

"What do you think about all this?" he asked the rabbi.

"Honestly?" she said.

"Is it too minor? Are you terribly disappointed?"

"I was thinking of an old story: that when the first human was created, God led him around the garden and warned him: 'See to it that you don't spoil and destroy my world. For if you do, there will be no one to repair it after you.' I was thinking that someone got to this little stretch of dirt at just the right moment."

Aileen walked up to them. "Isn't it fantastic?" she said. "Angie tells me we can take some produce from her plot anytime we feel like it. We'll make a salad entirely from veggies grown here. I can't wait. Isn't it wonderful?"

"Which one's Angie's plot?"

"On the right, in the middle."

Wishnasky looked at the rectangle to which Aileen was pointing. The vegetation seemed robust, not at all fragile or inadequate.

He put his arm around Aileen. "Those plants look strong," he said.

"That's what they are. Broccoli is hardy. And the zucchini can weather a typhoon. Cucumbers are about as tough as they come."

Wishnasky held her closer to him and took comfort from the warm, solid frame of her body. He had called the world a void once; now he noticed how substantial at least this speck of it was. What a change!

Just then, Willem walked over to them carrying an armful of greens. Aileen said, "Good job! They look splendid!" Willem smiled back but didn't speak.

Wishnasky looked around him and realized: there was Something, not Nothing. And it was growing, not vanishing. He hugged Aileen to him more closely. When they were together, anything might grow.

ACKNOWLEDGMENTS

I am grateful to the Holy One, who has kept me in life, sustained me, and allowed me to reach the season of this novel's publication.

So many people have encouraged me along the way; I fear that I'll offend by failing to name them all. But I should at least mention my good friends Samuel Anderson, Steve Saudek, and David Scheffer; my literary comrades Richard Dey and Michael Stephens; my sister, Trisha, nephew Leighton, and niece Faryn; my tennis nemesis and guitar hero, the late Bill Edwards; and my agent Laura Strachan.

I will always be thankful to the late Rabbi Ben Zion Gold of Harvard. His example is a light that continues to shine for me and for many others.

A few of the ideas in this novel came from my reading of the poet and professor Roger Kamenetz, the philosopher Charles Taylor, and the theologian John Hick.

I could have never risked pursuing the life of a writer without the cooperation of my parents, Lester and Harriet Leib, of blessed memory. Their love and support made *Image Breaker* possible.

VINE LEAVES PRESS

Enjoyed this book?
Go to *vineleavespress.com* to find more.
Subscribe to our newsletter:

CPSIA information can be obtained
at www.ICGtesting.com
Printed in the USA
BVHW031204020423
661604BV00001B/1